The Complete Leadership Collection (Vol. 3)

Politics, Nicomachean Ethics & Rhetoric —
Aristotle on Virtue, Governance and Persuasion

A Modern Translation

Adapted for the Contemporary Reader

Aristotle

Translated by Tim Zengerink

Table of Contents

Preface - Message to the Reader

What If You Could Help Rebuild the Greatest Library in Human History?

Thousands of years ago, the Library of Alexandria stood as the crown jewel of human achievement — a sanctuary where the collected wisdom of every known civilization was gathered, preserved, and shared freely.

And then, it was lost.

Through fire, conquest, and the slow erosion of time, humanity lost not just books — but ideas, dreams, discoveries, and stories that could have changed the world forever.

Today, the Library of Alexandria lives again — and you are invited to be a part of its restoration.

Our mission is simple yet profound:

To rebuild the greatest library the world has ever known, and to translate all timeless works into every language and dialect, so that no seeker of knowledge is ever left behind again.

By joining our movement to rebuild the modern Library of Alexandria, you become part of an unprecedented mission:

- **Unlimited Access to the Greatest Audiobooks & eBooks Ever Written:**

    Instantly explore thousands of legendary works—Plato, Shakespeare, Jane Austen, Leo Tolstoy, and countless more. All instantly available to read or listen, placing a complete literary universe at your fingertips.

- **Beautiful Paperback & Deluxe Editions at Printing Cost**

  Own any title as an elegant paperback, deluxe hardcover, or stunning collectible boxset—offered to you at true printing cost, delivered straight to your door. Build your personal Library of Alexandria, crafted for beauty, built for durability, and worthy of proud display.

- **Fresh Translations for Modern Readers—in Every Language & Dialect**

  Enjoy timeless masterpieces reimagined in clear, contemporary language—no more outdated phrases or obscure references. Alongside the original versions, we're tirelessly translating these classics into every language and dialect imaginable, ensuring accessibility and understanding across cultures and generations.

- **Join a Global Renaissance of Literature & Knowledge**

  You directly support expanding our library, publishing deluxe editions at true cost, translating works into all global languages, and bringing humanity's greatest stories to people everywhere. By joining today, you're not just preserving a legacy of masterpieces; you set in motion a powerful wave of literary accessibility.

Become a Torchbearer of Knowledge.

Join us for free now at **LibraryofAlexandria.com**

Together, we will ensure that the light of human wisdom never fades again.

With gratitude and a shared love of knowledge,
The Modern Library of Alexandria Team

Visit:

www.libraryofalexandria.com

Or scan the code below:

Introduction

Leadership as Ethical Practice, Civic Craft, and Persuasive Power

The Complete Leadership Collection (Vol. 3) offers a trilogy of foundational works by Aristotle—Politics, Nicomachean Ethics, and Rhetoric—that together form a comprehensive philosophy of leadership grounded in virtue, justice, and persuasion. Unlike modern leadership manuals that emphasize charisma or tactics, Aristotle's texts provide a holistic framework in which the leader is first and foremost a moral agent, a civic steward, and a thoughtful speaker.

These texts represent not merely philosophical abstraction, but deeply practical instruction for anyone seeking to lead with clarity, consistency, and purpose. Aristotle explores how individuals and communities thrive, what constitutes ethical excellence, and how language shapes judgment. His thought speaks as powerfully to heads of state as to entrepreneurs, educators, and activists, offering a model of leadership that prioritizes the cultivation of the soul, the harmony of the community, and the art of reasoned communication.

This introduction maps the key ideas of these three texts, showing how they interlock to form a unified vision of principled leadership that is as relevant today as it was in ancient Athens. For Aristotle, the leader is not simply a strategist—but a builder of lives, laws, and shared understanding.

Nicomachean Ethics and Politics: Virtue, Justice, and the Art of Statesmanship

At the heart of Aristotle's philosophy is a single premise: every action aims at some good. In Nicomachean Ethics, he seeks to define the highest good for human beings—what he calls eudaimonia, often translated as "flourishing" or "happiness." For Aristotle, this is not a passing feeling, but a life of rational activity in accordance with virtue over a complete life.

Leadership, then, is not a means to power or prestige, but a practice of virtue in the service of the common good. Aristotle distinguishes between moral virtues (like courage, generosity, temperance) and intellectual virtues (like wisdom and prudence). A good leader must possess both: character to inspire trust and judgment to make wise decisions.

The Ethics culminates in Book X with the claim that the highest form of human activity is contemplation. But Aristotle does not leave us in solitude. He links the personal to the political, leading directly into Politics, where he argues that humans are by nature political animals. The city-state (polis) exists not only to secure life, but to enable the good life.

In Politics, Aristotle examines various forms of government— monarchy, aristocracy, polity, and their corrupt counterparts: tyranny, oligarchy, and democracy. He critiques pure democracy for pandering to the masses, but also warns against the arrogance of oligarchy. His preferred system is a balanced polity, grounded in a strong middle class and guided by law.

Crucially, Aristotle sees leadership as an extension of citizenship. The ruler must be ruled in turn; law is above individual will. The good leader cultivates civic virtue, harmonizes interests, and upholds justice—not merely legal justice, but distributive and corrective justice. He must also be educated in philosophy, for only then can he govern wisely.

Together, the Ethics and Politics form the ethical and civic spine of leadership. They show that to lead well is to be deeply attuned to both human nature and political order—to know not only what is right, but how to enact it in a complex society.

Rhetoric: The Language of Leadership and the Persuasion of the Polis

If Ethics gives us the leader's character, and Politics the civic context, then Rhetoric gives us the tool of influence. For Aristotle, rhetoric is not manipulation or flattery. It is the art of using reasoned speech to persuade others toward truth and action. It is the civic expression of leadership—the bridge between mind and community.

Aristotle defines rhetoric as "the faculty of observing in any given case the available means of persuasion." He classifies persuasion into three modes:

- Ethos: the character of the speaker. Trustworthiness and credibility.
- Pathos: the emotion of the audience. Understanding their desires and fears.
- Logos: the argument itself. Logic, evidence, and structure.

A great leader, then, must command all three. He must speak with integrity (ethos), connect with his listeners' humanity (pathos), and offer sound reasons (logos). Rhetoric is not simply public speaking— it is applied ethics. It is how leaders align values with action, and how they forge consensus in a pluralistic world.

Aristotle also explores the types of rhetoric:

- Deliberative rhetoric: used in political or legislative contexts, arguing about future actions.
- Forensic rhetoric: used in courts, focusing on justice and the past.
- Epideictic rhetoric: used in ceremonial contexts, celebrating virtue or condemning vice.

Each requires a different tone, structure, and method of appeal. But in all, the aim is not to overpower, but to guide. Rhetoric, for Aristotle, is a public good when grounded in truth and used for the common benefit.

In an age of spin, branding, and manipulation, Aristotle's Rhetoric is a call back to responsible persuasion. It reminds us that language is not just a tool of power—but a duty of reason and a measure of our character.

The Leader as Philosopher, Citizen, and Orator

Taken together, these three works by Aristotle offer a complete model of ethical leadership:

- The Ethics teaches the cultivation of personal virtue.
- The Politics shows how to govern justly and structure communities.
- The Rhetoric equips the leader to persuade ethically and unify diverse voices.

This is not a leadership of slogans or short-term wins. It is a lifelong practice of excellence—a kind of spiritual craftsmanship rooted in moral clarity and civic responsibility. For Aristotle, leadership is not a role—it is a way of being.

In a world often divided between idealism and pragmatism, Aristotle offers a third path: practical wisdom (phronesis). This is the ability to choose well in complex, variable situations. It is not a formula, but a cultivated faculty—a habit of thoughtful action informed by experience, ethics, and empathy.

Welcome to The Complete Leadership Collection (Vol. 3). May Aristotle's enduring wisdom guide you not only to lead, but to live— virtuously, justly, and with persuasive clarity, in service of something greater than yourself.

Politics

Aristotle

Book 1

Every state is a type of community, and every community is formed with the aim of achieving some good. Humans always act to get what they believe is good. If all communities aim for some good, then the state or political community, which includes all other communities, aims for the greatest good. It does so to a higher degree than any other community.

Some people believe that the roles of a statesman, king, head of a household, and master are the same, and they only differ in the number of people they control. For instance, a master rules over a few people, a head of a household rules over more, and a statesman or king rules over even more, as if there were no difference between a large household and a small state. The distinction made between a king and a statesman is this: if the government is run by one person, he is called a king, but if citizens take turns ruling according to the rules of political science, then he is called a statesman.

However, this is a mistake. Governments differ in nature, which becomes clear if we break things down into their simplest elements. Just as in other sciences, in politics we must break things down into their basic parts. We should examine the basic elements that make up the state so we can understand how different types of rule differ from one another, and whether we can reach any scientific conclusions about them.

Anyone who looks at things from their very beginning, whether it's a state or anything else, will see them most clearly. First, there must be a union between those who cannot exist without each other—specifically, male and female so the race can continue. This union happens not by choice but because humans, like animals and plants, have a natural desire to leave behind something of themselves. There must also be a union between the natural ruler and the natural subject so that both may survive. For the one who can think and plan is naturally meant to be the ruler, and the one who can use their body to carry out these plans is naturally meant to be the subject, or the slave. Therefore, the master and the slave have a common interest. Nature has clearly distinguished between a woman and a slave, as she makes everything for a single purpose and not for many. But among barbarians, there is no distinction between women and slaves, as they have no natural rulers. They are a community of slaves, both male and female. That's why poets say, "It is right for Greeks to rule over barbarians," as if they believe that barbarians and slaves are naturally the same.

From these two relationships—between man and woman, and between master and slave—the family emerges. Hesiod is correct when he says, "First, a house, a wife, and an ox for plowing," as the ox is the poor man's slave. The family is a natural association created to meet people's everyday needs, and the members of the family are called 'companions of the cupboard' by Charondas and 'companions of the manger' by Epimenides the Cretan. When several families unite to achieve more than just daily survival, the first community formed is a village. The most natural form of a village seems to be a colony from the family, consisting of children and grandchildren who are said to be raised 'on the same milk.' This is also why early Greek states were originally ruled by kings because they were governed by kings before coming together as states, just like the barbarians today. Each family is ruled by the eldest, and so in these family colonies, a kingly form of government existed because they were all related by blood. Homer says, "Each man gives law to his children and wives," because in ancient times people lived apart from one another. Therefore, people say the gods have a king, because they imagine the lives of the gods to be like their own.

When several villages unite to form a complete community that is large enough to be nearly or entirely self-sufficient, a state comes into existence. It starts because of basic needs but continues for the sake of living a good life. So, if the earlier forms of society are natural, then the state is also natural because it is the end goal of those earlier forms. A thing's nature is its end goal. For example, the fully developed form of a person, a horse, or a family is its true nature. Furthermore, the final purpose of something is the best, and being self-sufficient is the highest goal.

Therefore, it's clear that the state is a creation of nature, and man is naturally a political animal. A person who lives outside the state by nature and not by accident is either a bad person or someone above human society, like the "tribeless, lawless, heartless one" that Homer condemns. Such a person is a natural outcast, like a piece removed from a game of checkers.

It is obvious that man is more of a political animal than bees or other social animals. Nature does nothing in vain, and man is the only animal with the gift of speech. Mere sounds, like cries of pleasure or pain, exist in other animals too, as they can sense pleasure and pain and communicate it to each other. However, speech allows us to express what is useful or harmful, just or unjust. It is human nature to have a sense of good and evil, right and wrong, and it is the sharing of these values that creates families and states.

The state is also naturally more important than the family and the individual, because the whole is always more important than its parts. For example, if the whole body is destroyed, there will no longer be a foot or hand, except in name, like a stone hand. The parts are defined by their function, and when they lose their function, they lose their true nature. This proves that the state is natural and more important than the individual because a person cannot be self-sufficient alone. A person is like a part of a larger whole. Someone who cannot live in society or who doesn't need society because they are completely self-sufficient is either a beast or a god. They are not part of a state. Humans have a natural social instinct, and the person who first founded the state was the greatest benefactor. When a person is fully developed, they are the best of animals, but without law and justice, they are the worst. Injustice with power is dangerous, and humans are born with weapons—intelligence and virtue—that can be used for both good and evil. Without virtue, a person becomes the worst of all animals, full of greed and violence. Justice is the bond that holds a state together, and the administration of justice is what creates order in political society.

Since the state is made up of households, we must first understand how a household is managed before we can understand the state. The parts of household management correspond to the people who make up the household, and a complete household consists of both slaves and free people. To understand household management, we must start by examining its simplest parts: master and slave, husband and wife, and parent and children. We need to consider what each of these relationships is and should be. There is also the part of household management known as acquiring wealth. Some say this is the same as household management, while others say it is a major part of it. We will need to consider the nature of this as well.

Let's first talk about the relationship between master and slave, looking at both practical life and how we can understand this relationship better. Some people think that mastering slaves is a science and that running a household, controlling slaves, and political or royal rule are all the same. Others argue that ruling over slaves is unnatural and that the difference between slaves and free people exists only because of laws, not nature, and is therefore unjust.

Property is a part of the household, and the skill of acquiring property is part of the art of managing a household. No one can live well, or live at all, without the basic necessities. Just as workers need tools for their work, managing a household requires its own set of tools. Some tools are lifeless, like a rudder, while others are living, like a lookout on a ship. In the household, a servant is like a living tool. Property is a tool for maintaining life. A slave is a living possession, and property consists of many such tools. A servant is an instrument that comes before all other tools. If all tools could do their own work, obeying or anticipating the will of others, like the statues of Daedalus or the tripods of Hephaestus that "walked by themselves into the assembly of the gods," then master craftsmen wouldn't need assistants, nor would masters need slaves. However, the tools we use for production are different from the possessions we use for action. For example, a shuttle is used to make something else, while a bed is only used for its function. Life is about action, not production, and the slave's role is to assist in action. A possession is part of something else, and the part fully belongs to the whole. In the same way, a possession fully belongs to its owner. The master is only the master of the slave; he does not belong to the slave. But the slave belongs entirely to his master. Therefore, a slave is someone who, by nature, belongs to someone else. A possession is an instrument of action, separate from its owner.

Is there anyone naturally meant to be a slave, for whom slavery is both good and right, or is all slavery against nature?

The answer is clear based on both reason and experience. It is necessary and beneficial for some to rule and others to be ruled. From birth, some people are marked for leadership, and others for following.

There are different types of rulers and subjects. The rule is better when it's over better subjects. For example, ruling over humans is better than ruling over wild animals because the work done by better workers is always better. Wherever one person rules and another is ruled, they are doing something together. This distinction exists in all living creatures, and it comes from the way the world is organized. Even in non-living things, like music, there's a guiding principle. But let's stick to living things. Every living creature is made of both soul and body, with the soul naturally ruling and the body naturally following. To understand nature, we have to look at things that are in their best form, not those that are corrupted. So, we must study someone who has both a healthy body and soul, for only in such a person will we see the correct relationship between the two. In people who are in bad shape, the body may seem to rule the soul, but this is not natural.

In living creatures, we can observe two kinds of rule. The soul rules over the body like a master over a slave, while the intellect rules over desires in a more balanced, constitutional way. The soul's rule over the body, and the mind's rule over desires, is natural and beneficial. When desires rule over the mind, it's always harmful. The same is true of animals in relation to humans. Tame animals are better off when ruled by humans because humans help them survive. Likewise, men are naturally stronger, and women weaker. Men are meant to rule, and women to follow. This principle applies to all human beings.

When there's a big difference between two things, like between soul and body or humans and animals, the lower kind is naturally a slave. This is especially true for people whose only role is to use their bodies and who can't do anything better. It's good for them, just like it's good for all lesser beings, to be ruled by a master. A person who belongs to someone else and who can understand reason but can't fully grasp it is a natural slave. On the other hand, animals can't even understand reason. They follow their instincts. The way we use slaves and tame animals is similar—they both serve life's basic needs with their bodies.

Nature seems to want to make a clear difference between the bodies of free people and slaves. Slaves should be strong for hard labor, while free people should be upright and fit for political life. But this doesn't always happen. Some people have the souls of free people but the bodies of slaves, and others the opposite. If people were as physically different from one another as humans are from statues of gods, everyone would agree that the weaker class should serve the stronger. And if this is true for the body, it's even more true for the soul. However, we can see physical differences easily, but differences in the soul are harder to see. It's clear that some people are naturally free, and others are naturally slaves. For those meant to be slaves, this is both beneficial and just.

Still, those who disagree also have a point. The words "slavery" and "slave" can mean different things. There is slavery by nature, and then there is slavery by law. The law I'm talking about is the idea that anything taken in war belongs to the victor. But many legal experts reject this idea. They don't think that one person should be a slave simply because another person is stronger. Philosophers also disagree on this point. The confusion comes from the fact that people often link power with virtue. They think that the strong should rule because they are better in some way. So, this debate about slavery is really a debate about justice. One side thinks justice is about goodwill, while the other thinks it's about the rule of the strongest.

If we look at these arguments separately, the view that virtuous people should rule is strong. But the other side believes that the law justifies slavery in war. However, they also admit that this only works if the war itself is just. No one would agree that a person who doesn't deserve to be a slave should be one simply because they were captured in war. This is why Greeks don't like calling other Greeks slaves; they reserve that term for barbarians. In reality, they are talking about natural slaves. Just like nobility, there are two kinds of slavery—one that is natural and one based on law.

Greeks think of themselves as noble everywhere, but barbarians are only noble in their own lands. In a play, Helen says, "Who would call me a servant, when I am descended from the gods on both sides?" This shows how they link freedom and nobility to good and bad. They think good people come from other good people, just like animals give birth to animals. But nature doesn't always make this happen.

So, there is some truth to both sides. Not everyone is naturally free or naturally a slave. In some cases, it is clear and right that some people should be slaves and others masters. When this relationship is natural, both benefit. The master and the slave are like parts of the same body. But when slavery is based only on law and force, the relationship is not beneficial.

From these points, it's clear that the rule of a master is not the same as the rule in a political system. The rule over free people is different from the rule over slaves. The head of a household rules like a king because there is only one leader. In a political system, free and equal citizens share power. A master isn't called a master because of any special skill, but because of who he is. The same applies to slaves and free people. However, there could be a skill in mastering slaves and a skill in being a slave. For example, a man in Syracuse taught slaves how to do their daily tasks for money. This kind of knowledge could even include skills like cooking. Some tasks are more necessary, while others are more honorable, like the saying goes: "slave before slave, master before master." But these kinds of knowledge are low-level skills.

There is also a skill in being a master, which is about using slaves effectively. This skill isn't particularly great, as the master only needs to know how to give orders that the slave must carry out. This is why wealthy people have managers to take care of their households while they focus on philosophy or politics. The skill of acquiring slaves, however, is different from the skill of ruling them—it's more like hunting or warfare. That's enough about the difference between masters and slaves.

Now let's explore property in general and the skill of getting wealth. We've already said that a slave is a kind of property. The first question is whether getting wealth is the same as managing a household, or just part of it. If it's part of it, is it like how making shuttles is part of weaving, or how casting bronze is part of sculpture? These two aren't the same: one provides tools, while the other provides the materials. For example, wool is the material for weaving, and bronze is the material for statues.

It's easy to see that managing a household is different from getting wealth. The household manager uses the things that wealth-getting provides. There is some debate about whether getting wealth is part of household management or a separate skill. If wealth-getting is about finding where wealth can be obtained, and there are many types of property and riches, then is farming and providing food part of wealth-getting or a separate skill? There are many types of food, which is why there are many types of lives for both animals and humans. Different creatures live in ways that suit the food they eat—some are social, some live alone, and they all live in ways that help them find the food they need.

Humans also have many different ways of living. The simplest are shepherds, who live quietly and get their food from their animals. They follow their flocks wherever they go to find food, living a wandering life. Others live by hunting, which can take many forms. Some are bandits, while others live by fishing in lakes, rivers, or seas, or by hunting birds and wild animals. Most people get their food from farming. These are the basic ways of living for people who don't rely on trade. There are shepherds, farmers, bandits, fishermen, and hunters. Some people combine two jobs, like a shepherd who is also a bandit or a farmer who is also a hunter. People adapt in whatever way is necessary to survive.

It seems that nature gives all living things the basic necessities of life. Some animals bring forth their young with enough food to last until they can care for themselves. Oviparous and viviparous animals are examples of this. Viviparous animals, for example, produce milk to feed their young for a time. Similarly, we might say that plants exist to provide food for animals, and some animals exist to provide food and materials for humans. If nature makes nothing incomplete or pointless, it seems that she made all animals for the sake of humans. Therefore, in one sense, war is a natural way of acquiring what we need, including hunting wild animals and forcing those meant to be ruled into submission. War of this kind is naturally just.

There is one kind of wealth-getting that is part of household management. This involves finding or providing what is necessary for life and what is useful for the household or the state. These are the elements of true wealth. There is a limit to how much property is needed for a good life, even though the poet Solon said, "No limit has been set on wealth." But there is a limit, just like there is for all other arts. The tools of any craft are never unlimited in number or size. Wealth can be defined as the tools needed for managing a household or a state. So, we see that there is a natural way of acquiring wealth, which is practiced by household managers and statesmen, and what is the reason of this.

There is another type of skill for getting wealth, and it's often called the art of making money. People commonly think that wealth and property have no limit because of this idea. This skill is closely related to what we've already talked about, but they're not exactly the same. The one we talked about before is more natural, while this one is learned through experience and skill.

Let's start by looking at this question with the following points in mind:

Everything we own can be used in two ways. Both uses are related to the thing, but they're not the same. One is the correct, main way to use it, and the other is a secondary, less proper use. Take a shoe, for example. You can wear it, or you can trade it. Both are uses of the shoe. If someone trades a shoe for food or money, they're using it, but that's not what it was made for. Shoes weren't created to be traded. The same is true for all things we own. The art of trading applies to all of them, and it began because some people had too little while others had too much. This shows that retail trade isn't a natural part of getting wealth. If it were natural, people would stop trading once they had enough. In the first community, which is the family, this art wasn't needed, but it became useful when society grew. Families originally shared everything. Later, when families divided, different parts had different things, so they had to trade for what they needed. This kind of barter is still used by some nations today. They trade just for life's basic needs, like exchanging wine for money. This kind of trade isn't part of the art of making wealth and isn't against nature. It's simply needed to meet people's natural needs. The more complex kind of exchange came from the simpler one. When people from one country started depending on those from another, they traded things they had too much of for things they needed. This led to the use of money, because it was hard to carry goods around. People agreed to use something useful in itself and easy to handle, like iron or silver. At first, its value was measured by weight and size, but later they put a stamp on it to avoid the trouble of weighing and to mark its value.

Once money was used, a new kind of wealth-making arose from the simple barter of necessities—retail trade. It probably started as something simple but became more complex as people learned where and how to make the biggest profit. Since money was now involved, people thought the art of making wealth was mostly about dealing with money. They believed that the goal was to collect money, thinking riches only meant having lots of coins. Since the art of getting wealth and retail trade dealt with money, people assumed money itself was wealth. But others argued that money isn't really wealth. It's just something we agree on. If people stopped using it, it would be worthless, and it's not something we need for life's necessities. A person could have lots of money and still starve, like King Midas, who, according to the story, wished for everything he touched to turn to gold. But even though he had a lot of gold, he couldn't eat any of it.

So, people look for a better understanding of wealth and how to get it than just collecting money, and they're right to do so. Natural wealth and the natural way of getting wealth are different. In their true form, they are part of managing a household. Retail trade, however, is about creating wealth through exchange. It's focused on money since money is used for trade and is the measure of that trade. There's no limit to the riches that can come from this kind of wealth-getting. Like how there's no limit to health in medicine or to achieving the goal in other skills, the goal in this kind of wealth-getting—riches— also has no limit. The art of managing a household, though, does have a limit. Its goal isn't to get unlimited wealth. So, in one way, wealth should have a limit, but in reality, people try to collect as much money as possible. The confusion happens because these two types of wealth-getting are so closely related. The tools used are the same, even though the way they're used is different. In one case, the goal is to collect as much as possible, and in the other, there's another purpose. This makes some people think that managing a household is all about collecting wealth, and their whole focus is either to increase their money or, at least, not lose it. This attitude comes from people being focused only on living, not on living well. Their desires are endless, so they want the means to meet their desires to be endless too. People who want to live well focus on getting the means to enjoy their lives. Since they believe that enjoyment depends on wealth, they focus on collecting money. This leads to the second kind of wealth-getting. Since their desire for enjoyment is excessive, they look for ways to create an excess of enjoyment. If they can't satisfy their desires with wealth-getting, they try other ways. They use their abilities in ways that go against nature. For example, courage is meant to inspire confidence, not to make money. Neither is making money the goal of a general's skill or a doctor's skill. A general aims for victory, and a doctor aims for health. Yet, some people twist every skill and quality into a way to make money. They believe money is the goal, and everything else should help them achieve that.

We've now talked about the unnecessary kind of wealth-getting and why people desire it, as well as the necessary kind of wealth-getting, which is part of managing a household and is focused on getting food. This kind of wealth-getting has limits, unlike the other kind.

We've answered the question of whether getting wealth is the responsibility of a household manager or a statesman. The answer is that wealth is something they use, but it isn't their main task. Just as political science doesn't create people but uses them as nature made them, so nature provides people with resources like land or the sea for food. This is where the job of the household manager begins. He has to make use of what nature provides, like a weaver uses wool. He doesn't make the wool but needs to know what kind is good and useful. If this weren't the case, we wouldn't know why getting wealth is part of managing a household while medicine isn't. After all, people in a household need to be healthy, just like they need to live. The answer is that the household manager does need to think about health in one way, but it's really the doctor's job. Similarly, wealth is considered by the household manager, but in a limited way, as part of a natural system. Nature provides the means of life, and the manager must use them, like food coming from plants and animals.

There are two kinds of wealth-getting. One is part of managing a household, and the other is retail trade. The first is necessary and respectable, while the second, which involves trading things for money, is often criticized because it's unnatural. Usury, or charging interest on money, is the most disliked form of wealth-getting because it takes money and makes more money from it, rather than using it for trade. Money was made to help trade, not to grow by itself. The word "interest" means the birth of money from money, and it's called this because it's like money giving birth to more money. This is why usury is seen as the most unnatural way to get wealth.

We've talked enough about the theory of getting wealth. Now, we'll move on to the practical part. It's not beneath philosophy to talk about these things, but actually doing them is not a noble or pleasant task. The useful parts of wealth-getting involve knowing which livestock—like horses, sheep, or oxen—are most profitable and where they'll thrive. A person should know which animals give the best return and which do better in certain places. Then, there's farming, which includes planting crops, keeping bees, raising fish or birds, or any animals that are useful to humans. These are the main parts of the natural way of getting wealth.

The second way, involving exchange, has several parts. The most important is commerce, which includes shipping, transporting goods, and selling them. Commerce can differ in safety and profitability. Then, there's usury, and finally, there's work for hire. This can involve either skilled mechanical arts or unskilled physical labor. There's also a middle ground between natural wealth-getting and exchange. This includes industries that make money from the land, like cutting timber or mining, even though they don't produce food. Mining itself has many branches, since there are different things to dig out of the earth. I've now covered these different ways of getting wealth in general. Going into more detail might be helpful in practice, but it would also be tedious right now.

The jobs that are the most respected involve the least amount of luck. The least respected jobs are those that wear down the body the most, and the most servile jobs are those that use the body the most. The least noble jobs are those that don't require much skill or virtue.

There are many books on these subjects, like those written by Chares of Paros and Apollodorus of Lemnos, who wrote about farming and planting. Others have written about different parts of wealth-getting. Anyone who's interested in these things can read their works. It would also be useful to gather stories of how individuals became wealthy because that information can help those who care about the art of making wealth. There's a story about Thales of Miletus and a clever way he made money. It's said he knew by studying the stars that there would be a big olive harvest that year, so during the winter, he used a small amount of money to rent all the olive presses in Chios and Miletus. When the harvest came and many people needed presses, he rented them out at a high price and made a lot of money. He showed that philosophers can be rich if they want to be, but that's not their main goal. His plan was a monopoly, something that's used often by cities when they need money. They control the supply of certain goods.

There's also the story of a man in Sicily. He used money deposited with him to buy all the iron from the mines. When the merchants came to buy, he was the only one selling. Without raising the price too much, he made a 200 percent profit. When Dionysius heard about it, he told the man to take his money and leave the city because he thought the man's way of making money was a threat to his own interests. Like Thales, this man figured out how to create a monopoly.

Statesmen should know about these things because cities often need money and have to use clever ways to get it, just like households do.

We've talked about how household management has three parts: managing slaves, which we've already discussed, being a father, and being a husband. A father and husband rules over his children and wife, but these roles are different. A father's rule is like that of a king, and a husband's rule is like that in a government. Even though there are exceptions, the male is naturally better suited to command than the female, just as an older person is superior to a younger one. In most governments, citizens take turns ruling and being ruled, since everyone is considered equal. But when one person is in charge and another is being ruled, we try to create a difference by using titles and signs of respect, like the story of Amasis and his foot-basin. The relationship between men and women is like this, but here the inequality is permanent. A father's rule over his children is royal because it's based on love and the respect that comes with age. That's why Homer called Zeus the "father of gods and men," since he was king of them all. A king is naturally above his subjects, but he should be related to them, just as a father is to his children.

It is clear that managing a household focuses more on people than on getting material things. It also values human excellence more than wealth, and the virtues of free people more than the qualities of slaves. A question might come up: can a slave have virtues like self-control, courage, or justice, or do they only have physical and servant-like qualities? And no matter how we answer, there's a challenge. If slaves do have virtues, how are they different from free people? But, on the other hand, since they are human and can reason, it seems wrong to say they don't have virtues at all.

The same question can be asked about women and children. Should women be considered brave, just, and self-controlled? Should children be called self-controlled or not? In general, we can ask whether natural rulers and natural subjects have the same virtues or not. If both need to have noble qualities, why does one always rule and the other always follow? And we can't just say it's a matter of degree because the difference between ruler and subject is a difference in kind, not just in amount.

It seems strange to think that one person should have virtue and the other shouldn't. If a ruler is unjust and lacks self-control, how can they rule well? And if a subject lacks self-control and is cowardly, how can they follow orders well? It's clear that both need to have some virtues, but they need different types of virtues, just like there are differences among natural subjects. The very makeup of the soul shows us the way. One part of the soul naturally rules, and another part naturally follows. The ruler's virtues are different from the subject's virtues. The ruler's virtue is based on reason, while the subject's virtue comes from following.

This same principle applies to almost everything. Most things in nature involve some form of ruling and following. But the type of rule is different: a free person rules over a slave in a different way than a man rules over a woman or an adult rules over a child. Even though all of them have the same parts of the soul, those parts work differently. The slave doesn't have the ability to make decisions. A woman has this ability, but it doesn't carry authority, and a child's ability is immature. So, the virtues should be different too. Everyone should have some virtues, but only the ones needed for their role.

This means the ruler should have complete moral virtue because their job requires a high level of skill. Rational thought is that skill. The subjects, on the other hand, need only the amount of virtue that fits their role. So, moral virtue belongs to everyone, but the self-control of a man and a woman, or the courage and justice of a man and a woman, are not the same. As Socrates said, a man shows courage by leading, while a woman shows courage by following. This applies to all other virtues too. If we look at them closely, we'll see that they aren't the same for everyone, even though some people say virtue is just about having a good attitude or doing the right thing.

They're mistaken. It's much better to think, as Gorgias did, that virtues should be listed separately for different types of people.

Different groups of people have different qualities. As the poet said, "Silence is a woman's glory," but that's not a man's glory. A child is still growing, so their virtue isn't just for themselves, but also in relation to adults and teachers. In the same way, a slave's virtue relates to their master. We said earlier that a slave is useful for daily needs, so they only need enough virtue to keep them from failing in their duties due to fear or lack of self-control.

Someone might ask if this means that craftsmen, too, need virtue, since they can fail in their work due to lack of self-control. But there is a big difference. A slave shares in their master's life, while a craftsman is more distant. A craftsman only reaches excellence if they become like a slave. The lower types of craftsmen have their own kind of slavery. Slaves exist by nature, but not shoemakers or other craftsmen.

So, it's clear that a master should be the source of the slave's virtue. The master should do more than just give orders; they should teach the slave how to do their duties. This is why it's wrong to think that masters shouldn't talk to their slaves and should just command them. Slaves need guidance even more than children do.

This is enough on this subject. The relationships between husband and wife, parent and child, their virtues, what's good and bad in their relationships, and how to pursue the good and avoid the bad will be discussed when we talk about different types of government. Since every family is part of a state, and these relationships are part of a family, the virtue of each part must match the virtue of the whole. Women and children must be educated with the state in mind because their virtues affect the state. They do matter because children grow up to be citizens, and women make up half of the free population in a state.

We've said enough about this for now. What's left to discuss can be covered later. With this part of our inquiry finished, we'll start on a new topic. First, we'll look at different ideas of a perfect state.

Book 2

Since we are trying to figure out what type of civil society is the best for people who have the freedom to live however they want, it's necessary to look at the governments of states that are known to be well-managed. If there are any other states that people say are properly run, we should note what is right and useful about them. And if we point out where they have failed, it's not to act like we know everything. It's because there are big problems with all the systems that already exist, which is why I've taken on this task. We will start with the part of the subject that naturally comes first. The members of any state must share everything in common, share some things but not others, or share nothing at all. Clearly, sharing nothing in common is impossible, because society itself is a kind of community. The first thing necessary for that is a common place to live—the city—which must be one, and every citizen must have a share in it. But in a well-founded government, is it better to make everything shareable, or only some things but not others? For example, citizens might share their wives, children, and property, as in Plato's Republic, where Socrates says this should be the case. Which should we prefer—the customs we already have, or the laws Socrates suggests?

Now, having wives in common brings many difficulties, and the reasons he gives for structuring society this way don't seem logical. It also wouldn't achieve the goal he aims for. He hasn't given any specific directions for how it should work either. I agree with Socrates' idea that a city should be as unified as possible, but if you reduce it too much, it stops being a city, since a city must have a lot of people. If we go too far, we will shrink a city into a family, and a family into one person. We admit that a family is more unified than a city, and one person is more unified than a family. If this is the result, it's clear it should never be put into practice because it would destroy the city. A city isn't just a large group of people; it must have different kinds of people. If everyone were the same, it wouldn't be a city. A city and a confederacy are two different things. A confederacy is valued for its numbers, even if everyone in it does the same job. This is because a confederacy is created for mutual defense, like adding weight to tip the scale. This difference is the same between a city and a nation when people don't live in separate villages but all together like the Arcadians.

Now, there are different ways in which a city can be united, and keeping a balance of power between these is where its safety lies (as I have mentioned in my treatise on Morals). Among free and equal people, this balance is necessary because not everyone can govern at the same time. People can govern for a year or some other period, meaning that everyone takes a turn in office. It's like if shoemakers and carpenters were to switch jobs, instead of always working in the same trade. But it's obviously better for them to keep doing their own jobs. Similarly, in civil society, it would be better for the same people to continue governing where possible. But where it's not possible, as nature made all men equal, it's only fair—whether the administration is good or bad—that everyone gets to take part. In such cases, the best approach is to rotate leadership, letting people take turns submitting to those who are in office. In time, they will switch, being both governors and the governed, as if they were different people taking on different jobs.

From this, it's clear that a city can't be unified in the way some propose. What they claim would be the city's greatest good would actually be its destruction, which cannot happen because the good of anything is what preserves it. Another reason it's clear that making a city too unified is not for the best is that a family is more self-sufficient than an individual, and a city is more self-sufficient than a family. Plato also thinks that a city exists because its members can provide for themselves. If this self-sufficiency is desirable, then the less unified the city, the better.

But even if we agree that it's best for a city to be as unified as possible, that doesn't mean it will happen if everyone says, "This is mine," or "This is not mine," as Socrates suggests as proof of a city being united. The word "all" is used in two ways. If it means each individual, then what Socrates proposes will nearly happen because each person will say, "This is my son, my wife, my property," and so on. But if wives and children are shared in common, they won't say that individually. Instead, everyone will say it together, which is misleading because the word "all" is used in both a distributive and collective sense. This causes confusion in reasoning. So, for everyone to say the same thing is theirs in a distributive sense would be ideal but impossible. In the collective sense, it wouldn't help the unity of the state. There's also another problem. When something belongs to many, it's taken care of the least. People care more about what is specifically theirs than about what is shared with others. They pay less attention to it than they should. People are often more careless about things they share responsibility for than about their own personal tasks, just like how a family is often worse served by many servants than by a few.

If every citizen in the state had a thousand children, but none of them were considered their individual child, then all the children would be neglected. Whenever any citizen acted well or badly, everyone might say, "This is my son," or "This is someone else's son," and in this way, they wouldn't know whose child it was. Which do you think is better: for everyone to say, "This is mine," when they might apply it to two thousand or ten thousand people, or for someone to say, "This is mine," in our current forms of government where one man calls another his son, another calls him his brother or nephew, and each cares for him according to their relationship? It's better for someone to be a nephew in his private capacity than a son in the shared manner Socrates describes.

It would also be impossible to prevent people from realizing they are brothers, sisters, fathers, or mothers to each other. From the natural resemblance between parents and children, they would know

28

their relationship, just like writers tell us happens in some parts of the world. For example, in Upper Africa, wives are shared in common, but they still give their children to their real fathers based on their likeness to them. Some animals, like certain mares and cows, also give birth to offspring that look so much like the male that it's easy to tell which one fathered them, as with the famous mare Just in Pharsalia.

Additionally, people who propose this kind of shared community can't easily avoid the problems that come with it, such as accidental or intentional harm, quarrels, and insults. It would be wrong to treat your father or mother or close relatives this way, but these problems happen more often among people who don't know how they're related to each other. When they do happen among these people, they allow legal consequences. But when these issues arise among close family, those legal actions are not possible. It's also absurd for those who suggest a shared community to forbid people who love each other from fully indulging in their desires, while not restraining them from the passion itself. This includes the most improper relationships, like between a father and son or a brother and brother. Preventing relations between close family members, not because of the intensity of the pleasure, but because of the relationship itself, is ridiculous.

It would make more sense for farmers to share wives and children than for soldiers to do so because there would be less love among them, and these people should be under the law to follow it and not seek change. Overall, a law like this would do the opposite of what good laws should, which is what Socrates aimed to establish with his rules about women and children. We believe that friendship is the greatest good a city can have because it prevents civil strife. Friendship in a city is something Socrates praises above all else. He says it is the effect of true friendship, as Aristophanes explains in the Erotics, where he says those who love each other intensely wish to be one and the same person, blending into one soul. But if this happens, one or both of them would have to disappear.

In a city that shares everything, the bond of friendship would be weak because no father can say, "This is my son," or no son can say, "This is my father." Just like how a little sweetness gets lost when mixed with a lot of water, family ties would fade away in such a society. The names and roles that come with family would be lost. It wouldn't matter if a father had any regard for who he called his son or brothers for those they call brothers. There are two things that make people care about and love their children: knowing they are their own and knowing they should be the focus of their love. Neither of these would happen in a shared society.

Switching the children of farmers with those of soldiers, and the reverse, would only cause more confusion, no matter how it's done. The people who move the children will always know where they came from and who they gave them to. This increases the chances of harm, inappropriate love, fights, and similar problems. For example, those who are taken from their real parents and given to the soldiers won't call each other brother, son, or father. The same thing would happen to soldiers placed among farmers, and everyone would be afraid of acting inappropriately toward someone they might be related to.

Next, let's look at how property should be handled in a state with the best form of government. Should property be shared or not? This is a separate question from what we discussed about wives and children. Should property stay separate, as it is now everywhere, or should both possessions and their use be shared in common? Another option is for the land to have individual owners, but for the produce to be gathered and used as common property, as some nations do today. Or should the land be shared, and should it be farmed in common, with the produce then divided among individuals for personal use, as is said to be practiced by some barbarians? Or should both the land and its produce be shared? When the citizens aren't the ones farming, it's easier to settle. But when those who farm also have a shared right to the land, there can be problems. There might not be an equal amount of work done compared to how much people consume. Those who work hard but get little will certainly complain about those who do less but take more.

Overall, sharing everything between people is difficult, and this is especially true when it comes to property. We can see this in new colonies, where settlers often have conflicts over minor things and even fight over trivial matters. We also see that the slaves we most often punish are the ones who do the common chores for the household. So, sharing property has these and other problems.

But the way of life we have now, especially when guided by good morals and fair laws, is far better because it combines the benefits of both shared and private property. In some ways, property should be somewhat shared, but overall, it should stay private. When everyone focuses on their own property, there will be fewer complaints. This will also encourage people to work harder to improve their private property. Then, through virtue, they will help each other according to the saying, "All things are common among friends." In some cities, traces of this custom can be seen, showing it's not impossible, especially in well-governed cities. In these places, some things are shared while others are private. In Sparta, for example, people share each other's slaves, as if they were their own. They also share their horses, dogs, and sometimes even food when traveling.

So, it's clear that it's best for property to be private, but for its use to be shared. It's up to the lawmaker to figure out how to make this happen. There's also great satisfaction in feeling like you own something. It's natural for people to have affection for themselves, and though being selfish is often criticized, it's natural. We don't mean someone who simply loves themselves, but someone who loves themselves more than they should. In the same way, we criticize those who love money, yet everyone loves both money and themselves. It also brings pleasure to help friends, companions, and those we're connected to through hospitality. This is impossible without private property.

In a society that's too unified, these opportunities are lost, and two key virtues—modesty and generosity—are also lost. Modesty is about respecting other people's relationships, and generosity depends on private property. Without private property, no one can be generous or do noble deeds because generosity is about giving away what belongs to you.

The system of shared property seems appealing at first because of its appearance of kindness and friendship. It might give someone the impression that it will create a strong bond between everyone, especially when people criticize the problems in society today, like disputes over contracts, fraud, perjury, and flattery of the rich. But these problems don't come from private property; they come from human vices. In fact, people who share everything are more likely to argue than those who have private property. There are fewer examples of conflict in shared-property systems only because so few people live that way. It's important to note not only the problems avoided by sharing property but also the benefits lost. When everything is considered, this way of life turns out to be impractical.

We should assume that Socrates made a mistake because the idea he started with was wrong. We agree that a family and a city should be united in some ways, but not completely. If a city goes too far in becoming just one, it will no longer be a city. There's also a point where a city could still be called a city but would be so close to not being one that it would be worse than nothing. It's like trying to make all the voices in a choir sound like one, or reducing a whole verse to just one word. The people should be united as a community, as I've said before, through education. At Sparta and in Crete, their lawmakers made property and public meals common to everyone. But anyone who thinks they can make their city excellent and respectable by introducing education alone is mistaken if they don't also shape it with good manners, philosophy, and laws.

Anyone trying to establish a government where goods are shared should look at the experience of many years, which would show whether or not this idea is helpful. Almost everything has already been discovered, but some things have been forgotten, and other things, though known, haven't been put into practice. This would be even more obvious if someone could see such a government actually working. It would be impossible to create such a city without breaking it into separate parts, like public meals, neighborhoods, and tribes. Here, the laws would only prevent the military from working in agriculture, which is what Sparta tries to do.

Socrates hasn't told us (and it's not easy to say) how the government should deal with individual people in a state where goods are shared. His citizens will mostly be people from different jobs, but he hasn't decided what to do about them. Should the farmers' property be shared or should each person have their own part? Should their wives and children be shared too? If everything is shared equally, what will set them apart from the military? What would they gain from accepting the rule of the military? Why would they do it unless they follow the wise idea of the Cretans, who allow their slaves to have everything except physical training and the use of weapons?

If these people don't have their property in common like other cities, then what kind of community would there be? In one city, you would end up with two separate groups opposing each other. Socrates makes the military the guardians of the state and the farmers, artisans, and others into citizens. But all the arguments, accusations, and problems that he says ruin other cities would be present in his city too. Socrates also claims they won't need many laws because of their education, only laws for basic things like streets and markets. However, he only focuses on educating the military and ignores everyone else.

Socrates makes the farmers pay a tax in exchange for owning property, but this would likely make them more troublesome and rebellious than the Helots, Penestae, or other slaves. He doesn't say if he would take care of these details, like their government, education, and laws. It's not a small issue and not easy to figure out how to organize these things while still keeping the military community intact.

Also, if wives are shared but property is kept separate, who will take care of household matters with the same care that men give their farms? The problem wouldn't be fixed by making both property and wives common. And it's absurd to compare humans to animals and say that the connection between a man and a woman should be like that of animals, which don't have family relationships.

Socrates's plan for government is risky because he suggests keeping people of the same rank in office forever. This can lead to rebellion even among people with little power, but especially among those with courage and a warrior mindset. It seems necessary for him to arrange his community this way because he believes that God mixed a small bit of gold into some people's souls, which stays with them from birth. He says some people are born with gold and others with silver, while farmers and artisans have brass and iron.

Even though Socrates denies happiness to the military, he says that a lawmaker should make all citizens happy. But it's impossible for a city to be happy unless all or most of it is happy. Happiness is not like numbers adding up to a certain sum, where none of the parts contain happiness on their own. Happiness must be in every individual, just like certain qualities belong to every whole thing. And if the military isn't happy, who else would be? The artisans and common people doing low-level jobs certainly aren't happy. The state Socrates describes has these problems and others that are just as serious.

This is also true in his later work on laws, so it makes sense to briefly consider what he says about government there. In that work, Socrates only deals with a few aspects of government in detail, like how to share wives and children, how property should be handled, and how the government should run.

He divides the people into two groups: farmers and soldiers. From these, he picks a third group to be senators and run the city. But he doesn't say whether the farmers and artisans will have a say in government or whether they'll have weapons and join in wars. He thinks that women should also fight in wars and be educated like the soldiers. As for other details, his work is filled with ideas unrelated to government. When it comes to education, he only talks about how the soldiers should be educated.

In his book about laws, he mainly focuses on laws, and he says little about the actual government. The system he wants would create more of a shared community than any other city, but it ends up being similar to the first system he described. Except for shared wives and goods, both systems are set up the same way. In both, the citizens have the same education, don't do menial work, and eat together in public meals. The only difference is that in one system, the women eat separately, and there are a thousand soldiers. In the other system, there are five thousand soldiers.

All of Socrates's arguments are impressive, clever, and full of new ideas. But it's probably too much to say that all of them are true. As for the number of soldiers he mentions, we have to admit that he would need a huge country, like Babylon, to support five thousand idle men, plus even more women and servants. Anyone can make up whatever plan they want, but it should at least be possible.

A lawmaker should consider two things when making laws: the land and the people. It's also wise to think about the neighboring states if the community is going to have any kind of political relations with them. They need to know how to defend themselves, not just in their own country but in other countries too. Even if someone chooses not to engage in public or private life, they still need to be a threat to their enemies, both when defending their land and when attacking others.

We might also consider if people's property could be divided up more clearly than Socrates suggests. He says that everyone should have enough to live moderately, as if someone had said they should live well, which is a broader idea. A person can live moderately and still live miserably at the same time. He should have proposed that people live both moderately and generously because if you don't balance these two things, either luxury or poverty will follow. These are the only two ways people use their money. We can't say that a person's fortune makes them kind or brave, but we can say that they are wise and generous, which are qualities related to their money.

It's also strange to make property equal without thinking about the increasing number of citizens. Leaving that uncertain, as Socrates does, assumes that things will work themselves out depending on how many women are childless. But this is not the same as how things happen in real cities. In real cities, no one goes without because the property is divided among everyone, no matter how many there are. But in Socrates's system, property can't be divided, so if there are too many people, some will have nothing at all. It's more important to control the growth of the population than to regulate property, and in doing so, you have to consider children who will die and women who will be barren. Ignoring this, as is done in many cities, leads to poverty, and poverty causes rebellion and crime. Phidon of Corinth, one of the oldest lawmakers, thought that families and the number of citizens should always stay the same, even if the amount of land they originally received didn't match their numbers.

In Plato's Laws, the situation is different. We'll talk later about what we think is best in these matters. Plato also didn't explain how the rulers should be chosen from the common people. He says that like wool is made into different threads, some people should govern, and others should be governed. But if Plato allows their property to increase fivefold, why doesn't he allow the country to grow in the same way? He should also think about whether his system of assigning houses will work. He gives two houses to each person, but it's not practical for someone to live in two houses.

He wants his government to be something between a democracy and an oligarchy, which he calls a polity. This is because it will be made up of soldiers. If Plato wanted to create a state where everything is more shared than in any other state, he's given it the right name. But if he meant for it to be the next best state after the one he described earlier, it isn't. Some people might prefer the Spartan system of government or another system that better achieves an aristocracy.

Some people say the best government is one that combines parts of all other types of government. That's why they praise Sparta. They say Sparta's government includes elements of oligarchy, monarchy, and democracy. The kings represent the monarchy, the senate represents the oligarchy, and the ephors, who are chosen from the people, represent the democracy. Others say the ephors have absolute power and that the common meals and daily life represent the democracy.

Plato says in his Laws that the best government is one that mixes democracy with tyranny, but no one else would call that a real government, and if it is, it would be the worst possible kind. Those who suggest mixing many types of government have a better idea because the most perfect government is one made up of many parts. But Plato's government shows no sign of a monarchy, only oligarchy and democracy. He seems to favor oligarchy, as seen in how he assigns the magistrates. Choosing them by lot is common in both oligarchy and democracy, but requiring that a rich man must be a member of the assembly, while others are left out, leans toward oligarchy. Plato also tries to ensure that most of the rich will hold office, and the rank of officials will match their wealth.

The same idea applies to how the senate is chosen. The election process favors an oligarchy. Everyone must vote for the first-class senators, then the same number from the second class, and then from the third class. But the lower classes aren't required to vote for the third and fourth classes. Only the first and second classes must vote for the fourth. He thinks this will create an equal number of senators from each class, but he's wrong. The majority will always be from the upper classes and the wealthiest people. This is because many of the common people won't be required to attend the elections and won't bother showing up.

It's clear that this state will not be a mix of democracy and monarchy. We will explain this further when we discuss this type of government in more detail. There's also a big risk in how the senate is chosen because the elected senators get to choose the others. If even a small group of people decide to work together, they can always control the election. These are some of the ideas Plato suggests in his book about laws.

There are also other types of government that have been suggested by private individuals, philosophers, or politicians. These come much closer to the governments that have been established or that exist today, unlike Plato's two systems. These suggestions don't include sharing wives and children or having public meals for women, but instead, they focus on the rules that are absolutely necessary.

Some people believe that the first goal of a government should be to manage private property well. They say that ignoring this leads to all kinds of conflicts. For this reason, Phaleas of Chalcedon suggested that the fortunes of the citizens should be equal. He thought this would be easy to do when a community is first set up, but it would be more difficult in one that has been established for a long time. However, he still believed it was possible by making the rich give marriage gifts but never receive them, while the poor would always receive but never give them.

But Plato, in his Laws, thinks that some differences in wealth should be allowed, as long as no one can have more than five times the amount of the poorest person, as we've already mentioned. Lawmakers who try to enforce these rules often forget something important. While they limit how much property someone can own, they also need to control how many children people have. If the population grows beyond what the available resources can support, the law would have to be changed. Even after the law is changed, many people would still end up poor. This shows how easy it is for those trying new ideas to make mistakes.

Some of the ancients understood that having some equality in wealth could help strengthen society. For example, Solon made a law, as did others, to stop people from owning as much land as they wanted. Similarly, there are laws that prevent people from selling their property, like in Locri, unless they can prove they suffered some serious misfortune. People were supposed to hold onto their inherited property. When the Leucadians broke this custom, it made their government too democratic, because it was no longer necessary to have a certain amount of wealth to be a magistrate. However, if wealth is distributed too equally, it could allow people to live in luxury, which might be too much. On the other hand, if it's too little, it could force people to live miserably. So, it's clear that lawmakers shouldn't aim for total equality, but instead, should find a balance.

Even if someone could divide up property so that everyone had enough, it wouldn't be enough to fix the problem. What matters more is that citizens share the same values, and that can't happen unless they are properly educated under the law. Phaleas might say that's exactly what he proposed, with both equal property and a single system of education. But he didn't explain what kind of education he meant, and even if there's only one type of education, it might teach people to be too focused on gaining honors or wealth, or both.

It's not just inequality in wealth, but also inequality in honors, that can cause unrest. The common people will cause trouble if wealth is unequal, while those with higher ambitions will rebel if honors are too equal.

"Both good and bad should not be treated the same."

People don't only commit crimes because they need the basics, like food or warmth (which Phaleas thought equal wealth would solve). They also steal to get what they want or to experience pleasures they wouldn't otherwise be able to afford. What solution is there for these three types of wrongdoing? First, to prevent stealing out of need, everyone should be given enough to live on, but they should also need to work for more. Second, to stop people from stealing to get luxury items, temperance should be encouraged. And third, those seeking pleasure for its own sake should look for it in philosophy, while everyone else will need to rely on other people for help.

Since people commit the worst crimes because of ambition, and not just to meet basic needs, no one tries to become a tyrant just to stay warm. That's why the highest praise goes to the person who kills a tyrant, not just a thief. Phaleas's system might help prevent minor crimes, but it wouldn't stop greater ones.

Phaleas was also very focused on creating rules to perfect the internal order of his city, but he should have done the same for its neighbors and foreign nations. When planning a government, it's important to think about military needs, so the city isn't defenseless in case of war, but Phaleas didn't mention that at all. Property should not only be distributed in a way that meets the city's needs, but also in a way that prepares it for external threats.

The amount of wealth shouldn't be so large that it tempts stronger neighbors to invade, but it shouldn't be so small that the city can't defend itself against equal powers. Phaleas didn't address this at all. It's true that it's better for a city to be rich than poor. A good rule to follow is to have enough wealth that a more powerful neighbor wouldn't bother attacking you, but not so much that they think it's worth the effort. This is like when Autophradatus wanted to besiege Atarneus, but Eubulus told him to think about how long it would take to capture the city. He advised him that even if it took less time than planned, it wouldn't be worth it, so Autophradatus gave up the siege.

It's true that equal wealth can help prevent conflicts, but not by much. People with great talents will resent being treated as equals with the rest of society. Because of this, they are often quick to start conflicts or rebellions. People's greed has no limits. While they may start by wanting just a little more, their desires grow and grow until they want everything. Many people live only to satisfy these endless desires.

The real solution isn't to focus on making everyone equally wealthy, but to stop good people from wanting more than what's theirs, and to prevent bad people from getting what doesn't belong to them. This can be done by keeping them in lower positions and ensuring they aren't treated unfairly.

Phaleas didn't do a good job with his idea of equal property because he only applied it to land. A person's wealth includes more than just land—it also includes slaves, livestock, money, and other possessions. There should be either equality in all of these things, or clear rules about them, or they should be left completely unrestricted. It also seems that Phaleas wanted to create a small state because he intended for all craftsmen to work for the public and not be considered citizens. If all public workers are to be owned by the state, this should be done like it was in Epidamnum or as Diophantus once organized it in Athens. From these points, anyone can judge whether Phaleas's plan was well-thought-out or not.

Hippodamus, the son of Euruphon of Miletus, invented the idea of designing city layouts and was the one who planned the division of the Piraeus. He was always looking for attention and seemed to live in an eccentric way. He had long hair, dressed in flashy clothes, and wore a heavy cloak even in the summer. He wanted to be known as an expert in many subjects and was the first person, without being involved in politics, to ask what the best form of government was. He designed a state with 10,000 citizens, divided into three groups: craftsmen, farmers, and soldiers. He divided the land into three parts, one for religious purposes, one for public use, and one for private citizens. The land for religious purposes was for supporting worship, the public land was for the soldiers, and the private land was for the farmers.

He also thought there only needed to be three kinds of laws, which would deal with assault, property damage, and death. He suggested that there should be a special court of appeal where cases could be reviewed if someone thought they were judged unfairly elsewhere. This court would be made up of older men chosen for this task. He also proposed that judges shouldn't cast their votes in the usual way. Instead, they should use a tablet to say whether they thought someone was guilty or not. If they found someone guilty of one part of the charge but not the other, they could write that on the tablet too. Hippodamus didn't like the usual way of deciding cases, which forced judges to make a decision one way or the other. He also made a law that anyone who came up with a good idea for the city should be rewarded, and that the children of soldiers who died in battle should be educated at the city's expense. This law hadn't been suggested by any previous lawmaker, though it is used now in Athens and other cities. He wanted the magistrates to be chosen from all three groups he mentioned earlier. The magistrates would be in charge of public matters, as well as taking care of strangers and orphans.

These are the most important points of Hippodamus's plan. However, some might question his decision to divide the citizens into three parts. The craftsmen, farmers, and soldiers all make up one community, but the farmers don't have weapons, and the craftsmen don't have either weapons or land, which makes them almost like slaves to the soldiers. It's also impossible for everyone in the community to share in the most important jobs, like generals or protectors of the state. These roles must go to the soldiers, who would hold the highest offices. But since the other two groups wouldn't have a part in the government, why would they care about it?

It's necessary for the soldiers to be stronger than the other two groups, and this won't be easy unless they outnumber them. If the soldiers do outnumber the others, why should there be any other groups at all? Why should these other groups have a right to elect the magistrates? Also, what role do the farmers play in this system? Craftsmen are needed because every city needs them, and they can live by working in their trade. If the farmers were providing food for the soldiers, then they would be a part of the community. But in

Hippodamus's system, the farmers are supposed to own private property and work it for themselves.

If the soldiers are supposed to work the land assigned to them for their own support, then there would be no difference between a soldier and a farmer, which Hippodamus didn't intend. If someone else is supposed to farm both the private property of the farmers and the common land for the soldiers, this would create a fourth group in the city. This group would have no part in the government and would likely be hostile toward it.

If someone suggested that the same people farm both their own land and the public land, then there wouldn't be enough food to support two households. The land wouldn't produce enough for both the farmers and the soldiers, and all this would lead to chaos.

I also don't agree with his method of handling legal cases, where he wants judges to divide up a simple case into parts. Instead of being judges, they would become arbitrators. When a matter goes to arbitration, several people usually discuss it together, but this doesn't happen when a case goes before judges. In fact, many lawmakers make sure that judges can't share their opinions with each other. Besides, what would stop confusion in court when one judge thinks a fine should be one amount, and another thinks it should be something else? One might propose a fine of twenty minae, another ten, another less, and another even less. In this way, they would all disagree, with some giving the full amount asked for and others giving nothing. How could their final decisions be settled?

A judge wouldn't be lying if they simply found someone guilty or innocent, as long as the case was fair. The judge who acquits someone isn't saying they shouldn't pay a fine at all, but that they shouldn't have to pay the full fine of twenty minae. However, a judge who finds someone guilty would be lying if they sentenced them to pay twenty minae when they believe the fine should be less.

As for rewarding those who suggest something useful for the city, this sounds good in theory, but a lawmaker shouldn't actually make it a rule. It would encourage informers and likely cause unrest in the city.

This suggestion raises even more questions. Some people wonder whether it's helpful or harmful to change the established laws of a country, even if it's for the better. For this reason, it's hard to say whether this idea would be useful or not. We know that it's possible to suggest improvements to both laws and government for the common good. Since I've mentioned this subject, it's worth exploring a little further because it's a difficult issue.

It might seem better to change the laws since it has been helpful in other fields. Medicine, for example, has advanced beyond its original methods, as have gymnastics and other arts. So, we can be certain that the same is true in the art of government. History shows us that the old laws were often too simple and primitive. For example, the Greeks used to carry swords in the city and bought their wives from each other. All the old laws that we still have are quite basic. In Cuma, there was a law about murder that said if a person could get a certain number of their relatives to testify against someone, that person would be found guilty.

In general, everyone should aim to follow what is right, not just what is traditional. The first people on earth, whether they came from the ground or survived some disaster, probably had little understanding or knowledge, as is said about early humans. It would be foolish to continue following their rules. It's also wrong to keep written laws unchanged forever. Just like in other fields, in politics it's impossible to write everything down perfectly. When we put things in writing, we have to use general terms, but every situation is different and unique. This shows that some laws can be changed when necessary.

However, looking at the issue from another angle, we see it's something that requires great caution. If the benefit of changing the law is small, it might be better to leave things as they are because making it too easy for people to change their laws can have bad consequences. It's often better to overlook some mistakes made by lawmakers or officials because the harm of changing the law could be worse than the benefit.

The example from other fields is misleading because changing a law is not the same as improving a craft. A law gets its strength from tradition, and that takes time to build. If we make it too easy to change the law, we weaken its authority. This brings up another question. If we are to change laws, should we change all of them? Should this happen in every government or just some? Should one person decide or should many? These are important differences, and for now, we'll leave this issue and explore it more at another time.

There are two main questions to consider about the government in Sparta and Crete, and in almost all other states: First, do their laws create the best government possible? Second, is there anything in the way the government is set up or run that stops it from following the original plan? In a well-organized state, it's agreed that people should be free from hard labor. But it's not easy to figure out how to make that happen. For example, the Penestae often revolted against the Thessalians, and the Helots frequently rebelled against the Spartans. The Helots were always looking for a chance to take advantage of any trouble that might weaken Sparta. However, this didn't happen with the Cretans. One reason is that although the Cretans were often at war with neighboring cities, none of those cities were willing to support the revolters because they had their own slaves to worry about. But in Sparta, there was constant hostility between them and their neighbors, such as the Argives, Messenians, and Arcadians. The first rebellion of slaves against the Thessalians happened while they were at war with their neighbors, the Achaeans, Perrhaebians, and Magnesians.

In my opinion, managing these slaves is always a difficult task. If you are too lenient, they become arrogant and think they are equal to their masters. But if you treat them harshly, they will hate you and plot against you. It's clear that no one has figured out the best way to deal with slaves yet.

Letting women have too much freedom in society is also harmful to the government and the city's well-being. A man and his wife are two parts of a family, and if you think of the city as divided in two, you'd expect the number of men and women to be equal. So, in any city where the women are not under proper rules, you could say that half of the city is not following the law. This was the case in Sparta. The lawmaker focused on making the men warriors, and he succeeded in that, but he completely ignored the women. The women lived without restraint, indulging in luxury and improper behavior.

Because of this, wealth became highly valued in Sparta, especially when men were influenced by their wives. This has happened to many brave and warlike people, except for the Celts and other nations that openly practiced male relationships. The first mythmakers probably had a reason for pairing Mars, the god of war, with Venus, the goddess of love, because nations like these are often either devoted to the love of women or to male lovers. In Sparta, the women held a lot of influence, which led to many decisions being made by them. It doesn't matter whether the power is in the hands of women or in the hands of those they control—the outcome is the same.

This boldness of the women wasn't helpful in everyday matters, and if it were useful, it would be in war. But even in war, the Spartan women were a huge disadvantage. This was proven during the Theban invasion, when they didn't contribute at all and caused more trouble than even the enemy did.

The reason Spartan women had so much freedom can be traced back to the long time the men spent away on military campaigns against the Argives, and later against the Arcadians and Messenians. When these wars ended, the men had learned a disciplined, military way of life and were prepared to follow the laws of their lawgiver. However, we are told that when Lycurgus tried to make the women follow his laws, they refused, and he gave up trying. It may be said that the women were to blame for this, but we're not focusing on blame here. The question is what is right and what is wrong. And when women's behavior isn't properly controlled, it not only brings disgrace to the state but also increases the desire for wealth.

Another issue was the unequal distribution of property. Some people had far too much, while others had too little, which led to land being concentrated in the hands of a few. Lycurgus made it shameful to buy or sell land, which was a good idea. But he allowed people to give away or bequeath their land, which caused nearly the same problems. It's estimated that almost two-fifths of the land was owned by women because they often inherited property and brought large dowries into marriages. It would have been better to limit what women could inherit or own, either giving them nothing, a small amount, or a set portion. As it stands, anyone can make a woman their heir if they want. And if someone dies without a will, the legal heir can give the property to anyone they choose.

Because of this, although the land is capable of supporting 1,500 cavalry and 30,000 infantry, the number of soldiers has dropped to less than a thousand. This clearly shows that the system was poorly managed, as the city couldn't withstand even one major crisis and was ruined because there weren't enough men.

It's said that during the reign of the ancient kings, foreigners were given citizenship to prevent a shortage of people while Sparta fought long wars. It's also believed that Sparta once had a population of 10,000. Whether this is true or not, it's clear that having more equal property helps increase the number of people. The law that was meant to encourage large families didn't fix this inequality. Lycurgus wanted the Spartans to have as many children as possible, so he made laws to encourage this. For example, a man with three children didn't have to stand night guard, and a man with four children didn't have to pay taxes. But it's clear that if the land was divided in such a way, having more people would only lead to more poverty.

Lycurgus also made mistakes with how he set up the ephorate (a council of five elected officials). These ephors were responsible for making important decisions, but they were chosen from the general population. This meant that a poor person could be elected and easily bribed. There have been many examples of this in the past, including the recent events in Andros. These corrupt men tried to bring down the city, and because their power was so great, almost tyrannical, the kings were forced to flatter them, which weakened the state. This turned Sparta from an aristocracy into more of a democracy.

The ephorate is the main support of the state, because people feel reassured knowing that they could be chosen for the highest office. Whether this was Lycurgus's plan or just happened by chance, it has helped the state. It's important for every part of the government to support the rest to keep it stable. This is why the kings always act to protect their honor, the wise and good protect the senate, and the common people support the ephors, since they come from the people.

It's good that the ephors are chosen from the whole community, but the way they are selected now is ridiculous. The ephors are in charge of judging the most important cases, but since anyone could be chosen by chance, they shouldn't rely on their own opinions. Instead, they should follow written laws or customs. Their lifestyle is also too lenient, while others in the city live too harshly. Because of this, some secretly break the laws to enjoy life's pleasures.

There are also problems with how the senators are selected. If they were truly trained in every human virtue, they could be very useful to the government. But even if they were good men, it could be debated whether they should remain judges for life, since the mind ages just like the body. However, since the senators weren't raised in such a way that they could be trusted to always do good, their power puts the state at risk. We know that senators have been guilty of taking bribes and showing favoritism in many public matters. It would have been much better if they were held accountable for their actions, but they are not.

Some might say that the ephors act as a check on all the magistrates, and it's true that they have a lot of power in this area. But I believe they shouldn't have as much control as they do. Additionally, the way the senators are elected is very childish. It's also wrong for people to campaign for an office they want. Everyone should serve in whatever role they are fit for, whether they want to or not. Lycurgus's goal was to fill his government with ambitious men seeking honors, which is why the senate is filled with men like this. However, most crimes are committed because of ambition or greed.

We can discuss whether kings are necessary for the state another time, but for now, it's clear that kings should be chosen based on their character, not in the way they are currently selected. Lycurgus himself didn't expect to make all his citizens perfectly honorable and virtuous, which is clear because he didn't trust them. He sent people who were in conflict with each other on the same mission, believing that their rivalry would keep the state safe.

The common meals, or public dinners, were also not well organized at first. These meals should have been provided at public expense, as they are in Crete. In Sparta, however, everyone was required to contribute their share, even if they were too poor to afford it. This had the opposite effect of what Lycurgus intended. He wanted these public meals to strengthen the democratic part of the government, but in reality, they excluded the very poor. Their ancestors warned that not allowing the poor to join the common meals would lead to the ruin of the state.

Others have criticized the laws about naval affairs, and they have a point. The head of the navy was almost set up as a rival to the kings, who were the generals of the army for life.

There's also another problem with Sparta's laws, which Plato pointed out in his Laws. The whole system was designed for war. It's great for making them good soldiers, but it's not good for anything else. The state's survival depended on war, but its downfall began with its victories because the Spartans didn't know how to do anything but fight. They thought that the things people fight over are better gained through virtue than through vice, and they were right. But they wrongly valued those things more than virtue itself.

Sparta's finances were also poorly managed. The state was practically worthless, even though they were involved in major wars. They raised funds in a careless way. The Spartans owned a lot of land, but they didn't hold each other accountable for paying their share. The result was the opposite of what Lycurgus intended: the state was poor, and the citizens were greedy. These are the main problems with the Spartan government.

The government of Crete is similar to Sparta's in many ways, though it's worse in some areas. Overall, it's a less well-thought-out system. In many ways, Sparta's system was modeled after Crete's, and usually newer systems improve on the old ones. It's said that when Lycurgus finished being the guardian of King Charilaus, he traveled and spent time with his relatives in Crete. The Lycians were a colony of the Spartans, and the early settlers there adopted the laws they found in Crete. Those who live nearby still follow the laws first set up by Minos.

Crete is in a position that naturally makes it the ruler of Greece, as it is surrounded by the sea. It's not far from either Peloponnesus or Asia, where Triopium and Rhodes are located. Minos used this position to control the sea and the surrounding islands, conquering some and settling others. He eventually died in Camicus while trying to capture Sicily.

There are several similarities between Sparta and Crete. The Helots farm the land for the Spartans, and domestic slaves do the same for the Cretans. Both states have common meals, though the Spartans used to call them andreia instead of psiditia, like the Cretans do, which shows where the custom started. Their governments are also alike in other ways. The ephors in Sparta have the same role as the kosmoi in Crete, though there are five ephors and ten kosmoi. The Spartan senate is the same as the Cretan council. There was once a king in Crete, but that position was later removed, and the kosmoi became the commanders of the army.

In both states, everyone has a vote in the public assembly, but this assembly can only confirm decisions already made by the council and the kosmoi.

Crete managed the public meals better than Sparta. In Sparta, each person had to provide their own share, and if they couldn't afford it, they lost their rights as citizens. But in Crete, the public meals were paid for by the community. All the grain, livestock, taxes, and contributions from the slaves were divided up to meet the needs of the gods, the state, and the public meals. This way, everyone, including men, women, and children, was supported by a shared fund. The lawmaker also made sure that people ate modestly, believing this was good for the citizens. He also tried to keep the population from growing too large by encouraging the love of boys, which reduced the connection with women. Whether this was a good or bad idea can be discussed another time. But it's clear that Crete's public meals were better managed than those in Sparta.

The system of the kosmoi was even worse than that of the ephors. It had all the problems of the ephorate, plus some of its own. In both states, it's uncertain who will be elected. But Sparta has an advantage because everyone is eligible, which gives all citizens a stake in the government's success. This makes everyone want to protect the state. In Crete, however, the kosmoi are chosen from certain families, and the senate is selected from the kosmoi. The same criticisms of Sparta's senate apply here. The senators have too much power, especially since they serve for life, and their decisions aren't guided by written laws but by their own judgment.

The fact that there are no revolts, even though the people don't have a say in the government, isn't proof of a well-run state. The kosmoi don't face the same opportunities for bribery as the ephors, because they live on an island far from those who might corrupt them. But the way they handle problems is foolish and tyrannical. It's common for fellow magistrates or private citizens to conspire against the kosmoi and remove them from office. The kosmoi are even allowed to resign before their term ends, which would be fine if it were done by law, but it happens at the whim of individuals, which is not a good practice.

Worst of all, the kosmoi often cause chaos by disrupting the legal system. This shows what kind of government they really have—it's not so much a government as it is lawless power. It's common for the leaders to gather their supporters and some of the common people, then rebel and fight against each other. What's the difference if a state is destroyed all at once through violent means or gradually falls apart over time until it's no longer the same government?

A state like this would always be vulnerable to attack from a stronger enemy. But as I mentioned earlier, Crete's location protects it, since it is free from foreign invaders. That's why the domestic slaves in Crete remain quiet, while the Helots in Sparta are always rebelling. The Cretans stay out of foreign affairs, and it's only recently that any foreign troops have attacked the island. When they did, it quickly became clear that Crete's laws were ineffective.

That's enough for now about the government of Crete.

The government of Carthage seems to be well-organized and, in many ways, better than others. In some aspects, it is similar to Sparta, and in other ways, to Crete, though there are many differences. One of the great things about their system is that even though the people have a role in the government, it has stayed stable. There have been no major revolts from the people, and it hasn't turned into a tyranny either.

Carthage shares some features with Sparta, such as having public meals for groups of friends, similar to Sparta's Phiditia. They also have a group of 104 magistrates, similar to Sparta's ephors, but chosen with more care. In Sparta, any citizen can become an ephor, but in Carthage, they are picked from the best families. There are similarities between the kings and senates of both governments, though

Carthage's method of selecting kings is better. They don't limit the position to just one family, and they don't base it on age. Instead, they choose the most capable person, even if they are younger than other candidates. This is important because, in Carthage, the kings have a lot of power, and if they are not competent, they could harm the state, as has happened in Sparta.

In Carthage, their government is a mix of aristocracy and democracy, and some parts lean towards democracy, while others tend to create an oligarchy. For example, if the kings and senate agree on something, they don't have to bring it to the people for a vote. But if they disagree, the people get to decide. The people not only hear what the senate has approved, but they have the final say, and anyone can speak out against any proposal. This is different from other places where such freedom of speech is not allowed.

The five officials who elect each other hold a lot of power. They choose the 100 top magistrates, and their influence lasts longer than any other officials because they hold power before and after their term. This makes the government more like an oligarchy. But since they are elected based on merit and can't take bribes, they help preserve the aristocracy.

In Carthage, all cases are decided by the same magistrates, unlike in Sparta where different cases go to different courts. This system helps keep things stable. However, Carthage's government is slowly shifting from aristocracy to oligarchy because of the belief that officials should not only be from good families but also be wealthy. People think that if someone is poor, they won't be able to handle the responsibilities of office or devote enough time to public duties.

Choosing wealthy people for office makes the government lean toward oligarchy, while choosing capable people makes it more aristocratic. In Carthage, they consider both wealth and ability when selecting officials, especially for the highest positions like kings and generals. But this approach has its problems. The lawmaker should have ensured that capable citizens wouldn't be forced to do anything beneath them and would always have time to serve the public, both in office and as private citizens. If wealth becomes the main requirement for holding office, important positions will soon be bought and sold, leading to corruption. Riches would become more important than virtue, and the love of money would dominate the city. What those in power value becomes what all citizens strive for. When virtue isn't honored, an aristocracy can't thrive.

It's likely that those who buy their way into office will use their power to make money. It's unreasonable to think that a good but poor person would want to make money in office, but a bad person wouldn't want to do the same, especially to recover their costs. For this reason, the government should be made up of people who are capable of supporting an aristocracy. It would have been better for the lawmaker to ignore the poverty of good men and make sure they had enough free time to focus on public duties while in office.

It's also a mistake to let one person hold multiple offices, which was allowed in Carthage. A job is best done when one person focuses on it. It's the lawmaker's duty to make sure this happens, not to allow one person to do several jobs, just like you wouldn't expect the same person to be both a musician and a shoemaker. In a large state, it's better and fairer to let more people share in the government, because when different tasks are given to different people, things get done better and faster. You can see this in both the army and navy, where people take turns leading and following orders.

But because Carthage's government leans towards oligarchy, they avoid its bad effects by appointing some common people to run the cities and make their fortunes. This helps fix the problem and keeps the government stable, but it's still risky. The lawmaker should have set up the government so that revolts couldn't happen in the first place. Right now, if a major disaster struck and the people turned against their rulers, there would be no way to restore order through the laws.

These are the most important things about the governments of Sparta, Crete, and Carthage that deserve praise.

Some of the people who wrote about government never actually took part in public life. They lived as private citizens. We've already discussed what's important in their works. Others were lawmakers, either in their own cities or hired to fix the governments of foreign states. Some only wrote laws, while others designed the entire system of government. Lycurgus did both, as did Solon, who saved Athens from becoming a complete oligarchy and prevented the people from falling into slavery. He brought back the ancient democratic system, and each part of it was well-balanced to fit with the rest. In the senate of Areopagus, there was an oligarchy; in the election of officials, an aristocracy; and in the courts of justice, a democracy.

Solon didn't change the basic structure of the government, either the senate or how officials were elected. But he gave the people a lot of power by putting them in charge of the courts, and some people criticize him for this, saying it disrupted the balance he was trying to create. By allowing the people, chosen by lot, to judge all cases, Solon had to appeal to their power, which eventually led to the pure democracy we see today.

Both Ephialtes and Pericles reduced the power of the Areopagus, and Pericles introduced pay for those who served in the courts. Every leader who wanted to be popular gave more and more power to the people until the government became what it is now. It's clear that this wasn't Solon's original plan, but it happened by chance. The people had won the naval battle against the Medes, and that victory made them feel powerful. They followed populist leaders, even though they were opposed by the better citizens.

Solon believed it was necessary to give the people the right to choose their officials and hold them accountable. Without this, they would have been slaves and enemies to the wealthier citizens. However, he limited the elections to those who had a certain amount of wealth. Officials had to be chosen from those worth 500 medimni, those called zeugitae, or those of the third census, who were called horsemen. The fourth class, made up of craftsmen, couldn't hold office.

Zaleucus was the lawgiver for the Western Locrians, and Charondas of Catana created laws for his own city and for other cities in Italy and Sicily that were founded by the Chalcidians. Some claim that Onomacritus, a Locrian, was the first to write laws, and that he did so while studying the prophetic arts in Crete. They say Thales was his companion, and that Lycurgus and Zaleucus were his students, and Charondas was a student of Zaleucus. But this timeline doesn't add up. Philolaus, from the Bacchiadae family, was also a lawmaker in Thebes. He was very close to Diocles, an Olympic victor, who left Corinth because of an inappropriate passion his mother had for him. Diocles moved to Thebes, and Philolaus followed him. They died there, and their graves can still be seen. They were buried facing each other, but Diocles's tomb doesn't look toward Corinth because of his hatred for his mother's feelings. Philolaus's tomb does face Corinth, and that's the reason they both lived in Thebes.

Philolaus made laws about many things, including adoption, which he created to preserve the number of families. Charondas didn't make many new laws, except for one about perjury, which he was the first to address specifically. His laws were written with more care and elegance than any others we have today.

Philolaus introduced the law for the equal distribution of property. Plato created the idea of shared women, children, and property, as well as public meals for women. He also made a law about not getting drunk, so people would stay sober at their banquets. He created a rule for military exercises so that people would learn to use both hands equally, believing it was important to make both hands useful.

As for Draco's laws, they were created when the government was already in place. The only thing that stands out about them is their harshness and the extreme punishments they imposed.

Pittacus made some laws, but he didn't design a whole system of government. One of his laws stated that if a drunk person hit someone, they should be punished more severely than if they were sober. He didn't excuse bad behavior caused by drunkenness, but instead focused on the good of society. Andromadas of Rhegium was also a lawgiver for the Chalcidians in Thrace. Some of his laws, such as those about murder and inheritance, still exist, but there's nothing particularly original in them.

And that's enough for now about the different types of governments, both those that exist and those that have been proposed.

Book 3

Anyone who wants to understand government and its different types should start by asking, "What is a city?" There is disagreement about this. Some say the city did something, while others say it wasn't the city, but the oligarchy or tyranny. The city is the main focus of politicians and lawmakers in everything they do, and a government is how the people living in the city are organized. Since a city is made up of different parts, we first need to understand what a citizen is because a city is made up of citizens. So, we need to figure out who should be called a citizen and what makes someone a citizen, because this isn't always clear. For example, someone who would be considered a citizen in a democracy might not be one in an oligarchy. We're not talking about people who become citizens through special honors, but only those who have a natural right to it.

Living in a city doesn't automatically make someone a citizen. Visitors and slaves live in cities, too, but that doesn't make them citizens. Having certain legal rights, like being able to use the courts, also doesn't make someone a citizen. People from other countries can sometimes do that through agreements, but they still aren't considered full citizens. Often, visitors need the protection of a patron to use the courts, showing that they aren't fully part of the community. The same applies to children who aren't yet registered as citizens or to old men who are no longer able to serve in the military. We consider them citizens in some ways but not fully because they either aren't old enough or are past the age of service. The situation is similar for people who are banished or who have lost their honor. The clearest sign of being a full citizen is having a role in the judicial or executive parts of the government.

Some government roles are temporary, meaning that a person can't hold the position twice or must wait a certain amount of time before doing so again. Other roles, like being a juror or a member of the general assembly, aren't limited in this way. Some might argue that these aren't really offices or that these citizens don't play an important role in the government, but that's wrong. It's silly to say that people who hold the most power in the state don't hold office. This is just a disagreement about words. There's no general term that covers both jurors and assembly members, but we can call it an indefinite office. I believe that people who can hold these offices are citizens. This is the best description of what it means to be a citizen.

Everyone should also understand that parts of different things that belong to different groups become less and less similar the more they change. We can see that governments come in different forms, with some being flawed and others as good as possible. It's obvious that governments with many flaws are much worse than those without them. I will explain what I mean by flawed governments later. The role of a citizen also changes depending on the form of government. In a democracy, a citizen has all the rights that come with being a citizen, but in other forms of government, this isn't always the case. In some states, the people have no power, and there is no general assembly. Only a few selected men make decisions.

In different governments, different people handle different types of cases. For example, in Lacedaemon, contracts are handled by the ephors, and the senate judges murder cases. In Carthage, specific magistrates decide all cases. We can adjust our earlier definition of a citizen because, in some governments, the role of a juror or assembly member is not indefinite. Specific people are chosen for these roles, and all or some citizens are chosen as jurors or assembly members. They may deal with all public business or just specific issues. This helps clarify what a citizen is. A citizen is someone who has the right to participate in the judicial and executive parts of the government. A city is simply a group of these people, large enough to manage all the needs of life.

In general, people say a citizen is someone born to citizen parents on both sides, not just on the mother's or father's side. Some take this even further and ask how many generations back their ancestors were citizens, like their grandfather or great-grandfather. But some people question how the first generation of a family could prove they were citizens if this definition were used. Gorgias of Leontium made fun of this by saying that just like a mortar is made by a mortar-maker, a citizen is made by a citizen-maker. This explanation is too simple. If citizens were defined this way, it would be impossible to apply it to the founders of cities, who couldn't claim citizenship through their parents. It's even harder to figure out the rights of those who became citizens after a political revolution. For example, in Athens, after the tyrants were overthrown, Clisthenes added many foreigners and freed slaves to the citizen rolls. The question wasn't whether they were citizens but whether they were legally made citizens.

Some people even wonder if someone can be a citizen if they weren't legally made one, as if an illegal citizen and someone who isn't a citizen at all were the same. But we see that some people rule unjustly, yet we still consider them rulers, even if they aren't ruling justly. Since we defined a citizen as someone who holds certain offices, it's clear that someone who was made a citizen illegally is still a citizen, but whether this was done justly or unjustly is a different question.

It's also been debated what counts as the actions of the city. For example, when a democracy replaces an aristocracy or tyranny, some people refuse to honor their contracts, claiming that the agreement was with the tyrant, not the state. There are other similar issues, like if a government official made an agreement based on force rather than for the common good. In a democracy, the actions of officials are considered the actions of the state, just as they are in an oligarchy or tyranny.

It's important to ask when we can say a city is the same and when it has become something different. It's not enough to just look at the location or the people. These things can change, and people can live in different places. A city can be defined in many ways, so the question can be answered in many ways. If people live in the same place, when do we say they are living in the same city or that the city is the same? It doesn't depend on the walls. For example, Peloponnesus could be surrounded by a wall like Babylon, which enclosed many nations rather than just one city. Some people in Babylon didn't even know it had been captured for three days. We'll figure out the right time to answer this question because the size of a city and whether it should include more than one group of people are things politicians should know about.

Another question is whether a city stays the same while the same group of people lives there, even though some die and others are born. For example, we say a river or spring is the same even though the water is always changing. But when a revolution happens, do we say the people are the same but the city is different? If a city is a community, and the type of government changes, it seems like the city must also be different. Just like we would call a tragic chorus different from a comic one, even if the same performers were in both. In the same way, if the type of government changes, we say the city is different, just as the same hands can play different musical harmonies. So, when we say a city is the same, we are really talking about the government that's in place, no matter what name it has or who lives in it. But whether it's right to dissolve a city when the government changes is another question.

Given what's been said, we should now consider whether the same virtues that make someone a good person also make them a good citizen or if they are different. To answer this, we need to first give a general description of the virtues of a good citizen. Just like sailors are part of a crew, citizens are part of a city. Sailors have different jobs—some row, some steer, and some are in charge of the equipment—but they all share one goal: the safety of the ship. In the same way, citizens may have different roles, but they all care about the safety of the community because the citizens make up the state.

Since there are different types of governments, it's clear that what makes a good citizen in one type of government may not be the same in another. This means that a citizen's virtue can't be perfect. We call someone a good person when their virtues are perfect, so a good citizen doesn't necessarily have the same virtues as a good person. This can be proven by looking at the best-organized states. It's impossible for a city to be made up entirely of excellent citizens. Everyone should be good at their own job, but not everyone can have the same qualities. It's impossible for all citizens to have the same virtues. A city is made up of different parts, just like an animal is made up of a body and soul, and a family includes a man and woman, and property includes a master and a slave. Since a city is made up of all these different parts, it's clear that the virtues of the citizens cannot all be the same. The person leading the dance is different from the other dancers.

It's clear that the virtues of a citizen aren't all the same. But can a good person also be a good citizen? We often say someone is an excellent leader and a wise and good person. Prudence is necessary for anyone involved in public affairs. Some people believe that those who are going to rule should have a different education than other citizens, like how the children of kings are taught how to ride and fight. As Euripides says, "Teach me what the state requires." This suggests that rulers need a special education.

If we agree that the virtues of a good person and a good ruler are the same, and a citizen is someone who obeys the ruler, then the virtues of a good citizen and a good person can't always be the same, though they might be the same for some citizens. The virtue of a ruler must be different from the virtue of a regular citizen. Jason once said that if he were no longer king, he would waste away because he didn't know how to live as a regular person. It's important to know how to command and how to obey. Being able to do both well is the mark of a good citizen.

If the virtue of a good person is only about being able to command, but the virtue of a good citizen is about being able to both command and obey, then these virtues are not the same. It seems that both the ruler and the follower need to learn their roles separately, but the citizen must know how to do both. In a household, the master doesn't need to know how to do the servant's work but just benefits from the servant's labor. Doing that work would be beneath him. I mean that regular family duties are the work of a slave.

There are different types of slaves because there are different kinds of work. Artisans, for example, make their living with their hands, and these kinds of workers include all mechanics. In some states, these people were not allowed to take part in the government until democracies were established. It's not proper for an honorable person or anyone involved in public life to learn these kinds of jobs unless they need them for personal use. If this distinction isn't maintained, the line between master and slave would disappear. But there is another kind of government where men rule over their equals and other free people. We call this a political government. In this type of government, men learn to command by first learning to obey, just like a good horse general or army commander learns their duty by being under someone else's command. This is true in any part of the army. As the saying goes, no one knows how to command unless they've been commanded first.

The virtues of rulers and followers are different, but a good citizen must have both. A good citizen should know how free people should rule and be ruled, and this is also the duty of a good person. If the justice and self-control of the ruler are different from those of the free person who is being ruled, then the virtues of a good citizen must also be different from the virtues of a good person. The virtues must change in these two situations, just like the courage of a man is different from the courage of a woman. A man who had only the courage of a woman would seem like a coward, and a woman who spoke as much as a man would seem like a gossip.

The household duties of men and women are also different. The man's job is to earn a living, while the woman's job is to manage the household. Leadership and understanding of public affairs are virtues unique to rulers, though both rulers and those being ruled need other virtues. However, those being ruled don't need to worry about ruling—they just need to have the right beliefs. They are like flute makers, while the rulers are the musicians who play the flutes. This is enough to show whether the virtues of a good person and a good citizen are the same or different, and how they are sometimes the same and sometimes different.

There's still some debate about who really counts as a citizen. Are only those who can participate in the government truly citizens, or do mechanics and workers count too? If people who don't have a say in running the city are still considered citizens, then not all citizens can have the same virtue. But if we say these workers aren't citizens, where do we place them? They aren't just visitors or foreigners. Maybe it doesn't cause a problem if they aren't citizens, since they aren't slaves or freedmen either. It's true that not everyone needed for a city to function is a full citizen, just like boys aren't citizens in the same way adults are. Boys are citizens, but not fully—they aren't old enough yet. In the past, some societies made mechanics either slaves or foreigners, and this is still true today in some places. The best-organized cities often don't allow mechanics to be citizens. But if mechanics are allowed to be citizens, then we can't expect the same virtue from every citizen, only from those who aren't doing servile work.

People who work for one master are slaves, and those who work for money are mechanics or hired workers. So, it's clear what their position is. In some places, mechanics and hired workers must be allowed to be citizens, but in others, like aristocracies, they can't be. In aristocracies, honor is based on virtue, and it's impossible for someone living as a mechanic or hired worker to practice the same virtues. In an oligarchy, hired workers also aren't citizens because offices are based on wealth. But mechanics might be citizens since many of them are rich.

Thebes had a law that no one could participate in government until they'd been out of trade for ten years. In some places, laws invite foreigners to become citizens, and in some democracies, the child of a free woman is also considered free. The same happens with children born outside of marriage. But this usually happens because there aren't enough citizens being born regularly. As the population grows, cities first stop giving citizenship to children of slaves, then to children of free women, and eventually, only those whose parents are both free are considered citizens.

There are clearly different types of citizens, and a person is most fully a citizen when they share in the honors of the state. Achilles, in Homer, complains that Agamemnon treats him like a dishonored stranger. A stranger or visitor is someone who doesn't share in the honors of the city. When the right to be a citizen isn't clear, it's done to protect the residents of the city.

From what's been said, it's clear whether the virtue of a good man is the same as that of a good citizen or not. In some places, they are the same, but in others, they aren't. This doesn't apply to all citizens, but only to those who lead or are capable of leading in public affairs, either on their own or with others.

Now that we've established this, we can consider whether only one form of government should be used or if there should be more. If there should be more than one, how many should there be, and what should they look like? What are the differences between them? A form of government is the way a city is organized, especially the offices that hold the most power. The government always holds this power. The way power is shared in a city is what makes up the government. In a democracy, power is in the hands of the people. In an oligarchy, power is held by a few. So, we can say that these governments are different, and the same is true for others.

First, we should determine why a city exists and explore the different types of leadership people accept in society. I've already mentioned in my writing on household management that humans are naturally social creatures. When people don't need help from others, they still want to live together, mostly because it makes life more pleasant for everyone. This desire for a better life is something all people feel, both as individuals and as a group. But it's not just a choice—they also come together to survive. People will even endure hardships just to keep living, because life is naturally sweet and desirable.

It's easy to describe the different types of government. I've already done so in other writings. The authority of a master, though useful for both the master and the slave, is mainly for the master's benefit. The slave benefits only indirectly—if the slave is lost, the master's power ends. The authority a man has over his wife, children, and household is different. This type of leadership benefits those being governed, or at least benefits everyone equally. It's like how a doctor or a coach works for the good of the patient or athlete, not for themselves. Sometimes the doctor or coach might benefit, but that's just a bonus—it's not the main goal. The same goes for political governments that aim to maintain equality among citizens. In these governments, it's fair to take turns leading. In the past, it was normal for citizens to take turns serving the public, expecting that others would do the same for them when their turn came. But now, people want to stay in power all the time so they can keep benefiting from holding office, as if being in charge solves all problems.

It's clear that governments aiming for the common good are rightly established and truly just. Governments that only aim for the good of the rulers are based on wrong principles. They're more like a master ruling over slaves, while a city is a community of free people.

Now that we've covered these points, we can look at how many types of governments exist and what they are. First, we'll talk about their good qualities, because once we know those, it'll be easy to see their flaws.

Every government has a supreme power that controls the entire state. This power must be held by either one person, a few people, or many people. When this power is used for the common good, the state is well-governed. But when the power is only used for the benefit of the one, few, or many who hold it, the state is poorly governed. If the people making up the state are truly citizens, they must share in the benefits of government. When one person governs for the common good, we call it a monarchy. When a few people govern for the common good, we call it an aristocracy—this might be because they are the best citizens or because it's the best system for the city. When many people govern for the common good, we call it a republic, though this term can apply to other governments too. These terms make sense because it's easy to find one or a few very capable people, but it's almost impossible to find a large group where everyone is equally good. The only virtue that can exist in large numbers is courage because it comes from strength in numbers. In these kinds of states, military power will always play a major role in the government.

The corrupt versions of these governments are as follows: a monarchy can turn into a tyranny, an aristocracy can become an oligarchy, and a republic can turn into a democracy. A tyranny is a government where one person rules for their own benefit. In an oligarchy, only the rich are considered, and in a democracy, only the poor are. None of these corrupt forms have the common good in mind.

We need to explain these forms of government more clearly because they can be difficult to understand. If we want to truly understand their principles, we can't just look at their surface features—we need to dig deeper into their true nature. A tyranny is a monarchy where one person has absolute power over the entire community and every person in it. An oligarchy is where the rich hold power, and a democracy is where the poor have control.

But here's the first problem with these definitions: what if the majority of the people in a democracy are actually rich? Or what if the poor are fewer in number, but because of their strength or skill, they control the government? This raises the question of whether our definitions are correct. Also, what if the majority of the people are rich but hold power as a group? What if the minority are poor but they still hold power? Our definitions seem to miss something.

It's clear that whether power is in the hands of the many or the few might just be a matter of chance. What really matters is that when power is in the hands of a few, it's an oligarchy, and when it's in the hands of many, it's a democracy. This is because there are always more poor people than rich people. So, it's not just the number of people in power that defines these governments—it's whether the people in power are rich or poor. When the rich are in charge, it's an oligarchy, and when the poor are in charge, it's a democracy. And, as we've said, there will always be more poor than rich, which leads to constant competition between wealth and liberty for control of public affairs.

Let's now figure out the limits of oligarchy and democracy and what justice looks like in each. All people have some idea of justice, but they only get part of it right. They often don't fully understand what is absolutely just. For example, equality seems just, and it is, but only among equals. Inequality also seems just, but only among those who are unequal. People often overlook this and make bad judgments because they only think about what's good for themselves. Most people are bad judges of their own cases.

Justice relates to people, so we need to make distinctions between different kinds of people just like we do with things. I've talked about this more in my work on ethics. People often agree about equality when it comes to things, but they disagree about equality among people. This is because they are judging their own cases, and people aren't good at judging what's fair for themselves.

If society were only about keeping property safe, then people's rights in the city would be based on their wealth. Those who support oligarchy would be right—someone who contributes just a little shouldn't have the same rights as someone who contributes much more. But society isn't just about preserving life or property—it's about living well. If it were just about staying alive, then a city could be made up of slaves or even animals, but this isn't the case. These creatures don't share in the happiness of the city, and they don't live according to their own choices. A city isn't just an alliance for defense or trade. If that were true, then trade alliances between different nations would make them into one city, but that's not how cities work. For example, Tyrrhenians and Carthaginians have trade agreements, but they don't share a government or work together to improve each other's morality. They only care about preventing harm and ensuring fair trade. But a lawmaker who wants to build a city that's more than just an alliance needs to focus on making the citizens virtuous.

A city is different from an alliance for protection because its main goal is to make its citizens good and happy. If the citizens aren't virtuous, then the city is just an alliance for survival, like any other agreement between groups of people. Law is just an agreement to do justice to one another, but it's not enough to make everyone in the city good.

If we built a wall around two cities like Megara and Corinth, they still wouldn't be one city, even if the people could marry each other and trade freely. A city isn't just a group of people living close together. A true city forms when people come together not just for survival, but to live well. They join with their families and raise their children together to create a community that helps everyone live the best life possible. That's why cities have social gatherings, religious ceremonies, and celebrations to build friendships and connections. These activities help make life better and happier for everyone.

A city is a community of families and villages working together to live well and independently. It's not just about living together—it's about living the right way. Those who contribute the most to this goal should have more power in the city than those who are equal in wealth and freedom but are less virtuous. From this, we can see that in any argument about government, each side has some part of the truth.

It might also be a question where the highest power should be placed. Should it be with the majority of people, the wealthy, a group of the best people, one person better than the rest, or a ruler with complete control? No matter which one we choose, there will be some issues. For example, should the poor be in charge just because they are the majority? If that happens, they might divide the wealth of the rich among themselves. Is this wrong? It might not be, if the top power has decided it's fair. But what good is it to say something is the height of injustice if this isn't one of those cases?

If the majority takes everything from the few, it's clear the city will collapse. Virtue doesn't destroy what's virtuous, and what's right shouldn't ruin the city. So, a law that allows this can't be right, just as a tyrant's acts can't all be wrong. If someone has absolute power, they force others to follow their commands, just like how the majority can overpower the rich.

Is it fair, then, that the rich, who are the few, should hold the highest power? What if they are just as guilty of stealing from the majority? That would be as unfair as the other case. It's clear that any behavior like this is wrong. So, should those who are better than the rest have the power? But does this mean that all the other citizens will live without honor, never sharing in the city's leadership?

The city's offices are its honors, and if one group is always in charge, the rest will be without honor. Should we give power to one person who is the best fit for it? This would shrink the power even more, leaving even more people unhonored. Some might argue that a person shouldn't have the highest power but that the law should, because a person is controlled by many emotions.

But if the law creates a government of the best or a democracy, will it help in solving these problems? The issues we've mentioned will still happen.

Other points will be discussed separately, but it seems important to prove that power should belong to the many rather than the few who are considered better. We should also explain what doubts might arise. Even if no individual in the majority is fit for the highest power, when they come together, they may actually be better qualified than the few. This is not true for each one separately, but for the group as a whole. It's like how public meals are better than those prepared by just one person. Since they are many, each person brings a bit of wisdom and virtue. When they combine, they're like one person with many hands, feet, and minds. In this way, the collective understanding and morals of the group are better.

For example, the public is the best judge of music and poetry because some people understand one part and others understand another. Together, they understand the whole thing. Important people are different from the majority, just like how beautiful people are different from those who aren't, or how good paintings collect the best parts of different people into one image. Even if the separate parts, like an eye or hand, are better in real life, the whole picture is more beautiful.

But if this difference exists between every group of people and the few who are important, it might be unclear whether this is always true. In fact, it's clear that, for some groups, it isn't true. The same could be said for animals. In what way are some men different from animals? Nothing stops this from being true in some places. So, the doubt we mentioned can be settled like this: the free citizens who make up most of the people should have power in some areas. However, since they are not wealthy and don't always act with virtue, it's not safe to trust them with the highest offices in the state. They might do wrong either because of dishonesty or because they don't know better.

Still, it would be dangerous not to give them any power or role in the government. If there are many poor people who can't take part in their country's honors, there will be many enemies of the state. So, they should be allowed to vote in public assemblies and decide cases. This is why Socrates and other lawmakers gave them the power to elect officers and examine their conduct after their term. But they weren't allowed to be magistrates themselves. When the majority is gathered together, they have enough wisdom for these tasks. By mixing with those of higher rank, they help the city. Sometimes things that aren't good by themselves are better when mixed with others.

However, there is a problem with this form of government. It seems like the person who can cure someone who is sick should be the best judge of who should be hired as a doctor. But this person must be a doctor himself. The same goes for any art or skill. A doctor should report his work to another doctor, and the same is true for other professions. Doctors, for example, can be divided into three groups: those who make the medicine, those who prescribe it (like how an architect plans while a mason builds), and those who understand the science but don't practice it.

These groups exist in other arts as well. We respect the opinions of those who understand the principles of a skill, even if they don't practice it. The same applies to elections. Choosing the right person in any skill is the job of those who know that skill. For example, mathematicians should choose the best in geometry, and sailors should choose the best in steering. Even if some people know something about certain arts, they don't know more than the professionals.

So, based on this, neither the election of officers nor the review of their work should be given to the majority. But maybe this isn't entirely right. If the people aren't completely unskilled, even if each person knows less than experts, when they come together, they might know better, or at least not worse. Besides, in some arts, the worker isn't the only one who can judge the work. For example, the person who lives in the house might be a better judge of it than the builder. Similarly, a ship captain knows more about the steering equipment than the person who made it, and someone hosting a meal knows more about it than the cook.

This seems to solve this problem, but another one arises: it seems strange to give power to people with average morals instead of those with excellent character. The power to elect and judge is very important, and in some places, it's given to the people. The public assembly is the highest court, and they make decisions in all public matters, judging all cases without regard to their social standing or age. But treasurers, generals, and other high officials are chosen from people with wealth and honor.

This difficulty can also be solved in the same way. The power is not in the individual assembly members but in the assembly as a whole, which includes the council and the people. The whole group, including the senator, adviser, or judge, shares the power. For this reason, it's right that the majority should have the greatest power because the people, council, and judges are made up of them. Together, they have more wealth than any one person or small group who holds high offices. This resolves the issue.

The first question we asked shows clearly that the highest power should be in well-made laws. The magistrates, whether one or more, should decide cases where the laws can't be specific. After all, it's impossible for laws to cover every possible situation. But we haven't yet explained what these best laws should be. This is still open to debate. The laws of each state will reflect the state itself, either good or bad. It's clear that good governments will have good laws, while bad ones will have bad laws.

In every art and science, the goal is always something good, and this is especially true in founding a society, where the goal is justice. Justice benefits everyone. Most people agree that justice involves some kind of equality, and philosophers agree on this when talking about morals. They say justice means giving equal things to equals.

But we need to know how to decide what things are equal and unequal. This is a difficult question that requires the wisdom of a politician.

Some people might say that government jobs should go to the best person in each category, as long as they are similar to others in every other way. Justice gives different things to people based on their merits. But if this is true, then someone's looks, height, or similar qualities could be reasons to give them more rights. This is clearly absurd. In music, the best flute player doesn't get the best instrument because he's from the best family. His playing won't be better because of that. The best flute should go to the best player.

To make this clearer, let's say there is a great flute player who isn't from a good family and isn't very attractive. Family and beauty are more valuable than musical skill, but the best flutes should still go to the best player. Strength and size shouldn't outweigh virtue. The point is that claims to office shouldn't be based on just any advantage. For example, being fast or slow doesn't make someone more or less qualified for government, even if it matters in a race. What matters for government offices is having the skills useful to the state.

So, it makes sense that people with family, wealth, and independence should compete for these offices. A city can't be made up only of poor people, just like it can't be made up only of slaves. If people like this are necessary, then people who are just and brave are also important. No state can survive without justice, and it can't be happy without bravery.

It seems necessary, then, for the establishment of a state, that most, if not all, of these details are thoroughly examined. Virtue and education have the strongest claim to be considered the key to making citizens happy, as we've said before. Since people who are equal in one way aren't necessarily equal in all ways, and those who are unequal in one way aren't unequal in all ways, it follows that any government based on such a principle is flawed.

As we've already said, all members of the community will argue over who should hold office; and they may be right in some ways, but not in all. For example, the rich argue that they should lead because they have the most land, and since the right to land is shared by the community, their wealth is seen as dependable. Free men and those from noble families also dispute who should hold power, as they see themselves nearly equal. These men argue that their heritage gives them a higher status than those from obscure backgrounds, as honorable ancestry is respected everywhere. It's also reasonable to think that descendants of virtuous men will be virtuous too, as noble birth is seen as the source of virtue. This is why virtue itself has the right to claim power. For instance, justice is a virtue so essential to society that all other virtues must come second.

Now, let's see what the majority has to argue against the few. They might say that, collectively, they are stronger, richer, and better than the few. But if it happens that the rich, the noble, and the good all live in the same city, like the majority, will there still be a reason to argue over who should govern, or will there not? In any community we've mentioned, there's no argument over who holds supreme power; as the communities differ, so do the ruling groups. In one state, the rich rule, in another, the virtuous do, and each rules based on their own customs. But what happens when all these different groups live in the same city at the same time? If the virtuous are very few in number, what should we do? Should we prefer the virtuous due to their abilities if they are capable of governing? Or should we choose them if they almost make up the entire state?

There's also a debate over the claims of those who argue they should govern due to their wealth or family status. They don't have a strong defense, since, based on their argument, if one person is richer than all the others, that one person would have the right to govern everyone. In the same way, one person from the best family would claim the right over others based on family merit. Likewise, in an aristocracy, the same argument might apply to virtue—if one person is more virtuous than all the others, then that person should rule. By the same logic, while the majority believes they should rule due to being stronger, if a small group is stronger than the majority, then the smaller group should rule instead.

All of this shows that none of these principles can fairly justify the right to supreme power, and no one can claim that all others must obey them. For those who claim to rule based on virtue or wealth, they might have objections, because it's possible that the majority can sometimes be better or richer than the few, not as individuals, but collectively.

To address the question some people have raised: should a legislator create laws that serve the best part of the citizens or the majority, in the circumstances we've discussed? The fairness of something lies in its equality, so what is equally right will benefit the entire state and every citizen.

In general, a citizen is someone who shares in governing and is also willing to be governed. This varies in different states, but the best system is one where a man can live a virtuous life, both publicly and privately. But if there is one person or a very small group who are extremely virtuous—so much that the virtue of the majority cannot compare—such a person or group shouldn't be considered part of the city. It would be wrong to treat them as equals to those who are so inferior to them in virtue and ability, as they would appear god-like compared to ordinary men. This shows that laws must be designed for those who are equal in nature and power. These exceptionally virtuous men are not subject to laws, for they are like a law unto themselves. It would be absurd to try to subject them to the penalties of the law. As Antisthenes said, when the lions were asked to share equal power with the hares, they refused. This is why democratic states use ostracism—to keep equality their main goal. They force those who become too powerful in wealth, influence, or other areas to leave the city for a time. As the story goes, Hercules wasn't taken aboard the ship Argo because of his superior strength. Those who dislike tyranny and criticize the advice Periander gave to Thrasybulus should realize that Periander's suggestion wasn't without reason. The story goes that Periander didn't say anything to the messenger sent to consult him. Instead, he simply struck down the tallest ears of corn in the field, reducing them to the same height. The messenger relayed this back to Thrasybulus, who understood the message—that he should eliminate the city's leading men. This isn't just helpful to tyrants; oligarchies and democracies also use similar tactics. Ostracism works in a similar way, by restraining and exiling those who grow too powerful. Even powerful governments, like Athens, imposed their will on places like Samos, Chios, and Lesbos after gaining control of Greece, violating previous agreements. The King of Persia also often suppresses the Medes and Babylonians when they try to regain their past power. Every government, even the best-run ones, keeps this principle in mind—some for private gain, others for the public good.

This is also seen in other fields, like the arts. A painter wouldn't draw an animal with a foot that's too large, no matter how beautiful it is otherwise. A shipbuilder wouldn't make one part of a ship larger than it should be. The leader of a band won't let someone who sings louder than everyone else dominate the performance. In the same way, a monarch might act in line with free states to maintain his own power, just as they do to benefit their own communities. When there's a recognized difference in the power of citizens, the idea behind ostracism is politically just. But it's better for a legislator to create a system from the start that doesn't need such measures. If problems arise later, they should fix them with careful correction. However, ostracism was often used improperly, not for the community's benefit but as a weapon for causing conflict.

It's clear that in corrupt governments, ostracism is partly just and useful to the individual, but it's also evident that it isn't entirely fair. In well-governed states, there's doubt about its usefulness—not because of differences in strength, wealth, or connections, but when the superiority lies in virtue. In that case, what should be done? It doesn't seem right to exile such a person, but it also doesn't seem right to govern them, as that would be like trying to share power with Zeus.

The only natural solution is for everyone to submit to the leadership of those who are truly virtuous and allow them to rule as kings forever.

It seems now appropriate to change our focus and look into the nature of monarchies. We've already accepted that monarchies are one of the valid forms of government. Let's consider whether a monarchy is suitable for a city or country focused on the happiness of its people or if another form of government would be better. First, let's determine whether monarchy is of one type or several. It's easy to see that there are many kinds and that governments don't all operate the same way. In Sparta, for example, the king's power is mostly regulated by law and isn't absolute in all matters. When the king leaves the state, he becomes the army's general and oversees religious affairs. In essence, the king there is more of a general, not to be held accountable for his actions, and his command is for life. He doesn't have the power of life and death except as a general, as we see in their military expeditions, something Homer describes. For example, when Agamemnon is insulted in council, he controls his anger, but on the battlefield, he has the power to say:

"Whoever I find avoiding the fight Will soon be prey for dogs and vultures, for I control death."

This is one type of monarchy, where a king rules as a general for life, and the position can be hereditary or elective. Another type is found among some barbarian tribes, where kings hold near-tyrannical power, though they are still bound by laws and customs. Since barbarians tend to be more submissive to authority, especially in Asia compared to Europe, they tolerate despotic governments. This is why their governments are tyrannical, but stable, as they are customary and legal. Their guards, like those in monarchies, are citizens, unlike tyrants, who rely on foreign guards. The monarch rules according to the law over willing subjects, while a tyrant rules arbitrarily over unwilling subjects. So, one king is guarded by citizens, and the other guarded from them.

These are two types of monarchy. Another type is the aesumnetes, which was an elective tyranny found in ancient Greece. This differs from barbarian rule not because it wasn't based on law, but because it didn't follow the traditional customs. Some aesumnetes ruled for life, others for a specific time or purpose, like Pittacus of Mitylene, who was elected to deal with exiles. Alcaeus, the poet, criticized the Mitylenians for making Pittacus their tyrant, praising him while he destroyed a misguided people. These governments are despotic because they are tyrannies, but since they are elective and over a free people, they are also monarchies.

A fourth type of monarchy existed in the heroic age, where free people accepted kings according to the laws and customs of their time. Those who benefited society—through their skills in war or the arts, or by organizing people—became kings of willing subjects and established hereditary monarchies. They were primarily generals and oversaw sacrifices, except for those performed by priests. They also acted as supreme judges, and sometimes took an oath while doing so, swearing by their scepter.

In earlier times, kings had absolute authority over everything, both public and private, but over time, they gave up some of these powers, and people took others. In some states, kings were left with only the right to preside over sacrifices. Even those who retained the title of king were reduced to being commanders of foreign wars.

These are the four main types of kingship: the first, from the heroic age, ruled over a free people with clearly defined rights. The king was a general, judge, and high priest. The second type is barbarian, an hereditary despotism governed by law. The third is the aesumnetic, an elective tyranny. The fourth is the Lacedaemonian, which is essentially a hereditary generalship. A fifth type of kingship exists where one person has supreme authority over everything, just as a city or state governs its public affairs. Just as a master rules over his household, this king rules over the entire city or state.

The different types of monarchies can basically be reduced to two main forms, which we'll look at more closely. The last one mentioned, and the Lacedaemonian form, are the two extremes. The others fall in between these two, having more power than the Lacedaemonians but less than an absolute monarchy. The main questions can be reduced to two points: one, whether it's good for a general's position to be held by one person for life and whether it should be limited to specific families or open to everyone; and two, whether it's good for one person to have total control over everything or not. However, discussing the position of a Lacedaemonian general is more about creating laws for a state than considering the nature and benefits of its constitution, since every state appoints generals. So, we'll skip that topic and focus on the second part, which is the structure of the state itself. This is something we need to look at in detail and address any questions that come up.

The first thing we need to consider is this: is it better to be governed by a good person or by good laws? People who prefer monarchy believe that laws can only speak in general terms and can't address specific situations. This is why they think it's foolish to follow written rules in any science. In Egypt, for example, doctors were allowed to change the treatment prescribed by law after the fourth day, but if they did it sooner, they took a risk. This shows that a government ruled by written laws isn't always the best. However, general rules are necessary for those who govern, and these rules are much better if they come from people who are free from emotions than from those who are naturally affected by them. Laws have this quality, while emotions are natural to the human soul. But someone might argue that a person would be a better judge of specific situations. So, a king would need to be a lawmaker, and his laws should be made public, but only the reasonable ones should have authority.

The question is whether it's better for the community to be governed by every worthy citizen, as happens now when public assemblies act as judges and advisors, making decisions on specific cases. For example, it's clear that one individual, no matter who they are, is less wise than the collective judgment of the whole community. Just like a large feast is better than one person's portion, the judgment of many people is often better than one. The larger group is also less likely to be corrupted because of its size, just like water is less likely to be polluted if there's more of it. An individual's judgment can be clouded by anger or other emotions, but it's unlikely that a whole community would be misled by anger. Furthermore, if the people are free, they will do nothing against the law except in cases where the law doesn't apply. And while what I'm about to suggest may be rare, if most of the state's citizens happen to be good people, and they have to choose between one uncorrupt ruler or many equally good rulers, isn't it clear that they should choose the many? However, divisions can occur among the many, which can't happen with just one. The answer to this is that all of them should be motivated by virtue just like the one good ruler would be.

If a government of many good people is called an aristocracy, and a government of one is called a monarchy, then it's clear that people should choose an aristocracy over a monarchy, especially if the state is powerful and there are enough good people to form it. This is probably why the earliest governments were usually monarchies—it was hard to find many virtuous people, especially since the world was divided into small communities. Also, kings were often chosen as a reward for the benefits they brought to society, and these actions were usually performed by good men. But when a large number of virtuous people appeared, they no longer accepted one person's superiority. Instead, they sought equality and established free states. Later, when people became corrupt, they treated public property as their own, which likely led to oligarchies. In these systems, wealth became the qualification for power, and government positions were reserved for the rich. These oligarchies eventually turned into tyrannies, and these, in turn, gave rise to democracies. Tyrants' power weakened because of their greed, and the people became strong enough to establish democracies. As cities grew, it became more difficult for them to be governed by anything other than a democracy.

But if someone prefers a monarchy, what should be done about the king's children? Should his family continue to rule? If his children turn out poorly, it could be harmful to the state. Some might say the king will prevent his unworthy children from succeeding him, but that's hard to guarantee and would require more virtue than is typically found in human nature. There's also the question of how much power a king should have. Should he have enough force to compel those who refuse to follow the law, and how should he maintain his authority? If he governs according to the law and does nothing against it, he will still need some power to enforce the law. This issue isn't too hard to solve, though: the king should have enough power to be stronger than any individual or large part of the community, but weaker than the whole community. This is why the ancients gave guards to aesumnetes, or tyrants, when they appointed them, and someone advised the Syracusans to give Dionysius only the number of guards he requested.

Next, we'll consider the absolute monarch, who does everything according to his own will. A king who follows laws that he must obey doesn't create any specific form of government by himself, as we've already said. In any state, whether aristocratic or democratic, it's easy to appoint a general for life, and many people entrust the administration of their affairs to a single individual. This is the case in Dyrrachium and similarly in Opus. Absolute monarchy, where the entire state is under the control of one person, seems unnatural to many. It doesn't make sense for one person to rule over citizens who are equal to him. Nature suggests that those who are equal in merit should also be equal in status. Just as it would be harmful for people with different physical constitutions to follow the same diet or wear the same clothes, it's harmful for those who are equal in virtue to be unequal in rank. This is why people should take turns ruling and being ruled, as this is the purpose of law—law creates order. And it's better for law to govern than for one citizen to do so. Even if some individuals are given supreme power, they should act as guardians and servants of the laws. But it's unfair for one person to hold supreme power when all are equal.

It's also unlikely that one person can make better judgments than the law in cases where the law cannot be specific. The law sets down the best general rules, leaving the application of specifics to the magistrate's discretion. Additionally, the law allows changes if experience shows there's a better way to do things. Those who believe the supreme power should rest in reason would entrust it to the laws and to God, but those who give it to a man hand it over to a wild beast, as human desires can sometimes overpower reason, even in the best people. This is why law represents reason without desire.

The argument about the arts seems flawed. It's said that a sick person shouldn't rely on books for treatment, but instead, trust experienced doctors. Doctors act according to reason and aren't swayed by friendship; they earn their money by curing the sick. In contrast, those who manage public affairs often act out of hatred or favoritism. As proof, when a sick person suspects their doctor of foul play, they might turn to books for a cure. Even doctors themselves call on other doctors when they fall ill, and those who teach gymnastics train with others in the same profession. This shows that those who seek justice look for a balance, and law provides that balance.

The moral law deals with higher principles than the written law, and the supreme magistrate is more trustworthy than the written law, even if he is inferior to the moral law. But since one person can't oversee everything, the supreme magistrate must employ several assistants. So why not do this from the beginning instead of appointing just one person? Besides, if, as we've already said, a virtuous person is fit to govern, two virtuous people are better than one. For example, Homer says, "Let two go together," and Agamemnon wished for "ten such faithful counselors." Even now, there are specific magistrates with the authority to decide cases where the law doesn't apply, and no one doubts their role. Since laws cover some things but not everything, we must ask whether it's better for the best person or the best law to govern. After all, it's impossible to make laws for every situation humans might face.

No one denies that there should be someone to decide cases that fall outside the law's reach. But we argue that it's better to have many such people rather than one. Although everyone who judges according to the law makes just decisions, it seems ridiculous to suggest that one person can see better with two eyes, hear better with two ears, or act better with two hands and two feet than many people can with many eyes, ears, hands, and feet. Absolute monarchs today have many eyes, ears, hands, and feet by entrusting power to their friends. If they aren't friends of the monarch, they won't act as he wishes. But if they are friends, they are also friends of his government. A friend is an equal, and if the king thinks such people should govern, then he believes that his equals should also govern. These are some of the common objections raised against monarchy.

It's likely that what we've said applies to some people but not to others. Some people are naturally suited to be ruled by a master; others by a king; and others are citizens of a free state, just and useful. But tyranny and other corrupt forms of government aren't natural, as they go against nature. It's clear that among equals, it's neither fair nor right for one person to rule over all, whether there are no laws and his will is the law, or even where laws exist. Nor should a good person rule over other good people, or a bad person over other bad people, unless in a very specific way, which we will explain, though we've touched on it already. Next, we will determine which people are best suited for a monarchy, which for an aristocracy, and which for a democracy. A monarchy is best for people who are naturally inclined to submit their civil government to a family known for its virtue. An aristocracy is best for those who are naturally inclined to be ruled by free men whose superior virtue makes them fit to manage others. A free state is best for a warlike people, naturally inclined to both govern and be governed by laws that allow even the poorest citizens to share in the honors of the state based on their worth.

But if a whole family or an individual stands out in virtue, excelling beyond all others, then it's right for them to hold kingly power, or for the individual to be king and ruler of all. This principle aligns with the foundation of all governments—whether aristocratic, oligarchic, or democratic—which seek to place supreme power in the hands of those with merit. And, as we've already said, it wouldn't be right to kill, banish, or ostracize someone for their superior merit. It wouldn't be right either for such a person to only hold power in turn. It goes against nature for the highest to ever become the lowest, which would happen if such a person were governed by others. So the only solution is to let them continuously hold supreme power. This is the conclusion we reach regarding monarchy in different states, and whether or not it benefits them.

Since we have said that there are three types of regular governments, the best one will naturally be the one that is led by the best people. This could be a government where one person, one family, or a group of people stand out in virtue and are capable of both governing and being governed in a way that makes life most pleasant. We've already shown that the virtue of a good man and that of a citizen in the best government are the same. It's clear, then, that the same qualities that make a person good would also make a government—whether it's an aristocracy or a kingdom—well-established. Therefore, it's education and morals that are almost entirely what make someone a good person. The same traits make a good citizen or a good king.

Now that we've discussed these details, we'll move on to consider what kind of government is the best, how it naturally comes about, and how it is set up. It's important to carefully examine these questions.

Book 4

In every art and science that deals with a whole subject and not just parts of it, it's the job of that art to decide what fits best with that subject. For example, in exercise, it's important to choose the right kind of exercise for a particular body to help it function best. A body that is naturally strong and perfect needs the best exercises, and it's also important to choose exercises that will work for most people. This is the role of the gymnastic arts. Even if someone doesn't want to become an expert in these exercises, it's still necessary for the teacher to be an expert if they're going to train others. We see this same principle in other areas like medicine, shipbuilding, and tailoring, as well as all other arts. This shows that it's the same art or science that should find out which form of government is the best and which matches what people would ideally want, without any outside interference. It should also find which type of government is best suited for different types of people, as some may not be able to handle the best form of government. This means that a lawmaker, or someone who understands politics well, should not only know about the best form of government but also know what type of government fits certain situations.

There's also a third category—an imaginary one—that the lawmaker should be able to recognize if it ever comes up. They should be able to see how such a government would start and how to keep it going for a long time. This could happen if a state doesn't have the best form of government or if it's missing something important, or if it only has part of what it needs. Additionally, it's important to know what kind of government works best for all cities. Most writers on this subject, even if they talk about it in interesting ways, don't describe how to make it work in practice. It's not enough to understand what's best; it must also be possible to put it into action. The system should be simple and something that everyone can achieve. Some people only focus on the most complicated forms of government. Others prefer to criticize the government they live under and praise the greatness of another state, like Sparta or others. But a lawmaker should create a government that fits the current state and mindset of the people it will serve, so they will be willing to follow it. Changing an existing government's mistakes can be just as difficult as forming a new one. It's as hard to recover something you've forgotten as it is to learn something new. Therefore, anyone aiming to be a lawmaker should also know how to correct the errors of an established government, as we've already mentioned. But this is impossible for someone who doesn't know how many different forms of government exist. Some people think there's only one type of democracy and one type of oligarchy, but this isn't true. It's important for everyone to understand how different these governments are and where their differences come from. It's also essential to know which laws are best and most suitable for each type of government.

All laws should be made to match the state they govern, not the other way around. Government is the way power is distributed within a state, especially when it comes to magistrates—how they are selected and where supreme power is placed, and what the main goal of the state is. Laws are something different from the government's structure. Their job is to guide the actions of the magistrates in carrying out their duties and punishing wrongdoers. Therefore, it's clear that lawmakers should understand both the number and the types of governments that exist. It's impossible for the same laws to work for every type of oligarchy or every type of democracy because both of these governments have many different forms, not just one.

Since we have divided regular governments into three types—the monarchy, aristocracy, and free states—and shown that each has its extremes, we now need to examine them more closely. Monarchies can turn into tyrannies, aristocracies into oligarchies, and free states into democracies. We've already discussed aristocracy and monarchy because deciding what form of government is best involves looking closely at these two, as they are both based on virtue. We've also explained how monarchy and aristocracy differ from one another and what it means for a state to be ruled by a king. Now we must examine the free state, as well as other forms of government such as oligarchy, democracy, and tyranny. It's clear which of these extremes is the worst, and which comes next after that. The worst excess comes from the best and most virtuous form of government. The name of king may remain, but if a king takes more power than he should, tyranny results, which is the worst possible form of government, being the opposite of a free state. The next worst is oligarchy because it differs a lot from aristocracy, and the least bad is democracy. One previous writer said that of all the excellent forms of government, like a good oligarchy, democracy was the worst, but of all the bad forms, democracy was the best.

I believe that all these types of states have fallen into excess at some point, and that the writer should not have said that one oligarchy was better than another but that it was just not as bad. We won't get into that question right now. First, we'll examine how many different types of free states there are, since democracies and oligarchies have many forms. We'll also look at which of these is most suitable and desirable after the best form of government, and whether there is another form similar to a well-established aristocracy. We'll also look at which form works best for most cities and which is best for specific groups of people. Some people might prefer an oligarchy over a democracy, and others the opposite. After this, we'll discuss how someone should go about establishing either a democracy or an oligarchy. Finally, once we've covered all the important points, we'll try to explain what causes governments to become corrupt or stay stable, both the things that apply to all governments and those that are unique to each type, and the main causes behind them.

The reason there are so many types of governments is that each state is made up of many different parts. First, we see that all cities are made up of families. Among these families, some people are rich, some are poor, and others are in the middle. Among both the rich and poor, some people are used to fighting and others are not. We also see that some common people are farmers, others are merchants, and others are craftsmen. There is also a difference among nobles in terms of their wealth and the status they live with, like how many horses they own, since horses can only be kept by the very wealthy. This is why, in the past, cities whose strength came from cavalry often became oligarchies. They used their cavalry to fight against neighboring cities, like the Eretrians, Chalcidians, and Magnetians, who lived near the Meander River, as well as many others in Asia.

In addition to differences in wealth, there are differences in family background and merit. If there are any other distinctions that make up the city, we've already talked about them when discussing aristocracy, where we considered how many parts a city must have. Sometimes all these different groups share in the government, sometimes only a few do, and other times more.

It's clear, then, that there must be many forms of government that differ based on their specific makeup because the parts that make them up are different from one another. Government is about how the magistracies of the state are organized, and the people share power among themselves, either by force or according to some common equality, like poverty, wealth, or something they both share. There must be as many forms of government as there are different ranks in society, depending on the superiority of some people over others and their different circumstances. These seem to fall into two main types, like the winds—the north and the south. All the other forms are variations of these. In politics, we have the government of the many and the government of the few, or democracy and oligarchy. Aristocracy can be seen as a type of oligarchy because it's also a government of the few. What we call a free state can be considered a type of democracy. In the same way, people see the west wind as part of the north and the east wind as part of the south. Some people also think there are only two types of music—the Doric and the Phrygian—and they group all other music under one of these names. Many people look at governments in the same way. But it's more practical and more accurate to divide governments the way I have— into two main categories: those based on sound principles, which can have one or two forms, and those that are excessive forms of the first.

We can compare the best form of government to the most harmonious music, oligarchy and tyranny to more violent tunes, and democracy to soft and gentle melodies.

We shouldn't define a democracy as some people do, saying it's simply a government where the majority of the people have the supreme power. Even in oligarchies, the majority can have supreme power. Nor should we define an oligarchy as a government where power is in the hands of a few. For example, if there are thirteen hundred people in a community and one thousand of them are rich and do not allow the three hundred poor people to have any say in the government, no one would call this a democracy, even though the rich are the majority. Similarly, if the poor, even though they are fewer in number, gained power over the rich, no one would call this an oligarchy just because a few poor people hold power.

Instead, we should say that a democracy is when power is in the hands of the free citizens, and an oligarchy is when it's in the hands of the rich. Usually, this means that in a democracy, the many will have power, and in an oligarchy, the few will, because there are usually more poor people than rich. If power were given based on size or beauty, as they say it is in Ethiopia, then it would still be an oligarchy because few people are large or beautiful.

What we've said so far isn't enough to fully explain these forms of government, though. There are many types of both democracies and oligarchies, so the matter needs more thought. For example, we can't say that a government is a democracy if a few free people hold power over the many who aren't free, like in Apollonia, Ionia, and Thera. In these cities, power is held by a few wealthy families who founded the colonies. Also, if the rich were in the majority, as they once were in Colophon before the Lydian war, this wouldn't make the government a democracy just because there were more rich people.

A democracy is when the majority of free citizens, including the poor, hold power. An oligarchy is when the wealthy and noble families, being fewer in number, control the government. Now that we've shown there are different forms of government and explained why they exist, we'll move on to show that there are even more variations and explain what they are and why. Let's start with the principle we've already discussed. Every city is made up of different parts. If we were trying to categorize different species of animals, we'd first look at the parts every animal has, like sensory organs, and the parts needed to eat and digest food, like the mouth and stomach. We'd also look at the parts needed for movement. If these were the only parts an animal had, and there were differences between them, like different types of stomachs and sensory organs, the combinations of these parts would make up the different species of animals.

The same thing is true for governments. A city is made up of many different groups, as we've said before. One group provides food, which includes farmers. Another group is made up of craftsmen who do manual work, which is essential for a city to function. Some work on basic needs, while others focus on luxuries and pleasures. Another group includes traders—those who buy, sell, and transport goods. Then there are the hired laborers who do various jobs. The next group is made up of soldiers, who are just as important as the others because, without them, the city would be defenseless and vulnerable to invaders. A city that can't defend itself isn't really a city because a true city is self-sufficient, unlike a slave who depends on others. So, when Socrates, in Plato's Republic, says a city is made up of four groups—weavers, farmers, shoemakers, and builders—he's speaking well but not quite correctly. He then adds more groups, like blacksmiths, herdsmen, merchants, and traders, as if a city exists only for necessity and not for happiness, or as if a shoemaker and a farmer are equally important.

He doesn't mention soldiers until later when he talks about expanding the city's territory and the need for war. Even among the groups he does mention, or in any group of people, there must be someone to distribute justice and resolve disputes between individuals. If the mind is more important than the body, then the things that benefit the mind should be more valued in the city than basic necessities like war or justice. You can also add wisdom and council to this, which fall under civil leadership. It doesn't matter if these jobs are done by different people or the same person, like someone who is both a soldier and a farmer. So, if the judge and council member are considered parts of the city, then the soldier must be as well.

The seventh group is made up of those who perform public services at their own expense; these are the rich. The eighth group includes those who fill the various offices of the state, without whom the city couldn't survive. It's necessary to have people who can govern and hold office in the city, whether for life or in rotation. The roles of senator and judge, which we've already discussed, are the only ones left. If a city is going to be happy and just, it needs citizens who are capable of managing public affairs. Many people believe that one person can do multiple jobs, like being both a soldier and a farmer or craftsman. Some also believe that the same people can serve as both senators and judges.

However, a person can't be both rich and poor at the same time, so the most obvious way to divide a city is into the rich and the poor. Most of the time, the rich are the few, and the poor are the many. These two groups are the most opposed to each other, and depending on which one is stronger, the city will either become a democracy or an oligarchy.

Now that we've discussed the causes of different governments, let's explain the different types of democracies and oligarchies. This should be clear from what we've said already. There are many types of common people and many types of nobles. Among the common people, there are farmers, craftsmen, and traders who buy and sell goods. There are also sailors, some who fight in wars, some who trade, some who transport goods and passengers, and others who fish. In some places, like Tarentum and Byzantium, there are many fishermen; at Athens, there are galley captains; at Aegina and Chios, there are merchants; and at Tenedos, there are those who rent out ships. We can also include those who live by manual labor and have little property, meaning they have to work to survive. Then there are those who aren't fully free citizens, and other types of common people.

Nobles are distinguished by their wealth, family background, talents, education, or some other excellence. The purest form of democracy is based on equality. In this kind of democracy, the law ensures that the poor aren't more controlled than the rich and that neither group holds supreme power. Instead, both groups share power. If liberty and equality are the main goals of democracy, as some say, then a democracy is at its strongest when all parts of the government are equally open to everyone. Since the people are the majority and their votes determine the law, this form of government is called democracy. This is one type of democracy. Another type allows magistrates to be elected based on a small property requirement, with everyone who meets it eligible for office. However, if someone's wealth drops below the requirement, they lose the right to hold office.

Another type allows any citizen who isn't dishonorable to participate in government, but the laws still hold the highest authority. Another type allows every citizen to participate, regardless of their wealth, and in this case, the people, not the laws, hold power. This happens when decisions are made by a majority vote rather than by following laws, and it occurs when demagogues influence the people. In democracies where laws govern, demagogues have no role, and the best people hold the highest offices. But when the people hold power, demagogues thrive because the people act as a collective ruler, not as individuals.

Homer criticized the rule of many, but it's unclear if he meant the type of government we're talking about or one where each person rules individually. When the people hold this kind of power, they want complete control and don't want to be limited by laws. This is when flatterers gain favor. There's no real difference between this type of democracy and a monarchy under a tyrant. Both rulers act the same way and have absolute power over people better than themselves. The decrees in such democracies are like the edicts of tyrants, and the demagogues are like the flatterers of tyrants. The greatest similarity is the way the demagogue and the people support each other. The demagogue leads the people, and the people give him power. As a result, the people's votes, not the laws, control the government. Demagogues bring all issues before the people because they influence the people's opinions, and the people follow their lead. The people enjoy accusing magistrates and use these accusations to weaken all offices.

So, we can say that this kind of government, which is a democracy in name but not a true free state, is flawed. When the laws don't hold power, there is no free state. The laws should rule over everything, and the magistrates should handle any issues that the laws don't cover. If a democracy is to be considered a free state, it's clear that a government where all power rests in the votes of the people cannot truly be called a democracy, because its decisions aren't general or based on the law. This is how we can describe the different types of democracies.

There are also different types of oligarchies. One type is when the right to hold office is based on a certain property requirement, so the poor, even if they are the majority, have no say in the government, while everyone who meets the requirement participates in public affairs. Another type is when officials are chosen from among people of modest wealth. If these officials come from the general population, the government leans toward an aristocracy. But if they come from a specific group, it's an oligarchy. Another form of oligarchy is when power is held by an inherited nobility. The fourth type is when power is in the hands of a few, and they aren't controlled by laws. This form of oligarchy is similar to a monarchy that becomes a tyranny, and it's also like the form of democracy we just described. This type of oligarchy is called a dynasty. These are the different forms of oligarchies and democracies.

It's important to note that sometimes a free state, where the laws hold power, might not be democratic. However, because of the customs and traditions of the people, it might function as if it were a democracy. On the other hand, a government with more democratic laws could function like an oligarchy, especially after a change in the government. People don't change easily and are attached to their old customs. Change happens gradually, so the old laws remain while power shifts to those who brought about the change.

From what has been said, it's clear that there are many kinds of democracies and oligarchies, as I have listed. In a democracy, either all the people I mentioned will have a share in the government, or only some will, and others will not. When farmers and those with moderate wealth hold the power, they will govern according to laws because they have to work for a living and don't have much free time for public business. They will create good laws and only call public meetings when necessary. They will also allow anyone who reaches the wealth requirement set by law to share in the government. Anyone who qualifies will have a role in the government. If some people are excluded, it would become an oligarchy, but not everyone has time to attend unless they have enough to live on. This is why this form of government is a type of democracy.

Another type of democracy is when officials are elected, and anyone is eligible, as long as there's no reason to disqualify them based on birth, and they have time to participate. In this type of democracy, the law holds the most power, because those attending public assemblies are not paid. A third kind of democracy is when all free citizens have the right to take part in the government, but they won't accept it for the same reasons mentioned before. So, here again, the law will hold the supreme power. The fourth type of democracy arose later when cities grew larger, and public revenue increased. At that point, even the poorest citizens were allowed to take part in public affairs because they were paid to do so. These poorer citizens had more time to attend public meetings since they didn't have personal wealth or businesses to worry about, unlike the rich, who often didn't attend. This resulted in the poor holding the most power, instead of the laws. These are the different types of democracies, and these are the causes that led to them.

The first kind of oligarchy is when most of the citizens have moderate property, which gives them enough time to manage public affairs. Since they are a large group, it's only natural that the laws, not individuals, hold the highest power. They are far from a monarchy and don't have enough wealth to ignore their personal business, and they are too many to be supported by the public. So, they will decide to be governed by laws, not by each other. But if only a few people in the state have large amounts of wealth, then a second type of oligarchy will form. Those with the most power will believe they deserve to rule over the others. To make this happen, they will include some people interested in public affairs. Since they aren't strong enough to govern without laws, they will create laws to help them. If the few rich people become even more powerful, the oligarchy will change into a third kind. They will pass laws allowing them to control all government offices, passing them down from father to son. As their wealth and influence grow, they will oppress others even more, and this will eventually lead to a monarchical dynasty where individuals hold all the power, not the laws. This is the fourth type of oligarchy, similar to the last type of democracy I mentioned.

There are also two other types of government, a democracy and an oligarchy, that people often talk about. These are usually considered part of the four types of governments. People count them as monarchy, oligarchy, democracy, and a fourth type they call aristocracy. There is also a fifth type, which is often called "the state." But because this type is rare, those who try to list all the types of governments usually miss it. Plato, in his Republic, also mentions only four types of government.

An aristocracy, as I talked about earlier, is rightly called so. This is a government where the best people, who follow the most virtuous principles, are in charge, not just people who have good ideas. In this type of government, a person can be both a good citizen and a good person, which isn't always true in other forms of government. In some governments, people are only considered good in relation to that particular state. Some other governments are also called aristocracies, but they differ from both oligarchies and free states. In these aristocracies, both the rich and virtuous share in the administration, which is why they are given the name aristocracy. In governments where virtue isn't a main focus, there are still good and honorable people. A state like Carthage, which values the rich, the virtuous, and all citizens, can be considered a form of aristocracy. When a state only values the virtuous and the citizens, like in Lacedaemon, this is a virtuous democracy. These are the two main types of aristocracies after the first, which is the best type of government. There's also a third type, which is when a free state leans toward the rule of a few people.

Now, we will talk about what is called a free state and about tyranny. The reason I discuss the free state here is because, like aristocracies, it seems like a good system, but to be honest, both have moved away from being truly perfect governments. They are both deviations from other forms, as I mentioned earlier. Tyranny is mentioned last because it is the least like a proper government. But since my goal is to discuss all forms of government, I will talk about tyranny when the time comes.

Now, I will explain what a free state is, and we will better understand it by comparing it to oligarchy and democracy. A free state is really just a mix of both. People often call a state that leans toward democracy a free state, and a state that leans toward oligarchy an aristocracy because the rich are usually from well-known families and have a good education. They also have things that others commit crimes to get, which is why they are considered honorable and important.

Since aristocracy aims to give the best citizens the most power, people say oligarchy is made up of the most worthy and honorable individuals. It seems impossible for a government where good people hold power to have bad laws, and it's just as unlikely that a government with bad leaders will have good laws. A government is not well-structured just because it has good laws. It's also important to make sure the laws are enforced. A sign of a well-structured government is one that makes sure its laws are followed and that those laws are suited to the people who live under them. If the laws are bad, they still need to be obeyed. This can happen in two ways: the laws can be the best for a specific state or the best in general.

An aristocracy is likely to give the honors of the state to virtuous people because virtue is the focus of aristocracy, while wealth is the focus of oligarchy, and freedom is the focus of democracy. What most people approve of will prevail in all three types of government. What seems good to most members of the community will prevail. What we call a "state" prevails in many communities that aim to balance the interests of the rich and the poor, as well as wealth and freedom. The rich are often considered to be in the same category as the worthy and honorable. Since freedom, wealth, and virtue are the three main things valued in a state (and the fourth, family rank, comes from virtue and wealth), it's clear that the combination of rich and poor creates a free state. But all three—freedom, wealth, and virtue—lean more toward an aristocracy than any other form of government, except for a true aristocracy, which holds the highest rank.

We have already explained that there are forms of government different from monarchy, democracy, and oligarchy, and we've shown how they differ from each other. We've also discussed aristocracies and states, and it's clear that they are quite similar to each other.

Next, we'll explain how a government called "the state" comes about alongside democracy and oligarchy, and how it should be structured. We'll also show where democracy and oligarchy differ from each other and how a state can combine parts of both.

There are three main ways to mix two forms of government. First, you can combine the rules of each. For example, in an oligarchy, the rich are fined if they don't show up as jurors, but the poor aren't paid for attending. In a democracy, the poor are paid, and the rich aren't fined if they don't show up. These practices, which are common to both, are suitable for a free state, which is made up of both types of citizens. This is one way to combine them. Second, you can create a middle ground between the two systems. For example, in a democracy, there is either no wealth requirement to vote or a very low one, while in an oligarchy, only those with a high amount of wealth can vote. Since these two systems are opposites, a free state can establish a middle ground between them. Third, you can adopt different laws from each system. In a democracy, officials are often chosen by lot, while in an aristocracy, they are elected. In one system, the choice is based on wealth, while in the other, it is not. A free state or aristocracy can take ideas from both systems, using elections from the oligarchy and removing the wealth requirement like a democracy.

The best sign of a successful mix between democracy and oligarchy is when people can call the same state both a democracy and an oligarchy. Those who speak this way do so because both systems have been combined well. This is true for all balanced systems—elements of both sides are present. In Lacedaemon, for example, some say it's a democracy because of the many ways it follows that system. For instance, rich and poor children are raised the same way, and the poor can access the same education as the rich. As adults, they are treated equally, and at public meals, everyone gets the same food. The rich also wear clothes that the poorest person can afford. In their two highest offices—the senate and the ephorate—everyone has the right to participate. Others say Lacedaemon is an oligarchy because of certain things it follows from that system, like choosing officials by vote and not by lot, and only allowing a few people to judge serious cases.

A state that successfully combines two systems should resemble both and neither at the same time. It should have the strength to maintain itself from within, not relying on external factors. By this, I mean that it shouldn't depend on the goodwill of its neighbors, as even a poorly governed state can be left alone by others. Instead, every member of the state should be committed to maintaining its constitution without any desire to change it. This is the way a free state or aristocracy should be structured.

Finally, let's discuss tyranny. Although there isn't much to say about it, we need to include it since we listed it among the different forms of government. At the start of this work, we looked into the nature of kingship and discussed in detail what a true kingship is, whether it benefits the state, how it should be set up, and how it works. We also mentioned two types of tyranny, which are somewhat similar to kingship because both are established by law. In some barbarian societies, they elect a king with absolute power, and in ancient Greece, there were similar leaders called sesumnetes.

These two systems are different, though. Some kings only have limited power under the law and rule over people who willingly accept their leadership. Others rule as tyrants, governing according to their own desires. A third type of tyranny, which is the most properly called tyranny, is the exact opposite of kingship. This is the government of one person who rules over his equals and superiors without being held accountable. His goal is his own benefit, not the benefit of the people he governs. Because of this, he rules by force since no free people would willingly accept such a government. These are the different types of tyrannies, their principles, and their causes.

Now we move on to explore what type of government and way of life is best for most communities, not focusing on the perfect virtue that only a few can achieve or an education that only those with great natural abilities and wealth can have. We are not talking about imaginary ideas, but rather about a way of life that most people can reach and a government that most cities can establish. The aristocracies we've mentioned are either too perfect for most states to maintain or so similar to the state we are about to examine that we will treat them as the same thing.

Our views on this topic must follow a basic principle: if what I said in my work on ethics is true, then a happy life comes from a constant practice of virtue. If virtue is about finding the middle ground, then a life lived in the middle is surely the happiest, and this middle ground can be reached by everyone. The same balance between good and bad in a person must also exist in a state because the government is the life of the city. In every city, there are three types of people: the very rich, the very poor, and those in the middle. If we agree that the middle is best, it's clear that in terms of wealth, the middle ground is the most desirable. People in the middle are more likely to follow reason. The very rich, very strong, very noble, or very wealthy often don't follow reason well, just like the very poor or very weak. The rich tend to be arrogant and commit crimes because of their excesses, while the poor often become mean and deceitful. Neither group is likely to take part in the offices of the state, which hurts the state overall. The rich and powerful are not willing to be ruled, and this starts early in life when they are raised without being taught to follow rules. The poor, on the other hand, are so focused on their lack of wealth that they live in a way that is too lowly.

In a city like this, where there are only masters and slaves, not free citizens, one group will hate the other, and there will be no possibility of friendship or unity in the political community. Friendship is essential in a community because we don't even travel with our enemies. A city should be made up of equals as much as possible, and this happens when most of the people are in the middle class. This means the best city will be made up of those who naturally belong to the middle class. These people will also be the most secure because they won't desire the property of others like the poor do, and others won't want to take what they have, like how the poor want to take from the rich. This way, they can live without fear of being plotted against or needing to plot against others. This is why the philosopher Phocylides wisely wished for the middle class, as it brings the most happiness.

It's clear that the most perfect political community comes from people in the middle class, and the best states are those where the middle class is the largest and most respected group, bigger than both the rich and the poor combined. If this isn't possible, the middle class should at least be larger than either group on its own, so it can balance the state and prevent either extreme from gaining too much power.

The greatest happiness for citizens is to have a moderate and comfortable amount of wealth. If some people have too much and others have nothing, the government will either fall into the hands of the poorest people or become a strict oligarchy. In extreme cases, it can even lead to tyranny, which often comes from a wild democracy or oligarchy. However, when the members of a community are roughly equal in status, tyranny is rare. We will explain this more when we discuss how states change.

The middle class is the best because it is the least likely to cause rebellions and unrest. Larger states are also less prone to these problems because they have more people in the middle class. In small states, it's easier to have extremes where most people are either very rich or very poor, leaving little room for the middle class. This is why democracies tend to last longer and are more stable than oligarchies. However, even in democracies, if there aren't enough people in the middle class, the poor can become too powerful, leading to problems and the collapse of the government.

As evidence of what I'm saying, we can look at the best lawmakers in history. They have often come from the middle class, such as Solon, as we can see from his writings, and Lycurgus, who wasn't a king, and Charondas, among others. What I've said explains why many free states have changed into democracies or oligarchies. When the middle class is too small, the larger groups—whether the rich or the poor—take control of the government. This leads to either a democracy or an oligarchy.

Moreover, when the rich and poor fight with each other, and one side wins, they don't set up a free state. Instead, they create a government that favors their side, making it either a democracy or an oligarchy.

Those who conquered Greece often set up democracies or oligarchies based on the governments of their home cities. They didn't think about what was best for the conquered state, but rather what was familiar to them. This is why governments that put power in the hands of the middle class are rare. Only a few conquerors have recognized the value of this group, and most cities don't aim for equality. Instead, people want to either rule or be ruled when they are conquered.

Now that we've explained what the best state is and why, it will be easier to understand which governments are the best among the many that exist. There are different types of democracies and oligarchies, and we can see which are better or worse based on how close or far they are from the best possible government. The best is the one closest to the ideal middle ground, while the worst is the one furthest from it. However, different governments might be better for different situations, so a government that is worse in general might still be the best for certain purposes.

After discussing this, we should now explain which form of government is best for different groups of people. The first rule is that those who want to keep the current government should always outnumber those who want to change it. Every city is made up of both "quality" and "quantity." By "quality," I mean things like freedom, wealth, education, and family background. By "quantity," I mean the number of people. It's possible that quality might be found in one group in the city, while quantity is found in another. For example, there might be more poor people than rich, or more people from unknown families than from noble families. However, the numbers should not outweigh the quality. These elements must be balanced, because if the poor outnumber the rich too much, a democracy will form. If the farmers have more power than others, it will be a democracy of farmers. The kind of democracy depends on which group is the largest. If the majority are farmers, it will be a democracy of farmers, which is the best kind. If the majority are craftsmen or hired workers, it will be the worst kind of democracy. The same applies to any other group.

When the rich and noble have more influence because of their status than they lack in numbers, an oligarchy will form. The type of oligarchy depends on the nature of the ruling group. Any lawmaker who wants to create a stable government should focus on the middle class. Whether it's an oligarchy or a democracy, the laws should be designed to support this group. If the middle class outnumbers both the rich and poor combined, or at least one of them, it will bring stability to the state. There's no risk that the rich and poor will team up against the middle class, because neither group wants to help the other.

Anyone who wants to build the most stable government should rely on the middle class. The rich and poor won't want to take turns ruling because of their mutual distrust. In contrast, the middle class can act as a fair judge for both groups, which is why it's often the best group to hold power.

Those who aim to create aristocratic governments often give too much power to the rich and end up tricking the common people. This creates real harm in the long run, as the actions of the rich are often more destructive to the state than those of the poor.

There are five key areas where the rich try to unfairly undermine the rights of the people: public assemblies, state offices, courts, military power, and athletic training. In public assemblies, they make the meetings open to everyone but only fine the rich for not attending, or they fine others very little. For state offices, they allow the poor to opt out but don't give the same option to those who meet the wealth requirement. In the courts, they fine the rich for not serving, but fine the poor either very little or not at all, as was the case under the laws of Charondas. In some places, every enrolled citizen had the right to attend public meetings and serve as jurors, and if they didn't, they faced a heavy fine. This fine made people avoid getting enrolled so they wouldn't have to serve.

The same approach applies to military service and athletic training. The poor are excused if they don't have weapons, but the rich are fined if they don't have them. The rich are also fined if they don't attend their training sessions, while the poor face no penalty. As a result, the rich make sure to have weapons and attend training, while the poor do neither. These are the sneaky tricks used by oligarchical lawmakers.

In contrast, democracy does the opposite. In democracies, the poor are paid to attend meetings and serve in court, while the rich are not. This shows that the best way to combine these practices is to extend both the payments and the fines to everyone in the community. Then, everyone would participate, whereas now only some do.

The citizens of a free state should be those who serve in the military. It's not easy to say exactly how much wealth a citizen should have, but the rule should be that the number of people who qualify for citizenship should be larger than those who don't. The poor, even if they don't hold office, will be content as long as they are left alone to manage their property. However, this isn't always easy because those in charge may not always act kindly.

In times of war, the poor usually don't fight unless they are provided with food. When they are fed, they are willing to fight. In some states, power is given not only to those currently serving in the military but also to those who have served in the past. For example, in Mali, only former soldiers held office, and all their officials were veterans.

The first states in Greece that replaced monarchies were military governments. At first, the power was with the cavalry because, back then, armies relied on horsemen. Heavy-armed foot soldiers were useless without proper training. The art of military tactics wasn't known to the ancients, so their strength was in their cavalry. As cities grew larger and foot soldiers became more important, more people gained freedom in the city. This is why what we now call republics were once called democracies. Early governments were either oligarchies or monarchies because there were so few people in each state. It would have been impossible to find enough middle-class people to form a government, so the few who were used to following orders accepted being ruled.

We've now shown why there are so many types of governments and why they differ. There are more kinds of democracies and oligarchies than one might think. We've also discussed their differences, their origins, and which form of government is best, both in general and for specific groups of people.

We will now continue to look at different types of governments and how each one works, starting with their key principles. There are three important things that a careful lawmaker must consider in every state. If these three things are properly managed, the state will be happy. These three things also cause one government to differ from another. The first is the public assembly. The second is the officers of the state—who they should be, what powers they should have, and how they should be chosen. The third is the judicial system.

The job of the public assembly is to make decisions about war and peace, forming or breaking alliances, passing laws, deciding punishments such as death or banishment, and holding officials accountable for their actions while in office. These powers can be given to all the citizens, or just some of them. They can be given to one official, to a group of officials, or split among different groups. When all the power is given to all the citizens, this is a democracy because democracy is about equality.

There are several ways to delegate these powers to the citizens. In one way, the citizens take turns in making decisions, as was done by Tellecles of Miletus. In another method, a council made up of different officials handles these decisions. People don't meet together unless they are making new laws, discussing a national issue, or hearing proposals from officials. Another method is for the people to meet as a group to make laws, discuss war and peace, and check the behavior of officials, while the rest of the public business is managed by different officials who are chosen by vote or lot. In a fourth method, everyone discusses every issue in public meetings, where the officials cannot decide anything on their own but can only give their opinions first. This method is used in the most direct form of democracy, similar to how power is distributed in strict oligarchies or tyrannies.

These are the different ways public business can be conducted in a democracy. When the power is held by only part of the community, it's an oligarchy, and there are different customs for this too. If officials are chosen from those with moderate wealth, and there are many such people, they will follow the law carefully. When everyone with the required wealth can participate, it's an oligarchy, but one based on fair principles. In another type, a few people are chosen to make decisions, and they govern according to the law. This is also an oligarchy. When officials are elected from among themselves, and their positions are passed down to their sons, allowing them to override the laws, this is a stricter form of oligarchy.

In some cases, different groups make decisions on different matters, like war and peace, while another group checks the behavior of officials. This type of government is either an aristocracy or a free state. In other cases, some officials are chosen by vote, others by lot, and they may come from either the whole population or just a selected group. When both voting and drawing lots are used, it's partly an aristocracy and partly a free government. These are the various ways the power to make decisions is divided in different governments, all following some version of these rules.

It benefits a democracy, where the people hold power even over the laws, to hold frequent public meetings. It's also a good idea for democracies to follow the example of oligarchies in their court systems, where they fine people for not attending when they're supposed to. In a democracy, they should reward poor people for attending public assemblies. The best decisions will come when both the citizens and the nobles discuss things together. If only part of the citizens are involved in the council, an equal number of nobles and citizens should be chosen, either by vote or by lot. If the common people outnumber the nobles, either not all of them should be paid for attending, or they should be reduced by lot.

In an oligarchy, it's a good idea to include some common people in the council, or to set up a court, as some states do, where officials called pre-advisers or guardians of the laws propose laws for the council to approve. This way, the common people can have a role in public affairs without causing disruption. The people can also be allowed to vote on proposals, but they can't suggest new laws themselves, or they can offer advice, but the final decision rests with the officials. It's also important to follow the opposite practice of democracies, where the people are allowed to forgive someone but not to condemn them. In an oligarchy, forgiving is left to a few people, while condemning is left to the public. This is how the power to make decisions is handled in different governments.

Now, let's consider how officials are chosen. This is an important part of government, involving many aspects: how many officials there should be, what their duties are, and how long they should serve— whether six months, a year, or longer. Some officials may be allowed to serve multiple terms, while others may not be allowed to serve more than once. It's also important to decide who can be chosen as an official, who will choose them, and how they will be chosen. We need to explore all these options and figure out which ones are best for different types of governments.

It's not easy to say who exactly should be called a "magistrate" (an official). Governments need many people to fill different roles, but not everyone chosen by vote or lot should be considered a magistrate. Priests, for example, are different from civil officials. Other roles, like choregi (who organize festivals) or heralds (messengers), are also chosen, but they aren't the same as magistrates. Civil officials are those who take part in making decisions or enforcing the law, and those who hold positions of authority, especially those who command others, are most properly called magistrates.

But deciding who qualifies as a magistrate is less important than figuring out which offices are necessary for a state, how many offices there should be, and which ones, though not necessary, would still benefit a well-governed state. This is important for all states, large or small.

In large states, each office should be given to one person, as there are enough people to fill these roles, and everything is done better when one person focuses on one task. In smaller states, however, one person may need to take on multiple roles because there aren't enough people to spread the work around. Smaller states may need the same officials and laws as larger ones but won't need to use them as often. So, it's sometimes necessary for one person to handle multiple roles in a small state without causing problems.

If we could figure out how many officials are necessary for each city and how many, though not essential, would still be useful, we could better determine how many roles one official could manage. We also need to know which courts should handle which issues in different places and what matters should always be handled by the same official. For example, should market inspectors handle cases of improper behavior if they happen in the market, while another official handles them elsewhere, or should the same official handle them everywhere?

In different types of governments, should the officials be the same or different? In an aristocracy, for instance, offices are given to those who are well-educated; in an oligarchy, they are given to the rich; and in a democracy, they are given to free citizens. The types of officials may also change depending on the needs of the state. In some cases, officials need great power, while in others, only small power is needed.

There are certain officials who belong to specific types of governments. For example, pre-advisers are not needed in a democracy, but a senate is necessary. The senate's job is to prepare bills for the people to vote on so they can focus on their own lives. When the senate is small, the government tends to lean toward an oligarchy. The power of the senate is reduced in democracies where the people handle all the business themselves in public meetings. This happens when people have enough money or are paid to attend, making them free to meet often and decide everything themselves.

Officials who control the behavior of boys or women are only found in aristocracies, not democracies. After all, who can stop poor women from going out in public? Such officials also don't exist in oligarchies because the women there are too delicate to be controlled.

Now that we've discussed this, let's talk more about how magistrates are chosen, starting from the basics. Magistrates are chosen in three different ways, and all the variations come from these. The first difference is in who gets to appoint the magistrates. The second is in who is appointed, and the third is in how they are appointed. Each of these three can be done in three ways. Either all the citizens can appoint the magistrates, or some of the citizens, or only a specific group of citizens chosen based on wealth, family, or virtue. They may also be chosen by vote or by lot. These methods can be combined in different ways, with some magistrates chosen by part of the community and others by the whole community.

There are also different ways to elect magistrates. In a democracy, all magistrates are chosen by all the people, either by vote or by lot, or some are chosen by vote and others by lot. In a free state, not all the magistrates are chosen by the whole community, but some are chosen by part of it, either by vote, lot, or both.

In an oligarchy, some officials may be chosen from the whole population, while others are chosen by vote, some by lot, and others by both methods. In a free aristocracy, some officials are chosen from the whole population, and others from a specific group, either by vote or lot. In a strict oligarchy, officials are chosen from a certain group of people, and this is done either by lot or vote, or both. Choosing from the whole community is not part of this type of government.

In an aristocracy, the whole community should choose magistrates from a specific group of people, and this should be done by vote. These are the various ways magistrates can be chosen, based on the type of government. What is best for each government and how the offices should be set up, along with the powers each official should have, will be discussed in detail later. When we talk about the powers of a magistrate, we mean what specific duties they are responsible for, like handling finances or enforcing the laws. Different magistrates have different powers, just as the role of a general in the army differs from that of a market inspector.

Now we turn to the judicial part of government, which we will divide into three parts just like we did with the officials. These three parts are: who the judges will be, what cases they will handle, and how they will be chosen. When we talk about "who," we mean whether the judges will be chosen from the whole population or just certain people. By "what cases," we mean how many different courts there will be. By "how," we mean whether the judges will be chosen by vote or by random selection (lot).

First, let's decide how many different courts there should be. There are eight main types. The first court is for reviewing the actions of officials after they leave office. The second is to punish those who harm the public. The third handles cases where the government is involved. The fourth is for disputes between officials and private citizens who appeal fines placed on them. The fifth court handles cases involving large contracts. The sixth deals with cases of murder, including different types like premeditated murder, accidental killing, and justified killing, where the fact of the crime is accepted but whether it was legal is debated.

There is another court in Athens called the Court of Phreatto, which handles cases where someone who has fled because of a murder wants to return. This kind of case happens rarely and only in very large cities. The seventh type of court deals with cases involving foreigners, whether it's a dispute between two foreigners or between a foreigner and a citizen. The eighth and last court handles small cases, like those involving sums of money between one and five drachmas, or a little more. These smaller cases should also be settled by law, but not by a large group of judges.

Without going into details about murder cases or cases involving foreigners, let's focus on the courts that deal with the community's main affairs, which, if not managed well, can cause unrest or revolts in the state. These cases must be handled by all the citizens, or by some citizens selected for this purpose, either by vote or by lot. Some judges may be chosen by vote for certain cases and by lot for others. This means there will be four types of judges. The same number of types also applies if judges are chosen from only part of the population. For example, all judges may be chosen from part of the population by either vote or lot, or some by vote and some by lot, depending on the case.

Different groups of judges may also be combined, meaning that judges from the whole population or from part of it, or both, can sit together in the same court. These judges may be chosen by vote, by lot, or by both methods. That covers the different kinds of judges.

The system where all citizens judge all cases is most suited for a democracy. The system where only certain people judge all cases fits an oligarchy. The system where the whole population judges some cases and specific people judge others is best for an aristocracy or a free state.

Book 5

We have now covered everything we planned to discuss. Next, we need to look at what causes changes in governments, how these changes happen, and what types of changes occur. We also need to understand what leads to the downfall of each type of government and which systems they are most likely to shift into. Additionally, we will examine what actions help preserve governments in general and which steps are useful for preserving specific types of governments. Furthermore, we will discuss how to fix corrupt governments, either as a whole or in specific cases.

First, we should establish this principle: many governments claim to support justice and equality but fail to achieve it, as we've already discussed. Democracies emerge because people think that if they are equal in one area, like freedom, they must be equal in all areas. Oligarchies arise from the belief that if some people are unequal in one thing, like wealth, they should be unequal in everything. As a result, those who are equal in some ways try to gain equality in all things, while those who are superior in some ways try to get even more. This drive for more creates inequality. Most governments, while having some understanding of justice, are largely mistaken, and when one side doesn't get the share of power they expect, they become rebellious. However, those who truly have the most right to rebel, the people of the highest virtue, are the least likely to do so because they are genuinely superior.

There are also people from well-known families who refuse to be treated as equals because they believe their noble lineage makes them better than others. These attitudes are the main sources of rebellion. There are two main types of changes people might try to make to a government: either they want to replace the existing system with a different one, such as turning a democracy into an oligarchy or the other way around, or they are fine with the current system but want to take control for themselves, either by concentrating power in the hands of a few or one person. People also argue about how much power a government should have. For example, if a government is already an oligarchy, they may want to make it more purely oligarchical, or the same goes for a democracy. People may also want to either expand or reduce the government's powers, or make specific changes like adding or removing a certain office, such as how Lysander tried to end the king's rule in Sparta, or how Pausanias tried to eliminate the ephors. In Epidamnus, one part of the constitution changed when they replaced the philarchi with a senate.

At Athens, all magistrates must attend court at the Helisea whenever a new magistrate is created. The power of the archon in Athens has an oligarchical nature. Inequality is always a cause of rebellion, but this doesn't happen when those who are unequal are treated in a way that corresponds to their inequality. For example, monarchy is unequal when exercised over people who are equals. In general, it is the desire for equality that causes rebellions. There are two kinds of equality: one based on number and one based on value. Numerical equality is when two things are the same in terms of parts or amount. Value-based equality is proportional, like how four is twice as much as two, and two is twice as much as one. This kind of equality is based on ratio.

Now, while everyone agrees on what is absolutely just, people argue over proportional value. Some believe that if they are equal in one thing, they should be equal in everything, while others believe that if they are superior in one thing, they should be superior in everything. This is how democracies and oligarchies mainly arise. Nobility and virtue are found in only a few people, while the opposite traits are found in the majority. You won't find hundreds of noble or virtuous people, but you will find plenty of the others. Building a government based entirely on either of these equalities is wrong, and history proves this. None of these governments have lasted because if something is wrong from the start, it will eventually fail. This is why, in some cases, numerical equality should prevail, and in others, equality in value should be considered.

However, democracy is generally safer and less prone to rebellion than oligarchy. In an oligarchy, rebellion can arise from two causes: either the ruling few conspire against each other, or they plot against the people. In a democracy, rebellion usually occurs only against the few who want exclusive power. There's hardly ever a case of the people rebelling against themselves. Also, a government made up of moderately wealthy people is more like a democracy than an oligarchy and is the most stable of all types.

Since we're looking into the causes of rebellions and political changes, we should start by identifying the main factors that lead to them. These can be broadly divided into three main categories. First, we must understand the situations that make people start rebellions. Second, we must consider the reasons for these rebellions. Finally, we need to examine how political conflicts and tensions begin between different groups.

The main reason people want to change the government is what I've already mentioned: people who want equality are always ready to rebel if they see that others they consider their equals have more than they do. Similarly, those who want superiority over others will rebel if they feel that those beneath them have the same or more. Whether their reasons are fair or not, those who feel inferior will rebel to become equal, while those who feel equal will rebel to become superior. People will start rebellions for the sake of gaining profit or honor, or to avoid shame or losing wealth, either for themselves or their friends. The original causes that lead people to seek these things can be categorized into seven main factors, though they could be more. Two of these are the same as already mentioned but affect people in different ways. For example, profit and honor lead to conflict, not just to gain these things for themselves, but when they see others, whether justly or unjustly, hoarding them. The other causes are pride, fear, a desire for distinction, contempt, and an imbalanced growth in some part of the state.

There are also other causes that, in different ways, lead to political changes, such as election rigging, negligence, lack of citizens, and extreme differences in circumstances.

The impact of poor treatment and the pursuit of profit on causing rebellion is almost obvious. When leaders are arrogant and try to take more than their position allows, they cause conflict, not just among themselves but also with the state that gave them their power. Their greed is aimed at either private property or state property. The desire for honor also causes rebellion when people see others being honored while they themselves are not. When honors are given or denied unfairly, either by giving someone too much or not enough, it leads to rebellion. Excessive honors can also lead to rebellion if one or more people become more powerful than the state can handle, leading to a monarchy or dynasty. This is why some places, like Argos and Athens, use ostracism to prevent this. But it's better to avoid this kind of power imbalance when founding a state than to try to fix it later.

Those who commit crimes will rebel out of fear of punishment, just as those who expect to be harmed will rebel to prevent it, like in Rhodes, where the nobles rebelled because they feared the new laws that would be passed against them. Contempt also causes rebellion and conspiracies, such as in oligarchies where many people have no share in government. The wealthy in democracies may also rebel, thinking they can improve their position through the same means that caused the downfall of democracies in places like Thebes, Megara, Syracuse, and Rhodes, where poor administration and disorder led to rebellion.

Rebellions can also be caused by imbalanced growth. Just as a body should grow proportionally to stay in harmony, a government should grow in balance. If one part grows too much, it disrupts the system, like a foot growing to four cubits while the rest of the body stays small. This kind of imbalance can change the government into something else, especially when the imbalance occurs without being noticed, like when the number of poor people grows in democracies or free states.

Rebellions can also happen by accident. For example, after the Median War, many of the nobles in Tarentum were killed, which led to a free state becoming a democracy. The same thing happened in Argos after Cleomenes, the Spartan, killed many citizens, forcing the state to grant citizenship to many farmers. In Athens, after battles reduced the number of nobles, more common soldiers were selected from the citizen rolls during wars with Sparta, which also weakened the power of the aristocracy. Sometimes, revolutions happen even in democracies, though this is rarer. When the rich increase in number or gain more property, these democracies can become oligarchies or dynasties.

Governments can also change without rebellion when people of lower status unite. For example, in Hersea, the mode of election was changed from voting to lots, allowing common people to take power. Negligence can also lead to political changes, as happened in Orus when outsiders were allowed into high office, ending the oligarchy of the archons and turning the government into a democratic free state.

Sometimes, small unnoticed changes can lead to large political shifts over time. In Ambracia, for instance, the property census was initially low, but over time it became irrelevant, as if a small change was as good as none. States composed of different groups are also prone to rebellions until their differences are merged. No city can be built from just any group of people, nor can it do so at any given time. This is why republics that either start with different people or later include neighboring groups are the most prone to rebellion.

For example, after the Achaeans and Traezenians founded Sybaris, the Achaeans grew more powerful and expelled the Traezenians, leading to the saying about Sybarite wickedness. Similar disputes occurred in Thurium between the Sybarites and their allies, and in Byzantium, new citizens who were caught plotting against the state were forced out by the army. The same thing happened in other places where outsiders were brought into the citizenry. These situations often cause conflict because one group assumes superiority over the other due to their origins or status.

In oligarchies, many people feel mistreated because they are excluded from honors, as we've mentioned. In democracies, it's often the most prominent citizens who feel resentful because they don't receive more than an equal share with others who are not their equals.

Even the layout of a city can lead to unrest if the geography divides people, as in Clazomene, where those living in one part of town fought with those on the island, or in Athens, where citizens in the Piraeus were more supportive of democracy than those in the city center. Just as a small stream can disrupt a line of soldiers, even small disagreements can lead to rebellion. However, nothing leads to rebellion more than the tension between virtue and vice, followed by the divide between rich and poor. These are the most powerful sources of conflict.

Conflicts in governments don't usually start because of small matters, but they often come from small beginnings. Major disagreements arise from these small issues, especially when they involve people of high status in the government. For example, in ancient Syracuse, a government was overthrown because of a personal quarrel between two young men in office over a romantic relationship. One of them, while away, had his mistress seduced by the other. To get back at him, he convinced his friend's wife to live with him. Soon, the whole city picked sides, and the government collapsed. This shows how important it is to stop these disputes early before they grow, as small problems can lead to major consequences. Disputes between prominent people often involve the entire city. In Hestiaea, after the Median war, two brothers fought over their father's estate. The poorer brother, angry that the wealthier one had hidden some of their father's money, got the common people on his side, while the wealthier brother rallied the upper class. In Delphos, a wedding-related quarrel led to a series of seditions. The bridegroom, scared off by a bad omen on his way to the wedding, fled without marrying the bride. Her relatives, feeling insulted, secretly planted sacred money in his pocket while he was making a sacrifice, then accused him of sacrilege and killed him. In Mitylene, a dispute over inheritance led to a major conflict and a war with the Athenians, during which Paches captured the city. Timophanes, a wealthy man, left behind two daughters, and when Doxander was tricked out of arranging their marriages for his sons, he started a rebellion and encouraged the Athenians to attack.

A similar conflict over inheritance happened in Phocea between Mnasis and Euthucrates, leading to the Sacred War. The government of Epidamnus also changed because of a quarrel over a planned marriage. One man had arranged to marry off his daughter, but the archon, who was the father of the groom, punished him for an unrelated offense. The insulted father then joined forces with others who had been left out of the government and overthrew it.

A government can shift into an oligarchy, democracy, or a free state when certain groups in the city gain more power or influence, such as when the Areopagus court in Athens gained great influence during the Median war, which strengthened their control. On the other hand, the navy, made up of common people, secured the victory at Salamis and boosted the power of the democratic faction. At Argos, the nobles gained credit after winning the Battle of Mantinea against the Spartans and attempted to overthrow the democracy. In Syracuse, after the common people won the war against Athens, they changed the government into a democracy. In Chalcis, after the people overthrew the tyrant Phocis and expelled the nobles, they took control of the government. The same happened in Ambracia, where the people expelled the tyrant Periander and took power.

In general, whenever a person, group, or institution is responsible for making a state powerful—whether they are private citizens, officials, a particular tribe, or any segment of the population—they often become the cause of disputes. Either others envy them for the honors they've received, or they themselves are no longer satisfied with the equality they once had. Conflicts also arise when opposing groups, such as the rich and the common people, grow closer to each other in power. If one side is clearly stronger, the weaker side won't risk a confrontation. That's why those who are superior in virtue and excellence don't usually cause rebellions—they are too few in number to challenge the many.

In general, revolutions and changes in government happen in two main ways: either through force or through deceit. If by force, the ruling powers are compelled to submit to the change, and if by deceit, the people are initially tricked into agreeing to a change in government and are later forced to stick with it. For example, the Four Hundred in Athens misled the people by claiming that the King of Persia would provide money for the war against Sparta. After deceiving the people, they tried to keep control of the government. In some cases, people are first persuaded and later agree to be ruled.

We should now look at what these causes lead to in different types of governments. Democracies are most prone to revolutions because of dishonest leaders. They may target wealthy individuals, forcing them to band together for protection since common fear unites even enemies. These leaders also turn the common people against the wealthy, which can be seen in many states. For instance, in Cos, the democracy fell because of corrupt leaders, as the nobles formed a coalition. In Rhodes, leaders bribed the people, causing them to refuse to pay the trierarchs what they owed. The trierarchs, burdened by lawsuits, conspired together and overthrew the democracy. A similar thing happened in Heraclea, where, after the city was founded, the influential citizens were mistreated by the leaders. They left the city but later returned and destroyed the democratic government. In Megara, democracy was overthrown in a similar way. Leaders confiscated property to gain wealth and exiled the nobles until a large group of exiles returned, defeated the people in battle, and set up an oligarchy.

A similar event occurred in Cumae, where Thrasymachus destroyed the democracy. If you look at other cities, you'll find that revolutions happen for the same reasons. Leaders trying to gain favor with the people either divide the property of the wealthy, force them to spend it on public services, or exile them so they can confiscate their wealth. In earlier times, when the same person acted as both leader and general, democracies often turned into tyrannies. This was the case with most ancient tyrannies. In those days, leaders gained power not through speeches but through military action. Now, with the art of public speaking, leaders are more often skilled orators than generals, so they are less able to become tyrants, though there are a few exceptions.

Tyrannies were more common in the past because certain magistrates were given broad powers, such as the prytanes in Miletus, who held control over many important matters. Additionally, cities were smaller, with most people living in the countryside and working as farmers. This gave leaders in the city a chance to become tyrants if they were good at war and could gain the people's trust by opposing the rich. This was how Pisistratus in Athens rose to power by opposing the Pedieis, and how Theagenes in Megara became tyrant after slaughtering the cattle of the rich. Dionysius also became tyrant by accusing Daphnaeus and other rich men, earning the people's trust through his enmity with them.

A democracy can also change into something entirely new if there's no system to regulate how magistrates are chosen. If elections are controlled by the people, then leaders, eager to gain power, will do everything they can to make the people more powerful than the laws. To prevent this, magistrates should be chosen by tribes rather than by the people at large. These are the main ways that democracies experience revolutions and the causes behind them.

There are two main causes of revolutions in oligarchies: one is when the people are mistreated, making them ready for rebellion, especially if one of the oligarchs becomes their leader. This was the case with Lygdamis, who became tyrant of Naxos. Revolutions also arise when the wealthy, who are excluded from power, feel wronged. In some cities like Massilia, Ister, and Heraclea, those who were left out of government kept fighting until they gained a share. First, the older brothers were included, then the younger ones. In some places, fathers and sons were not allowed to hold office at the same time, and in others, only the eldest brother was allowed in power. In these cases, the oligarchy became somewhat like a free state. At Ister, the government changed into a democracy, and in Heraclea, instead of being ruled by a few, the government was expanded to include six hundred citizens.

In Cnidus, the oligarchy was destroyed when the nobles fought among themselves because too few people held power. Only one member of a family, usually the eldest, could hold office at a time. The people took advantage of this division and chose one of the nobles as their leader, eventually gaining control.

In Erithria, during the rule of the Basilides, although the city thrived under their leadership, the people grew dissatisfied with power being held by so few and changed the government. Oligarchies can also fall because of internal conflicts among their leaders. Some demagogues flatter the ruling few, as Charicles did with the Thirty Tyrants in Athens, or Phrynichus did with the Four Hundred. Others flatter the people to gain power, like the state-guardians in Larissa, who flattered the people because they were elected by them.

This happens in oligarchies where officials are not self-elected but chosen from wealthy or prominent families by the soldiers or the people, as was the custom in Abydos. If the judicial power isn't controlled by the ruling party, demagogues may side with the people in legal cases, which can lead to the downfall of the government, as happened in Heraclea in Pontus. Oligarchies can also be weakened when some try to concentrate power into even fewer hands. In these cases, those trying to maintain equality must appeal to the people for support.

Oligarchies are also prone to revolution when the ruling class spends too much on luxuries. These individuals may seek to become tyrants themselves or support others in doing so, as Hypparinus supported Dionysius in Syracuse. In Amphipolis, a man named Cleotimus brought in a colony of Chalcidians and used them to stir up conflict with the rich. In Aegina, a man who brought a lawsuit against Chares attempted to use the case to change the government.

At times, oligarchs will start disputes to cover up theft from the public or to fight against those who try to expose them. This happened in Apollonia in Pontus. However, if the members of an oligarchy remain united, the government is harder to overthrow without outside interference. Pharsalus is an example of this, where, despite being a small city, the people maintained power through wise governance.

An oligarchy can also collapse if it creates another oligarchy within itself. This happens when the government is controlled by a few, but not all members share equally in power. For instance, in Elis, the general government was controlled by a small group, but out of this group, a senate of ninety members was selected, holding their positions for life. Their election process ensured that power stayed within certain families, much like the senators in Sparta.

Oligarchies are vulnerable both in times of war and peace. During war, they may rely on mercenaries instead of citizens, and these mercenaries' commanders may seize power, as Timophanes did in Corinth. If they appoint multiple generals, it could lead to the establishment of a ruling dynasty. In some cases, oligarchies are forced to give more power to the people because they need their help in wars.

In times of peace, distrust among the oligarchs may lead them to rely on mercenaries and their general, who may end up controlling both sides, as happened in Larissa when Simos and the Aleuadae had the most influence. A similar situation occurred in Abydos during the rule of political clubs, like the one led by Iphiades.

Oligarchies can also fall apart when one group becomes too dominant or when there are conflicts over lawsuits or marriages. For example, in Eretria, Diagoras overthrew the oligarchy of the knights because of issues related to marriage. A similar sedition occurred in Heraclea when someone was condemned by the courts, and at Thebes when a man committed adultery.

Although the punishments in these cases were just, they were carried out in ways that caused unrest. At Thebes, for instance, enemies tried to publicly humiliate Archias. Oligarchies have also fallen when people could no longer tolerate the despotism of the ruling class, as in Cnidus and Chios.

Sometimes changes happen gradually in free states or oligarchies where senators, judges, and officials are chosen based on a certain wealth requirement. Initially, only a few people may meet the requirement, but as the city grows wealthier, more people can participate in the government, leading to a shift in power. These changes can happen slowly over time or more rapidly, depending on circumstances.

These are the types of revolutions and seditions that occur in oligarchies, and the causes behind them. Both democracies and oligarchies can sometimes change not into completely different forms of government, but into variations of the same form, such as shifting power from the law to the ruling party, or the reverse.

Revolts can also happen in aristocracies because only a small number of people hold power, just like in oligarchies. This makes aristocracies similar to oligarchies, even though the reasons for this power imbalance might be different. Problems are more likely to occur when most people are confident and believe they are equal in ability, such as in the case of the Partheniae in Sparta. They were the descendants of citizens who conspired against the state but were caught and sent to found the city of Tarentum. Trouble can also arise when highly respected individuals are dishonored by others who have gained more power than they have, even though they are equally capable. For example, Lysander was disgraced by the Spartan kings. Revolts also occur when an ambitious person can't rise to power, like Cinadon, who led a conspiracy against the Spartans during the reign of Agesilaus.

Moreover, issues arise when some people become too rich and others too poor, which is especially common during wars. This happened in Sparta during the Messenian War, as described in a poem by Tyrtaeus called "Eunomia," where some people wanted the land divided because they had been impoverished. Conflicts also occur when someone of very high status wants to increase their power and rule alone. This seemed to be the case with Pausanias in Sparta during the Median War and Anno in Carthage.

Both free states and aristocracies often fail when there isn't a clear structure for running public affairs. This happens because the balance between democratic and oligarchic elements is not properly managed. In aristocracies, the problem also comes from a lack of balance between virtue and power. States that lean more toward oligarchy are called aristocracies, and those that lean toward democracy are called free states. Free states are more stable because the broader the foundation of a government, the more secure it is. It's always better to live in a place where equality is emphasized. However, when the rich are given special status, they often try to dominate others. In general, whichever direction a government leans, that's where it will end up. A free state will become a democracy, and an aristocracy will become an oligarchy, or the opposite may happen. For instance, if the poor feel mistreated, they will side with the opposite faction, and an aristocracy may turn into a democracy, or a free state into an oligarchy. The only truly stable government is one where everyone has the equality they deserve and where people fully possess what belongs to them.

This is what happened in Thurium. The magistrates were originally elected based on a high property qualification, but the requirement was lowered, and more courts were created. However, because the nobles owned most of the land against the law, the government leaned too much toward oligarchy, allowing them to take advantage of the rest of the people. Eventually, the people, strengthened by their experience in war, overthrew their rulers and expelled those who owned more than their fair share. Aristocracies, which are essentially free oligarchies, often face problems when the nobles try to seize too much power, as in Sparta, where property is concentrated in the hands of a few. The nobles have too much freedom to make alliances as they please. For instance, the city of the Locrians was ruined because of an alliance with Dionysius. Their government was neither a democracy nor a well-balanced aristocracy.

Aristocracies tend to collapse slowly, as we've seen with other forms of government. This happens when small, seemingly insignificant changes gradually lead to larger ones. Once a minor issue is treated lightly, something more important will be more easily changed, until the entire structure of the government is destroyed. This happened in Thurium, where the law required soldiers to serve for five years. A group of young, ambitious soldiers, who were well-regarded by their officers, despised the officials in charge of public affairs. They believed they could change the law so they could remain in the military indefinitely, knowing the people would elect them. The magistrates, called counselors, initially resisted this change but eventually agreed to it, thinking that if they allowed this law to be changed, they would retain control over other public matters. However, when they tried to prevent further changes, they found they had no power to stop them, and the government turned into a ruling faction of those who had introduced the changes.

In short, all governments can be destroyed from within or from external forces. External threats arise when neighboring states have opposing policies, or even when a powerful state far away is at odds with their system. The Athenians and Spartans serve as examples of this. The Athenians overthrew oligarchies when they were victorious, and the Spartans did the same with democracies. These are the main causes of revolutions and conflicts in governments.

We now need to consider how governments can be preserved, both in general and in specific types of states. First, if we understand the causes of a government's downfall, we can also understand the means of preserving it, since opposites produce opposite results. Destruction and preservation are opposites. In well-ordered governments, it's especially important that nothing is done against the law, and this is particularly true with small matters. Small violations can gradually destroy a state, just as small expenses can drain a person's income over time. The mind is often deceived by this faulty reasoning: if each small part is insignificant, then the whole is also insignificant. But while each part may be small, together they add up to something significant.

The first step is for the state to prevent small violations from occurring. Second, people should not trust those who try to deceive them with false claims, as they will eventually be proven wrong by the facts. The various ways in which this deceit happens have already been discussed.

Aristocracies and oligarchies often last not because their systems of government are strong but because their leaders are wise in dealing with both those who hold power and those who do not. They avoid harming those who aren't involved in government and instead offer important roles to the most influential among them. They also avoid offending those who seek honor and refrain from taking individuals' property. For those who are in power, leaders treat each other as equals. This desire for equality is both just and convenient for those of the same status. If many people share power, democratic principles can be useful, such as limiting how long someone can hold office. Rotating leadership ensures that all people of the same rank have their turn, which prevents any one person from gaining too much power. This method helps prevent both aristocracies and democracies from turning into dynasties because leaders don't hold power long enough to cause significant harm.

Governments are sometimes preserved by keeping the means of corruption far away, but at other times, a nearby threat can strengthen a government. When people are worried about a danger, they pay more attention to the state's needs. Leaders must be able to raise alarm when necessary to protect the government, rather than being like a guard who fails to keep watch. Even a distant danger should be made to seem close at hand.

It's also crucial to manage the conflicts and disputes among nobles through laws, and to prevent those not yet involved from getting drawn in. Recognizing problems early is the skill of a true statesman. In both oligarchies and free states, it's important to prevent problems related to the census. If the census remains the same while the overall amount of wealth increases, it can create issues. The total amount of wealth should be compared over time, either annually in small cities or every three to five years in larger ones. If the wealth has greatly increased or decreased compared to when the census was first established, the law should adjust the census accordingly. If wealth increases, the census should be raised, and if wealth decreases, the census should be lowered. If this adjustment isn't made, oligarchies will turn into dynasties, and free states will become democracies, or oligarchies will shift into free states.

In all types of governments—whether democracies, oligarchies, or monarchies—it's important not to allow any one person to rise far above the rest. Instead, it's better to give moderate honors over a longer period rather than great honors for a short time. Most people can't handle sudden success, which corrupts them. If great honors are given all at once, they should be taken away gradually rather than suddenly. Above all, the law should ensure that no one gains too much power through wealth or connections. If someone does, they should be required to leave the country.

Since some people push for changes in order to live according to their own desires, there should be an official responsible for monitoring everyone's behavior. This person should ensure that people's behavior aligns with the character of the state, whether it's an oligarchy, democracy, or any other form of government. The state should also be cautious of those who are overly successful and assign them to public duties to keep their power in check. It's important to balance the interests of the rich and the poor by uniting them into one body and increasing the number of people in the middle class. This helps prevent rebellions caused by inequalities in status.

In every state, it's also essential to ensure that public officials aren't corrupt. This is especially important in oligarchies, where the people may not mind being excluded from government as long as they aren't being cheated. But if they suspect that public officials are stealing from them, they will be angry for two reasons: they're being excluded from power and robbed at the same time.

One way to combine elements of democracy and aristocracy is to remove financial incentives from public office. When there's no money to be made from holding office, both the rich and the poor will get what they want. Allowing everyone to share in government is democratic, while having the wealthy hold office is aristocratic. If public offices don't offer financial rewards, the poor won't want the positions since they won't make any money, but the rich will still want them since they don't need the income. The poor will focus on improving their own finances, and the majority of the people won't be ruled by those of lower status.

To prevent public funds from being misused, all government money should be distributed openly for everyone to see, and copies of the accounts should be kept in different districts. Since magistrates aren't benefiting financially from their positions, the law should provide honors for those who do their jobs well.

In democracies, the rich should be protected by preventing their land or its produce from being divided. This is sometimes done without being noticed. It would also help if the people stopped the wealthy from hosting unnecessary and expensive public events, like plays, music performances, and parades.

In an oligarchy, it's important to take care of the poor by giving them profitable public jobs. If a rich person insults a poor person, the punishment should be harsher than if they insulted someone of their own rank. Inheritance laws should also prevent someone from owning multiple estates, so wealth is more evenly distributed, and the poor have a chance to improve their circumstances.

In both democracies and oligarchies, people who don't take part in public affairs should be given equality or preference in other areas. In a democracy, this means helping the rich, and in an oligarchy, this means supporting the poor. However, the most important offices should always be filled by those best qualified for the job.

There are three important qualities that people need to have to hold the highest positions in government. First, they must be loyal to the constitution of the state. Second, they must be fully capable of handling the duties of their office. Third, they must have the kind of virtue and sense of justice that fit the type of state they are serving. Justice doesn't look the same in every state, so it's clear that there are different kinds of justice depending on the state.

But what if all these qualities don't exist in the same person? How should we choose? For example, suppose one person is a skilled military leader but has poor morals and doesn't support the constitution. Another person is just and loyal to the constitution but lacks military skill. Which one should we choose? In these cases, we should look at which qualities are rarer and more valuable. For a general, courage might be more important than virtue, since fewer people have the ability to lead an army than there are good people in general. But when it comes to managing finances or protecting the state, we should prioritize virtue because more people are capable of handling these tasks, but fewer have the necessary level of virtue.

Some might ask if a person has the ability to do their job and supports the constitution, why is it necessary for them to be virtuous? Wouldn't these two qualities be enough to make them useful to the state? The answer is no, because people who are knowledgeable and loyal often lack good judgment. Just like some people neglect their own affairs even though they understand them and love themselves, they might treat the state's business the same way.

In short, everything that the laws say is good for the state helps to preserve it, but the most important thing is to have more people who want to keep the government intact than those who wish to overthrow it. One key thing that many governments, which are now corrupt, forget is to maintain a balance. Many things that seem helpful to a democracy can actually destroy it, and the same goes for an oligarchy. People often take one idea too far. It's like a nose that's only slightly crooked can still be beautiful, but if it becomes too crooked or too flat, it stops looking like a proper nose. In the same way, an oligarchy or democracy can stray a little from its perfect form and still work well, but if it is taken to an extreme, the government becomes worse, and eventually, it might not even be a government at all.

The lawmaker and the politician need to understand what preserves and what destroys both democracies and oligarchies. Neither type of government can exist without both rich and poor people. If complete equality is forced on everyone, the government will change into something else. So, when laws that allow for inequality in wealth are destroyed, the government itself is destroyed. It's also a mistake in democracies for leaders to make the common people more powerful than the law, which divides the city into two opposing sides: the rich and the poor. Instead, leaders should encourage harmony between the classes. In oligarchies, it's wrong to support those in power when they are in conflict with the people.

The oaths taken in oligarchies should also change. In some places, people swear, "I will oppose the common people and do everything I can against them." Instead, they should swear not to harm the people.

Out of everything I've mentioned, the most important thing to preserve the state is something that is often ignored: educating children for the sake of the state. No law, no matter how wise or approved by political leaders, will work unless citizens are raised with the values of the constitution. If the government is a democracy, children should be educated for a democracy. If it's an oligarchy, they should be taught accordingly. If individual people have bad morals, the whole city will, too. But this education shouldn't cater to the desires of those in power, whether in an oligarchy or democracy. It should prepare them to lead in either type of government. Currently, in oligarchies, the children of the wealthy are raised too softly, and the children of the poor are raised too tough, with lots of physical labor. This makes both groups eager and able to cause political changes.

In pure democracies, they often act in ways that are against their own best interests because they misunderstand freedom. There are two main ideas in a democracy: first, that the people should have the most power, and second, that everyone should enjoy freedom. But they make the mistake of thinking that freedom means everyone can do whatever they want. In this kind of democracy, people think they should be able to live however they choose, as Euripides said, "according to their own desire." But this is wrong. People shouldn't see living under the government as slavery, but as protection.

I've explained the causes of corruption in different types of states and how they can be preserved.

Now, we'll talk about monarchies, how they fall apart, and how they can be preserved. In many ways, the things I've already said about other forms of government also apply to monarchies and tyrannies. A kingdom is similar to an aristocracy, and a tyranny is like a mix of the worst parts of an oligarchy and a democracy. This makes tyranny the worst form of government because it combines all the flaws of both oligarchy and democracy.

These two forms of monarchy, kingdoms and tyrannies, come from opposite ideas. A kingdom is meant to protect the best citizens from the masses. Kings are chosen either for their great virtue and noble actions or because they come from a distinguished family. A tyrant, on the other hand, is often chosen from the lowest classes because the people want someone who will stand against the elite. Most tyrants start out as demagogues, gaining favor with the people by attacking the nobles.

Some tyrannies were established after cities became large and powerful, while others were created earlier by kings who took more power than they were allowed, trying to rule as despots. Still, others came from people who were elected to important positions in the state. In the past, people sometimes chose officials for life who handled both civil and religious matters. One person was given supreme power over all the officials, and this made it easy for them to become tyrants if they wanted to. This is how Phidon of Argos and other tyrants rose to power. Phalaris and others in Ionia gained power through their roles in the state, and others, like Pansetius in Leontium, Cypselus in Corinth, Pisistratus in Athens, and Dionysius in Syracuse, came to power as demagogues.

A kingdom, as I said, is similar to an aristocracy. It is given to those who deserve it based on their virtue, family, good deeds, or power. Kings are often people who have saved their cities from slavery in war, like Codrus, or freed them from oppression, like Cyrus. Founders of cities or colonies, like the kings of Sparta, Macedon, and Molossia, also became kings.

A king's goal is to protect his people, ensuring that property owners are secure in their possessions and that citizens are free from harm. A tyrant, on the other hand, cares only for his own benefit. His main goal is pleasure, while a king's goal is virtue. A tyrant wants wealth, but a king seeks honor. Kings are guarded by citizens, while tyrants rely on foreigners for protection.

A tyranny combines all the worst features of oligarchies and democracies. Like an oligarchy, it focuses on gaining wealth, which helps the tyrant maintain his guards and live a luxurious life. A tyrant also doesn't trust the people and often disarms them to prevent rebellion. He persecutes the masses and forces them out of the city, just as an oligarchy might. Like a democracy, a tyranny fights against the nobles, either killing them or driving them into exile because they are seen as rivals.

Both kingdoms and tyrannies can fall for the same reasons that cause other types of governments to collapse. Injustice, fear, and disrespect often lead people to conspire against monarchies. Of these, disrespect is usually the strongest reason. Sometimes people plot against the ruler because they've lost their wealth or property. The end of both kingdoms and tyrannies often looks the same because monarchs have both wealth and honor, which many people want for themselves.

Some plots are aimed at killing the ruler, while others target the government itself. Personal hatred is usually the reason for plots against a ruler's life, and there are many causes for this hatred. People who are motivated by anger often don't seek power themselves but want revenge. For example, the plot against the sons of Pisistratus started because they insulted Harmodius's sister and treated Harmodius poorly. Periander, the tyrant of Ambracia, was killed because he took liberties with a boy during a drunken feast. Philip of Macedon was killed by Pausanias because Philip failed to avenge an insult Pausanias received. Amintas the Little was killed by Darda because he mocked his age. Similarly, an eunuch killed Evagoras of Cyprus in revenge for taking his son's wife.

Many rulers have been killed by those they insulted or mistreated, even when they held kingly power. For example, at Mitylene, Megacles and his friends killed the Penthelidae family because they would roam around striking people with clubs. Later, Smendes killed Penthilus for whipping him and dragging him away from his wife. Decamnichus also led the plot against Archelaus because he had been handed over to Euripides to be whipped.

Fear also causes conspiracies in monarchies, just as it does in other governments. Artabanes conspired against Xerxes because he feared punishment for hanging Darius, even though he did it on Xerxes's orders. Artabanes thought Xerxes had changed his mind and was going to pardon Darius. Some kings have been overthrown because they were despised. Sardanapalus, for example, was reportedly caught spinning wool with his wife, and his people conspired against him. Dion plotted against Dionysius the Younger because Dionysius was always drunk, and the people wanted a change.

Even a ruler's friends may conspire against him if they despise him, especially if they feel confident they won't be caught. People who think they can take over the throne also plot against rulers because they see the danger as worth the risk. Military leaders, in particular, may attempt to overthrow a king. Cyrus, for example, overthrew Astyages because he saw that Astyages's forces were weak from inactivity and that Astyages himself lived an indulgent lifestyle. Similarly, Suthes, a Thracian general, conspired against Amadocus.

Sometimes multiple reasons, like contempt and greed, drive people to conspire, as in the case of Mithridates against Ariobarzanes. Bold individuals with military honors are especially likely to lead rebellions. Their courage and strength make them ready to take on such risks.

Some people conspire against tyrants for the sake of honor and glory, rather than for wealth or power. These individuals aren't motivated by personal gain but by the desire for fame. They see taking down a tyrant as a noble act, and they want to be remembered for their bravery. Although there aren't many people like this, those who act on this principle care little for their own safety. They are willing to die for the chance to make even a small difference, as Dion did when he attacked Dionysius with just a few troops. He said that even a small victory would be enough for him, and if he died right after gaining a foothold in his country, he would still consider his death honorable.

Tyrannies can also be destroyed by powerful neighboring states. Democracies, in particular, oppose tyrannies. As Hesiod said, "a potter against a potter," meaning similar systems naturally oppose each other. This is why the Spartans overthrew so many tyrannies, and the Syracusans did the same when their state was strong. Tyrannies can be brought down from within as well, especially when people who aren't involved in the government lead a revolution. This happened to Gelon and Dionysius, who were overthrown by the people.

Two main causes lead people to conspire against tyrants: hatred and contempt. Hatred seems to be unavoidable for tyrants, but contempt is also a common cause of their downfall. Many tyrants lose power because they become lazy and weak after inheriting their position, unlike those who originally rose to power by their own strength. As a result, they become despised and vulnerable to conspiracies.

Anger often plays a role in these conspiracies. While anger is different from hatred, it can be an even stronger motivator because it doesn't rely on reason. Many rulers have been brought down because of personal insults, as was the case with the Pisistratidae and others.

In summary, the same causes that destroy pure oligarchies and extreme democracies can also destroy tyrannies because they share many of the same characteristics.

Kingdoms are rarely destroyed by external forces, which is why they tend to be more stable. However, they can still be brought down by internal problems. The two main causes of a kingdom's downfall are either when those in power cause a rebellion or when they try to turn the kingdom into a tyranny by taking more power than the law allows.

In modern times, we don't often see true kingdoms being formed, but rather monarchies and tyrannies. A true kingdom is one that people willingly submit to, giving supreme power to a ruler in times of great need. But when many people are equal, and no one stands out as being clearly better than the rest, they won't agree to be ruled. If someone takes power by force or trickery, that's a tyranny, not a kingdom.

Finally, we should talk about the causes of revolutions in hereditary kingdoms. One cause is that many rulers are naturally weak and easy to disrespect. Another is that they often act arrogantly, even though their power isn't absolute. A king's power depends on the people's willingness to obey, but a tyrant's power relies on force. These are some of the reasons why monarchies fall apart.

Monarchies are preserved in ways that are opposite to what causes their downfall. To break this down more clearly: the stability of a kingdom depends on keeping the king's power within reasonable limits. The less absolute the king's power is, the longer the government will last because the king will be less tyrannical and more on equal footing with the people. This will cause less envy and resentment from the people.

For example, the kingdom of the Molossi lasted a long time because of this balance. In Sparta, the power was divided between two kings, and moderation was introduced by Theopompus, who set up the ephors. By taking away some of the king's power, he actually extended the life of the kingdom. As he famously told his wife when she asked if he was ashamed to pass down a kingdom weaker than what he inherited, he replied, "No, I am making it last longer."

Tyrannies, on the other hand, are preserved in two completely opposite ways. One method is to delegate power among multiple people. Many tyrants have used this method, and it's said that Periander founded several of these types of governments. Another way to preserve a tyranny is to do the opposite of what preserves a healthy government. Tyrants should keep down anyone with ambition and eliminate those who refuse to submit. They should prevent people from gathering for public meals, forming clubs, or receiving education—anything that might inspire high spirits or mutual trust. Tyrants should also ensure that the people remain isolated from each other because familiarity breeds trust, which could lead to plots. To keep the people submissive, tyrants should require all strangers to be visible in public and live near the city gates, so their actions can be monitored. People who are treated like slaves rarely have noble ambitions.

In short, tyrants should mimic the practices of the Persians and other so-called "barbarians," who excel at keeping people oppressed. Tyrants should use spies to watch over everyone. For example, the Syracusans had women called potagogides who acted as spies, and

Hiero would send out listeners to eavesdrop on any group discussions. This made people afraid to speak freely, and if they did, it was less likely to stay secret. Tyrants should also stir up conflict between different groups: friends against friends, commoners against nobles, and the wealthy against each other.

It's also helpful for tyrants to keep their subjects poor so they have no time or resources to organize against the government. This is why projects like the Pyramids in Egypt and the grand buildings of tyrants like the Cypselids and Pisistratids served not just as monuments but as ways to keep the people occupied and impoverished. Heavy taxes can also achieve this, as Dionysius of Syracuse did when he collected the people's wealth over five years. Tyrants should also involve their people in wars to keep them busy and dependent on their leader.

A king is supported by friends, but a tyrant can't trust anyone— not even his closest allies, since they have the greatest power to overthrow him.

A tyrant should also follow some practices seen in extreme democracies. For example, he should give great freedom to women and slaves because they are unlikely to plot against him. If treated well, women and slaves become loyal supporters of tyrants. In extreme democracies, the people also desire absolute power, which is why flatterers become important. In democracies, the demagogue flatters the people, and in a tyranny, the flatterer tells the tyrant whatever he wants to hear. Tyrants tend to surround themselves with the worst kind of people because they love to be flattered—something honorable people refuse to do. Dishonest people are also useful for carrying out evil deeds, as the saying goes, "like attracts like."

Tyrants should avoid showing favor to men of character or those who value freedom because they will naturally challenge the tyrant's authority. Instead, tyrants prefer to associate with outsiders rather than citizens, as the former are less likely to conspire against them.

These methods help tyrants maintain power, and their rule is often characterized by evil actions. However, all of these tactics can be grouped into three main goals: keeping the citizens poor and submissive, ensuring they don't trust each other, and leaving them powerless. If a tyrant can achieve these three things, his rule will be secure.

There is also another way to maintain a tyranny, which is the opposite of everything mentioned above. This method involves making the government appear more like a kingdom, while still maintaining the tyrant's absolute power. The key is to make the people think they are being ruled by a just and fair king while keeping the necessary force to maintain control. The tyrant should seem focused on public welfare and avoid spending money in ways that anger the people. He should keep careful records of income and spending, like some tyrants already do, so that he appears more like a responsible family head than a greedy ruler. The people should believe that taxes and services are collected for the good of the state, not for the tyrant's personal gain.

A tyrant should also avoid appearing harsh. He should aim to inspire respect rather than fear, and if possible, develop some political skills so his people see him as capable. He should avoid any actions that might offend others' sense of decency and should never allow those around him to act arrogantly. Many tyrants have been brought down by the haughty behavior of their wives and family members.

In terms of personal behavior, a tyrant should avoid indulging in excessive pleasures and showing off his luxuries. Instead, he should appear moderate and disciplined. People are less likely to plot against someone they see as responsible and sober rather than lazy and indulgent.

A tyrant should also make improvements to the city, so he seems more like a protector than an oppressor. Additionally, he should be seen as especially pious, which will make people less likely to believe he would commit unlawful acts. If the people think their leader is religious and respectful of the gods, they will be less inclined to criticize or rebel against him. However, this show of piety must be genuine to avoid suspicion of hypocrisy.

It's also important for a tyrant to honor and reward people of merit so that they don't believe they could be treated better in a free state. Honors should come directly from the tyrant, while any criticism or punishment should be delivered by his officials. Tyrants should avoid making any one person too powerful, especially not several people at once, as they might support each other in a rebellion. If a powerful person needs to be removed from office, it should be done gradually to avoid stirring up resistance.

Tyrants should also avoid humiliating or insulting people of honor. Just as people who value money are most upset when their wealth is taken, people who value honor are most hurt when they are publicly shamed. If punishment is necessary, it should be more like a father correcting a son than a master punishing a slave. If a tyrant does cause offense, he should make up for it by offering even greater honors to that person.

Above all, tyrants should be wary of those who are willing to risk their own lives to achieve their goals. People motivated by anger or revenge are the most dangerous because they are willing to sacrifice themselves to take down the tyrant. As Heraclitus said, "It is dangerous to fight with an angry man who will buy his victory with his own life."

A city is made up of both rich and poor people, so a tyrant must ensure that both groups are treated fairly. He should not allow either group to dominate the other. If the tyrant can win over the most powerful group, he won't need to free the slaves or disarm the citizens to stay in control. The strength of that group, combined with his own forces, will make him safe from any conspiracy.

In summary, a tyrant should try to appear as much like a king as possible. He should act as a protector of the people rather than their oppressor. By doing this, he will make his rule more honorable and less hated. Not only will this gain him the loyalty of his people, but it will also make his reign last longer. At the very least, even if he cannot be fully virtuous, he should try to appear half-virtuous.

Oligarchies and tyrannies are generally the shortest-lived forms of government. The tyranny of Orthagoras and his family in Sicyon lasted longer than most because they ruled with moderation and followed the laws in many ways. Clisthenes, in particular, was a skilled general who never lost the respect of the people. He even made his government more popular by rewarding someone who ruled against him in a judgment.

Another long-lasting tyranny was that of the Cypselids in Corinth, which lasted seventy-seven years and six months. Cypselus ruled for thirty years, Periander for forty-four, and Psammetichus for three years. Cypselus managed to stay popular and ruled without the need for bodyguards. Periander, on the other hand, ruled more like a traditional tyrant, but he was an effective general.

The Pisistratids ruled Athens for about thirty-three years, although Pisistratus himself was expelled twice. His son, Hippias, ruled for eighteen years. In total, their reign lasted thirty-three years, although it wasn't continuous.

Other notable tyrannies, like those of Hiero and Gelo in Syracuse, didn't last as long. Gelo ruled for eight years, Hiero for ten, and Thrasybulus only lasted eleven months. Many other tyrannies were even shorter-lived.

We have now discussed the main causes of corruption and the ways to preserve both free states and monarchies.

In Plato's Republic, Socrates discusses the ways in which governments change, but his argument has some flaws. He doesn't specifically address what causes the best governments to change, and he only gives a general explanation that nothing stays the same forever. He argues that human nature will eventually produce bad leaders who won't accept proper education, and in this, he's probably correct. Some people simply cannot be made into good leaders, no matter how much they are taught. But why should this kind of change happen more in the best government than in any other?

Socrates also suggests that all governments will eventually transform in a predictable cycle, from one form to another. He says a well-ordered government will first change into a Spartan-style government, then into an oligarchy, then into a democracy, and finally into a tyranny. However, he doesn't explain what will happen to a tyranny or what will cause it to change. According to his logic, all governments should eventually return to their original form, creating a continuous cycle.

In reality, tyrannies often change into something else. For example, the tyranny of Myron in Syria changed into that of Clisthenes. Some tyrannies, like Antileon's in Chalcas, turned into oligarchies. Others, like Gelo's in Syracuse, changed into democracies, and still others, like Charilaus's in Sparta and in Carthage, became aristocracies. Similarly, oligarchies have sometimes turned into tyrannies. Many of the ancient tyrannies in Sicily, like those of Panaetius in Leontini, Cleander in Gela, and Anaxilaus in Rhegium, started as oligarchies.

It's also incorrect to say that governments change simply because those in power are greedy for money. In many oligarchies, making money is not allowed, and strict laws prevent it. Yet, in Carthage, which is a democracy, money-making is considered respectable, and their government has remained stable.

It's also wrong to say that oligarchies are divided into two cities, one for the rich and one for the poor. This division can happen in any state where people don't have equal wealth or character, not just in oligarchies.

Governments can change for many reasons, and while Socrates focuses on just one—people becoming poor through luxury and debt—this is only part of the story. Oligarchies can change even when the rich grow stronger than the poor or when those who are excluded from power are treated unfairly.

Though there are many types of oligarchies and democracies, Socrates only discusses each as if there is just one form.

Book 6

We have already explained the nature of the supreme council in the state, how different councils might work, and how various officials should be managed. We've also talked about the role of the courts and what kind of court system fits different types of states. Finally, we've discussed the causes of both the downfall and the preservation of governments.

Since there are many kinds of democracies, just as there are many other types of governments, it's important to look at anything we might have missed regarding each of them. We need to give each form of government the rules and structures that best suit it and are most useful for it. We also need to examine how different types of governments can be combined, because when governments combine, they can change from one form to another, like from an aristocracy to an oligarchy or from a free state to a democracy.

I mean the combinations where, for example, the decision-making part of the government works like an oligarchy, while the court system works like an aristocracy. Or maybe only the decision-making part is like an oligarchy, while the officials are chosen like in an aristocracy. Sometimes, not every part of the government is organized according to the overall nature of that state. But first, we'll consider what kind of democracy fits a particular city and what kind of oligarchy fits a particular people. We'll also look at what's beneficial for other types of states. We need to show clearly which government is best for a particular state and how it should be established. We will also cover these topics briefly.

First, let's talk about democracy. This will help us understand its opposite, oligarchy. As we do this, we need to look closely at all the parts that make up a democracy and the things connected to it. The way these parts are combined creates different types of democracies, and that's why there are more than one kind, each with its own nature.

There are two main reasons why democracies come in different forms. The first is because the people themselves are different. In one country, most people are farmers, while in another, they might be mechanics or hired workers. If a country has both farmers and hired workers, their democracy will not only be better or worse, but also different in how it operates. The second reason we'll talk about now. The different elements connected to democracies, when combined, make one democracy different from another. Sometimes only a few elements are involved, sometimes many, and this affects how the government functions.

Anyone who wants to build a government they approve of or improve one that already exists needs to understand all these details. Most founders of states try to fit as many similar elements into their government plan as possible, but they often make mistakes, as I explained earlier when discussing how governments are preserved and destroyed. Now I'll explain the key principles and practices that every democracy needs.

The foundation of a democratic state is liberty, and people often say that only in democracy can true liberty be found. They believe liberty is the main goal of every democracy. One part of liberty is taking turns ruling and being ruled. According to democratic justice, equality is based on numbers, not on merit. Since this is seen as fair, it means the people, as a whole, should have the highest power, and what the majority decides should be final. So in a democracy, the poor should have more power than the rich because they are the majority. This is one key idea of liberty that all designers of democracies believe in.

Another is the idea that everyone should live as they like because they see this as a right that comes from liberty. They say someone who can't live as they want is like a slave. This is another basic principle of democracy. It also leads to the belief that no one should be forced to obey anyone else, except in turn, just as that person must obey when it's their turn to do so. This supports the idea of equality that liberty requires.

Since this is how the government is set up, certain rules must be followed. First, all officials should be chosen from all the people, and everyone should take turns ruling. Most officials should be chosen by lottery, except for roles that require special skills or knowledge. There shouldn't be a property requirement to hold office, or if there is, it should be very small. No one should hold the same job more than once, or only very rarely, except in the military. Most appointments should be for short terms, or as many as possible should be. The whole population should be able to judge legal cases, whether they are public issues or private contracts. For example, in Athens, the people judge officials when they finish their term and also decide on both public and private matters. The highest authority should be the public assembly, and no official should have much personal power, except in very limited and unimportant cases.

A senate is best suited to a democracy, where the whole population isn't paid for attending meetings. Without pay, the people will bring all cases before the senate, as we discussed before. If possible, there should be a fund to pay everyone who has a role in public affairs, whether in the assembly, the courts, or as officials. If that's not possible, then at least the officials, judges, senators, and assembly members should be paid, as well as those required to eat at a common table.

Just as an oligarchy is said to be a government of the wealthy and well-educated, democracy is a government run by people without high birth, wealth, or special skills. In a democracy, no office should be held for life. If any such offices remain after the government has changed to a democracy, their power should be gradually reduced, and officials should be chosen by lottery rather than election.

These ideas apply to all democracies. The key principle of democracy is that the number of people should determine equality.

This is what defines a government run by the people. The rich should not have more of a say in government than the poor, and the government should not be controlled only by the wealthy. Everyone should be equal based on the number of people, as this is seen as the best way to preserve equality and liberty in the state.

Next, we need to figure out how this equality can be achieved. Should we divide the population so that 500 rich people have the same power as 1,000 poor people? Or should the 1,000 poor have the same power as the 500 rich? Or should we not do it this way? Instead, we could take an equal number from both groups to choose officials and judges. Would this be true democratic justice, or would it only reflect the rule of numbers? Those who defend democracy say that whatever the majority agrees on is fair, while supporters of oligarchy argue that the opinion of the wealthiest is what matters. They believe the government should be guided by property value.

Both views are unjust. If we follow the idea of the wealthiest, we risk creating a tyranny, because if one person happens to be richer than everyone else, then, by oligarchic logic, he should have all the power. On the other hand, if the majority's opinion always prevails, it would be unfair to the rich, since they are fewer in number, as I've already said.

To find a fair solution that both sides can agree on, we need to start with a definition of justice that works for both sides. They both agree that what most people in the state support should be established as law. But this rule should not apply fully. Since a city is made up of two groups—rich and poor—the laws should be approved by both groups, or at least by a majority from both. If they disagree, then the decision should be based on the side with the higher total wealth. For example, if there are 10 rich people and 20 poor people, and 6 of the rich and 15 of the poor agree on something, while the remaining 4 rich and 5 poor oppose it, the group with the higher total wealth should have their way. If the wealth is equal on both sides, it should be treated like a tie in a court case, where the decision is made by lot or some other method.

Even though it's hard to define exactly what's fair and just, it's easier to understand than to convince those in power to follow these principles. The weak always want equality and fairness, but the strong often ignore these ideals.

There are four kinds of democracies. The best is the one made up of people like farmers, which is also the oldest type. I call this the first kind because most people would place it first when dividing the population. The best part of this group is made up of farmers. A democracy can be formed where most people are farmers or herders, because they don't have much property and are too busy working to constantly hold public meetings. They'll spend their time on their work, not on political offices, which don't offer much reward. Most people prefer wealth to honor.

This is shown by how people in the past and even now have accepted tyrannies or oligarchies, as long as they aren't disturbed in their daily work or deprived of their property. Some of them become rich quickly, while others escape poverty. The right to vote and hold officials accountable when they finish their term will satisfy their desire for honor if they have any. In some states, even though the common people don't elect the officials, they are represented by a part of the assembly. It's enough for the people to have the power to make decisions. This should be considered a form of democracy, as it was in the past at Mantinea.

In this type of democracy, people should have the power to criticize their officials when they leave office and to make decisions on legal cases. The top officials should be elected, either based on property or skill, depending on the role. A state like this will be well-run because the best people will hold office with the approval of the people, who won't envy them. The wealthy and powerful will be satisfied because they aren't being ruled by their inferiors. They will also be careful with their power because others can hold them accountable. It benefits the state for officials to answer to others and not have total freedom to do whatever they want. Without limits, people would abuse their power.

It's clear that this is the best type of democracy because the people have the right amount of power. To create a democracy of farmers, it's helpful to have laws that limit how much land anyone can own or how close it can be to the city. In some ancient states, no one was allowed to sell their original land. There's also a law by Oxylus that forbids people from increasing their wealth through loans. We should also look at the laws of the Aphytaians, who had little land but a large population of farmers. They divided their land in a way that gave more power to the poor than the rich.

Next to farmers, the best group for a democracy is herders, as they are similar to farmers in many ways and make strong soldiers because of their lifestyle. The worst kind of people for a democracy are those who live in poverty and have no connection to virtue in their work. These are the mechanics, tradesmen, and hired laborers. They spend their time in the city, making it easy for them to attend public meetings, while farmers, who live in the country, have a harder time getting there and are less interested in going.

In countries where much of the land is far from the city, it's easier to establish a good democracy or free state because most people will live in the country. In these democracies, even though there may be many people near the city center, no official meeting should be held without the country people present. We've explained how the first and best democracy should be set up, and this will serve as a guide for other types of democracies. In each case, the lowest class should be kept separate from the rest.

The worst kind of democracy is the one that gives every citizen a share in every part of the government. Few people can handle this kind of democracy, and it's hard to keep it stable for long unless it's well-supported by laws and customs. We've already talked about almost every cause that can destroy this type of government or any other.

Leaders of this kind of democracy try to keep it going by gathering as many people as they can and giving them citizenship, even to those born outside the city. This method works well for this kind of government, and it's what demagogues typically do. However, they should stop once the common people become more powerful than the nobles and middle class, because if they go further, the state will become disorderly. The nobles won't tolerate the power of the common people and will resent it, as happened in Cyrene. Small problems can be ignored, but when they grow large, they are harder to miss.

It's also helpful in this type of democracy to do what Clisthenes did in Athens when he wanted to increase the people's power, or what was done in Cyrene to establish democracy. This involves creating many tribes and brotherhoods, reducing private religious ceremonies, and making religious practices more public. Every effort should be made to blend the people together and break old customs.

Many things that are done in a tyranny are also useful in this type of democracy. For example, the freedom of slaves, women, and children to act as they please is useful to a certain extent. In this type of government, it's also common to let people live however they want. Many people will support such a system because it's more appealing to live without rules than to live under strict control.

It is also the job of lawmakers and those who support this kind of government not to make it overly ambitious or too perfect. Instead, they should aim for stability. Even if a state is poorly designed, it can still survive for a short while. Therefore, they should focus on preserving it through the methods we've already discussed, explaining the causes of how governments last or fall. They should avoid harmful things and create both written and unwritten laws that encourage what helps keep the state stable. They shouldn't think that what's good for a democracy or an oligarchy is making them purely one or the other, but rather what helps them last longer. However, modern demagogues, who flatter the people, cause frequent confiscations in the courts. For this reason, those who truly care about the welfare of the state should do the opposite of what these demagogues do. They should pass laws preventing forfeitures from being shared among the people or put into the treasury. Instead, these should be set aside for sacred purposes. This way, people with bad intentions will still be cautious, as the punishment would be the same, but the public wouldn't be so eager to condemn those on trial if they don't gain anything from it.

They should also ensure that the number of public trials is as few as possible, and those who bring lawsuits recklessly should be punished harshly. It's usually the nobles, not the common people, who are prosecuted. Citizens in the same state should care for one another, at the very least not treat those in power like enemies. In many of the democracies formed recently, it's hard to get people to attend public meetings unless they're paid for it. When there isn't enough public money for this, it harms the nobles. The shortfall is made up by taxes, confiscations, and fines imposed by corrupt courts, and these practices have destroyed many democracies.

So, when the state has little revenue, there should be fewer public meetings and fewer courts. However, those that exist should cover a wide range of issues but only operate for a few days. This way, the rich won't fear the cost, even if they don't get paid for attending, and the poor still receive pay. Judgments will also be fairer because the wealthy won't want to be away from their own affairs for long, but they won't mind for a short time. When there's plenty of public money, the approach should differ from what demagogues do now. Today, they distribute extra public funds to the poor. The poor take it, but soon they need more again, making it like pouring water into a leaky bucket. A true patriot in a democracy should ensure that most of the population isn't too poor, as poverty causes greed in that system. He should strive to help them enjoy lasting abundance. Since this benefits the rich too, any money saved should be set aside and then distributed to the poor in a way that helps them buy a small piece of land. If that isn't possible, at least give them enough to get the tools they need for farming or trade. If there isn't enough for everyone to receive a lot at once, it should be divided among groups or tribes.

In the meantime, the rich should pay the poor for necessary work but not be required to fund their leisure activities. This system was somewhat similar to how things were managed in Carthage, where they kept the people's loyalty by sending some of their community into colonies, which brought prosperity. It's also wise and generous for the nobility to divide the poor among themselves and give them what they need, encouraging them to work. Or, they could follow the example of the people of Tarentum, who allowed the poor to share in what they needed. This approach won over the common people. In their system, magistrates were selected in two ways: some by vote and others by lottery. The lottery allowed the people to have a role in the administration, while voting ensured good governance. The same balance can be achieved if some magistrates are chosen by vote and others by lot. This explains how democracies should be structured.

The principles discussed earlier also show how an oligarchy should be set up. To design such a state, one must consider how to oppose democracy since every type of oligarchy is based on principles that are the opposite of some form of democracy. The best type of oligarchy is the one that most closely resembles what we call a free state. In this system, there should be two different property qualifications: one high and one low. The lower class can be chosen for ordinary government offices, while the upper class provides the top officials. No one within the property qualification should be excluded from participation, and the qualifications should be set up so that the common people who meet them have more power than those who don't. People who manage public affairs should always come from the best citizens. A similar structure should be used in the second-best oligarchy. But in the worst type of oligarchy, which is closest to a dynasty or tyranny, it's much harder to maintain. As in a weak body or a leaky ship, where even small problems can cause disaster, poorly designed governments need the most care. In contrast, a well-constructed government can withstand many challenges, just as a healthy body or a well-built ship can endure more damage.

In a democracy, the number of citizens helps preserve it, as they balance the privileges based on wealth or rank. But in an oligarchy, preservation comes from regulating the various classes within society.

Most communities are made up of four types of people: farmers, craftsmen, merchants, and laborers. Those who serve in war are also divided into four groups: horsemen, heavily-armed soldiers, lightly-armed soldiers, and sailors. When a region can support many horsemen, a strong oligarchy can easily be formed, as the safety of the people depends on that force. Only those with considerable wealth can afford to maintain horses. In places where heavily-armed troops are more common, a less powerful oligarchy can be established since these soldiers tend to be wealthier but not necessarily rich. On the other hand, lightly-armed soldiers and sailors support democracy. When these groups are numerous and a conflict breaks out, the other parts of society are at a disadvantage. A solution to this problem can be learned from experienced military leaders, who always mix light troops with horsemen and heavily-armed soldiers. It's with these forces that the common people gain an advantage over the wealthy in an uprising. Lighter troops are more agile and can hold their own against horsemen and heavily-armed soldiers. If an oligarchy recruits soldiers from these groups, it's preparing for its own downfall.

Since cities consist of people of different ages, both young and old, fathers should teach their sons easy, light exercises while they are young. When the sons grow up, they should become skilled in all military exercises. Allowing the people to participate in the government should either be based on a property qualification, as mentioned earlier, or, like in Thebes, by allowing those who have stopped working in a trade for a certain period to take part, or as in Massalia, by selecting them based on merit, whether they are citizens or foreigners.

The duties of the highest-ranking officials in a state should be clearly defined to prevent the common people from wanting their jobs. When the people know what the officials have to do, they will respect them. These officials should also perform public sacrifices and build monuments to serve the state. When the people see the city adorned with these public gifts and structures, they will appreciate the stability of the government. Additionally, the generosity of the nobles will be remembered. Unfortunately, this is not the approach taken by those in power in modern oligarchies. Instead, they seek profit more than honor, which is why these oligarchies could more accurately be called small democracies.

We've now explained how democracies and oligarchies should be structured.

Next, we'll discuss the magistrates—what kind they should be, how many are needed, and their purposes. No state can exist without necessary magistrates, and it can't be happy without those who contribute to its dignity and order. Small states need only a few magistrates, while large states need more. It's also important to understand which offices can be combined and which should remain separate. First, proper officials must be appointed to oversee the markets. A magistrate should be responsible for ensuring good order in the markets since cities rely on both buyers and sellers to meet their needs. This is one of the main contributors to a comfortable life, which is why people form communities.

A second duty, closely related to the first, is to oversee both public and private buildings to ensure they are well-maintained and safe. These officials should ensure buildings don't collapse and that roads are in good condition. They should also protect property boundaries to prevent disputes. In larger cities, these responsibilities may be divided among different officials, with one overseeing buildings, another responsible for fountains, and a third in charge of harbors. These officials are called city inspectors.

A third task, similar to the previous one but dealing with rural areas, is to ensure proper care of the countryside. Officials responsible for this are called land or forest inspectors. Despite their different titles, their duties are the same as those of city inspectors.

There must also be officials in charge of managing public revenue and distributing it to various departments within the state. These officials are called treasurers or receivers. Another official is needed to record private contracts, court judgments, and legal declarations. This task is sometimes divided among many officials, but one person usually oversees them all. These officials are called clerks or secretaries.

Another vital, though unpleasant, office is that of the official responsible for enforcing judgments, collecting fines, and overseeing prisoners. This role is difficult and often unpopular, so people are usually unwilling to take it on unless it's made profitable. Even then, they may not carry out their duties properly. However, it's essential because passing judgment is pointless unless it's enforced. Without enforcement, human society couldn't function. For this reason, it's best if this office isn't handled by a single person but by several magistrates from different courts. Similarly, the collection of fines ordered by judges should be divided among different officials.

As different magistrates handle different cases, younger officials should handle cases involving young people. For cases that have already gone to trial, one person should pass judgment, and another should enforce it. For example, officials overseeing public buildings could enforce the judgments made by market inspectors. By dividing these duties, the officials responsible for enforcing laws will face less public anger, making it easier to carry out their duties. If the same person both passes and enforces judgments, they'll become widely hated, and if they handle all cases, they'll be seen as enemies of the people.

In some cases, one official holds the prisoner, while another carries out the sentence, as was done by the Eleven in Athens. It's wise to separate these roles and give them as much attention as anything else we've discussed. People of good character may avoid this job, while untrustworthy people can't be trusted with it, as they may need to be guarded themselves. Therefore, this office should never be separate from others, nor should it be continuously assigned to the same individuals. Instead, it should be taken on by young men as part of their civic duties.

These are the most necessary magistrates. Next, we have other essential officials of higher rank who must be skilled and trustworthy. These officials are responsible for the city's defense and must ensure the walls and gates are secure. They must also organize and train citizens for both war and peace. Some cities have many officials overseeing this, while smaller cities may only have one, called a general or polemarch. In larger cities, where there are horsemen, lightly-armed troops, archers, and sailors, separate commanders are often appointed for each group, with others serving under them. All of these officials work together to form one military body.

Because many magistrates deal with public money, there must be officials whose sole job is to audit them and correct any mismanagement. Additionally, there is often one official who is in charge of all the others. This person may control public revenue and taxes, preside over the people when they hold the supreme power, and summon the assembly. Sometimes this role is held by a group of officials called preadvisers, but when there are many, they're more accurately called a council.

These are the main civil magistrates required in a government, but there are also officials responsible for religious matters, such as priests and those who oversee the temples, ensuring they're maintained or rebuilt if they fall into disrepair. In some cities, this responsibility is given to one person, while in others, it's divided among many officials distinct from the priests. These officials are in charge of public worship and the sacred revenue. There are also officials responsible for overseeing public sacrifices to the state's protective gods, a task not always assigned to priests. Different states use different names for these officials.

To sum up, the various magistrates handle matters related to religion, war, taxes, expenditures, markets, public buildings, harbors, highways, and courts. There are also clerks who record private contracts and guards to watch over prisoners. Other officials ensure that the laws are enforced and advise the courts.

In especially fortunate states that have the leisure to focus on finer details and are dedicated to good order, there are even more specialized magistrates. For example, some officials oversee women, ensuring they follow the laws, while others are responsible for boys and their education. Other officials manage gymnastic exercises, theaters, and public spectacles. However, not all of these offices are necessary in every state. For example, poorer states can't afford officials to manage women since the wives and children of the poor must work, as they can't afford slaves.

Some states have three main officials with supreme power: guardians of the laws, preadvisers, and senators. Guardians of the laws are best suited for aristocracies, preadvisers for oligarchies, and senators for democracies. This concludes our discussion of magistrates.

Book 7

Whoever wants to figure out what the best government is should first understand what kind of life is the best to live. If this remains unclear, it will also be unclear which government is best. It's likely that, as long as no unexpected events happen, those who live under the best government will live the happiest lives, given their circumstances. So, we need to first figure out what kind of life is most desirable for everyone. After that, we should ask whether this best life is the same for both the individual and the citizen or if it's different. I believe I've already explained well enough what sort of life is best in my popular talks on this subject, so I think it's appropriate to repeat it here. No one has ever questioned one important point: that what is good for a person can be divided into three types—external goods, those that benefit the body, and those that benefit the soul. It's clear that all of these things must come together to make someone truly happy. No one would say that a person is happy if they lack courage, self-control, justice, or wisdom. It wouldn't make sense to say someone is happy if they're afraid of flies, would steal the smallest thing if hungry or thirsty, or would even kill a dear friend for a small amount of money. It also wouldn't make sense to say that a person is happy if they're as confused as a baby or fool. These points are so obvious that everyone agrees with them, even though people may argue over how much and what kind of virtue is necessary for happiness. Some believe that only a little virtue is enough, but when it comes to things like wealth, property, power, and honor, they try to increase them without limit. To them, we reply that it's easy to prove, based on what we learn from experience, that external goods do not create virtue, but rather, virtue helps to bring about external goods.

Now, as for whether a happy life is found in pleasure, virtue, or a combination of both, it's clear that those who are most moral and have well-trained minds enjoy more happiness, even if they aren't extremely wealthy. In fact, they are happier than those who are rich but lack morality and wisdom. Anyone who thinks carefully can see this for themselves because everything external has a limit, just like a machine. Any external good in excess can either be harmful or, at best, useless to the person who has it. But every good quality of the soul becomes even more valuable the more it is developed, if we may use the word "useful" in the same sense as "noble" when describing these qualities. It's also clear that different things bring about different kinds of outcomes, depending on how valuable they are. So, if the soul is nobler than any external possession, like the body, both in itself and in relation to us, then it follows that the best qualities of the soul are also the most valuable. Besides, it's for the sake of the soul that these other things are desirable, not the other way around. Wise people should desire external things for the sake of the soul, not desire the soul for the sake of external things. Therefore, we can be sure that the more virtue and wisdom a person has, the more happiness they will experience by living according to these virtues. We have an example of this in God, who is perfectly happy, not because of anything external but because of His own nature. Good luck, or fortune, is different from happiness because anything that isn't based on the mind comes from chance or luck. But wisdom and justice don't come from luck. This means that the city with the best government is the happiest one because it acts in the best way. No one can act well without being virtuous, and no city can do anything praiseworthy without virtue and wisdom. Whatever is just, wise, or prudent for an individual is the same for a city.

This is just an introduction, as I felt it was necessary to touch on this topic briefly, though I can't fully examine it here because it relates more to another question. For now, let's assume this: that the happiest life for a person, both as an individual and as a citizen, is a life of virtue, accompanied by the benefits that usually come with virtue. If there are those who aren't convinced by what I've said, their doubts will be addressed later. For now, let's move forward with our plan.

Now, we need to ask whether the happiness of a person and that of a city are the same or different. But this is clear enough. Anyone who believes that wealth makes a person happy must also believe that a wealthy city is the happiest. Those who think that having power over others brings happiness will think that the happiest city is the one that rules over many others. In the same way, if someone praises a person for their virtue, they will think the most virtuous city is the happiest. There are two things we need to consider here. The first is whether it's better to be a member of a community and have the rights of a citizen or to live as an outsider who doesn't get involved in public affairs. The second is what form of government is best and how the state should be organized. Should everyone have a role in governing, or just the majority, or only a few? This is a political question, and it's not directly related to the individual. The second point is the focus of my current discussion. It's clear that the best government is the one that allows everyone to act virtuously and live happily. However, some people who agree that a life of virtue is best still wonder whether an active public life or a private life of contemplation is better. Some believe that a life of contemplation is the only life suitable for a philosopher. Throughout history, the most virtuous men have chosen one of these two ways of life—either the public or the philosophical. This question is important because a wise person will naturally lean toward the better choice, both as an individual and as a citizen. Some argue that ruling over others is the greatest injustice, while others believe that political rule is not unjust but is a burden on the pleasures and peace of life. Others have the opposite view and think that a public and active life is the only life worth living. They believe that private citizens have no chance to practice virtue compared to those engaged in public affairs.

These are their beliefs. Some even argue that tyrannical and despotic governments are the only ones that bring happiness. Even among some free states, the goal of their laws seems to be to dominate their neighbors. In fact, many political systems, wherever they may be, seem to have one common goal: to conquer and rule. We see this in the laws of the Spartans and Cretans and in the way they trained their children. Their goal was to make them soldiers. Across many nations, those who have enough power to enslave others are honored because of it. This was true for the Scythians, Persians, Thracians, and Gauls. Some nations even have laws to encourage bravery. For instance, in Carthage, people could wear rings to show how many military campaigns they had participated in. In Macedonia, a man who hadn't killed an enemy had to wear a rope around his neck. Among the Scythians, during festivals, only those who had killed an enemy could drink from a special cup that was passed around. Among the Iberians, a warlike people, they put up as many pillars on a man's tomb as the number of enemies he had killed. Different nations have different customs like these, some of which are established by law and others by tradition.

It may seem absurd to some people to ask whether it's the job of a legislator to teach a state how to rule over or enslave its neighbors, whether the neighbors want this or not. How could this be the task of a politician or a legislator when it's unlawful? Something can't be lawful if it can be done both justly and unjustly because some conquests are made unjustly. In the arts, we see nothing like this. For example, a doctor or a captain of a ship doesn't use force or persuasion to get people to follow their orders. Still, many people think a despotic government is a political one. They would never allow such a government to rule over them but wouldn't hesitate to rule over others this way. They want to be governed wisely themselves but don't care if others are. However, despotic power is only justified when nature has made one group of people to rule and another to be ruled. No one should try to rule over everyone, but only over those who are meant to be ruled. Just as no one hunts people for food or sacrifice, but only wild animals that are suitable for those purposes.

Now, a city that is well-governed can be happy by itself, even if it has no contact with other states, as long as it has a good system of laws. Even if its government isn't focused on war or conquest, it wouldn't need these things. It's clear that war is only praiseworthy as a means to an end, not as an end in itself. A good legislator must carefully study their state and the nature of the people to see how they can enjoy all the aspects of a good life and the happiness that comes with it. In this respect, some laws and customs are better than others. A legislator must also think about how to deal with neighboring states, whether to resist them or offer them help.

Now, we will address those who, while agreeing that a life of virtue is best, disagree on how to live it. We speak to both sides. Some believe that all political governments are bad and that the best life is one of complete freedom, outside of citizenship. Others think the life of a citizen is the best, and that happiness comes from virtuous activity. Both groups are partly right and partly wrong. They are right in saying that the life of a free person is better than that of a slave because a slave has no honorable work. The tasks they are ordered to do have no virtue in them. However, it's wrong to say that living under any government is the same as slavery. The government of free people is as different from the government of slaves as slavery is from freedom itself, which I've already discussed.

It's also wrong to think that doing nothing is better than being active in virtuous deeds. Happiness comes from action, and many noble things come from the actions of the just and wise. Based on what we've discussed, someone might believe that the greatest good is having supreme power because that allows a person to demand many useful services from others. Therefore, such a person might think they should not give up that power but instead should seize it. They might even believe that, for this reason, a father should have no concern for his son, or a son for his father, or a friend for a friend because the best thing is the most desirable. But the best life is to be a part of the community and share in its happiness.

What these people argue might seem true if the supreme good really did belong to those who use violence to get it. But this is highly unlikely. Just because someone gains power over others doesn't mean their actions are honorable, unless they are naturally as superior to others as a man is to a woman, a father is to a child, or a master is to a slave. Once someone abandons the path of virtue, they cannot easily return to it. Among equals, what is fair and just should be mutual. This is what equality is. It's not right for equals to not receive equal treatment, nor for similar people to not be treated in a similar way. Whatever is contrary to nature is not right. Therefore, if one person in a community is superior in virtue and ability to others, then it is right for everyone to follow and obey that person. But even that person cannot lead alone; they need others to help.

If we are correct in what we've said so far, then happiness comes from virtuous activity. Both for the community and the individual, the most active life is the happiest. However, being active doesn't necessarily mean interacting with others, as some people think. Not all practical activities are about teaching others what to do. The most practical activities are often the ones that improve a person's own judgment and understanding. Virtuous activity has a goal, so it is practical. In fact, those who create the plans that others follow are said to act more than those who carry out the plans. They are superior to the workers who execute their designs. Even cities that choose not to engage with other states don't have to remain inactive. The members of those cities can interact with each other. The same is true for individuals. Otherwise, neither God nor the universe could be perfect because neither of them relies on anything external. Therefore, it is clear that the same life that brings happiness to an individual also brings happiness to the state and its members.

Now that I've finished introducing the topic and talked about different kinds of states, I'll start by saying what a city should be like if we could design it exactly how we wanted. No good state can exist without having just the right amount of what's needed. Many things are worth aiming for, but none of them should be impossible. I'm talking about the number of citizens and the size of the land. Just like a weaver or a shipbuilder needs the right materials for their work, because the better the materials, the better the final product, the same is true for the lawmaker and politician. They must aim to get the right people for the job. The first and most important tool for a politician is the number of people. They need to know how many people there should be and what kind of people they should be. They also need to know how big the land is and what kind of land it is.

Most people think a city needs to be big to be happy. But if this is true, they don't know what makes a city large or small. They often judge by the number of people living there, but they should be looking at its strength instead. A state has a goal, and its size should be measured by how well it can reach that goal, not by the number of its inhabitants. It's like saying that a great doctor like Hippocrates is better, even if he isn't a larger person, than someone bigger but less skilled. If we're going to measure a city's strength by its population, we shouldn't just count everyone living there. Cities often have many slaves, visitors, and foreigners. The real strength of a city comes from the people who are truly part of it—those who are citizens. A large number of these citizens proves that a city is large. However, a city filled with many craftsmen and few soldiers cannot be truly great, because the greatness of a city isn't about numbers but about the kind of people living in it.

This is also clear from experience. It's hard, if not impossible, to properly govern a very large number of people. In fact, in all the well-governed states, we don't find any where the rights of citizenship are given to just anyone. This makes sense because, just like the law brings order, good laws bring good order. A huge number of people can't be governed easily, unless by some divine power that rules the universe. It's true that having a certain size is important for beauty, and a city's perfection includes being large as long as it can still maintain that order. But everything, whether animals, plants, or machines, has a proper size. When they are either too small or too large, they don't work as they should. A ship that's too short isn't really a ship, and neither is one that's too long. In both cases, it's useless. The same goes for a city. One that's too small can't defend itself, which is essential for a city. One that's too large can defend itself, but then it's a nation, not a city. It would be hard to govern such a large group. Who would want to lead such a massive crowd or speak to them without having a voice as loud as a herald like Stentor?

The first thing a city needs is a population large enough for the people to live happily in their political community. If the population grows beyond what's needed, the city can still grow, but this growth must have a limit. What that limit is will be clear from experience, and this experience comes from both the rulers and the citizens. Since it's the job of the rulers to guide the lower officials and to judge fairly, they can't make good decisions or give proper orders unless they know the character of their fellow citizens. If they don't know them well, they won't be able to manage the city well, and things will fall apart. Rulers need to avoid making hasty decisions without proper knowledge, and this will certainly happen if there are too many citizens to know personally. In addition, it will be easier for outsiders to pretend to be citizens and go unnoticed in such a large crowd.

So, it's clear that the best size for a city is one where the population is large enough to be self-sufficient but not too large to be properly governed by the leaders. This is how we should decide the size of a city.

What I've said about a city also applies to the land. The land should be enough to make the people happy, meaning it should provide them with everything they need for life. If they have all they need in abundance, they will be content. As for how large the land should be, it should be enough for the people to live comfortably with freedom and self-control. Whether I've set the right limit for the land is something we will discuss later when we talk about property and how much wealth a person needs to live well. We'll also consider how they should use that wealth. There are many disagreements on this topic, as some believe life should be strict while others believe it should be more indulgent.

Deciding the location of the land isn't hard. We should take advice from military experts for some of the details. The land should be difficult for enemies to reach but easy for the people to access. Just as I said the population should be small enough to be manageable by the rulers, the land should also be manageable so it can be easily defended.

If we could place a city wherever we wanted, it would be useful to place it near the sea. The land should be positioned in a way that it can easily support itself and receive supplies from other areas, like food, wood, and other materials the country might need.

There are some who question whether placing a city near the sea is good or bad for a well-run state. They argue that bringing in people from different backgrounds could harm the state by interfering with the laws and overwhelming the population. A large number of merchants would come and go, and this could make governing harder. But if this problem doesn't arise, then it's clear that being near the sea is better, both for safety and for making it easier to get the necessities of life. It's important for a city to be able to defend itself from enemies, both by land and sea. If possible, it should be able to defend itself in both ways, but if not, it should at least be strong where it has the most power. Being near the sea is also helpful for trading with other places when the land doesn't provide enough or has an excess of certain goods. However, a city should trade only to meet its own needs, not to supply the needs of others. Cities that open markets to everyone do so for profit, but this isn't the right approach for a well-ordered state. They shouldn't encourage this kind of trade.

In many places, cities have docks and harbors that are convenient for trade but are separated from the main city by walls or other fortifications. In such cases, if the trade brings benefits, the city will get them, but if it causes harm, the city can control it with laws about who is allowed to trade and who isn't.

When it comes to naval power, there's no doubt that a city needs a navy to some degree. This is necessary for the city itself and also for dealing with neighboring states, either to be seen as strong or to help others by land and sea. The size of the navy should depend on the city's strength. If the city is strong and can take the lead among other states, its navy should match its ambitions.

The large population that often comes with naval power isn't essential for a state, and they shouldn't be considered citizens. The sailors and soldiers in command should be free men, and the success of a naval battle depends on them. But in places with many workers and farmers, they will always have enough sailors, as we see in some states today, like Heraclea, where they man many ships, even though the city is smaller than others. This is what we should decide about the land, ports, city, sea, and naval power. As for the number of citizens, we've already discussed what it should be.

Next, we need to consider the natural qualities of the citizens. This can be seen by looking at the most well-known Greek states and other nations in the world. People in cold northern regions, like Europe, are brave but lack intelligence and the arts. Because of this, they fiercely protect their freedom, but they aren't skilled enough to conquer their neighbors. On the other hand, the people of Asia are clever and skilled in the arts, but they lack bravery, which is why they are often conquered and enslaved. The Greeks, being in the middle of these two groups, have both bravery and intelligence. This is why Greece remains free and is governed in the best way possible. If they could agree on a single system of government, they could rule the world.

This is the main difference between the Greeks and other nations. The Greeks combine both qualities, while others only have one. So, it's clear that people need to have both intelligence and bravery to follow a lawmaker whose goal is virtue. Some people say that soldiers should be gentle with people they know and harsh with strangers, but bravery is what makes a person admirable. It's the quality of the soul that we respect the most. We get angrier at friends who wrong us than at strangers, and that's why Archilaus said to himself, "Shall my friends insult me?"

The spirit of freedom and leadership comes from this type of character because courage is commanding and unbeatable. It's wrong to say we should be harsh to strangers because that's not appropriate for anyone. Those with noble character are not usually harsh, except with wicked people. When they are harsh, it's often towards friends who have wronged them. This makes sense because, when you expect a favor from someone and don't get it, you not only feel wronged but also feel the loss of what you were expecting. That's why people say, "Brothers' wars are the worst," and "Those who once loved deeply now hate deeply."

We have now mostly decided how many citizens a city should have, what their character should be, and how large and what kind of land they need. I say "mostly" because there's no need to be as exact in these matters as we would be with things that are studied by reason alone.

Just like in living bodies, where nothing is considered a part unless the whole wouldn't exist without it, it's clear that in a political state, not everything necessary to it is a part of it. Similarly, not every other group that helps make a whole can be seen as part of it. Something should be common to the community, whether shared equally or unequally, like food, land, or similar things. But when something benefits one person and not another, there's no real sense of community, except for the fact that one makes it and the other uses it. This is like the relationship between a tool and the worker who uses it. There's nothing shared between a house and the builder except the skill the builder uses to work on the house.

So, while property is necessary for states, it isn't a part of the state itself, though many types of property are alive. A city is a community of equals that aims to live the best life possible. The best and happiest life is one that involves practicing virtues perfectly. Since some people have more or fewer opportunities to engage in these virtues, this creates differences between various cities and communities. Each of them tries to achieve the best life through different means, leading to different lifestyles and forms of government.

We need to consider what things are absolutely necessary for a city to exist. We can figure this out by knowing how many things a city needs. First, the people need food. Second, they need tools because many things are required for life. Third, they need weapons to defend themselves both against their own members who might rebel and against outside enemies who might attack. Fourth, they need a source of income for the state's internal needs and for war. Fifth, and most importantly, they need religious institutions. Sixth, they need a court system to judge criminal and civil cases.

These are the things that are essential for every state. A city isn't just a random group of people coming together; they come together to secure their independence and protect themselves. Without these necessities, the city can't achieve those goals. It's essential that a city can acquire all these things. For this, it needs enough farmers to provide food, workers to make tools, soldiers to defend the state, wealthy citizens, priests, and judges to decide what's right and wrong.

Now that we've figured this out, we need to decide whether all of these different jobs should be open to everyone or if we should assign them to different groups of people. Should some jobs be reserved for certain groups, while others are shared among everyone? Not every state handles this the same way. In some states, everything is shared, while in others, only some things are. This is the main difference between types of governments. In democracies, the entire community shares everything, but in oligarchies, it's different.

Since we are discussing the best form of government, which is the one that makes the citizens happy, and since happiness can't exist without virtue, it follows that in the best-governed states, the citizens must be truly virtuous people. In these states, no one should be allowed to work in trades or commerce, as these jobs are seen as dishonorable and harmful to virtue. Citizens also shouldn't be farmers, so they can focus on improving themselves and serving the state.

As for the roles of soldiers, senators, and judges, which are clearly necessary, should these jobs be assigned to different people, or should one person do multiple jobs? This question is easy to answer. In some cases, the same person can do different jobs, but in other cases, the jobs should go to different people if they require different skills. For example, courage is needed for one role, while judgment is needed for another. In these cases, the jobs should go to different people. But when it's clear that the people who have weapons can't be forced to always follow orders, the same person should be trusted with both roles. This is because those with weapons can decide whether they want to take power or not.

The government should be entrusted to those who have both courage and judgment, but not in the same way. Young people are better suited for roles that require courage, while older people are better suited for roles that require judgment. This way, each person is given the job they are best suited for, based on their strengths. It's also necessary for these people to own land because citizens need to be wealthy. These people are the right ones to be citizens. No tradesperson should be given the rights of citizenship, nor should anyone whose job isn't considered noble, honorable, and virtuous. This follows the principle we started with: to be happy, a person must be virtuous.

We shouldn't judge a city's happiness by looking at just one group of citizens; we must examine all of them. So, it's clear that land should belong to these citizens, though they may need farmers, either slaves, foreigners, or servants, to work the land.

Of the different groups of people we've mentioned, the priests form a separate class. They aren't counted among the farmers or tradespeople because respect for the gods is an important part of every state. Since the citizens have been divided into soldiers and council members, and since proper worship must be given to the gods, it's necessary that those who serve as priests have no other responsibilities. Let this job be given to older citizens.

We've now explained what's necessary for a city to exist, what parts it's made up of, and that farmers, tradespeople, and servants are necessary for a city. But the essential parts of the city are the soldiers and sailors, and while they are different from the others, they are only occasionally different from each other.

It seems that, even in the past, philosophers who studied politics didn't realize that a city should be divided into different groups of people based on their roles. The farmers and soldiers should be kept separate from each other. This custom is still followed today in places like Egypt and Crete. In Egypt, Sesostris established this, and in Crete, Minos did the same. The practice of common meals also seems to be ancient. It was established in Crete during Minos' reign and even earlier in Italy. According to the best sources, a king named Italus in Italy, who ruled the AEnotrians, made them switch from being shepherds to being farmers and gave them new laws. He was also the first to introduce common meals, which is why some of his descendants still follow this practice.

The custom of dividing the citizens into groups likely came from Egypt, as the reign of Sesostris was long before that of Minos. Just like many other things were discovered over a long period because people needed to figure out how to survive, we should conclude that political organization also took a long time to develop. Since Egypt seems to be the oldest civilization and had laws and order before others, we should learn from their example and try to improve upon what they left out.

We've already said that land should belong to the soldiers and those who participate in the government, which is why farmers should be a separate group. We will now discuss how the land should be divided and how many farmers there should be. We don't believe that property should be entirely shared, as some have suggested. However, in the spirit of friendship, no citizen should go without the basics for survival.

It's generally agreed that common meals are appropriate in well-organized cities. I'll explain my reasons for supporting them later. All citizens should take part in them. However, it will be difficult for poorer citizens to contribute to the meals while also providing for their families. The cost of religious worship should also be covered by the entire state.

Because of these needs, the land should be divided into two parts. One part should belong to the community as a whole, and the other part should be owned by individuals. Each of these parts should be further divided. Half of the public land should be used to support religious worship, and the other half should support the common meals. Half of the private land should be on the outskirts of the country, and the other half should be near the city. This way, everyone will have land in both places, which would be fair and help the citizens work together more harmoniously, especially during times of war.

When the land isn't divided like this, some people won't care about border attacks, while others will overreact. This is why some places have laws that prevent people living on the borders from voting on matters of war, as their personal interests might make them biased.

If we had a choice, the farmers should be slaves, not from the same country and not too spirited. This would make them hardworking and less likely to cause trouble. The next best choice would be barbarian servants who have a similar temperament. Some of these slaves should work on private land, while others should work on public land. Later, we will discuss how these slaves should be treated and why it's a good idea to promise them freedom as a reward for their service.

We've already said that both the city and the land should be connected to both the sea and the mainland as much as possible. There are four main things to consider when choosing the city's location. First, the health of the citizens is the most important thing. A city that faces east and catches the eastern winds is considered the healthiest. After that, a northern location is best for winter. Next, the city's position should be good for both governing and defending in war. The city should be easy for its citizens to access but difficult for enemies to reach or capture.

The city should also have plenty of water, with rivers nearby. If there aren't any rivers, large cisterns should be built to collect rainwater, so there's enough water during a siege. Since health is so important, the first thing to consider is the city's location and position. The second thing is having good drinking water, and this shouldn't be neglected. Water is something we use all the time, and it has a big impact on our health. Both air and water affect health, which is why wise governments set aside different waters for different uses. If there isn't enough high-quality water, drinking water should be kept separate from other water used for other purposes.

As for fortifications, what works for some governments won't work for others. A high citadel is good for a monarchy or an oligarchy, while a city on a plain works better for a democracy. For an aristocracy, neither of these is ideal. Instead, it's better to have multiple strong places.

Regarding private homes, the best and most useful ones are those that are separate from each other and follow a modern design like the one Hippodamus suggested. However, for safety during war, the older style of buildings, which are hard for strangers to navigate and difficult for enemies to besiege, might be better. A city should have both types of buildings, and this can be arranged by laying them out like rows of vines. The buildings shouldn't be detached from each other throughout the city, just in some parts, so that both elegance and safety are ensured.

When it comes to walls, those who say that a brave people don't need them are holding onto outdated ideas. In fact, we often see those who take pride in this idea proven wrong. It is shameful for a people who are equal to or almost equal to their enemy to hide behind walls, but sometimes the attackers are too strong for the defenders to resist. If you don't want to suffer the horrors of war or the enemy's arrogance, it's better to take refuge behind walls. This is especially true now, with so many new weapons and machines designed to attack cities.

Choosing not to have walls is like choosing a land that's easy for enemies to invade or flattening the hills of your land. It's like someone deciding not to build a wall around their house because they don't want to be seen as a coward. But you should also consider that if your city has walls, you can choose to act as though it does or doesn't. Without walls, you don't have this option. So, it's not only necessary to have walls, but they should also serve as a defense during war and be an ornament to the city. Modern improvements should be included along with traditional methods. Just as attackers try to gain every possible advantage over their enemies, defenders should use all available means, both old and new, to protect themselves. Those who are well-prepared are rarely attacked first.

Since citizens are expected to eat together at public tables, and the city walls should have defensive towers at the right places and distances, it's clear that some of these public tables should be located in the towers. These buildings should be made to decorate the walls as well. For the temples used for public worship and the halls for the magistrates' public tables, they should be built in the right locations and close to each other. The only exception should be those temples which, by law or through oracles, must be kept separate from other buildings. These should be placed on a noticeable high point so they have a good view and are near the best-fortified part of the city.

Next to this area, there should be a large square, similar to what they call "The Square of Freedom" in Thessaly, where nothing is bought or sold. No tradespeople, farmers, or others like them should be allowed in this area unless they are called by the authorities. It would also make this area more beautiful if the older citizens performed their gymnastic exercises there. For these exercises, citizens should be divided into groups according to their age. Younger people should have officers in charge of them, while older citizens should stay near the magistrates. This setup would inspire true modesty and a sense of respectful fear in the younger ones.

There should also be another square, separate from the first one, for buying and selling. It should be placed so that goods can easily come in by both sea and land. Since the citizens include magistrates and priests, the public tables for the priests should be located near the temples. The tables for magistrates who deal with contracts, lawsuits, and similar matters, as well as those in charge of markets and public streets, should be near the square or along some main road. I mean the square where business is conducted, as the other one is meant for leisure and this one for necessary business.

The same arrangement should be followed in the countryside. The officials there, like forest wardens and land overseers, must also have their public tables and towers for protection against enemies. Temples for both gods and heroes should also be built in the proper locations, but it's not necessary to go into more detail on these points. Planning these things is not hard; it's carrying them out that's more difficult. Theory is shaped by our wishes, but the practical part depends on fortune. For this reason, we will stop discussing these subjects here.

We will now consider what number and type of people a government needs to have in order to make the state happy and well-run. There are two things that determine how excellent and perfect something is. First, the goal or purpose must be appropriate. Second, the means used to achieve that goal must fit the purpose. These two things may or may not align. For example, the goal we choose might be good, but we could make mistakes in how we try to achieve it. Other times, we might have the right methods, but the goal itself might be bad. And sometimes, we could be wrong about both the goal and the means, like a doctor who doesn't know what a healthy body should look like or how to make it healthy.

In every art and science, we need to understand both the right goal and the correct way to achieve it. It's clear that everyone wants to live well and be happy, but not everyone has the ability to make that happen. Some people lack the means either because of nature or fortune. Many factors are needed for a happy life, but fewer are needed for those with good character than for those with bad character. Some people have everything they need for happiness but fail to use it properly.

Since we are asking what the best form of government is—the one that makes a state well-run and its people the happiest—it's important to understand what happiness is. I've already said in my work on morals (if I can refer to it here) that happiness comes from the active and perfect practice of virtue. And this virtue isn't just relative to circumstances but is simply good in itself. By relative, I mean something that's necessary in certain situations. By simply good, I mean something that is good and beautiful in itself. For example, just punishments and necessary restrictions arise from virtue and are therefore virtuous, though it's better if neither the state nor any individual needs them. Actions aimed at gaining honor or wealth are simply good. The others are only useful for removing a problem, but these actions form the foundation of what's simply good.

A good person can endure poverty, sickness, and other misfortunes with a noble spirit, but happiness consists of avoiding these things. As I've already said in my work on morals, a good person considers what is good because it's virtuous as simply good. Therefore, all of this person's actions must be worthy and simply good. This has led some people to think that external goods cause happiness. But this would be like saying that playing the lyre well is because of the instrument, not the skill.

From what has been said, it's clear that some things should be readily available, and others must be provided by the lawmaker. This is why, when founding a city, we hope that many things under the control of fortune will be plentiful (because we admit that fortune controls some things). However, making a state worthy and great is not only the work of fortune but also of knowledge and good judgment. To have a worthy state, the citizens who run it must also be worthy. But since, in our city, every citizen is expected to be worthy, we need to figure out how to make that happen. It would be ideal if everyone could be worthy, not just some individuals. If one person can do something, it's better if everyone can do it.

People can be worthy and good in three ways: by nature, by habit, and by reason. First, a person must be born human, not some other animal. That means they must have both body and soul. But just being born with certain qualities isn't enough. Habit has a great impact because some things in our nature can be shaped for better or worse by habit. Other animals mostly live according to their nature, with very little influence from habit. But humans live according to reason, which only they have. Therefore, a person should make nature, habit, and reason work together. If people followed reason and believed it was best to do so, they would often act against nature and habit.

I've already said what kind of people should naturally make good members of a community. The rest of this discussion will focus on education because some things are developed through habit and others through learning.

Every political community consists of rulers and the ruled. We need to consider whether the same people should be rulers and ruled for their entire lives or whether different people should fill these roles at different times. The system of education should be based on this distinction. If people were as different from each other as we imagine gods and heroes are from ordinary men, being superior in both body and soul, then it would be clear that the superior should always rule, and the others should always be ruled. But since this isn't possible, and rulers aren't so superior to their subjects as Scylax describes kings in India, it's clear that for many reasons, it's necessary for everyone to both govern and be governed at different times.

It's only fair that equals should have equal shares in everything. A state founded on injustice is hard to sustain. Those who want change will join forces with those who feel they are being ruled unfairly, and they will become such a large group that the rulers won't be able to control them. But it's also clear that rulers should be superior to those they govern. The lawmaker must figure out how to make this happen while ensuring that everyone gets an equal share of governing.

Nature has already given us a guide for this: she makes some people young and others old. The young should obey, and the old should rule. No young person is upset about being governed, especially when they know they will receive the same honors once they reach the right age. In some ways, rulers and the ruled are the same; in others, they are different. This means their education should be partly the same and partly different. As people say, the best rulers are those who have first learned to obey.

Some governments are set up for the benefit of the ruler, like the relationship between a master and a servant. Others are for the benefit of those who are ruled, like the relationship between free citizens.

Some commands differ from others not because of the work but because of the goal. This is why some tasks, even those that seem like servile work, are not shameful for young free people to do. Many things that are commanded aren't honorable or dishonorable by nature, but the reason for doing them makes the difference.

Since we've established that the virtue of a good citizen and a good ruler is the same as that of a good person, and that everyone should first learn to obey before they command, it's up to the lawmaker to figure out how to make citizens good people, what kind of education is needed, and what the ultimate goal of a good life is.

A person's soul can be divided into two parts: the part that has reason and the part that doesn't but can follow reason's guidance. A person is considered good based on the virtues of these two parts. Of the virtues that are ends in themselves, it's easy to determine which they are based on this division. The inferior part exists for the sake of the superior, just as we see in both nature and art. The superior part is the one that has reason. Reason itself is divided into two parts: the theoretical and the practical. This division is also important here.

Actions follow the same pattern. Those that are superior should always be chosen by those who have the ability. What's most desirable is what leads to the best outcome. Life is divided into work and rest, war and peace. The goals of our actions are either necessary and useful or noble. We should value noble actions more than necessary ones, just as we value the superior parts of the soul and its actions. War exists to bring peace, work exists to bring rest, and the useful serves the noble.

A lawmaker should consider everything, including the different parts of the soul and their actions, especially focusing on the higher and nobler aspects. The same approach applies to life and its actions. People should be prepared for both work and war, but even more so for rest and peace. They should be trained to do what's necessary and useful, but even more so to do what is fair and noble. The education of children and young people should focus on these goals.

Many Greek states that are now well-governed, and the lawmakers who founded them, didn't create their laws and education systems with the best goals in mind or aim to promote every kind of virtue. Instead, they focused on what was useful and profitable. Some more recent writers have had similar views. They praise the Spartan state, showing they agree with the lawmaker who made war and victory the main goal of the government. But this thinking is wrong and can easily be proven both by argument and by looking at the facts. People like Thibron and others who wrote about the Spartan state seem to admire the lawmaker for training the citizens to endure all kinds of dangers and hardships to gain power over their neighbors.

But it's clear, now that the Spartans have no hope of holding supreme power, that they are not happy, and their lawmaker wasn't wise. It's ridiculous that they lost their chance to be honorable while they still followed their laws and no one challenged their authority. These people don't understand what kind of government reflects well on a lawmaker. A government of free people is nobler and more in line with virtue than a despotic government.

A city shouldn't be considered happy, and a lawmaker shouldn't be praised, just because the citizens have been trained to conquer their neighbors. This approach has a big problem: it encourages every citizen to seek supreme power in their own city, just as the Spartans accused Pausanias of doing, despite the great honors he received. This kind of reasoning and these laws are neither political, useful, nor true. A lawmaker should teach people laws that benefit them both in their public and private lives.

The lawmaker's goal shouldn't be to prepare people for war just so they can enslave others. Instead, the goal should be to ensure they don't become enslaved themselves. Next, the lawmaker should focus on the safety of the citizens, not on ruling over everyone else. Finally, only those who are naturally suited to be slaves should be enslaved. Both reason and experience show that the lawmaker's attention to war and all the other rules should aim at achieving rest and peace.

Many states are preserved through war, but once they gain power over others, they fall apart. Like a sword that loses its shine when not in use, these states weaken during peace. This happens because the lawmaker never taught them how to live in peace.

Since a man has the same goal both as an individual and as a citizen, it's clear that a good man and a good citizen must have the same purpose in mind. It's obvious that all the virtues that lead to rest are necessary because, as we've often said, the goal of war is peace, and the goal of work is rest. But the virtues that aim for rest and those that aim for work are both important for living a free and restful life. We need many necessities so that we can enjoy rest.

A city, therefore, needs to be temperate, brave, and patient. As the saying goes, "Rest is not for slaves." People who can't bravely face danger will become slaves to those who attack them. So, courage and patience are needed for work, philosophy is needed for rest, and temperance and justice are needed for both. These virtues are especially important during peace and rest because war forces people to be just and temperate. But the pleasures of peace and rest often lead to arrogance. People who are comfortable and have everything they need for happiness have a great need for the virtues of temperance and justice.

So, if there are, as poets say, people living in the "happy isles," these people would need a higher level of philosophy, temperance, and justice because they live comfortably with all the pleasures they could want. It's clear, then, that these virtues are necessary for any state that wants to be happy or honorable. A person without worth can never enjoy true goodness, and even less can they enjoy rest. They can only appear good through hard work and war, but during peace and rest, they become the lowest of creatures.

This is why virtue should not be cultivated the way the Spartans did. They didn't differ from others in their idea of what the highest good is. Instead, they thought this good could be achieved through a specific type of virtue. But since there are greater goods than those gained through war, it's clear that we should aim to enjoy things that are valuable on their own, rather than virtues that are only useful in war. We now need to consider how and by what means we can acquire these greater goods.

We've already said that three factors influence this: nature, habit, and reason. We've also explained what kind of people nature must produce for this purpose. Now, we need to decide whether education should begin with reason or habit because both should work together in harmony. Sometimes reason can stray from its purpose and be corrected by habit.

First of all, it's clear that, as with other things, the beginning of education comes from one source, while its end comes from another source, which is also its goal. For us, reason and intelligence are the end of nature, so our upbringing and behavior should be directed toward these goals.

Next, just as the body and the soul are two different things, the soul itself is divided into two parts: the reasoning part and the non-reasoning part. Each of these parts has its own habits: one focused on desires and the other on intelligence. Just as the body develops before the soul, the non-reasoning part of the soul develops before the reasoning part. This is clear because emotions like anger, will, and desire appear in children almost as soon as they are born, while reason and intelligence develop as they grow older. So, we must take care of the body first, then focus on the desires for the sake of the mind, and care for the body for the sake of the soul.

If the lawmaker is to ensure that children's bodies are as perfect as possible, their first priority should be marriage—when and under what conditions citizens should marry. When considering marriage, the lawmaker should think about the age and condition of both the man and the woman. The goal is for them to grow old around the same time and for their physical abilities to be in harmony. This way, the man won't be able to have children while the woman is too old to bear them, or the woman won't be able to have children while the man is too old to be a father. Situations like this often lead to arguments and disputes.

There should also not be too great an age difference between parents and children. If there is, the parent will gain no benefit from the child's affection, and the child will not receive any help from the parent's care. However, there should also not be too little of an age difference, as this can cause problems. A boy who sees his father as almost his age may not show him proper respect, and this can lead to disputes in the family.

To return to the main point, care must be taken to ensure that children's bodies meet the lawmaker's expectations. This can also be achieved through the same means. The time for producing children is roughly determined—not precisely, but in general terms. For men, this lasts until around age seventy, and for women, until age fifty. Marriage should be timed with these periods in mind.

It is very bad for children if the father is too young. In all animals, young offspring tend to be weaker, smaller, and more likely to be female. The same is true for humans. You can see this in cities where men and women marry very young; the people tend to be smaller and less well-formed. Women also suffer more during childbirth, and many die young. This is what some people think the oracle at Traezenium was referring to—not that they were gathering their crops too early, but that they were marrying too young.

Marrying too young also tends to lead to a lack of self-control, especially in women. It also prevents men's bodies from growing to their full size if they marry before they have finished growing, as marriage stops further growth. For this reason, the best age for a woman to marry is eighteen, and for a man, thirty-seven, give or take a little. When they marry at this time, their bodies will be at their best, and they will stop having children at the right time. Also, in terms of the children, they will likely be reaching their full potential just as their parents are approaching old age, around seventy.

This is the best time for marriage, but the time of year is also important. Many people already follow this idea and choose winter as the best time to marry. Married couples should also follow the advice of doctors and naturalists who have written on these topics. We will discuss the best physical conditions for this when we talk about educating children, but for now, we'll briefly touch on a few points.

It's not necessary for anyone to have the body of a wrestler to be a good citizen or to have good health or healthy children. But they should also not be weak or overly affected by hardship. They should be somewhere in the middle. A person should be used to hard work, but not too much, and not focused on just one thing like a wrestler. Instead, they should engage in activities suitable for free people. This applies equally to both men and women. Pregnant women should make sure their diet is not too limited, and they should get enough exercise. This is something the lawmaker can easily encourage by requiring them to attend daily worship of the gods who oversee marriage.

However, while it's important for the body to be active, the mind should remain as calm as possible. Just as plants are influenced by the soil they grow in, children are influenced by their mothers' emotional state.

As for whether a child should be exposed to or raised, let it be a law that no child who is imperfect or deformed should be raised. Just as we have discussed the best time for men and women to marry, we should also determine how long it benefits the community for them to have children. Just as children born to parents who are too young are physically and mentally weak, the same is true for children born to parents who are too old. While the body is still in its prime, which some poets say lasts until age fifty or a little more, children are likely to be at their best. But after this age, it's better for parents to stop having children.

Any improper relationship between a man and a woman, or a woman and a man, when either party is betrothed, should be strongly condemned. If someone is guilty of this after marriage, they should be shamed as much as they deserve for their offense.

When a child is born, their physical strength will depend largely on the quality of their food. If you study animals and observe people who are determined to raise warlike children, you'll find they mostly feed them milk because it is best suited to their bodies. They avoid giving them wine to prevent illness. The natural movements of children are also very helpful for their growth. To prevent their limbs from becoming crooked, since their bodies are still very flexible, some people even use special devices to keep their bodies straight.

It's also helpful to get children used to the cold at a young age because this strengthens their health and prepares them for the challenges of war. This is why many barbarian groups dip their children in cold rivers or dress them lightly, as the Celts do. Whatever we want to accustom children to, it's best to start them early and gradually. Boys naturally like the cold because their bodies are warm.

These are the things we should focus on first. The next stage of life lasts until the child is five years old. During this time, they shouldn't be taught anything serious, not even necessary tasks, so as not to hinder their growth. They should be encouraged to move around enough to avoid becoming lazy, and this can be done through various activities and play. Their play should not be too serious, but also not too easy or lazy.

Their caregivers should also monitor the stories they hear and the tales they are told. These should prepare them for the lessons they will learn later in life. For this reason, most of their play should imitate the things they will do when they grow older. Some people are wrong to forbid boys from arguing and quarreling because these activities help them grow. Such struggles serve as exercise for the body because the tension and strain that comes with these quarrels make boys stronger.

Their caregivers should also keep an eye on their lifestyle and the people they spend time with, making sure they never associate with slaves. Until they turn seven, children should be raised at home. During this time, they should be kept away from anything inappropriate. In fact, it is just as important for the lawmaker to remove all indecent speech from the state. If shameful words are allowed, shameful actions will soon follow, especially among young people. For this reason, they should never speak or hear anything inappropriate.

If any free person says or does something forbidden before they are old enough to join the public meals, they should be punished with disgrace and whipping. If an older person does this, they should be treated like a slave because of their dishonorable behavior. Since we are banning inappropriate speech, we should also make sure children don't see any improper images or stories. The authorities should ensure that there are no statues or pictures of such things, except for certain gods, as allowed by law. Only people of a certain age should be allowed to worship these gods, along with their wives and children.

It should also be illegal for young people to watch iambic or comedic performances before they are old enough to enjoy the pleasures of life. A good education will protect them from the bad influences of these things.

We have only briefly touched on this subject for now. Later, when we return to it properly, we will determine whether educating children is necessary, and if so, how it should be done. For now, we have only mentioned it as something important.

The tragic actor Theodoras once said something wise: he wouldn't let anyone, not even the lowest actor, go on stage before him because he wanted to be the first to catch the audience's attention. The same applies to our interactions with people and things: whatever we experience first tends to please us the most. This is why children should be kept away from anything bad, especially things that are offensive to good manners.

When children reach the age of five, the next two years should be spent watching the activities they will later have to learn. Education should be divided into two stages based on the child's age. The first stage is from age seven to puberty, and the second is from puberty until age twenty-one. Those who divide age into seven-year periods are usually wrong. It's much better to follow nature's divisions because every art and lesson is meant to complete what nature leaves unfinished.

We should first consider whether any rules are needed for raising children. Next, we should decide if it's better to make this a shared responsibility or to leave it up to individuals, as is commonly done in most cities. Lastly, we should determine what those rules should be.

Book 8

No one can doubt that the government should take a great interest in the care of young people. When this is neglected, it harms the city because every state should be governed according to its unique character. The form and habits of each government are special to it, and just as they first created it, they usually continue to preserve it. For example, the ways of a democracy create a democracy, and the ways of an oligarchy create an oligarchy. But in general, the best habits lead to the best government.

Just like in any business or art, there are things that people must first learn and get used to in order to do their jobs well. It's clear that the same is true for practicing virtue. Since every city has one common goal, education should be the same for everyone, and it should be a public responsibility, not just a private one. Right now, each person takes care of their own children individually, and they teach them whatever they want. But what children need to learn should be common to everyone. No one should think of any citizen as belonging just to them; instead, each person belongs to the whole state. Each citizen is part of the state, and each part naturally has a duty to care for the good of the whole. For this reason, the Spartans are to be praised because they pay great attention to education and make it a public concern. It is clear, then, that there should be laws about education, and it should be public.

It is important to know what education is and how children should be taught. There are disagreements about the purpose of education because not everyone agrees on what children should be taught to improve their virtues or to live a happy life. It's also not clear whether education should focus on improving reason or fixing moral behavior. Based on how education is done today, we can't say for sure whether the goal is to teach children useful life skills or to help them develop virtue and excellence. Different people defend different views.

As for virtue, not everyone agrees on what it is. Since not everyone values the same virtues equally, it makes sense that they wouldn't teach the same virtues either. It's clear that everyone should learn what is necessary. However, what is necessary for one person is not necessary for everyone. There should be a difference between what a free person learns and what a slave learns. Free people should be taught everything useful that does not make them lowly. Any kind of work or art that damages the body, mind, or character of a free person is considered lowly because it makes them unfit for the practice of virtue. This is why any art that harms the body is considered lowly, as are all jobs done for profit. These jobs take away the freedom of the mind and make it focused on money.

There are also some arts that are acceptable for free people to learn to a certain degree, but trying to become an expert in them leads to the problems we just mentioned. There is a big difference between why someone does or learns something. It is not lowly to do something for yourself, your friend, or for the sake of virtue. However, doing it for someone else can seem like the work of a servant or a slave. The way children are taught today seems to include both approaches.

There are four main things that are usually taught to children: reading, physical exercises, music, and, in some cases, painting.

Reading and painting are both very useful in life, and physical exercises help develop courage. As for music, some people might question its purpose because most people use it for pleasure. But those who originally made it part of education did so because, as we have already said, nature requires that we not only work properly but also know how to spend our free time honorably. Of all things, this is the most important.

Although both work and rest are necessary, rest is more important than work. We must learn what to do when we are at rest because we should not spend our free time just playing. If we did, playing would become the main business of our lives. If this is not possible, then play is more necessary for people who work than for those who are at rest. People who work need relaxation, which play can provide. Because work brings pain and stress, play is like medicine for the mind. It gives the mind a break and brings pleasure.

Rest itself seems to be linked to pleasure, happiness, and a good life. But this kind of rest is not for those who are working; it belongs to those who are at rest. People who work do so for the sake of something they don't have yet, but happiness is an end in itself. Everyone agrees that happiness brings pleasure, not pain. However, not everyone agrees on what pleasure consists of because each person's idea of pleasure is influenced by their habits. But the best person seeks the best pleasure, which comes from the noblest actions.

It's clear, then, that in order to live a life of rest, a person must learn and be taught certain things. The purpose of this learning is the enjoyment of rest. On the other hand, the learning that prepares us for work has a different purpose. This is why the ancient people made music a part of education. It's not necessary in the way reading is for managing a household or doing something useful in public life. It's not like painting, which helps a person appreciate the fine arts. It's also not like physical exercises, which contribute to health and strength. We don't see these benefits come from music. So, music is meant to be part of how we spend our rest.

This was the intention of the people who introduced music into education. They thought it was a proper activity for free people, so they made it part of their education. Homer even writes about this when he says, "How right to call Thalia to the feast," and in other parts, he describes how Ulysses says the happiest part of life is "when at the festal board, in order plac'd, they hear the song."

It's clear that there is a certain kind of education that a child should receive, not because it's useful or necessary, but because it is noble and fitting for a free person. Whether there is one type of education or several, and how these should be taught, will be discussed later. For now, we can say that we have the support of the ancients, who included music as part of education, which shows that they understood its importance.

Moreover, it's necessary to teach children useful things, not just because they are useful, but also because they lead to other kinds of learning. For example, children should learn to read, not only because it's useful, but because it helps them gain other types of knowledge. They should also learn painting, not just so they don't get cheated when buying art or vases, but more importantly, because it helps them appreciate the beauty of the human form. Chasing after only what is profitable does not suit great and free souls.

Since it's clear whether boys should first be taught morals or reasoning, and whether their bodies or their minds should be trained first, it's obvious that boys should first be placed under the care of physical trainers to develop their bodies and teach them physical exercises.

Some states that seem to focus on their children's education put the most emphasis on wrestling, even though it can limit body growth and affect its form. The Spartans did not make this mistake. Instead, they made their children tough through hard physical labor because they believed this would make them courageous. But as we have often said, courage is not the only thing or the most important thing that should be taught. Even when it comes to courage, the Spartans may not achieve their goal.

We don't see that the most fierce animals or nations are the most courageous. In fact, it's often the gentler ones, like lions, that show true courage. Many cruel people kill and even eat other humans, like the Achaeans and Heniochi in Pontus, and many others in Asia. Some of these people are just as bad or worse than these examples. They live through tyranny, but they have no courage. We also know that the Spartans themselves, when they focused on hard labor and were superior to all others, didn't gain this superiority through their physical training. Instead, it was because they faced opponents who were not trained at all. Now, the Spartans are inferior to many other nations, both in war and physical exercises.

What is noble and honorable should be the focus of education, not what is fierce and cruel. A good man, not a wolf or any other wild animal, is the one who faces noble dangers. So, allowing boys to focus too much on these physical exercises without teaching them what's necessary makes them base and narrow-minded. They may excel in one part of being a citizen, but in everything else, they are useless.

We should not base our judgments on the past, but on what we see today. In the past, the Spartans didn't have any competition in their education, but now they do. Physical exercises are useful, and it's agreed how they should be used. During youth, it's best to focus on the gentler exercises and avoid the strict diets and harsh exercises that are often prescribed. This way, the body's growth won't be hindered. A clear sign that harsh training stunts growth is the fact that hardly any Olympic athletes have won as both boys and men. The exercises they did when young took away their strength.

After spending three years on other parts of education, starting from puberty, boys will then be at the right age to endure hard work and follow a regulated diet. It's impossible for the mind and body to work hard at the same time because they interfere with each other.

The work of the body hinders the progress of the mind, and the work of the mind hinders the body.

Regarding music, we've already talked a bit about it, though not very clearly. It's a good idea to go over what we said before in more detail, which can be a starting point for others to add their thoughts. Because it's hard to clearly explain what power music has, or why we should use it. Is it for fun and relaxation, like sleep or wine? These things aren't serious but are enjoyable and help us forget our worries, as Euripides says. That's why people group together sleep, wine, music, and sometimes dancing, using them all for the same purpose. Or should we think that music helps us become virtuous, like how exercise shapes the body, and that it can influence our character so we learn to enjoy things in the right way?

Or should we say that music helps us in life and makes us wiser? Some people think this is another benefit of music. It's clear that boys shouldn't learn music just as a game, because learning isn't playing— it's actually hard work. Also, it's not right to let boys have complete free time, because stopping learning isn't good for someone who isn't fully grown. But maybe we think that boys focus on music now so they can enjoy it as fun when they become adults. But if that's true, why should they learn it themselves? Why not be like the kings of the Medes and Persians, who enjoy music by listening to others play and showing them its beauty? Because those who spend all their time studying music will be better at it than those who just learn the basics.

But if that's a reason for kids to learn something, then they should learn cooking too—but that's silly. We have the same question if music improves character: why should they learn it themselves? Can't they get all the benefits of controlling emotions or judging performances by listening to others, like the Spartans do? Because they, without learning music, can still tell what's good and bad. The same goes if music is just for fun for those who live comfortably— why should they learn it themselves instead of enjoying others' skills?

Let's think about what we believe about the gods in this matter. We see that poets never show Jupiter himself singing or playing music. In fact, we often look down on professional musicians and say only drunkards or clowns would do that. But maybe we can talk more about this topic later. The first question is: should music be part of education or not? And among the three purposes given to music, which one is correct? Is it for teaching, for fun, or to fill the free time of those who are not working? Or could all three be suitable purposes for music?

Because it seems to involve all of them. Play is needed for rest, and rest is pleasant, acting like a cure for the stress from work. Everyone agrees that a happy life must be honorable and pleasant, because happiness includes both. And we all agree that music is very enjoyable, whether instrumental or with singing; as Musaeus says, "Music is man's sweetest joy." That's why music is rightly included in all gatherings and happy lives, because it can bring joy.

From this, one might think it's necessary to teach young people music. Because all harmless pleasures not only help us reach life's ultimate goal but also serve as relaxation. And since people rarely achieve that final goal, they often stop working and turn to amusement just to enjoy the pleasure it brings. So it's helpful to enjoy pleasures like these. Some people make play and fun their goal, and maybe that goal has some pleasure attached, but not the right kind. But while people aim for one thing, they settle for another because human actions resemble their goals in some way.

Because we pursue the goal for its own sake, not for anything else that comes with it. And pleasures like these are sought not because of what comes after them, but because of what came before, like work and hardship. That's why they look for happiness in these kinds of pleasures; and anyone can easily see this. Probably no one doubts that music should be pursued not only for this reason but also because it's very helpful during breaks from work. We should also ask whether music might have another, higher purpose besides this.

And we shouldn't just enjoy the ordinary pleasure it gives (which everyone feels, since music naturally gives pleasure and is agreeable to all ages and personalities), but also look at whether it helps improve our character and our souls. And we'll easily know this if we feel our moods influenced by it. And it's clear that they are, from many examples, like the music at the Olympic games, which obviously fills the soul with excitement. But enthusiasm is a feeling that strongly stirs our mood.

Also, everyone who hears imitations feels empathy, even when they're given without rhythm or poetry. Furthermore, since music is pleasant, and since virtue means enjoying, loving, and hating the right things, it's clear that we should train ourselves to judge correctly and to take joy in good character and noble actions. But feelings like anger and calmness, courage and modesty, and their opposites, and all other moods, are best imitated by music and poetry. This is obvious from experience, because when we hear them, our soul is changed.

And someone who feels joy or sorrow from an imitation is almost in the same state as if they were affected by the real thing. So, if someone likes seeing a statue just because it's beautiful, it's clear that seeing the real person would also be pleasing. Now, in our other senses, like touch and taste, there is no imitation of character. In sight, there is a little, but these are just images of things, and the feelings they cause are mostly the same for everyone.

Also, statues and paintings don't really imitate character, but are signs that show the body showing some emotion. However, the difference isn't big, but young people shouldn't look at the paintings of Pauso, but those of Polygnotus or other artists who show character. But in poetry and music, there are imitations of character; and this is clear because different harmonies are naturally so different that listeners feel different and are not in the same mood when one is played compared to another.

For example, one kind might cause sadness and shrink the soul, like the mixed Lydian; others soften the mind and sort of melt the heart; others steady it and make it firm, like Doric music does; while Phrygian music fills the soul with excitement, as those who have studied this part of education have well described; they give examples from the music itself. The same is true for rhythm; some steady the mood, others change it; some affect us strongly, others more gently.

From all this, it's clear how much music affects our mood and how it can influence it in different ways. And if it can do this, then certainly young people should be taught music. And learning music is especially suited to them, because at their age they don't like to pay attention to things that aren't enjoyable. But music is naturally very enjoyable, and there seems to be a link between harmony and rhythm; that's why some wise people thought the soul itself is harmony, or that it contains harmony.

We will now determine whether it's right for children to be taught to sing and play instruments, which we have previously questioned. It's well known that if you want someone to be skilled in any art, it helps if they learn the practical part themselves. Because it's very hard, if not impossible, for someone to judge well what they can't do themselves. It's also very important that children have something to do that will entertain them. That's why the rattle invented by Archytas seems clever—they give it to children to play with, so they don't break things around the house.

Because at that age they can't sit still. So this toy suits babies, and as they grow up, teaching should be their toy. So it's clear that they should be taught music in a way that lets them practice it. It's not hard to say what's appropriate or not for their age, or to answer people who say this activity is low or vulgar. First of all, they need to practice so they can judge the art; that's why this should be done when they're young.

But when they're older, they can stop the practical part; they'll still be able to judge what's good in the art and enjoy it properly because of what they learned when they were young. Regarding the criticism that some people make that music is low or vulgar, it's not hard to respond if we think about how much we want those who are being educated to become good citizens to be taught in this art, and what kind of music and rhythms they should know, and what instruments they should play, because there is probably a difference in these.

That's the right answer to that criticism: we must admit that in some cases, nothing can prevent music from having some of the bad effects people attribute to it. So it's clear that learning music should never interfere with the tasks of adulthood, or make the body weak and unfit for war or government work. But it should be practiced by the young and judged by the old. For children to learn music properly, they shouldn't be involved in the parts that music experts argue about.

They also shouldn't perform pieces that are impressive because they're hard to play, and which, after being shown in public contests, have now become part of education. Instead, let them learn enough to be able to properly enjoy good music and rhythms. And not just the kind of music that all animals, slaves, and boys feel, but something more. So it's clear what instruments they should use: they should never be taught to play the flute or other instruments that need great skill, like the harp, but instead ones that will help them be good judges of music or any other learning.

Also, the flute isn't a moral instrument; instead, it stirs up the emotions and is better used when we want to excite the soul, not when we want to teach. Also, there's something about it that's opposite to what education needs: when someone plays the flute, they can't speak. That's why our ancestors rightly banned its use by young people and free citizens, even though they themselves used it at first.

Because when their wealth gave them more free time, they became more enthusiastic about virtue; and both before and after the Persian war, their noble deeds lifted their minds so much that they focused on every part of education, not just one, trying to learn everything. That's why they included the flute as one of the instruments they were to learn. In Sparta, the leader of the chorus played the flute himself; and in Athens, it was so common that almost every free man knew how to play, as shown by the tablet that Thrasippus dedicated when he was chorus leader.

But later they rejected it as dangerous, having become better at judging what helped promote virtue and what didn't. For the same reason, many old instruments like the dulcimer and the lyre were set aside, as well as those meant to give pleasure to the player and needed a delicate touch and great skill to play well. What the ancients say in the myth about the flute makes sense: that after Minerva discovered it, she threw it away.

And they're not wrong who say the goddess disliked it because it made the player's face look distorted. But more likely, she rejected it because knowing how to play it didn't help improve the mind. Now, we think of Minerva as the goddess who invented arts and sciences. Since we don't approve of a child being taught to master instruments (we'd limit that to those competing for prizes in that art; because they play not to improve their virtue, but to please listeners and satisfy their demands), therefore, we think such practice is unsuitable for free citizens; it should be limited to those who are paid to do it.

Because it often gives people low ideas, since their goal is bad. Because the rude audience member makes them change their music, so the performers who pay attention to him adjust their actions according to his movements.

We are now going to discuss harmony and rhythm—whether all types should be used in education or if only certain ones should be chosen. Also, should we give the same guidance to those learning music for education as to those who are learning it for other reasons, or is there a difference between them? Since music is made up of melody and rhythm, we need to understand the role each plays in education. Should we focus more on melody or rhythm? However, since many people, including musicians and philosophers skilled in this area, have already written extensively on this subject, we will refer those seeking detailed information to their works. Here, we will only give a general overview without going into too much detail.

Some philosophers, whose views we agree with, divide melody into three categories: moral, practical, and the kind that stirs deep emotions. Each of these types of melody is matched with a specific kind of harmony that naturally fits it. We believe music should not serve just one purpose but several—helping to teach, purify the soul, and offer enjoyment and relaxation from mental stress. I use the word "purify" here without fully explaining it but will cover it in more detail in my Poetics. Music clearly has a role in all these areas, but not all types of harmony are suitable for every purpose. The most moral harmonies should be used in education, while the more active and emotional ones can be used for entertainment or performance.

Some people have a natural passion for strong emotions like pity, fear, or enthusiasm, though the intensity of these feelings varies between individuals. In some, these emotions can be overwhelming. But we can see that sacred music can calm even those whose emotions are out of control, bringing them peace, much like a physician's treatment. This same calming effect can be seen in people who are compassionate, fearful, or overwhelmed by their emotions. Music has the power to ease their minds and bring them back to a state of calm, offering pleasure along with relief. Music that can purify the soul in this way brings harmless pleasure to everyone.

Therefore, the harmony and music performed in public settings, like theaters, should include this kind of calming and purifying quality. However, because theater audiences consist of two types of people—the educated and free-minded, and the unrefined or working-class, such as hired laborers and others like them—there needs to be some music and entertainment that appeals to both groups. Just as their tastes in life have been shaped in different ways, their tastes in music are also different. Some music caters to more base tastes, while others appreciate natural, refined harmonies. What is natural brings pleasure to everyone, so music in the theater should lean toward this type of harmony.

In education, we should use melodies and harmonies that shape good character, such as the Doric harmony, which is serious and helps develop courage. Experts in the field of music education have also supported this view. But Socrates, in Plato's Republic, made a mistake by allowing both the Phrygian and Doric harmonies while banning the flute. The Phrygian harmony has the same emotional power as the flute—it can stir up the mind and emotions. This is shown by how poets use the flute in their songs about wild, intense feelings, like in Bacchic rituals. The Phrygian harmony fits these situations perfectly.

It's widely agreed that the dithyrambic style of music is Phrygian, and experts provide many examples to prove this. For instance, when Philoxenus tried to compose dithyrambic music in the Doric style, he naturally ended up using Phrygian, because it was better suited for that purpose. Everyone agrees that Doric music is the most serious and best for inspiring courage. Since the Doric harmony sits in the middle between two extremes, it's clear that this is the type of music that young people should learn.

When teaching music, we must consider what is possible and what is appropriate. Everyone should aim for what combines both of these qualities, but it also depends on their age. For example, it's difficult for older people to sing songs that require high notes, so they should focus on gentler music that doesn't require much vocal strength. Some music experts criticize Socrates for saying that young people shouldn't learn softer harmonies, as if it would make them lazy, like getting drunk. But this is not true—these harmonies are more appropriate for those who are older.

If there is a type of harmony that is both elegant and instructive for children, it should be used—perhaps the Lydian harmony, which seems to fit this description. So, we can say that education should be guided by three principles: moderation, what is possible, and what is appropriate.

Nicomachean Ethics

Book 1

Every art and every study, as well as every action and choice, is believed to aim at some good. For this reason, the good has been rightly described as what everything seeks. However, there is a difference among these goals: some are activities, while others are products that come from these activities. When there are goals separate from the actions, the products are naturally seen as better than the activities. Since there are many types of actions, arts, and sciences, their goals are many as well. The goal of medicine is health, that of shipbuilding is a ship, that of strategy is victory, and that of economics is wealth. But when different arts are connected under one skill—like bridle-making and the other arts related to horse equipment fall under the skill of riding, and this, along with all military activities, falls under the skill of strategy—it is clear that the goals of the master skills are better than those of the subordinate ones. After all, the subordinate actions are done for the sake of the higher goals. It doesn't matter whether the activities themselves are the goals or if they lead to something else, as is the case with the sciences mentioned.

Now, if there is one ultimate goal of everything we do, something we desire for its own sake (and not for the sake of something else), and if we don't choose everything for some other reason (which would go on forever, making our desires pointless), then this ultimate goal must be the greatest good. Knowing this should have a huge effect on our lives. Wouldn't we, like archers aiming at a target, be more likely to hit the right mark? If this is true, then we must try to figure out what this goal is and which of the sciences or abilities it belongs to. It seems to belong to the most authoritative art, the one that truly leads all others. Politics appears to be this type of art because it decides which sciences should be studied in the state and which subjects different classes of citizens should learn and how much they should learn. We see that even the most important skills, like strategy, economics, and rhetoric, fall under politics. Since politics uses the other sciences and makes laws about what we should and should not do, its goal must include the goals of all other sciences. This means the goal of politics must be the good for humanity. Even if the greatest good is the same for one person as it is for a state, the good of the state is greater and more complete. Whether we are trying to achieve or preserve the good, it's better to do it for a whole nation or for city-states than for one person. These are the goals our study focuses on since we are discussing political science in one sense of the term.

Our discussion will be enough if it is as clear as the topic allows. Precision shouldn't be expected the same way in every discussion, just as it's not expected in every craft. Fine and just actions, which political science studies, can vary greatly and be seen differently by different people. This leads some to think they exist only because of custom, not nature. Goods also vary in this way because they can sometimes bring harm to people. For example, people have been ruined because of their wealth, and others because of their courage. So, when speaking about such topics and using such ideas, we should be satisfied with indicating the truth roughly and in general terms. When discussing things that are only mostly true and starting with similar ideas, we can't expect perfect conclusions. Therefore, each statement should be accepted in the spirit it is given. It is the mark of an educated person to look for precision in each subject only as far as the topic allows. It is clearly foolish to expect mathematical certainty from a speechmaker and to demand scientific proof from a storyteller.

Each person judges well what they know, and they are good judges of the things they are familiar with. So, the person who is trained in a subject is a good judge of that subject, and the person with a well-rounded education is a good judge in general. This is why a young person isn't the best audience for lessons on political science. They are inexperienced in life's actions, which are the starting point for these discussions. Also, since young people tend to follow their emotions, their study will be useless because the goal is not knowledge but action. It doesn't matter whether they are young in years or young in character. The problem isn't age but living in a way where they pursue each passing desire as their emotions guide them. For such people, as with those who are lacking self-control, knowledge brings no benefit. But for those who want to live and act based on reason, knowledge about these subjects will be very useful.

These thoughts about the student, the kind of treatment to expect, and the purpose of our study can serve as our introduction.

Let's return to our study and, considering that all knowledge and every pursuit aims at some good, ask what we say political science aims at and what the highest good achievable by action is. In words, there is broad agreement: most people and those of higher understanding say that it is happiness. They agree that living well and doing well are the same as being happy. But they disagree about what happiness is. Many people don't agree with the wise on this. Most think it's something obvious like pleasure, wealth, or honor. However, they often change their minds—thinking happiness is health when they're sick or wealth when they're poor. Still, knowing they don't know, they admire those who speak of great ideas beyond their understanding. Some believe that there is another good beyond these obvious ones, something that exists on its own and causes the goodness of all other things. It may not be necessary to examine every opinion ever held, but it is enough to look at those that are most common or seem worth considering.

Let's not forget, though, that there's a difference between arguments from first principles and arguments toward first principles. Plato was right to ask whether we are coming from or going toward first principles. It's like a race where you either run from the starting line to the turn or from the turn back to the starting line. We must begin with what is known, but knowledge can mean two things: what is known to us and what is known without conditions. We should begin with what is known to us. So, anyone who wants to understand what is noble, just, and generally related to political science must have been brought up with good habits. The facts are the starting point, and if these are clear enough to him, he won't need the reasoning right away. A person who has been well brought up has or can easily gain these starting points. As for someone who neither has them nor can get them, let him listen to the words of Hesiod:

"Best of all is the one who knows everything for himself;
Good is he who listens to wise advice from others;
But he who neither knows nor listens to others
Is a useless fool."

Let's now return to the main point of our discussion. Looking at how people live, most people—especially those of lower desires—seem to equate the good, or happiness, with pleasure. This is why they love a life of enjoyment. There are, we might say, three main types of life: the life of pleasure, the political life, and the contemplative life. Most people are quite base in their tastes, preferring a life suitable for animals, but they get this idea because many powerful people share the same desires.

Looking at the main types of life, people of higher refinement and active nature tend to identify happiness with honor. Roughly speaking, this is the goal of the political life. However, honor seems too shallow to be what we are truly looking for, as it depends more on those who give honor rather than the one who receives it. But the good we seek should be something that belongs to a person and can't be easily taken away. Furthermore, people seem to seek honor to be assured of their goodness. They seek honor from wise people who know them and value their virtue. Clearly, then, virtue is better than honor, at least according to these people. One might even say that virtue, rather than honor, is the true goal of the political life. Yet, even this seems incomplete because having virtue is compatible with being asleep or inactive, and it can even exist alongside great suffering and misfortune. But no one would call a person happy if they were living like that unless they were just stubbornly defending their argument. But enough about this—it has been discussed at length in other debates. The third type of life is the contemplative life, which we will discuss later.

The life of money-making is one pursued out of necessity, and wealth is clearly not the good we are searching for. Wealth is useful for getting something else. So, we might instead say that the earlier-mentioned things (like pleasure and honor) are true goals because they are loved for themselves. But it's clear that even these aren't the ultimate goals. Many arguments have been made to support them, but we should now move on from this subject.

Next, we should consider the idea of the universal good and carefully examine what it means. This inquiry is made difficult by the fact that the idea of Forms has been introduced by friends of ours. Still, it is better—and indeed our duty—to pursue the truth even if it means criticizing ideas that are dear to us, especially since we are philosophers and lovers of wisdom. While both truth and friends are important, piety demands we honor truth above our friends.

Those who introduced the idea of Forms did not propose Ideas for categories that included levels of priority and order. For this reason, they did not suggest there was an Idea for all numbers. But the term "good" is used in different ways in different categories, such as substance, quality, and relation. Substance is more fundamental in nature than relation because relation is like an offshoot or an accident of being. So, there cannot be one common Idea of good across all these categories. Furthermore, "good" has many meanings, just like "being" does. It is used for substances like God and reason, for qualities like the virtues, for quantities like moderation, and for relations like usefulness. It is also used for time, like the right moment, and for place, like the right location. Clearly, it cannot be one thing present in all cases. If it were, it could not be used in all these different categories. Also, since each science studies one thing, there would be one science of all goods, but instead, we see many sciences studying things within the same category. For example, strategy studies opportunity in war, and medicine studies opportunity in illness. Medicine also studies moderation in food, while gymnastics studies moderation in exercise.

One might also ask what is meant by "the thing itself," as when we say "man himself" or a particular man, the definition of man is the same. If they are both men, they don't differ in that respect. The same should be true of "good itself" and particular goods—they shouldn't differ as far as their goodness is concerned. Furthermore, something doesn't become better just because it lasts longer. Something that lasts a day isn't necessarily less good than something that lasts forever. The Pythagoreans seem to give a better explanation of the good when they place "the One" in the column of goods. This is the view that Speusippus seems to have followed.

But we should discuss these things elsewhere. However, we should consider that the Platonists haven't been talking about all goods. They say that the goods we pursue for themselves are good in relation to a single Form, while things that produce or preserve these goods, or prevent their opposites, are only secondarily called good. Clearly, then, goods must be spoken of in two ways: some are good in themselves, and others are good because they lead to these. Let's separate goods that are good in themselves from those that are useful and see if the former are all good because of one Idea. What kind of things would we call good in themselves? Is it things we pursue even when they are not connected to other things, like knowledge, sight, and certain pleasures and honors? Certainly, even if we pursue these for something else, we would still place them among things that are good in themselves. Or, is nothing good in itself except the Form of good? If that's the case, the Form would be empty. But if the things we've mentioned are good in themselves, then there must be some common quality that makes them all good, just like there is something common in both snow and white lead that makes them white. But when we consider things like honor, wisdom, and pleasure, their goodness seems to come from different sources. So, the good is not one single thing that applies to all these different cases.

Then, what do we mean by the good? It's not like things that only have the same name by chance. Are goods one because they come from one good or because they all contribute to one good? Or are they one by analogy? Certainly, reason is in the soul just as sight is in the body, and so on in other cases. But maybe we should leave these subjects for now. Perfect accuracy about them belongs to another area of philosophy. The same goes for the idea of the universal good. Even if there is one good that applies to all goods or exists on its own, it clearly can't be achieved by humans. But right now, we're looking for something that can be achieved. Still, some might think it's worth recognizing this idea of the universal good as a way to better understand the goods we can achieve. If we know the universal good, we can use it as a guide to help us achieve the goods that are good for us. This argument sounds reasonable, but it seems to go against the methods used in the sciences. All sciences aim at some good and try to supply what is missing, but they don't start by studying the universal good. It's hard to believe that experts in different fields don't know about such a great help as the universal good. It's also difficult to see how a carpenter or a weaver would benefit in their craft by knowing about the universal good, or how someone who understands the Idea of the good would be a better doctor or general. A doctor seems to study not general health, but the health of a particular person. After all, it's individuals that doctors treat. But we've said enough about these topics for now.

Let us once again focus on the idea of the good we are trying to find, and ask what it could be. It seems to vary depending on different actions and skills. For example, in medicine, strategy, and other arts, it differs. So what is the good in each case? Surely, it is the thing for which everything else is done. In medicine, it's health; in strategy, it's victory; in architecture, it's a house; and in other areas, it's something else. In every action and effort, it is the end goal, because it is for this goal that people do everything else they do. So, if there is one goal for everything we do, this goal will be the good we can achieve through action. And if there are more than one, these will be the goods we can achieve through action.

This reasoning leads us, in a different way, to the same point. But we should try to explain this more clearly. Since there are clearly multiple goals, and we choose some of them (for example, wealth, flutes, or tools) for the sake of something else, it is clear that not all goals are final ends. The highest good is clearly something final. So, if there is only one final end, that will be what we are looking for. If there are more than one, the most final of these will be what we are searching for. We say that what is worthy of being pursued for its own sake is more final than something pursued for another reason, and what is never desired for something else is more final than things desired both for themselves and for another reason. Therefore, we call "final" without any limits that which is always desired for itself and never for something else.

Happiness, more than anything else, seems to be this kind of thing. We always choose it for ourselves, not for something else. But honor, pleasure, reason, and every virtue we choose for themselves (because even if nothing else came from them, we would still choose each one of them), yet we also choose them because they lead to happiness. Happiness, on the other hand, no one chooses for the sake of these or for any other reason.

From the perspective of self-sufficiency, the same result appears. The final good is thought to be self-sufficient. Now, by self-sufficient, we do not mean something that only one person needs, like someone living alone, but also something for their family, friends, and fellow citizens, because humans are social beings. But we must set a limit to this, because if we include our ancestors, descendants, and friends' friends, we will be dealing with an infinite chain. Let us leave this for another time and now define self-sufficient as that which, when alone, makes life desirable and complete, lacking nothing. We believe happiness to be like this. We also think it is the most desirable thing of all, not just one good thing among others. If it were one of many, even the smallest addition would make it more desirable, because the added good would make it better, and greater good is always more desirable. So, happiness is something final and self-sufficient, and it is the goal of action.

However, saying that happiness is the highest good might seem obvious, and people might still want a clearer explanation of what it really is. We could explain it more clearly if we could first figure out the function of a human being. Just as for a flute-player, sculptor, or artist, and generally for all things that have a purpose or activity, the good is thought to reside in that purpose, so it seems to be with humans, if they also have a function. Do the carpenter and the leatherworker have specific functions or tasks, but not humans? Were we born without a purpose? Or, just as the eye, hand, and foot have functions, does humanity, too, have a specific role apart from these? What might it be? Life itself seems common to both plants and animals, but we are searching for what is unique to humans. Therefore, let's rule out the life of nutrition and growth. The next possibility is a life of perception, but this also seems to be shared with horses, oxen, and every animal. What remains is the active life of the part of us that has reason. One part of reason follows principles, and the other part has and exercises them. Since "life of reason" has two meanings, we should clarify that we mean life in the sense of activity because that seems to be the truer meaning of the term. If the function of a human is an activity of the soul that follows or implies a rational principle, and if we say that both a person and a good person share the same function—like a lyre and a good lyre-player—and if, in all cases, the function is the same but excellence makes it better, then we must add to this definition the idea of performing that function well. For example, the function of a lyre-player is to play the lyre, and the function of a good lyre-player is to do so skillfully. If this is the case, and if the function of a person is a kind of life, this life will involve actions of the soul that follow a rational principle, and the function of a good person will be to perform these actions nobly and well. Since any action is performed well when it is done in line with its excellence, human good turns out to be activity of the soul in accordance with virtue. If there are many virtues, the good follows the best and most complete ones.

But we must add "throughout a complete life." One swallow does not make a summer, nor does one day. Likewise, one good day or short time does not make someone blessed and happy.

Let this be a rough outline of the good. We should first sketch it out roughly, then fill in the details later. It seems that anyone can carry on and explain something that has been well outlined, and time is a good helper in such tasks. The growth of the arts happens this way—anyone can add what is missing. We should also remember what has been said before and not seek the same level of precision in all subjects. Instead, in each area, we should aim for the kind of accuracy that fits the topic. A carpenter and a mathematician study the right angle in different ways. The carpenter looks at how useful it is for his work, while the mathematician is interested in what it actually is. We must act the same way in all subjects, ensuring that our main task does not get bogged down by minor questions. Nor should we always demand to know the cause of everything. Sometimes, it's enough that the facts are well-established, especially in the case of first principles. First principles are the most important thing. We come to know them in different ways—some by induction, others by observation, habit, or other methods. But we should try to understand each principle in the right way, putting effort into explaining them clearly, as they greatly influence everything that follows. The beginning is said to be more than half of the whole, and many of the questions we ask are cleared up by it.

We must also consider this matter in light of both our conclusions and what is commonly believed. When our view is correct, all the facts fit together, but when it is wrong, the facts start to clash. Goods have been divided into three types: some are external, some are related to the soul, and some to the body. We consider those related to the soul as the truest goods, and we classify actions and activities of the soul in this category. Therefore, our argument must be correct according to this view, which is an old one agreed upon by many philosophers. It is also correct because we define the goal in terms of certain actions and activities. This places it among goods of the soul, not among external goods. Another common belief that fits our account is that a happy person lives well and acts well because we have basically defined happiness as living and acting well. The traits that are usually associated with happiness all seem to match our definition of it. Some people say happiness is virtue, some say it's practical wisdom, while others believe it's a kind of philosophical wisdom. Some say it's one or all of these things, either with or without pleasure. Others include external prosperity. Many of these ideas have been held by both ordinary people and important thinkers, and it's unlikely that all of them are completely wrong. Instead, they are probably right in at least one way, or even in most ways.

Our account fits with those who say that happiness is virtue or a specific virtue, because virtuous activity belongs to virtue. However, there is an important difference between putting the highest good in having virtue or in using it, in the state of mind or in the action itself. The state of mind might exist without leading to any good results, like when someone is asleep or otherwise inactive, but action cannot. If someone is engaged in virtuous activity, they will act, and act well. Like in the Olympic Games, it is not the most beautiful or strongest people who win crowns, but those who actually compete. It is some of these who are victorious. Likewise, it is those who act that win the good things in life.

Their life is also naturally pleasant. Pleasure is a state of the soul, and to each person, what they love is pleasant to them. For example, a horse is pleasant to someone who loves horses, and a spectacle is pleasant to someone who loves sights. In the same way, just actions are pleasant to someone who loves justice, and virtuous actions are pleasant to someone who loves virtue. For most people, their pleasures conflict with each other because their pleasures are not naturally pleasant, but for lovers of the noble, the things that are naturally pleasant are also pleasant to them. Virtuous actions are like this. So for them, these actions are pleasant in themselves, and also naturally pleasant. Therefore, their life does not need any extra pleasure to make it enjoyable—it is already pleasant. Also, a person who does not enjoy doing noble things is not truly good. No one would call someone just if they didn't enjoy acting justly, or call someone generous if they didn't enjoy generous acts. This applies to all other virtues as well. If this is true, then virtuous actions are naturally pleasant. They are also good and noble, and have all these qualities to the highest degree, because a good person judges them to be so. Their judgment is as we have described. So happiness is the best, noblest, and most pleasant thing in the world. These qualities are not separated from one another, as in the old inscription at Delos:

The noblest is what is most just, the best is health, but the most pleasant thing is to get what you desire.

All these qualities belong to the best activities, and we believe that one or all of these activities are connected with happiness.

But as we said, happiness also needs external goods. It is either impossible or difficult to do noble deeds without the proper resources. In many cases, we use friends, wealth, and political power as tools, and there are some things that, if missing, take away from happiness. For example, good birth, good children, and beauty. A person who is very ugly or poorly born, or who is isolated and without children, is unlikely to be very happy. A person would be even less likely to be happy if they had very bad children or friends, or if they lost good children or friends to death. So, as we said, happiness seems to need a certain level of good fortune. This is why some people connect happiness with luck, while others link it with virtue.

For this reason, people also ask whether happiness is something we learn or develop through habit or some other kind of training, or whether it comes from divine intervention or luck. If it is a gift from the gods, it would make sense that happiness is something they give, as it is the best thing a person can have. But this question might be better for another discussion. Even if happiness is not a gift from the gods but instead comes as a result of virtue or some kind of learning or training, it still seems to be one of the most godlike things. The reward and goal of virtue seem to be the best things in the world, something divine and blessed.

According to this view, happiness will also be widely shared because everyone who has the potential for virtue can achieve it with the right study and effort. If it is better to be happy because of our actions rather than because of chance, it makes sense that this is the way it works. Everything that depends on nature is as good as it can be, and the same goes for anything that relies on art or reason. This is especially true when it depends on the best cause of all. It would be a very poor arrangement if the greatest and most noble thing in life were left to chance.

The answer to this question is also clear from the definition of happiness. We said that happiness is a virtuous activity of the soul, of a certain kind. Of the other goods, some must exist beforehand as conditions for happiness, and others are helpful and useful as tools. This agrees with what we said at the beginning. We said the goal of political science is the best end, and political science focuses on making the citizens good and capable of noble actions.

It makes sense, then, that we do not call an ox, horse, or any other animal happy because none of them can take part in this kind of activity. For this reason, a boy is not happy either, because he is not yet able to act this way due to his age. When we call boys happy, it is because of the hopes we have for their future. As we said, not only is complete virtue needed for happiness, but also a complete life, because many changes and chances happen throughout life. The most fortunate people may experience great misfortune in old age, like Priam in the Trojan story. No one would call someone who ended their life in misery happy.

Should we not call anyone happy while they are still alive, as Solon says, and wait until they die to judge? But even if we accept this idea, does that mean someone is happy only when they're dead? Isn't that an odd thing to say, especially since we believe that happiness involves activity? If we don't call a dead person happy, and Solon didn't mean that, maybe what he meant is that once someone dies, we can safely say they were blessed because they are no longer at risk of misfortune. However, this raises another question. We think good and bad things can still happen to a dead person, just like they can happen to someone who is alive but unaware of them—like when children or descendants experience good or bad fortunes, or receive honors or dishonors.

This creates a problem. What if a man lived a happy life and died in a way that honored his life, but later his descendants faced many hardships or some did well while others did not? The closeness of the relationship between the man and his descendants can also vary a lot. It would seem strange if the dead person's happiness changed based on what happens to their descendants—sometimes being happy and other times being sad. But it also seems strange if their descendants' fortunes had no effect on the dead person's happiness.

Let's go back to the main problem. Maybe looking at it again will help us solve this issue. If we must wait until a person dies to call them happy, not because they are happy now but because they were happy before, this seems like a paradox. How could we not call someone happy while they're alive, if happiness is something that belongs to them at that time? We might hesitate to call living people happy because life is full of changes, and happiness seems like something that should be stable and not easily altered. One person might experience many ups and downs in life. If we judged them based on every turn of events, we might call them happy at one moment and unhappy the next, making happiness seem as changeable as a chameleon. But maybe it's wrong to let a person's happiness depend so much on their changing fortunes. Happiness doesn't depend on things like wealth or power but on a person's virtuous actions, which define happiness.

This discussion actually supports our definition of happiness. No part of a person's life is as lasting as their virtuous actions. These actions are thought to last even longer than knowledge of the sciences. Among these actions, the most valuable ones last the longest because happy people tend to live their lives consistently in line with virtue. This may be why we don't forget them. So, we can say the happy person will remain happy throughout their life because they will always or most often be engaged in virtuous activities and contemplation. They will handle life's ups and downs with nobility and grace, especially if they are truly good and morally strong.

Many things in life happen by chance, but these events differ in importance. Small strokes of good or bad luck don't affect life much, but if many big events turn out well, they can make life happier. Not only do they add beauty to life, but the way a person handles these events can show their nobility and goodness. On the other hand, if these events go badly, they can harm happiness because they bring pain and can stop people from doing many things. Even then, a person's nobility can still shine through when they endure great misfortunes with dignity—not by ignoring the pain, but by showing greatness of soul.

If, as we said, a person's actions define their life, a truly happy person can never become miserable. They won't do things that are disgraceful or mean. We believe that a truly good and wise person will handle whatever life brings in the best possible way, like how a good general uses the army he has or a good shoemaker works with the leather he's given. The same goes for all other craftsmen. If this is true, a happy person cannot become miserable, although they may not reach the highest level of happiness if they face extreme misfortunes like those of Priam.

A truly happy person is not constantly changing in their happiness. They won't lose their happiness easily or because of ordinary bad luck.

Only a series of very great misfortunes could shake their happiness. Even if they do face many great misfortunes, they won't regain their happiness quickly. If they regain it at all, it will only be after a long period of time and after they've had many great successes.

So, should we not say that someone is happy if they live according to complete virtue and have enough external goods—not just for a short time, but for their entire life? Or should we add that they must also die in a way that reflects how they lived? The future is unknown to us, but happiness, as we've said, is the final goal and something complete in every way. If this is true, we will call happy those among the living who meet these conditions and who will continue to do so, but we will only call them truly happy once their life is complete. That settles these questions.

The idea that the fortunes of a person's descendants and friends don't affect their happiness at all seems a bit harsh and goes against what people generally believe. But since there are many events, and these events can vary greatly in how much they matter, it would take too long to go through each one in detail. A general outline should be enough. Just as some of the misfortunes a person experiences have a bigger impact on their life than others, the same is true for the misfortunes of their friends and descendants. It also makes a difference whether these misfortunes happen to people who are alive or those who are already dead. For example, in a tragedy, it matters whether horrible deeds happen on stage or are just talked about. Whether or not the dead are affected by the fortunes of the living is something people still debate. It seems that if good or bad things do reach the dead, the effects are weak or small, or at least not enough to make a happy person unhappy or change the situation of someone who is blessed. The fortunes of friends and descendants may have some impact on the dead, but only in a way that doesn't make the happy unhappy or cause any major change in their state.

Now that we've answered those questions, let's consider whether happiness is something to be praised or something to be valued. It's clear that happiness isn't just a potential thing. Everything that is praised seems to be praised because it's a certain kind of thing and is related to something else. For example, we praise a just or brave person because of their actions and what they do. We praise someone strong or fast because they are good at something important. This is clear when it comes to the gods, too. It seems strange to compare the gods to human standards, but we do this in praise because praise involves comparing one thing to another. However, we don't praise the best things, we value them more highly. Instead of praising the gods and the most godlike humans, we call them blessed and happy. The same goes for good things like happiness. No one praises happiness in the same way they praise justice. Instead, they call it blessed because it's more divine and better than things that are praised.

Eudoxus seems to have been right in arguing that pleasure is the highest good. He believed that the fact that pleasure, though good, is not praised shows that it is better than the things that are praised. He thought that God and the good were similar because all other things are judged in comparison to them. Praise is fitting for virtue because virtue leads people to do good deeds, but we celebrate virtuous acts themselves. This might be something that those who study praise and celebration focus on, but for us, it's enough to understand that happiness is something to be valued and complete. This seems clear because happiness is the first principle. It is the reason we do everything we do, and we consider the first principle of anything to be the most valuable and divine.

Since happiness is an activity of the soul according to perfect virtue, we need to examine what virtue is. Maybe this will help us better understand the nature of happiness. The true student of politics is thought to study virtue above all things because they want to make their fellow citizens good and obedient to the law. This is shown by lawgivers like those in Crete and Sparta, and others like them. If this inquiry belongs to political science, then it fits with our overall plan. But clearly, the virtue we need to study is human virtue because the good we are looking for is human good, and the happiness we are concerned with is human happiness. By human virtue, we don't mean bodily virtue but virtue of the soul, since happiness is also an activity of the soul. If this is true, the student of politics must know something about the soul, just as a doctor must know about the body if they are to heal it. And politics is more important than medicine. Even the best doctors spend much time learning about the body. So, the student of politics must study the soul, but only enough to answer the questions we are discussing. Going deeper would require more precision than our purpose demands.

Some things about the soul are already discussed well enough in other works, and we can use them here. For example, people say that one part of the soul is irrational, and one part follows reason. Whether these parts are physically separate, like parts of the body, or only separated in how we define them, doesn't matter for our current discussion.

Of the irrational part, one part seems to be shared by all living things and is responsible for nutrition and growth. This is the power of the soul we find in all plants and animals, including humans. It's more reasonable to think of this as a common power than to assign different powers to different creatures. The excellence of this part of the soul seems to be shared by all living things, not just humans. This part of the soul seems to be most active during sleep, and since goodness and badness aren't obvious during sleep, there's a saying that happy people are no better off than unhappy people for half of their lives. This happens naturally because sleep is when the soul is inactive in the part where it can be good or bad. However, perhaps some movements of the soul happen during sleep, and in that case, the dreams of good people might be better than those of others. But let's leave this topic aside for now, as the nutritive part of the soul has no part in human excellence.

There seems to be another irrational part of the soul that, in a way, listens to reason. For example, we praise the rational part of a person who has self-control and the person who lacks it. We praise the part of their soul that listens to reason because it guides them in the right direction toward the best things. But we also find another part of the soul that seems naturally opposed to reason and fights against it. Just as paralyzed limbs may move in the opposite direction when we try to move them, so it is with the soul. The impulses of those who lack self-control often pull them in opposite directions. In the body, we can see what goes wrong, but in the soul, it's less visible. However, we must assume that the soul, too, has something that goes against reason. Exactly how it is distinct from other parts of the soul doesn't concern us right now.

Even this part of the soul seems to listen to reason in some way. In a person with self-control, it obeys reason, and in the brave and temperate person, it listens even more closely to reason. In these people, the irrational part and the rational part speak with the same voice.

So, the irrational part of the soul seems to have two parts. The part responsible for nutrition doesn't follow reason at all, while the part responsible for desires and appetites does, in a way, listen to and obey reason. This is the same way we talk about following the advice of a father or a friend, not in the same way we discuss following a mathematical rule. The fact that the irrational part of the soul listens to reason is shown by how we give advice, reproof, or encouragement. If we say this part of the soul listens to reason, then the part of the soul that follows reason and the part that doesn't will each have two parts. One part follows reason strictly, while the other part follows reason like a person follows the guidance of their father.

Virtue is also divided into two kinds based on this difference. Some virtues are intellectual, and others are moral. For example, wisdom, understanding, and practical judgment are intellectual virtues, while generosity and temperance are moral virtues. When we talk about someone's character, we don't say they are wise or have understanding, but that they are good-tempered or temperate. Yet, we also praise the wise person for their state of mind. States of mind that deserve praise are called virtues.

Book 2

Virtue, as we know, is of two types: intellectual and moral. Intellectual virtue mainly comes from teaching, which is why it requires both experience and time. Moral virtue, on the other hand, comes from habit, which is why the word for moral virtue (ethike) comes from the word for habit (ethos). This shows that none of the moral virtues are naturally within us, because nothing that exists by nature can develop a habit that goes against its nature. For example, a stone, which naturally moves downward, can't be trained to move upward, even if you throw it up ten thousand times. The same goes for fire—it naturally rises and can't be trained to move downward. In the same way, nothing that behaves naturally in one way can be trained to behave in the opposite way. So, virtues don't come to us by nature or against nature. Instead, we are naturally able to acquire them, but they are perfected through habit.

For all things that come to us naturally, we first have the potential for them, and only later do we actually use them. This is clear with the senses: we didn't develop our ability to see or hear by using these senses many times. On the contrary, we had them before we used them. But we develop virtues by practicing them, just like with skills. For the things we need to learn before we can do them, we learn by doing them. For example, we become builders by building, and we become musicians by playing music. In the same way, we become just by doing just acts, temperate by doing temperate acts, and brave by doing brave acts.

This idea is also supported by what happens in cities. Lawmakers make citizens good by forming good habits in them. This is the goal of every lawmaker, and those who fail at this miss their target. This is the difference between a good and bad constitution.

In addition, the same causes that produce a virtue can also destroy it, just like with skills. A person becomes a good or bad musician by playing well or poorly. The same applies to builders and all other trades. People become good or bad at their craft based on how well they practice it. If this weren't true, there would be no need for teachers, and everyone would simply be born good or bad at their craft. The same goes for virtues. By behaving a certain way in our interactions with others, we become either just or unjust. By behaving a certain way when faced with danger, and by getting used to feeling either fear or confidence, we become either brave or cowardly. The same is true for our desires and feelings of anger: some people become temperate and calm, while others become self-indulgent and irritable, based on how they act in different situations. In short, our character develops from our repeated actions. That's why the actions we take must be of a certain kind, because our character reflects the differences in our actions. It makes a huge difference whether we develop good or bad habits from a young age.

Since we aren't trying to gain theoretical knowledge (like in other studies), but instead to become good, we must focus on actions—specifically, how we should do them. The way we act shapes the kind of character we develop, as we've already said. We all agree that we must act according to the right rule, and we'll discuss what this rule is later and how it connects to the other virtues. But for now, we should agree that when we talk about conduct, we are speaking in general terms, and we shouldn't expect exact details. Just like in matters of health, what is good for us doesn't have a strict set of rules. The same goes for specific cases, which are even less precise, as they don't follow any strict laws or rules. It's up to each individual to decide what is appropriate for the situation, just like a doctor or a navigator must do in their work.

Even though this is the nature of our discussion, we can still provide some help. First, let's consider that things can be destroyed by either deficiency or excess. This is true for both strength and health. To better understand this, we can look at things we can sense. For example, both too much or too little exercise can destroy strength, and both too much or too little food or drink can destroy health. However, the right amount of these things will both produce and maintain strength and health. The same is true for temperance, courage, and the other virtues. A person who runs from everything or fears everything becomes a coward. A person who is afraid of nothing and faces every danger becomes reckless. A person who indulges in every pleasure and avoids none becomes self-indulgent. Meanwhile, a person who avoids every pleasure, like someone who is insensitive, also misses the mark. So, temperance and courage are destroyed by both excess and deficiency, but they are maintained by moderation.

The same things that help virtues grow can also destroy them. This is true for all things we can sense. For example, strength comes from eating well and exercising, and strong people are better able to continue doing these things. The same is true for the virtues. By avoiding pleasures, we become temperate, and once we've become temperate, we are better able to avoid pleasures. The same applies to courage. By getting used to facing frightening things and standing our ground, we become brave, and once we are brave, we are more capable of standing our ground in the face of danger.

We can use pleasure and pain as a sign of our character. A person who avoids bodily pleasures and takes joy in doing so is temperate, while a person who is bothered by this is self-indulgent. A person who stands firm in the face of fear and either takes joy in doing so or is not troubled by it is brave, while a person who is troubled by it is a coward. Moral excellence is connected to pleasure and pain because we do bad things for pleasure and avoid noble things because they cause us pain. That's why we should be brought up from a young age, as Plato suggests, to take pleasure in the right things and feel pain for the right things. This is the proper way to be educated.

If the virtues are connected to our actions and feelings, and every action and feeling is tied to pleasure and pain, then virtue must also be connected to pleasure and pain. This is further proven by the fact that punishments use pleasure and pain, and punishment is a kind of cure. Cures work through opposites, so this shows the importance of pleasure and pain in shaping our character.

As we mentioned earlier, every state of the soul is influenced by the things that can make it better or worse. People become bad by chasing the wrong pleasures or avoiding the wrong pains, either at the wrong time or in the wrong way. This is why some people define virtues as being free from emotion and stillness. However, this definition isn't quite right because it doesn't include important details like doing things at the right time, in the right way, and for the right reasons. We assume that excellence in virtue means doing what is best in relation to pleasure and pain, while vice is doing the opposite.

We can also see that virtue and vice deal with these same things through other facts. There are three things we can choose and three things we can avoid: the noble, the beneficial, and the pleasant, as well as their opposites, the disgraceful, the harmful, and the painful. The good person tends to make the right choices in all of these areas, while the bad person makes the wrong choices, especially when it comes to pleasure. This is because pleasure is something all animals experience, and it is connected to all of our choices. Even the noble and beneficial things can feel pleasant.

Pleasure has been with us since we were born, which is why it's hard to remove it from our lives. We use pleasure and pain to measure our actions—some people more than others. For this reason, our whole study must focus on these feelings, because how we feel pleasure and pain has a big impact on our actions.

It's harder to fight against pleasure than against anger, as Heraclitus said, but both art and virtue deal with difficult things. Goodness is even better when it is more challenging. For this reason, both virtue and political science deal with pleasure and pain. A person who uses pleasure and pain correctly will be good, while a person who uses them incorrectly will be bad.

So, we can say that virtue is connected to pleasure and pain, and that it is strengthened by the actions that created it. If these actions are done differently, it can be destroyed. The actions that created virtue are the same ones that maintain it.

Some might ask what we mean when we say that we become just by doing just acts and temperate by doing temperate acts. After all, if people are doing just or temperate acts, aren't they already just and temperate? This seems to be like saying that if people follow the rules of grammar or music, they are already grammarians or musicians.

But this isn't even true for the arts. It's possible to follow the rules of grammar by chance or at someone's suggestion. A person is only a grammarian if they not only follow the rules but also understand them and apply them with knowledge.

The same goes for the virtues. The products of the arts have their value in themselves, so it's enough that they have a certain quality. But if acts of virtue have the right qualities, that doesn't mean they are done with justice or temperance. The person doing the act must also be in the right state when they do it. First, they must know what they are doing. Second, they must choose to do it, and choose it for its own sake. Third, their action must come from a firm and unchanging character. These conditions don't apply to the arts. In the arts, knowledge is enough, but for virtue, knowledge is only a small part. The other conditions are far more important and come from repeatedly doing just and temperate acts.

Actions are called just and temperate when they are the kinds of actions a just or temperate person would do. But just because someone does these actions doesn't mean they are just or temperate themselves. Instead, they must do them in the way a just or temperate person would do them. So it is true that we become just by doing just acts, and we become temperate by doing temperate acts. Without doing these things, no one would ever become good.

Most people, however, don't do these things. Instead, they turn to theory, thinking that by studying philosophy, they will become good. They behave like patients who listen carefully to their doctors but don't follow any of the instructions. Just as these patients will never be healthy this way, people will never improve their character by simply studying philosophy.

Next, we need to consider what virtue is. Since the things that are found in the soul are divided into three types—passions, faculties, and states of character—virtue must be one of these. By passions, I mean things like appetite, anger, fear, confidence, envy, joy, friendship, hatred, longing, and pity—in general, any feelings that come with pleasure or pain. By faculties, I mean the things that make us able to feel these emotions, like the ability to feel anger, pain, or pity. By states of character, I mean the way we relate to our emotions—whether we manage them well or poorly. For example, we manage anger poorly if we feel it too strongly or too weakly, and we manage it well if we feel it moderately. The same goes for all the other emotions.

Virtue and vice, however, are not passions. We are not called good or bad because of our passions, but because of our virtues or vices. We also aren't praised or blamed for simply feeling a certain way. A person isn't praised for feeling fear or anger, nor is someone blamed for feeling angry. Instead, we are praised or blamed for how we manage our virtues or vices.

Also, we don't choose to feel emotions like anger or fear, but virtues involve choice. In respect to our passions, we are said to be moved, but in respect to our virtues and vices, we are said to be in a certain state.

For these reasons, virtues are not faculties. We aren't called good or bad for simply having the capacity to feel emotions. Also, our faculties are natural, but we aren't naturally good or bad. We've already discussed this. So, if virtues are neither passions nor faculties, they must be states of character.

This explains what virtue is in terms of its category.

We also need to explain what kind of state virtue is. Every virtue brings something into good condition and helps it do its work well. For example, the virtue of the eye makes the eye and its work good. The virtue of a horse makes it good and capable of running, carrying its rider, and facing enemies. If this is true in every case, then the virtue of a person is the state of character that makes a person good and helps them do their work well.

We've already explained how this happens, but we can also clarify this by considering the specific nature of virtue. In everything that is continuous and divisible, we can take more, less, or an equal amount, either in terms of the thing itself or in relation to us. The equal amount is a middle point between excess and deficiency. The middle point in the object is equally distant from the extremes, and this is the same for everyone. But the middle point in relation to us is different. It is neither too much nor too little, and this varies for each person. For example, if ten pounds of food is too much and two pounds is too little, the middle point for one person might be six pounds, but that might still be too much or too little for another person. The same applies to running or wrestling. A skilled person will avoid both excess and deficiency and aim for the middle point, not in the object, but in relation to themselves.

If this is true for all the arts, where the best work is done by aiming for the middle point, then virtue must also aim for the middle. We often say that good works of art can't have anything added or taken away, because excess and deficiency ruin the work, while the middle point preserves it. Good artists focus on this in their work, and since virtue is better and more exact than art, it must aim at the middle as well. I'm referring to moral virtue here, which deals with emotions and actions. In both, there can be excess, deficiency, and a middle point. For example, we can feel fear, confidence, desire, anger, pity, and pleasure too much or too little, and in both cases, this is bad. But to feel them at the right time, in the right way, and for the right reasons is to find the middle point, and this is what virtue aims for. The same is true for actions. In all actions, excess is a kind of failure, as is deficiency, while the middle point is praised and successful. Since being praised and being successful are qualities of virtue, virtue is a kind of middle.

It's easy to fail in many ways because evil is limitless, as the Pythagoreans said, while good is limited. It's easier to miss the target than to hit it, which is why excess and deficiency are signs of vice, while the middle point is a sign of virtue.

People can be good in only one way, but they can be bad in many ways.

Virtue, then, is a state of character that involves choice and lies in a middle point, which is determined by reason and by how a wise person would determine it. It is a middle point between two vices: one of excess and one of deficiency. In both emotions and actions, vices go too far or not far enough, while virtue finds and chooses the middle.

However, not all actions or emotions have a middle point. Some are inherently bad, such as spite, shamelessness, and envy. In terms of actions, things like adultery, theft, and murder are always wrong, no matter how they are done. You can't be right with these actions by committing adultery with the right person, at the right time, and in the right way. These actions are always wrong. There is no middle point for unjust, cowardly, or indulgent actions. It would be absurd to think that there could be a middle, an excess, or a deficiency in such things. Just as there is no excess or deficiency of temperance or courage, since the middle point is actually an extreme, there is no middle, excess, or deficiency for the actions we mentioned. They are always wrong, no matter how they are done. There is no middle point for actions that are inherently bad.

We need to apply what we've discussed to specific situations. General statements about behavior apply broadly, but when it comes to actions, specific examples are more accurate since actions involve individual situations. We'll take our examples from our list. When it comes to feelings like fear and confidence, courage is the middle ground. Those who are too fearless don't have a name, while people with too much confidence are called reckless, and those with too much fear and too little confidence are called cowards.

For pleasures and pains (mainly pleasures), the middle is called temperance, and the excess is self-indulgence. People who are deficient in feeling pleasure are rare and don't have a common name, but we'll call them "insensible."

When it comes to giving and taking money, the middle is called generosity, and the excess and deficiency are wastefulness and stinginess. Wasteful people spend too much and take too little, while stingy people take too much and spend too little. (We're giving a summary here and will explain these more precisely later.) When dealing with larger amounts of money, we call the middle magnificence, and the excess is called tastelessness or vulgarity, while the deficiency is called meanness. These are different from generosity, which deals with smaller amounts, and we'll explain the differences later.

When it comes to honor and dishonor, the middle is proper pride. Too much pride is vanity, and too little is humility. Just as generosity relates to magnificence, dealing with small and large amounts, proper pride relates to honors, with some people aiming for small honors and others for large ones. You can desire honor in the right way, too much, or too little. The person who wants too much honor is called ambitious, while the person who wants too little is unambitious. The middle person doesn't have a specific name, but the extreme positions are often labeled ambition. Because these people are at the extremes, they both claim to be in the middle. That's why we sometimes call people ambitious and other times unambitious, and sometimes praise one group or the other. We'll explain this later, but for now, let's continue.

Anger also has a middle, an excess, and a deficiency. Though these don't have clear names, we call the person in the middle good-tempered. The person who gets too angry is irascible, and the person who doesn't get angry enough is inirascible (not easily angered).

There are three other qualities that are similar but slightly different because they deal with how we interact with others. One is about truthfulness, and the other two deal with being pleasant, either through joking or in everyday life. We'll discuss these to show that in everything, the middle is good, while the extremes are bad and deserve blame. Many of these qualities don't have names, but we'll create some for clarity. When it comes to truthfulness, the middle is honesty, the excess is exaggeration, and the deficiency is false modesty. In terms of joking and amusement, the middle is ready-wittedness, the excess is buffoonery (being overly silly), and the deficiency is boorishness (being dull or boring). When it comes to being pleasant in everyday life, the middle is friendliness, the excess is flattery (if done for personal gain) or being overly agreeable (without an ulterior motive), and the deficiency is being quarrelsome or surly (constantly unpleasant).

Some traits, like shame, are not virtues but are still praised. For example, someone who feels shame at everything is overly bashful, while someone who never feels shame is shameless. The middle is modesty. Righteous indignation is the middle between envy and spite, and these traits relate to how we feel about other people's fortunes. A person with righteous indignation is upset by undeserved good fortune, an envious person is upset by all good fortune, and a spiteful person is happy when others suffer. We'll explain these traits more later. When it comes to justice, which has multiple meanings, we'll explore its types and how it relates to the idea of the middle. We'll also discuss rational virtues in a similar way.

There are three kinds of dispositions: two vices (excess and deficiency) and one virtue, which is the middle. They are all opposed to each other in some way. The extreme states are opposed to each other and to the middle, just as something large is bigger than something small, but both are larger and smaller than something equal.

For example, a brave person might seem reckless to a coward and cowardly to a reckless person. Similarly, a temperate person might seem self-indulgent to someone who is insensible and insensible to someone who is self-indulgent. The same goes for someone who is generous; they may seem wasteful to someone stingy and stingy to someone wasteful. Because of this, people at the extremes tend to accuse those in the middle of being at the opposite extreme.

Since these states are opposed, the greatest opposition is between the two extremes, not between the extremes and the middle, because the extremes are farther apart. For example, recklessness might seem somewhat similar to bravery, and wastefulness to generosity, but the extremes are furthest from each other, and opposites are defined by how far apart they are.

In some cases, one extreme is more opposed to the middle than the other. For example, it's not recklessness (the excess) but cowardice (the deficiency) that is most opposed to bravery. Likewise, it's not insensibility (the deficiency) but self-indulgence (the excess) that is most opposed to temperance. This happens for two reasons. First, one extreme is often closer to the middle than the other, so we focus on the extreme that's farther away. For example, recklessness seems more similar to bravery, while cowardice seems more different. Second, people naturally tend toward certain extremes, and we oppose the one we tend toward more. Since we're more likely to seek pleasure, self-indulgence (an excess) is more opposed to temperance than insensibility (a deficiency).

So, moral virtue is a middle between two extremes, one involving excess and the other deficiency. It focuses on finding the middle ground in both feelings and actions. This shows that being good is not easy. It's hard to find the middle in everything, just like it's hard to find the exact center of a circle. Anyone can get angry or spend money, but doing it in the right way, for the right reasons, and at the right time is much harder. That's why being good is rare, praiseworthy, and noble.

To aim for the middle, we should first move away from what's most opposed to it, just like Calypso advises in The Odyssey, "Steer the ship away from the waves." Since one extreme is usually more wrong than the other, and hitting the middle is very difficult, the next best thing is to choose the lesser of two evils. The best way to do this is to think about where we tend to go wrong, and steer ourselves in the opposite direction. This will help us get closer to the middle, like straightening a bent stick.

We also need to be especially careful with pleasure, because it's something we don't judge fairly. We should treat pleasure like the elders treated Helen of Troy, blaming her for the chaos she caused. By rejecting pleasure in this way, we're less likely to make mistakes. If we do this, we'll be able to hit the middle.

But this is difficult, especially in specific situations. For example, it's hard to say exactly when and for how long it's right to be angry or whom we should be angry with. Sometimes we praise people for being mild and not getting angry, and other times we praise them for getting angry and being brave. A person who only deviates a little from the right path isn't criticized, but someone who deviates a lot is noticed and blamed. However, it's hard to say exactly where the line is, and that's something that depends on experience. What's clear is that the middle is always praiseworthy, and we should lean toward either excess or deficiency as needed to stay as close to the middle as possible.

Book 3

Since virtue is concerned with feelings and actions, and praise or blame is given for feelings and actions that are voluntary, while those that are involuntary receive pardon or sometimes pity, it is important to know the difference between voluntary and involuntary actions. This distinction is necessary for understanding virtue and is also useful for lawmakers when deciding on rewards and punishments. We consider actions involuntary if they happen due to force or ignorance.

An action is considered forced if its cause is completely outside the person, and they contribute nothing to it, like being carried somewhere by a strong wind or by other people who have control over them.

However, there are actions done out of fear of greater harm or to achieve a noble goal (for example, if a tyrant orders someone to do something shameful, threatening to kill their family unless they comply). It's debated whether such actions are voluntary or involuntary. The same question arises with throwing goods overboard during a storm. In general, nobody would throw their goods away voluntarily, but if doing so would save their life and the lives of their crew, any sensible person would choose to do it. These actions are a mix of voluntary and involuntary, but they are closer to being voluntary because they are chosen as the best option at that moment. The decision at the time of the action makes it voluntary. The person acts voluntarily because the source of movement that controls their body is within them, and they have the power to do or not do these things. Therefore, while these actions might seem involuntary in some ways, they are more voluntary when considering the circumstances.

People are sometimes praised for such actions, especially when they endure something bad or shameful for the sake of a noble cause. On the other hand, they may be blamed if they go through terrible things for no good reason. Some actions aren't praised, but people might be excused for them when they are forced to do things that push beyond what human nature can withstand. In some cases, however, there are things that should never be done, no matter how extreme the circumstances, and people should face death instead of committing such acts. For instance, the story of Euripides' Alcmaeon being forced to kill his mother seems absurd. It can be difficult to determine what is worth enduring and at what cost, and it's even harder to stick to those decisions. Usually, people are expected to endure pain, while the things they are forced to do are seen as disgraceful. As a result, people are either praised or blamed for how they respond when faced with force.

So, what kinds of actions should be called forced? We can say that actions are truly forced when the cause comes entirely from outside, and the person does not contribute anything to them. However, actions that are undesirable on their own, but are chosen because they bring about some benefit, and where the cause comes from the person, are in themselves involuntary but are now voluntary because of the circumstances. They are more like voluntary actions because in specific cases, the individual acts voluntarily. It's hard to say what should be chosen and what shouldn't be, as there are many differences depending on the situation.

If someone were to say that pleasant and noble goals have the power to force us, then all actions would be considered forced because people do everything for these goals. But those who act under force do so unwillingly and with pain, while those who act for pleasure or nobility do so willingly and with joy. It would be strange to blame outside circumstances for disgraceful actions while praising oneself for noble ones. It seems, then, that forced actions are those where the cause is outside the person, and the person contributes nothing.

Not everything done out of ignorance is involuntary. Only actions that cause regret or pain are involuntary. Someone who acts out of ignorance but feels no regret about what they did isn't considered to have acted involuntarily, since they didn't know what they were doing, but they also aren't called voluntary, because they don't feel pain over their actions. If someone acts out of ignorance and later regrets it, they are considered to have acted involuntarily. But if they don't regret it, they are not considered involuntary actors, though we might say they acted without knowing.

Acting out of ignorance is different from acting while being ignorant. For example, someone who is drunk or angry is not acting out of ignorance, but they are acting without full knowledge of their actions.

Every wicked person is ignorant of what they should and shouldn't do, and it's this kind of mistake that leads people to become unjust or bad in general. However, the word "involuntary" is not used when someone is ignorant of what benefits them personally, because acting from mistaken judgment doesn't make an action involuntary—it makes someone wicked. Rather, involuntary actions arise from ignorance of specific circumstances related to the action. This is where pity and pardon come in, as someone who is unaware of these particulars acts involuntarily.

It's helpful to understand what specific things someone can be ignorant of. A person can be ignorant of who they are, what they are doing, who or what they are affecting, what tool they are using, or what result they expect their action to bring. Additionally, they might not know how they are doing something, such as whether they are acting gently or violently. No one can be ignorant of all of these things without being mad. It's especially hard for someone to be ignorant of themselves. However, someone might be unaware of what they are doing, like saying something without realizing it or not knowing they were revealing a secret, as Aeschylus did with the mysteries. Or someone might accidentally discharge a weapon while only intending to show how it worked. Someone might mistake a person for an enemy, as Merope did, or think a spear has a safety tip when it doesn't, or believe a rock is light and harmless when it's not. A person might give someone a drink to heal them but accidentally cause harm, or they might try to tap someone in sparring and actually wound them. Ignorance could relate to any of these aspects of an action, and the person is seen as acting involuntarily, especially if they were unaware of the most important details, such as the goal of the action. Additionally, if the action was painful and caused regret, it is considered involuntary.

Since actions done by force or ignorance are involuntary, voluntary actions are those where the cause lies within the person, and they are aware of the specifics of what they are doing. It seems wrong to say that actions done out of anger or desire are involuntary. If that were true, animals and children would never act voluntarily, and we'd have to say that noble actions are done voluntarily while bad actions are done involuntarily. But this doesn't make sense because the same source—anger or desire—causes both types of actions. It would be strange to call actions involuntary when they are driven by desires we should have, like the desire for health or learning. Also, involuntary actions are usually painful, but actions that come from desire are generally pleasurable. There isn't much difference between mistakes made from calculation and mistakes made from anger, as both are considered human traits. Therefore, actions driven by anger or desire are still our actions, and it would be strange to call them involuntary.

Now that we have distinguished between voluntary and involuntary actions, we need to discuss choice. Choice is thought to be closely connected with virtue and is a better way of understanding character than actions are.

Choice seems to be voluntary, but it is not the same thing as voluntary action. Voluntary actions are more widespread. Both children and animals can act voluntarily, but they cannot make choices. We might describe actions done suddenly as voluntary, but we wouldn't say they are done by choice.

People who say that choice is the same as appetite, anger, wish, or a kind of opinion are wrong. Choice is not shared by animals, but appetite and anger are. An impulsive person acts on appetite, but not on choice. A self-controlled person acts with choice, but not appetite. Appetite can be opposed to choice, but not to itself. Appetite is concerned with pleasure and pain, while choice is not.

Anger is even less connected with choice because actions done out of anger are thought to be less deliberate.

Choice is also not the same as wish, though they are related. We can wish for impossible things, like immortality, but we don't choose them because choosing implies a belief that the action can be accomplished. We might wish for something we have no control over, like a particular athlete winning a competition, but we don't choose it. Choice is focused on actions we believe we can achieve ourselves. We wish for goals, but we choose the means to reach them. For instance, we wish to be healthy, but we choose the actions that make us healthy. We wish to be happy, but we don't choose happiness in the same way. Choice is connected to things that are in our power.

Choice is also different from opinion. Opinion deals with all kinds of subjects, even things that are impossible or eternal. It is judged based on whether it is true or false, while choice is judged based on whether it is good or bad.

We don't become good or bad people just by having certain opinions, but we do by making certain choices. Opinions are about what is true or false, while choices are about what we pursue or avoid. Opinion is praised for being accurate, while choice is praised for aiming at the right target. When we choose, we focus on what we know to be good, while opinions are often about things we are unsure of. Some people make good choices but have bad opinions, and others have good opinions but make bad choices because of their character. Whether opinion comes before or alongside choice is not important here. What matters is that they are not the same thing.

So, what exactly is choice, if it's not any of the things we've discussed? Choice seems to be voluntary, but not all voluntary actions involve choice. Could it be something that follows deliberate thinking? Choice involves reasoning and thought. Even the word "choice" suggests that it involves selecting something over other options.

Do we deliberate about everything, and is everything something we can deliberate about, or are there some things we can't? We should probably say that only what a sensible person would deliberate about is something worth deliberating on, not what a fool or madman would think about. For instance, no one deliberates about things that are eternal, like the material universe or whether the diagonal of a square is equal to its side. Similarly, we don't deliberate about things that involve movement but always happen the same way, whether by necessity or nature or some other cause, like the solstices or the rising of the stars. Nor do we deliberate about things that happen differently each time, like droughts or rain, or about random events like finding treasure.

We also don't deliberate about all human matters. For example, no Spartan deliberates about what the best government for the Scythians would be. These things can't be influenced by our efforts. We deliberate about things that are within our power and that we can actually do. Everything else, like nature, necessity, or chance, is not up to us. People deliberate about things they can do by themselves. For example, there's no need to deliberate about exact sciences, like writing letters of the alphabet—we know how to do that. But we do deliberate about things that involve our efforts and don't always have a fixed outcome, like medical treatment or making money. We deliberate more about navigation than about gymnastics, because navigation hasn't been worked out as exactly. We also deliberate more about the arts than the sciences because we tend to have more doubts about arts.

Deliberation deals with things that usually happen in a certain way but where the outcome is unclear, or things where there is uncertainty. We ask others to help us deliberate on important matters when we don't trust ourselves to make the right decision.

We don't deliberate about ends, only about means. A doctor doesn't deliberate whether he should heal people, nor does an orator deliberate whether he should persuade people. A statesman doesn't wonder whether he should create law and order. They take their goals for granted and think about how to reach them. If there are several ways to reach the goal, they deliberate about which way is best and easiest. If there's only one way, they think about how to use that method and what steps are needed to achieve it. It's like solving a geometry problem—the person who deliberates breaks down the problem into steps. Deliberation is a form of investigation, though not all investigation is deliberation, such as mathematical studies. What comes last in deliberation seems to come first in the process of doing things. If something seems impossible, like if money is needed but can't be obtained, we stop deliberating. If something seems possible, we try to do it.

By 'possible,' I mean something that can be done through our own efforts, and this includes things we can achieve with the help of friends since the source of the action is still within us. Sometimes we deliberate about tools, other times about how to use them. In the same way, we deliberate about the means to achieve our goal and how to use those means. As was said earlier, human beings are the source of their own actions. Deliberation is about the things a person can do themselves, and actions are done for the sake of something else. The end goal is not something we deliberate about, only the means to achieve it. We don't deliberate about basic facts, like whether something is bread or if it has been baked properly. Those are matters of perception. If we were always deliberating, we'd never stop.

The same thing is both deliberated about and chosen. However, the thing we choose is already decided upon because it's what we concluded after deliberating. We stop investigating how to act when we've traced the source of the action back to ourselves. The part of ourselves that rules is what makes the choice. This can be seen in ancient governments, as described by Homer. Kings would announce their decisions to the people.

The object of choice is something within our power that we desire after deliberating. So, choice is a deliberate desire for things that are in our control. Once we've deliberated, we desire things in line with our deliberation.

We've now given an outline of choice, explained what kinds of things it deals with, and shown that it concerns the means to an end.

Wish is for the end. Some people think it's for what is truly good, while others think it's for what seems good. Those who say it's for the good must admit that what a person who doesn't choose rightly wishes for isn't really a wish. If they wish for something bad, then it wasn't a true object of wish. Those who say wish is for what seems good must admit that there's no single natural object of wish—only what seems good to each person. Different things seem good to different people, and sometimes even opposite things seem good.

If these ideas seem unsatisfying, we could say that the true good is the object of wish for everyone, but for each person, their wish is based on what seems good to them. The truly good thing is wished for by the good person, while anything could be wished for by a bad person. This is like the way healthy things are good for healthy bodies, but other things might seem healthy to someone who is sick. The good person sees the truth in everything, while others don't. Different people have different ideas of what is noble and what is pleasant, but perhaps what makes a good person different is that they see the truth in these matters. People often make mistakes because of pleasure, thinking something is good when it isn't. This is why we sometimes choose pleasure as though it were good and avoid pain as though it were evil.

The end is what we wish for, and the means to that end are what we deliberate about and choose. Actions that concern the means to an end must be voluntary and based on choice. The exercise of virtues involves choosing the right means, so virtue is in our control, just like vice. If we can choose to act, then we can also choose not to act. So if doing the right thing is in our power, then not doing the wrong thing is also in our power, and vice versa.

If it's within our power to do noble or base acts and we can choose not to do them, then being good or bad is also in our power.

The saying that "no one is wicked voluntarily or happy involuntarily" is partly false and partly true. No one is involuntarily happy, but wickedness is voluntary. Otherwise, we would have to deny that a person is the cause of their own actions, just as they are the cause of their children. If it's clear that actions come from within us, then the actions whose source is within us must also be in our control and voluntary.

This is supported by individuals and by lawmakers, who punish people for wicked acts (unless they were forced or acted out of ignorance that wasn't their fault). They honor people who do noble acts, as if to encourage them and discourage others. No one encourages people to avoid things that are out of their control, like being hot or in pain. We will experience these things anyway. In fact, we punish people for ignorance when it's their fault, like doubling penalties for drunkenness. The person had the power not to get drunk, and their drunkenness caused their ignorance. We also punish people for not knowing the law when they should know it. We assume they could have avoided ignorance if they had been more careful.

A person might say that all people desire what seems good, but they can't control how things seem to them. The way things appear depends on their character. But if people are responsible for their own state of mind, then they are also responsible for how things appear to them. If not, then no one is responsible for their bad actions, and everyone does bad things because they are ignorant of the true end, thinking they will get what is best. It's like being born with an eye for seeing what is truly good—some people are naturally gifted with this, and others are not.

Whether it's natural or not, virtue is voluntary because the good person chooses the right means voluntarily. Vice is also voluntary because the bad person's actions also depend on themselves, even if not their end goal. If the virtues are voluntary, then vices must be voluntary too, since we are responsible for our character and how we see things.

We've described the virtues in general—they are means, states of character, and involve doing the acts by which they are produced. They are in our control and voluntary, following the right rule. Actions and states of character are not voluntary in the same way, though. We control our actions from beginning to end if we know the facts. But while we control the start of our character, its development is less obvious, just like with illnesses. Because it was in our power to act a certain way, our character is voluntary.

Let's now look at the individual virtues, explain what they are about, how they work, and how many there are. Let's start by discussing courage.

It has already been shown that courage is about how we handle feelings of fear and confidence. Clearly, the things we fear are the terrible things, and these are, without a doubt, evils. That is why people often define fear as expecting something bad to happen. We fear all kinds of evils, like disgrace, poverty, illness, loneliness, and death, but not all of these are what a brave person deals with. In fact, it is right and honorable to fear certain things, and it would be wrong not to fear them—such as disgrace. A person who fears disgrace is seen as good and modest, while someone who doesn't fear it is shameless. Sometimes people mistakenly call a shameless person brave because they don't fear disgrace, and in a way, they seem like the brave person, since a brave person is also fearless. However, things like poverty and illness are not the kinds of things we should fear, and they don't come from vice or wrongdoing. Yet, even someone who is unafraid of these things is not considered brave. We sometimes still call them brave because of a similarity—just as some people who are cowards in war can still be generous and confident when it comes to losing money.

A man is not a coward if he fears his wife or children being insulted, or if he fears envy or similar things. Nor is someone brave just because they stay confident when they are about to be beaten. So, what kinds of terrible things does the brave person face? Surely, it is the most frightening things, because no one is more likely to stand firm against something truly terrifying than the brave person. Death is the most terrible thing of all because it is the end, and once someone is dead, nothing can be good or bad for them anymore. However, even the brave person does not face death in every situation, like at sea or when dealing with illness. In what situations, then? Surely, in the most noble ones. The noblest deaths are those that happen in battle because they occur in the greatest and most honorable danger. These deaths are honored both in city-states and at royal courts. So, a brave person is one who is unafraid of a noble death and of all situations that involve death, especially those in war, which are the most honorable of these situations. Even at sea or in sickness, the brave person is fearless, but in a different way from the sailor, for example. The brave person has lost hope for safety and dislikes the thought of dying this way, while sailors are more hopeful because of their experience. We show bravery when there is a chance to demonstrate skill or when dying is noble, but these situations do not offer either.

What is frightening is not the same for all people, but we can say that there are some things that are beyond human strength and terrifying for everyone—at least for anyone sensible. However, the frightening things that are not beyond human strength vary in size and degree, and the same is true for the things that give us confidence. The brave person is as fearless as a human can be. Therefore, while they will fear things within human strength, they will face them properly and as the rule of honor dictates, because the purpose of virtue is honor. But it is possible to fear these things either too much or too little, or to fear things that aren't actually frightening at all. The mistakes people make involve fearing what they shouldn't, fearing in the wrong way, or fearing at the wrong time, and the same goes for the things that give us confidence. The brave person faces and fears the right things, at the right time, and for the right reasons, while also feeling confidence in the right way and under the right conditions. This person is brave because they act according to what is right and how the rule directs. In everything, the goal is to match our actions to the state of character. This applies to the brave person as well. Courage is noble, and so the goal is noble too, because everything is defined by its goal. Therefore, the brave person endures and acts courageously for the sake of a noble goal.

For those who go to extremes, the person who has no fear of anything has no name (as we've already said, many character traits have no names), but this person would be like a madman or someone insensible if they feared nothing—not even earthquakes or storms, as it is said the Celts do not. A person who is overly confident in the face of real dangers is rash. The rash person is seen as boastful, pretending to be brave. They want to appear brave just like the brave person, so they imitate bravery when they can. Because of this, most rash people are a mix of rashness and cowardice. They act confident in certain situations but fail to stand firm against truly frightening things. The person who fears too much is a coward because they fear what they shouldn't, or they fear things in the wrong way. All these descriptions apply to the coward, who also lacks confidence. However, the coward's excessive fear is especially noticeable in painful situations. The coward is a despairing person, fearing everything, while the brave person is the opposite. Confidence is a sign of hopefulness. So, the coward, the rash person, and the brave person deal with the same situations, but they react to them differently: the first two overreact or underreact, while the third holds the right balance. Rash people are eager for danger ahead of time, but back out when faced with it. Brave people, on the other hand, are calm beforehand but ready when the time comes for action.

As we have said, courage is about finding the right balance between fear and confidence in the situations we've described. The brave person chooses or endures things because it is noble to do so or because it would be shameful not to. However, dying just to escape poverty, heartache, or any other painful situation is not the act of a brave person. In fact, it's cowardly, because it shows weakness in the face of hardship, and such a person faces death not because it's noble, but just to avoid suffering.

Courage is like this, but the name also applies to five other types of behavior.

First, there is the courage of a citizen-soldier, which is most like true courage. Citizen-soldiers seem to face danger because of the punishments they'd receive by law or the shame they'd face if they didn't, and also because of the honors they gain from acting bravely. This is why the bravest nations are those where cowards are dishonored and the brave are rewarded with respect. This type of courage is what Homer describes in characters like Diomede and Hector:

"First will Polydamas heap disgrace on me," and
"For Hector will speak to the Trojans,
'Tydeides was afraid and fled from my face.'"

This courage is the closest to true courage because it comes from virtue. It is based on feelings of shame, the desire for honor, and avoiding disgrace, which is shameful. We might put in this same category those who are forced by their leaders to fight. They are inferior, though, because they do what they do not out of shame but out of fear, and they are not avoiding disgrace but avoiding pain. They are forced by their rulers, as Hector says:

"But if I spy any coward hanging back from the fight,
That man will have no hope to escape the dogs."

The people who assign these men to their positions and beat them if they retreat do the same thing, as do those who put trenches behind the troops to prevent escape. All of these methods are forms of compulsion. But true bravery comes from acting nobly, not from being forced to act.

The second kind of courage is based on experience in certain situations. This is why Socrates thought that courage was knowledge. Different people show this in different situations, but professional soldiers show it in war. There are often false alarms in battle, and these soldiers are familiar with them, which makes them appear brave. Their experience gives them confidence because they know how to use their weapons well and have the best ones for both attack and defense. Therefore, they fight like armed men against unarmed men or like trained athletes against beginners. In these cases, it isn't the bravest who fight best, but those who are the strongest and in the best condition. However, professional soldiers often turn cowardly when the danger is too great and they are outnumbered or outmatched. They are the first to flee, while citizen-soldiers die where they stand, as happened at the temple of Hermes. For the citizen-soldier, running away is disgraceful, and death is better than living with shame. The professional soldiers, on the other hand, always expected to be the stronger ones, so when they realize they're not, they run away. They fear death more than disgrace, which is not how a brave person behaves.

Third, some people act bravely because of passion. They charge into danger like wild animals attacking those who have wounded them, and this is sometimes mistaken for bravery. Brave people also act with passion because passion drives us to rush into danger. This is why Homer uses phrases like "put strength into his passion" or "aroused their spirit" or "hard he breathed panting" and "his blood boiled." All these expressions suggest the stirring of passion. Brave people, however, act for honor, and passion helps them, but wild animals act out of pain. They attack because they've been hurt or because they are afraid. For example, if they're in the woods, they don't approach anyone. Wild animals are not brave because they rush into danger without thinking of the risks—they act out of pain and passion. If that were bravery, even a donkey would be brave when it's hungry, because no amount of beating can drive it away from food. Lust also drives adulterers to take risks. So, being driven by pain or passion doesn't make someone brave. The kind of bravery that comes from passion seems the most natural, and it would be true bravery if it were combined with choice and a noble goal.

Men, like animals, feel pain when they are angry and feel pleasure when they take revenge. Those who fight for these reasons are aggressive, but not truly brave, because they don't act for honor or according to the rules—they act out of strong emotion. They are somewhat like brave people, but not exactly.

Fourth, optimistic people are not brave either, though they seem confident in danger because they have won many times and defeated many enemies. They are similar to brave people because both feel confident, but brave people are confident for the right reasons, while optimistic people are confident because they think they are the strongest and cannot be hurt. Drunk people also behave this way—they become overly confident. However, when things don't go as they expected, they run away. A truly brave person faces dangers that are real and terrifying because it is noble to do so, and shameful not to. This is why it is considered braver to remain calm and fearless in sudden emergencies rather than in situations that are expected. In unexpected situations, actions come more from a person's character, because there is less time to prepare. Expected actions may be planned and calculated, but sudden actions must come from a person's state of character.

Fifth, people who are unaware of the danger may also appear brave, but they are not far removed from optimistic people, except that they lack the same self-confidence. Optimistic people can hold their ground for a while, but those who realize the danger or suspect that things are different from what they thought, flee, as happened with the Argives when they mistook the Spartans for Sicyonians.

So, we have described the character of truly brave people and those who are only thought to be brave.

Although courage involves feelings of both confidence and fear, it deals more with fear. Someone who remains calm and acts as they should in the face of fear is considered braver than someone who simply feels confident. Bravery is about facing what is painful, and because of this, courage is justly praised. It is harder to face pain than to resist something pleasant.

Even though the goal of courage is something pleasant, it is often hidden by the painful circumstances that come with it. This is similar to athletic competitions. Boxers aim for the pleasant outcome—the victory and honors—but the blows they take along the way are painful and exhausting. Because the pain and effort are great, the pleasant goal seems small and insignificant. In the same way, death and wounds are painful and something the brave person does not want, but they face them because it is noble to do so and shameful not to.

The more virtuous and happier a person is, the more painful the thought of death will be because life is most valuable to them, and they know they are losing the greatest goods. This is painful, but it makes them even braver, because they still choose noble deeds in war at this cost. So, not all virtues are pleasant when practiced, except in the sense that they reach their goal. The best soldiers may not always be those with the greatest virtue, but those who have nothing else good in their lives. These people are willing to face danger and even sell their lives for small rewards.

This, then, is a summary of courage. It is not hard to understand its nature, at least in outline, from what has been said.

Now that we've talked about courage, let's discuss temperance, since these seem to be the virtues of the parts of us that aren't controlled by reason. We've said that temperance is about finding balance when it comes to pleasures (it's less concerned with pains and not in the same way), and self-indulgence also deals with the same things. So, let's now figure out what kind of pleasures temperance and self-indulgence are concerned with. We can distinguish between physical pleasures and those of the mind, such as the love of honor or learning. People who love these things enjoy them with their mind, not their body. But those who are focused on these pleasures aren't called temperate or self-indulgent. Similarly, those who enjoy other types of non-physical pleasures, like those who love hearing or telling stories or spend their days on random things, are called gossips, but not self-indulgent. The same goes for people who are upset about losing money or friends—they aren't called self-indulgent either.

Temperance is related to physical pleasures, but not all of them. For example, those who enjoy looking at things like colors, shapes, or paintings aren't called temperate or self-indulgent, even though it's possible to take pleasure in them in the right amount, or too much, or too little.

The same goes for things we hear. No one calls someone self-indulgent for enjoying music or acting too much, and those who enjoy these things appropriately aren't called temperate either.

We also don't use these terms for those who enjoy smells, unless it's in a certain way. For instance, we don't call someone self-indulgent for enjoying the smell of apples, roses, or incense, but we do call them self-indulgent if they enjoy the smell of perfume or rich food. This is because self-indulgent people like these smells since they remind them of the things they crave. You can even see other people, when they're hungry, enjoying the smell of food, but it's the self-indulgent person who loves this kind of thing because it's what they crave.

There aren't any animals other than humans who enjoy these kinds of senses, except accidentally. For example, dogs don't enjoy the smell of a hare, but they enjoy eating it, and the smell just tells them the hare is nearby. Similarly, a lion doesn't enjoy the sound of an ox, but enjoys eating it; the ox's sound just tells the lion the ox is near, which makes it seem like the lion enjoys the sound. And it's the same when the lion sees a stag or goat—it's not the sight that pleases the lion, but the meal that's coming.

Temperance and self-indulgence, however, are concerned with the kinds of pleasures that humans share with other animals, which seem more basic and animal-like. These are the pleasures of touch and taste. But even taste doesn't play a big role here, since taste is about recognizing flavors, which is what wine tasters or chefs do. Self-indulgent people don't enjoy making these distinctions; they enjoy the physical pleasure, which always comes through touch—whether with food, drink, or sexual contact. This is why a certain glutton once wished his throat were as long as a crane's, because he wanted to enjoy the contact for longer. So, the sense most connected to self-indulgence is the sense of touch, which is the most common of all the senses. Self-indulgence is rightly criticized because it connects us more to our animal side than to our human side. To love these kinds of pleasures more than anything else is animal-like. Even of the pleasures of touch, the most acceptable ones have been eliminated, like the pleasure that comes from rubbing in the gym or the heat that results from it. The kind of touch a self-indulgent person enjoys doesn't affect their whole body, just certain parts.

Some desires seem to be natural to everyone, while others are unique to individuals and are learned. For example, the desire for food is natural, because anyone who is hungry craves food, and the same goes for drink, and for love, especially if someone is young and strong, as Homer says. But not everyone craves the same type of food or love, and that's what makes personal desires seem more individual. However, these personal desires still have a natural element, because different things are more pleasing to different types of people, and some things are more pleasing to everyone than others.

With natural desires, most people make mistakes in only one way—by going too far. To eat or drink more than necessary until you're overfull is to go beyond what your body naturally needs, since natural desire is about filling a lack. People who do this are called gluttons, which suggests they fill their stomachs beyond what is right. It's people with a very servile character who behave this way. But with personal desires, people make many mistakes in many different ways. For example, someone who is "fond of something" might like it too much, or like something they shouldn't, or like it more than most people do. Self-indulgent people go wrong in all these ways. They either enjoy things they shouldn't because they're harmful, or they enjoy the right things but do so more than they should or more than most people.

Clearly, then, overindulgence with pleasure is self-indulgence and is wrong. But with pain, it's not like courage where you're praised for facing it or blamed for avoiding it. The self-indulgent person is called that because they are more upset than they should be when they don't get something pleasant, even though their upset is caused by the pleasure they crave. The temperate person, on the other hand, is praised for not being upset when something pleasant is absent or when they have to avoid it.

The self-indulgent person craves all pleasant things or at least the most pleasant ones, and they are led by their desires, even if it means sacrificing everything else. That's why they are upset both when they don't get what they want and even while they're still craving it (because desire itself involves pain). But it seems ridiculous to be upset in the pursuit of pleasure. People who don't enjoy pleasure as much as they should are rare, because that level of insensitivity is not human. Even other animals can tell the difference between different kinds of food and enjoy some more than others. If there were someone who found no pleasure in anything, they would be something very different from a human. This type of person doesn't have a name because they almost never exist.

The temperate person, however, takes a balanced approach to these things. They don't enjoy the things the self-indulgent person does, or if they do, they enjoy them less. They also don't crave what they shouldn't, or if they do, they don't crave it too much or feel pain when it's absent, or they do so only to a small degree and at the right times. Instead, they enjoy the things that bring health or good condition, and they do so in moderation. They may enjoy other pleasant things as well, but only if they don't interfere with health or nobility or go beyond what they can afford. A person who ignores these limits loves pleasure more than it's worth. The temperate person, however, is the kind of person who follows the right rules.

Self-indulgence is more voluntary than cowardice because it's driven by pleasure, while cowardice is driven by pain. Pleasure is something we choose, and pain is something we avoid. Pain messes with the person who feels it, while pleasure doesn't. That's why self-indulgence is more voluntary and also more blameworthy. It's easier to get used to the things that lead to self-indulgence because there are many of them in life, and getting used to them doesn't involve any danger. But the opposite is true for terrifying things.

Cowardice seems voluntary in some ways but not others. Cowardice itself is painless, but in specific situations, pain causes us to act, such as when we throw down our weapons or disgrace ourselves in other ways. In these cases, it seems like our actions are done under pressure. But for the self-indulgent person, specific acts are voluntary because they act out of desire, even though the overall state of being self-indulgent is less voluntary. No one desires to be self-indulgent.

The term self-indulgence is also used for childish faults because these resemble the things we've been discussing. It doesn't matter which one was named after the other for our purposes—the point is that childish faults are called after self-indulgence. This comparison isn't a bad one because the desire for what is base and which grows quickly should be kept in check. This is especially true for appetite and children, since children live by their appetites and have the strongest desires for pleasure. If this part of ourselves is not controlled by reason, it can go too far. In an irrational being, the desire for pleasure is never satisfied, even if it tries every source of gratification, and the more it indulges its appetite, the stronger the desire grows. If these appetites are powerful, they can even drive out reason. That's why they should be limited and few, and they should not conflict with reason—this is what we call a controlled state. Just as a child should follow the guidance of a tutor, our appetites should follow reason. In a temperate person, the appetites should align with reason, because both aim at what is noble. The temperate person desires the right things, in the right way, and at the right time. This is what reason tells us to do.

And this concludes our discussion of temperance.

Book 4

Let's now talk about liberality. It seems to be the balance when it comes to wealth. A liberal person is praised not for their skills in war, or for being moderate, or for making legal decisions, but for how they give and receive wealth, especially for how they give it. By "wealth," we mean anything that is valued by money. Prodigality and stinginess are extremes related to wealth. We call someone stingy when they care too much about money, but sometimes we use the word "prodigal" in a more complicated way. We call people prodigal when they lack self-control and spend money on things that are indulgent. That's why these people are considered to have poor character, as they show more than one vice. So, this is not the proper way to use the word "prodigal." A prodigal person has one bad trait: wasting their wealth. A prodigal person is ruining themselves, and since life depends on having some wealth, wasting it is like ruining your own life.

This is how we'll understand the word "prodigality" here. Now, anything that can be used can either be used well or poorly, and wealth is something useful. Anything useful is best used by someone who has the virtue related to it. So, wealth will be best used by someone who has the virtue related to wealth—this is the liberal person. Spending and giving seem to be how wealth is used, while taking and keeping it are about possession. So, it's more important for a liberal person to give to the right people than to take from the right sources, or to avoid taking from the wrong ones. Doing good is more virtuous than receiving good, and doing what's noble is better than not doing something shameful. Giving is clearly a way of doing good and acting nobly, while taking is more about receiving good or avoiding shameful behavior. We feel grateful toward someone who gives, not to someone who simply doesn't take, and we praise givers more. It's also easier not to take than to give, as people are more likely to give too little of what's theirs than to take from others. Givers are called liberal, but those who don't take aren't praised for being liberal—they're praised for being just. Those who take aren't really praised at all. Liberality is one of the most loved virtues because liberal people are generous, and their generosity is helpful, depending on their giving.

Virtuous actions are noble and done for the sake of nobility. The liberal person, like all virtuous people, will give for the sake of nobility and will do it rightly. They will give to the right people, the right amounts, at the right time, and in the right way. They will also do it with pleasure, or at least without pain, since virtuous acts are either pleasant or not painful. A person who gives to the wrong people, or not for the sake of nobility but for some other reason, is not considered liberal. And someone who gives with pain is not liberal either because they value their wealth more than the noble act, and this isn't typical of a liberal person.

A truly liberal person also won't take from wrong sources, as this doesn't fit with someone who doesn't care too much about wealth. They also won't be eager to ask for things because it's not typical of someone who gives to others to want benefits for themselves. They will, however, take from the right sources, like their own wealth, not because it's noble but out of necessity—so they can continue to give. They won't neglect their own property, as they use it to help others. They won't give to just anyone, but will give to the right people at the right time, when it is noble to do so. It's very typical of a liberal person to give too much, leaving little for themselves. This is because a liberal person doesn't focus on their own needs. The term "liberality" relates to a person's resources. Being liberal isn't about the number of gifts but about the character of the giver, and this depends on how much wealth they have. So, someone who gives less can still be more liberal if they have less to give.

People who inherited their wealth, rather than earning it, are often thought to be more liberal. First, because they've never experienced a lack of resources, and second, because people tend to value what they've created themselves, just like parents love their children. A liberal person usually doesn't become wealthy because they're not focused on taking or keeping wealth but on giving it away. They don't value wealth for its own sake but as a way to give. This leads to the common complaint that the people who deserve wealth the most often have the least of it. But it's not surprising because wealth, like anything else, can't be had without effort. Even so, a liberal person won't give to the wrong people or at the wrong time, because that wouldn't be true liberality. If they spent money on the wrong things, they wouldn't have anything left for the right causes.

As we've said, a liberal person spends according to their means and on the right things. A person who goes beyond this is called prodigal. We don't call rulers prodigal because it's hard for them to spend more than they have. Liberality is a balance in giving and receiving wealth. A liberal person will give and spend the right amount, on the right things, whether big or small, and do so with pleasure. They will also take the right amounts from the right sources. Since virtue is a balance between both, the liberal person will do both as they should. Proper giving and taking go hand in hand, while improper giving and taking don't happen together. If a liberal person ends up spending in a way that isn't right or noble, they will feel some pain, but only a little, and as they should. Virtue involves feeling both pleasure and pain at the right things and in the right way.

A liberal person is easy to deal with in money matters because they don't care too much about money. They get more upset if they haven't spent on something they should have, rather than feeling bad about spending on something they shouldn't have. They don't agree with the saying of Simonides.

A prodigal person also makes mistakes here because they aren't pleased or upset by the right things or in the right way. This will become clearer as we continue. Prodigality and stinginess are extremes when it comes to giving and taking. Prodigality goes too far in giving and doesn't take enough, while stinginess falls short in giving and takes too much, except in small things.

The traits of prodigality don't often go together because it's hard to keep giving if you're not taking. Private individuals quickly run out of money if they keep giving, and these are the people we usually call prodigal. Still, a person like this seems much better than a stingy person. Prodigality can be cured with age or poverty, and this can help the person move toward a middle state. Prodigal people have some traits of a liberal person because they give and don't take, even though they don't do these things well. If they learned to do these things properly, they could become liberal because they would then give to the right people and avoid taking from the wrong sources. This is why prodigals are thought to have a less bad character—it's not evil to give too much and take too little, but it is foolish. A person like this is considered much better than a stingy person because they benefit others, while a stingy person benefits no one, not even themselves.

Most prodigals, however, do take from the wrong sources, and in this way, they're similar to stingy people. They take because they want to keep spending, but their resources run out quickly, so they're forced to find money from other places. Since they don't care about honor, they take from any source, however wrong. Their giving isn't liberal because it's not noble, and it's not done properly. Sometimes they give to the wrong people, like flatterers, and neglect those with good character. Because of this, most prodigals are also self-indulgent, spending their money on pleasures instead of living for what's noble.

The prodigal person, if left unchecked, will continue this way. But with guidance, they can become more balanced. Meanness, on the other hand, is harder to cure. Old age and hardship tend to make people stingy. Most people are more interested in gaining money than giving it. Stinginess comes in many forms and seems to cover many different behaviors.

It has two parts: not giving enough and taking too much. Not all stingy people are the same, though. Some people take too much, while others don't give enough. People we call "miserly" or "stingy" don't give much but don't covet other people's property either. Some of these people hoard money to avoid doing anything shameful in the future. Others avoid taking from others because they know that if they do, others will take from them. So, they prefer to neither give nor take.

There are others who take from any source, like people in shady businesses, pimps, or moneylenders who charge high interest. These people take more than they should and from the wrong places. Their love of gain is their main fault. They'll accept a bad reputation if it means they can make money, even if it's just a little. People who make big gains from wrong sources, like tyrants who rob cities or temples, aren't called stingy—they're called wicked or unjust. But gamblers and thieves are considered stingy because they love gain and endure shame for the sake of money. They're both willing to take from wrong sources, making them greedy.

Meanness is considered the opposite of liberality. It's worse than prodigality, and people are more likely to be stingy than prodigal.

This covers liberality and its opposing vices.

It seems fitting to discuss magnificence next. This also deals with wealth, but it's different from liberality. It doesn't cover all uses of wealth but focuses on spending large amounts. As the name suggests, magnificence involves spending on a grand scale. However, the scale depends on the situation. For example, outfitting a ship is not the same as leading a sacred procession. Magnificence is about spending appropriately for the person and the occasion. A person who spends properly on small or moderate things isn't called magnificent, but the person who spends properly on big things is. A magnificent person is liberal, but a liberal person isn't necessarily magnificent. The lack of magnificence is called stinginess, while the excess is called vulgarity or bad taste. These vices don't involve spending too much on the right things but spending extravagantly on the wrong things. We'll discuss these vices more later.

A magnificent person is like an artist who knows how to spend large amounts in a tasteful way. As we said earlier, a person's character is shown by their actions and their goals. The magnificent person spends large amounts appropriately, and the result is fitting. The result should match the expense, or even surpass it. The magnificent person spends for honor's sake, which is true of all virtues. They will do so gladly and generously because careful calculation is a sign of stinginess. They'll focus on making the result as beautiful as possible, rather than on how cheaply it can be done. The magnificent person must also be liberal. A liberal person spends what they should, but a magnificent person does this on a grander scale, creating something even more impressive. Possessions and works of art aren't valuable in the same way. A possession's value is based on its cost, while a work of art's value comes from its beauty and greatness. Magnificence applies to spending on important and honorable things, like offerings to the gods, temples, or public projects. Magnificent people spend their money to support the city or the people, not for themselves.

A magnificent person will also make their house reflect their wealth because even a house is a public symbol. They prefer to spend on things that last because those are the most beautiful. They spend appropriately on everything. What's right for gods is not the same as what's right for humans, and what's right in a temple is different from what's right in a tomb. Each expenditure has its own greatness. What's most magnificent is spending a large amount on something great, but what's magnificent in one case may be small in another. The magnificent person makes sure everything they create matches the size of the expense.

The person who goes too far and is vulgar spends too much on the wrong things, showing bad taste. They might host a dinner party on the scale of a wedding banquet or use purple robes for a comedy, like they do in Megara. They do these things not for honor but to show off their wealth, thinking they'll be admired. Where they should spend a lot, they spend too little, and where they should spend a little, they spend too much. The stingy person, on the other hand, spends too little on everything. After spending a lot, they'll ruin the result by skimping on a small detail. They always try to spend as little as possible and regret even that.

Both vulgarity and stinginess are vices, but they don't bring as much disgrace because they aren't harmful to others or very shameful.

The goods that come from fortune, such as wealth and power, are also thought to add to a sense of pride. People who are well-born, wealthy, or powerful are considered worthy of honor because they are in a better position than others. When someone has something good that sets them apart, they are usually honored more. This is why people with these advantages tend to be prouder since others honor them for these things. However, in reality, only a truly good person deserves honor. A person who has both virtue and good fortune is seen as even more deserving of honor. But those who have wealth and power without virtue have no right to make great claims or to be called "proud" because true pride requires perfect virtue.

People without virtue often become disdainful and arrogant when they have good fortune. Without virtue, it's hard to handle the advantages of fortune with grace. They look down on others because they think they are better, and they act however they please. These people try to imitate a proud person, but they don't really understand what true pride is. The proud person looks down on others in a just way because they know their true worth, while most people look down on others for no good reason.

A proud person does not rush into small or trivial dangers, nor do they enjoy danger for its own sake, because they value only a few things. But they will face great dangers, and when they do, they won't hesitate to risk their life, knowing that sometimes life isn't worth living under certain conditions. A proud person is the kind who gives help to others but is ashamed of receiving help, because giving is a sign of superiority, while receiving is a sign of inferiority. When they do receive help, they tend to return the favor with even greater kindness, making the original giver feel indebted to them, which allows the proud person to stay in control of the relationship. They also tend to remember the help they have given but not the help they've received because the giver is superior, and the proud person always wants to be in a superior position. This is why Thetis didn't remind Zeus of the help she gave him, and why the Spartans didn't talk about how they helped the Athenians but focused on what they had received.

A proud person also doesn't ask for much from others, if anything, but is quick to give help when needed. They act with dignity toward people who are in high positions or who are fortunate, but they are humble toward people of the middle class. It's difficult to be superior to those in high positions, but easy to be above those in lower positions, and it isn't seen as rude to act superior to the powerful, but it would be rude to act that way toward the weak. A proud person doesn't aim for the things that others value or excel in, and they are often slow to act unless something great and honorable is at stake. They don't do many things, but the things they do are great and worthy of note.

A proud person must also be open about their feelings, whether love or hate. Hiding one's feelings or caring more about what others think than about the truth is seen as cowardly. A proud person speaks and acts openly because they are confident and don't need to hide anything. They tell the truth unless they are using irony to mock those who are beneath them. A proud person won't revolve their life around someone else unless that person is a friend because that would be like being a servant. For this reason, flatterers are seen as having no self-respect, and people who lack self-respect often become flatterers.

A proud person isn't easily impressed because nothing seems great to them. They don't hold onto grudges because that's not what proud people do—they overlook wrongs. They don't gossip, either about themselves or about others, because they don't care to be praised, nor do they care to blame others. Similarly, they aren't in the habit of praising others and don't speak ill of their enemies unless out of a sense of superiority.

When it comes to small or necessary matters, a proud person doesn't complain or beg for favors. This is because they don't take such things too seriously. A proud person would rather have beautiful but useless things than useful and profitable ones because this better fits their self-sufficient character.

A slow and deliberate step, a deep voice, and calm speech are all seen as traits of a proud person. Someone who takes few things seriously won't be in a hurry, and someone who thinks nothing is great won't get easily excited. A shrill voice and fast movements come from being in a rush or getting excited.

This, then, is the proud person. The person who falls short of this is overly humble, and the person who goes too far is vain. However, neither of these types of people is considered bad, just mistaken. An overly humble person denies themselves what they deserve, even if they are worthy of good things, and this shows a lack of self-awareness. If they knew their worth, they would seek out the things they are worthy of since these things are good. These people aren't thought to be foolish but rather too shy. However, this attitude can make them worse because people usually aim for what matches their worth, and these overly humble people avoid noble actions and even good things because they feel unworthy.

On the other hand, vain people are foolish because they don't know themselves. They attempt to do honorable things they aren't capable of, and then they fail. They also like to show off with fancy clothes and outward displays, and they talk about their good fortune as if that will make them more honorable. However, being overly humble is more opposed to pride than vanity because it's both more common and worse.

Pride, then, is concerned with great honor, as we've said. There seems to be another virtue related to honor that is like generosity compared to magnificence. Neither deals with the grand scale, but both guide us to act rightly in smaller matters. Just as there is a balance in giving and receiving wealth, there is a balance in seeking honor. Some people want honor too much or from the wrong sources, while others don't seek honor even for noble reasons. Sometimes we praise the ambitious person as someone who loves what is noble, and other times we praise the unambitious person for being moderate and self-controlled.

It's clear that there is more than one way to be "fond of" honor. When we praise ambition, we are thinking of someone who loves honor more than most people, and when we blame it, we are thinking of someone who loves it too much. Since the balance here doesn't have a name, it seems like the extremes compete to take its place. However, just as people can desire more honor than they should or less than they should, it's also possible to desire the right amount, and this state of character is praised. This balanced state doesn't have a name, but it is still virtuous. It seems unambitious compared to ambition and ambitious compared to being unambitious. This is true of other virtues as well.

Good temper is a balance when it comes to anger. The middle state doesn't have a name, and the extremes don't have clear names either, but we place good temper in the middle, although it leans toward the side of not being angry enough. The excess of anger might be called "irascibility" because the emotion involved is anger, but there are many causes for anger.

A person who gets angry at the right things, with the right people, in the right way, at the right time, and for the right length of time is praised. This is the good-tempered person because good temper is praised. A good-tempered person is calm and doesn't act on their emotions. They get angry only as the situation requires, but they tend to lean more toward being too calm than being too angry. A good-tempered person is not vengeful and tends to be forgiving.

On the other hand, those who don't get angry when they should are blamed. People who don't get angry in the right way or with the right people at the right time are seen as foolish because it seems like they don't care or don't feel pain when they are wronged. Since they don't get angry, they are also seen as unlikely to defend themselves. People who endure insults or allow their friends to be insulted are seen as weak.

The excess of anger can show up in many ways. A person might get angry with the wrong people, at the wrong things, too often, too quickly, or for too long. Not all of these traits show up in the same person because too much anger can destroy itself. Quick-tempered people tend to get angry too fast and with the wrong people or for the wrong reasons, but their anger doesn't last long, which is their best trait. They don't hold back their anger, so they express it quickly and then it's over.

People who are choleric, or quick to anger, get angry at everything and everyone, earning their name. Sulky people are harder to calm down and hold onto their anger for a long time. They don't express their anger right away, so it builds up inside them, and they won't feel better until they get revenge. If they don't, they carry the anger with them because no one knows they are upset, and that takes time to process. These people are difficult for both themselves and their close friends to be around. We call people bad-tempered if they are angry at the wrong things, too much, and for too long, and if they can't be calmed down until they have punished someone.

Good temper is more opposed to the excess of anger than to the lack of it because excessive anger is more common (since revenge is more natural to humans), and bad-tempered people are harder to live with.

It's clear from what we've already said that it's not easy to define exactly how much anger is appropriate, with whom, about what, or for how long. It's hard to say at what point right action becomes wrong. We don't blame someone who strays only a little, either toward too much anger or too little. Sometimes we praise people who seem too calm, calling them good-tempered, and sometimes we praise people who seem too angry, calling them strong and capable of leadership. It's hard to say exactly how far someone can go before they are blamed, and this depends on the situation and requires good judgment. However, it's clear that the middle state is praiseworthy—being angry in the right way, at the right time, with the right people. The extremes are blameworthy, either a little or a lot, depending on how far someone goes. Clearly, the middle state is best.

In social life, some people are seen as too eager to please. These people always agree with others and never cause conflict because they think it's their job to avoid upsetting anyone. On the other hand, people who argue about everything and don't care if they upset others are seen as rude and argumentative. It's clear that both of these extremes are wrong, and the balanced approach is better—where someone is pleasant and helpful, but also stands up for what is right. This middle state doesn't have a name, but it is similar to friendship. The person who holds this middle position is like a good friend, but without the emotional attachment of friendship. This person acts rightly not because they love or hate anyone, but because they are a good person. They act the same way toward both close friends and strangers, though they adjust their behavior to fit each relationship. They don't treat everyone the same but respond to each person appropriately, based on what's right.

This person tries to bring pleasure to others and avoid causing pain when it's honorable and good to do so. But if their actions would bring dishonor or harm to someone, they will choose to cause a little pain instead of agreeing with something wrong. This person will act differently toward those in higher positions and those in lower ones, and they will adjust their behavior depending on the situation.

This balanced person doesn't have a name, but people who are too eager to please are called "obsequious," and those who do it for personal gain, like money, are called "flatterers." People who argue all the time are called "contentious" or "churlish." These extremes seem to be opposites, and the middle state is without a name.

There's also a balance when it comes to boasting. The person who tells the truth about themselves without exaggeration or understatement is in the middle. The boaster, however, claims to have qualities they don't really have or exaggerates what they do have. On the other hand, the overly modest person downplays their qualities or denies them. Both of these extremes are wrong, but the person who tells the truth about themselves is praiseworthy.

Each person acts and speaks according to their character. A truthful person speaks and lives in a straightforward way because of their character, not for some other purpose. Lying is generally seen as bad, and truth is seen as good. Therefore, the truthful person is praised, while both the boaster and the overly modest person are criticized, though the boaster is usually seen as worse.

Now, let's discuss the boaster first. We aren't talking about someone who breaks promises or lies in serious matters—that falls under justice. We're talking about someone who is truthful in everyday life because of their character. This kind of person is seen as fair because they value the truth, and if they avoid lying even when nothing important is at stake, they are likely to be truthful when something important is on the line.

A boaster is seen as someone who claims more than they have, especially when they do it to gain something. The boaster who seeks fame or honor is less blameworthy than the one who does it for money, but both are wrong. A boaster who exaggerates their skills for money, like pretending to be a doctor or fortune-teller, is more blameworthy because they are lying for personal gain.

On the other hand, someone who is overly modest and downplays their good qualities is seen as more likable. This person isn't lying for personal gain but is avoiding showing off. However, if someone downplays their qualities too much, especially things that are obvious, they are seen as deceitful, and this can be a form of boastfulness in disguise.

The person who finds the middle ground—neither exaggerating nor downplaying their qualities—is the one who deserves praise. Both the boaster and the overly modest person are wrong, but the boaster is the worse of the two.

In life, there is also a balance between seriousness and playfulness. Some people are too serious, while others are too eager to joke around. A person who jokes too much and doesn't care if they hurt others is seen as vulgar, while someone who can't take a joke or make one is seen as rude or unapproachable. The person who finds the middle ground is considered witty because they know how to say the right thing at the right time, and their humor is appropriate for the situation.

A well-bred person's jokes are different from those of a vulgar person. You can see this difference in old and new comedies. The old comedies often focused on indecency, while the newer ones rely more on clever humor. This shows the difference between good taste and poor taste.

The person who jokes well does so in a way that is fitting for a well-bred person. They don't seek to hurt others with their humor, and their jokes are enjoyable for the listener. This person will also only make jokes that are appropriate and avoid ones that are mean-spirited.

The person who finds the right balance in humor is praiseworthy. The person who jokes too much and in bad taste is like a buffoon, while the person who can't take a joke is no fun to be around. Relaxation and amusement are important parts of life, but they need to be done in the right way.

So, these middle states in life are three in number, all dealing with how we interact with others in words and actions. They differ in that one is about truth, while the other two are about being pleasant.

Shame, however, is not a virtue. It's more like a feeling than a state of character. Shame is a kind of fear of dishonor, like how people feel fear in the face of danger. For example, people blush when they feel ashamed, just like they turn pale when they are afraid. Both are physical reactions, and this is more characteristic of a feeling than a character trait.

Shame is more appropriate for young people because they live more by their feelings and are more likely to make mistakes. Young people who feel shame are praised because it shows they care about their mistakes. However, we wouldn't praise an older person for feeling shame because we expect them to avoid actions that would make them feel ashamed. A good person doesn't need to feel shame because they don't do bad things, and shame is only felt when someone does something wrong. Feeling ashamed of bad actions doesn't make you a good person. It's better to avoid bad actions altogether.

So, while shame might be a good thing in certain situations, it's not the same as a virtue. A good person won't do anything shameful, so they don't need to feel shame. We'll talk more about continence and other related states later, but for now, let's move on to justice.

Book 5

When talking about justice and injustice, we need to (1) look at what actions they focus on, (2) figure out what kind of balance justice is, and (3) understand what extremes justice lies between. We will follow the same path as we did in previous discussions.

We know that everyone sees justice as a way of thinking that makes people want to do the right thing and act fairly. They also see injustice as a way of thinking that makes people act unfairly and desire what's unfair. Let's start with that. This is different from how we view science and skills. A science or skill can relate to opposite things, but a state of character only leads to one type of result. For example, being healthy means we only do things that are good for our health, like walking in a healthy way.

Often, we understand one thing by comparing it to its opposite, or by looking at the people who show these qualities. For example, (A) if we know what good health is, we can also understand bad health. (B) We know good health from those who are healthy, and vice versa. If good health means firm flesh, then bad health would mean flabby flesh, and something that creates firmness would be considered healthy. If one opposite is unclear, the other usually is too. For example, if the word "just" is unclear, "unjust" will be too.

The terms "justice" and "injustice" can have more than one meaning, but because the meanings are so close, we often don't notice. This is different from words with very different meanings, like how "kleis" can mean a collarbone or the tool to lock a door. Let's look at the different meanings of "an unjust person." We call both the lawbreaker and the greedy, unfair person unjust, so it's clear that both law-abiding and fair people are just. So, the just person is both law-abiding and fair, while the unjust person is both lawless and unfair.

Since the unjust person is greedy, they focus on certain goods— not all goods, but those that affect success or failure. These are always good in general, but they're not always good for a specific person. People often pray for and chase these things, but they should really pray that these things are good for them, and they should choose what is good for them specifically. The unjust person doesn't always choose the bigger thing, but sometimes they choose the smaller, especially when it's something bad. Since the smaller evil is still considered somewhat good, and greed focuses on the good, the unjust person is seen as greedy. They are also unfair, which is true in both cases.

Since the lawbreaker is unjust and the law-abiding person is just, all lawful actions are, in a way, just actions. The laws, set up by legislators, are considered lawful, and we say each of these actions is just. The laws are meant to benefit everyone or the best people or those in power, depending on the case. So, in one sense, we call those actions just that help create and maintain happiness and its parts for the whole community. The law tells us to act bravely, like not running away from danger or giving up our weapons. It also tells us to act with self-control, like not committing adultery or giving in to every desire, and to be good-tempered, like not hitting others or speaking badly of them. The law does this for other virtues and vices too, commanding some actions and forbidding others. A well-made law does this well, while a hastily made law does it less effectively. So, this kind of justice is complete virtue, but not in every sense—only when it comes to how we treat others. That's why justice is often seen as the greatest virtue, and there's a saying that "justice holds all virtues." It's considered complete virtue because it involves practicing all virtues, and it's complete because the person who has it uses it both for themselves and in their interactions with others. Many people can be virtuous in their own lives but not with others. This is why people say, "power reveals the person," because a ruler has to deal with others and be part of a community.

This is also why justice is called "another's good," since it's about treating others well. The worst person is someone who acts badly toward both themselves and their friends, while the best person isn't the one who's only good to themselves, but the one who's good to others. This is harder to do. Justice, in this sense, isn't just part of virtue—it's the whole of virtue, and the same goes for injustice. The difference between virtue and justice is clear from what we've said. They are the same, but their essence isn't the same. Justice is about how we treat others, while virtue is about the kind of person we are.

What we are studying now is justice as a part of virtue because we believe there is a kind of justice like that. The same goes for injustice in the particular way we're looking at it.

There is this kind of justice, and we can see it when we notice that someone can do wrong without being greedy, like throwing away their shield out of cowardice or speaking harshly out of anger. But when someone acts greedily, they are unjust, even if they don't show these other vices. So, there's another kind of injustice that's just part of the wider idea of injustice, which means "against the law." For example, if someone commits adultery for money and gains from it, they are unjust. But if someone does it because of their desires and loses money or gets punished, they are more self-indulgent than unjust. The person who profits from it is unjust but not self-indulgent, showing that greed is linked to injustice.

All other unjust acts are connected to some other vice. Adultery is linked to self-indulgence, leaving a comrade in battle is tied to cowardice, and hitting someone is linked to anger. But when someone gains from their actions, it's not connected to any specific vice except injustice. So, there's another, specific type of injustice, which is part of the broader kind because it shares the same basic idea. Both forms of injustice relate to others, but the specific one is about honor, money, safety, or all three, driven by the pleasure of gaining something. The general kind of justice involves all the things that matter to a good person.

It's clear, then, that there are different kinds of justice, and that one is separate from full virtue. We need to understand its type and differences.

We divided injustice into lawbreaking and unfairness, and justice into law-abiding and fairness. Lawbreaking connects to the broader sense of injustice, but unfairness is different from lawbreaking, like a part is different from the whole. All unfair acts are lawbreaking, but not all lawbreaking acts are unfair. So, injustice in the sense of unfairness is just a part of the wider idea of injustice, and the same goes for justice. This is why we need to talk about specific justice and injustice.

The kind of justice that covers all virtues and the injustice that covers all vices toward others can be set aside for now. We already know how "just" and "unjust" are used in this broad sense. Most of the laws focus on what's virtuous overall. The law tells us to practice every virtue and avoid every vice. Laws that aim to create virtue overall are those made for the common good. But when it comes to making an individual a good person in general, we need to figure out whether that's the role of politics or something else. It may not be the same thing to be a good person and a good citizen in every state.

When it comes to specific justice and what's just in this sense, (A) one type is about dividing things like honor, money, or anything else that people share in a society, where people can get either equal or unequal parts. (B) The other type deals with making things right between people in transactions. These can be divided into two groups: (1) some transactions are voluntary, like buying, selling, lending, and renting, which are voluntary because they start by choice, and (2) some are involuntary, like theft, adultery, poisoning, bribery, and murder. These can be either done in secret or violently, like physical assault or robbery.

(A) We've shown that both unjust people and unjust actions are unfair or unequal. So, it's clear that there's something in between these two extremes, and that's what's equal. In any case where there's a more and a less, there's also something that's equal. If injustice is inequality, then justice is equality, as people generally think. Since equality is in the middle, justice must also be in the middle. Equality means at least two things are being compared, so justice is both about balance and being equal for certain people. Equality is in the middle of greater and less, and it involves two people and the things being compared. If the people are unequal, they won't receive equal shares, and this is what causes conflicts. People argue when equals get unequal shares, or unequals get equal shares. This is clear because rewards should be given based on merit. Everyone agrees that justice in distribution must be based on some type of merit, though people don't all agree on what kind. Democrats say merit is based on being free, oligarchs say it's based on wealth or noble birth, and aristocrats say it's based on excellence.

So, justice is a kind of proportional equality, and proportion applies not just to numbers but to relationships between things. Proportion means the ratios are equal, and it always involves at least four terms. Continuous proportions can involve repeating terms, like saying, "as line A is to line B, so is line B to line C." Here, B is mentioned twice, so there are still four terms. Justice involves at least four terms, where the ratio between one pair is the same as the ratio between the other. As A is to B, so C is to D, and similarly, as A is to C, B is to D. So, the whole is in the same ratio to the whole. This kind of proportion makes distribution fair, and when terms are matched this way, justice is achieved. This fairness is the balance between the extremes, and injustice violates this balance. Mathematicians call this kind of proportion "geometrical" because it keeps the same ratio between parts and the whole.

So, what's just is proportional, and what's unjust breaks that proportion. When someone acts unjustly, they get too much, and the person treated unjustly gets too little of what's good. In the case of bad things, the reverse is true. The person with the lesser evil is considered to have more good because the lesser evil is better to choose than the greater one, and what's worth choosing is good. Therefore, the lesser evil is considered a greater good.

This, then, is one type of justice.

The other type is about correcting wrongs in both voluntary and involuntary dealings between people. This form of justice is different from the kind that deals with sharing common goods. The justice that deals with sharing is always based on a certain proportion (for example, in dividing up the money of a business partnership, it will be based on the amount each partner contributed). The injustice here happens when someone breaks this proportion. But justice in dealings between people is about equality, and injustice is about inequality— not in the same proportion as before, but in equal parts. It doesn't matter if a good person cheats a bad person, or a bad person cheats a good person, or if a good or bad person commits adultery. The law only looks at the wrong that was done and treats both people as equal—if one person is wrong and the other was wronged, if one person caused harm and the other received it. Since this type of injustice creates inequality, the judge's job is to restore equality. For example, if one person was wounded and the other did the wounding, or one person was killed and the other did the killing, the harm and the act are unequal. The judge's role is to equalize this by giving a penalty, taking away from what the wrongdoer gained. Even if the wrongdoer didn't gain in every situation (like wounding someone), we still call the harm "gain" for the wrongdoer and "loss" for the victim. After the judge determines the extent of the harm, one person is seen as having lost, and the other as having gained. Therefore, justice is the middle ground between gain and loss, and justice will correct things so that both sides are equal.

This is why, when people argue, they go to a judge. To go to the judge is to seek justice because a judge is like a living form of justice. People seek the judge as a neutral party, and in some places, they even call judges mediators because they believe that if they get a fair middle ground, they will get justice. So, justice is a middle point, and since the judge aims for fairness, justice is also a middle point. The judge tries to restore equality, like dividing a line into two unequal parts and taking from the longer part to make both sides equal. When the whole is divided equally, then people say they have what is rightfully theirs. The equal part is the middle point between the larger and smaller parts, according to simple mathematical equality.

This is also why justice is called "sikaion" because it means splitting something into two equal parts. It's similar to calling a judge "sikastes," which means a divider or equalizer. When you take something from one equal part and add it to the other, one part ends up being greater than the other by two units; if nothing had been added to the larger part, it would only be bigger by one unit. So, one part exceeds the middle by one unit, and the middle exceeds the smaller part by one unit. This helps us understand how much we must take from the bigger part and how much we must add to the smaller part. We need to add to the smaller part what the middle exceeds it by, and take from the larger part what exceeds the middle.

Let's say the lines AA', BB', and CC' are equal. If we take a segment AE from line AA' and add a segment Cd to line CC', the whole line DCC' will exceed the line EA' by the segments CD and CF, and therefore it also exceeds the line Bb' by the segment CD. (See diagram.)

The terms "loss" and "gain" come from voluntary exchanges, like buying and selling. To have more than your share is called gaining, and to have less is called losing. When people get neither more nor less than their fair share, they say they have what's rightfully theirs, and that they neither lose nor gain.

Justice, then, is the middle point between gaining and losing, specifically in cases that aren't voluntary. Justice is about having the same amount before and after the event.

Some people think that equality in return, or reciprocity, is always just, like the Pythagoreans believed. They defined justice as reciprocity. But reciprocity doesn't always fit either distributive or corrective justice—though people think Rhadamanthus' justice was based on this idea:

"If someone suffers what they caused, justice is done."

However, reciprocity and corrective justice don't always align. For example, (1) if an official has wounded someone, they shouldn't be wounded in return, and if someone wounds an official, they should be punished more than just being wounded. Also, (2) there's a big difference between acts done on purpose and acts done by accident. But in business, reciprocity works—people exchange fairly based on what's agreed. This proportional exchange keeps society together. People try to give back either good for good or bad for bad. If they can't do this, they feel powerless, like slaves. If they can't return good for good, no exchange happens, and without exchange, society can't function. This is why the temple of the Graces is important—it encourages people to give back favors. Grace means helping someone who helped you, and sometimes taking the lead in showing kindness first.

Fair exchange is based on proportion. Let's say A is a builder, B is a shoemaker, C is a house, and D is a shoe. The builder should receive shoes from the shoemaker and give the shoemaker a house in return. First, there must be proportional equality in what's being exchanged, and then the trade happens. If the work of one person is better than the other, the trade isn't equal, and the agreement doesn't hold. This applies to all professions. For example, two doctors don't trade with each other; instead, a doctor trades with a farmer or another person who provides a different service. Their work is different and unequal, so they need to find a way to balance it.

This is why money exists—it acts as a way to compare everything. It's like an intermediate that measures the value of all goods. It allows us to determine how many shoes are worth a house or how much food is worth a house. The number of shoes that trade for a house depends on the value of the builder's work compared to the shoemaker's work. Without money, there would be no exchange, and without exchange, people wouldn't interact. Proportion can't happen unless things are made equal. So, everything has to be measured by something, and that's why money was created.

In truth, it's not easy to make such different things equal, but they can be made equal enough by looking at how much they're needed. Money represents demand, and because of this, it allows things to be compared. That's why it's called "nomisma" (money)—because it exists by law (nomos) and can be changed or made useless if people decide. So, reciprocity happens when the value of the goods is equal—when the shoemaker's work equals the builder's work. We don't compare them after they've been traded, but while they still have their goods. This makes them equal partners. If not for this balance, no trade would happen.

Money ensures people can exchange even if they don't need something right now, by acting as a guarantee for future trade. Even though the value of money can change, it's usually more stable than goods. Because of this, everything needs a price so that trade can always happen. If there's trade, people can work together.

Money, as a measure, makes things equal by allowing them to be compared. Without money, there wouldn't be exchange, and without exchange, people couldn't cooperate. Although it's impossible to make such different things truly equal, they can be made comparable based on demand. Money acts as this comparison because everything is measured by money.

Let's say A is a house, B is ten minae, and C is a bed. If A is worth five minae, the house is half of B. If C is a bed worth one-tenth of B, then it's clear how many beds are worth one house—five. It didn't matter if people exchanged five beds for a house or the value of five beds in money.

Now, we have defined what is just and unjust. It's clear that just action is a middle point between acting unjustly and being treated unjustly. One person gets too much, and the other gets too little. Justice is a balance, but not in the same way as other virtues—it relates to an intermediate amount, while injustice is about the extremes. A just person does what is fair by choice and will share fairly with others, giving neither more good to themselves nor more harm to others. This fairness follows a proportion. Injustice, on the other hand, involves either taking too much or too little of what's good or bad, which leads to imbalance.

Justice helps create equality by making sure everyone gets what they deserve. Injustice causes either excess or lack, and just action is about finding that middle ground.

Acts done out of anger are rightly judged not to be done with evil intent. It's not the person acting in anger who starts the wrongdoing, but the person who made them angry. Also, the argument isn't whether the action happened or not, but whether it was fair. It's the clear unfairness that causes the anger. People don't argue about whether the act occurred, as they might in business disputes where one of the two parties must be dishonest—unless they forgot. But they agree on the fact and argue about who is in the right. A person who deliberately hurts another knows they've done so, so one person believes they were wronged while the other disagrees.

If someone harms another on purpose, they act unjustly. These are the actions of an unjust person if they violate fairness or equality. Likewise, someone is just when they act fairly by choice, but they act fairly if they simply act voluntarily.

Some involuntary actions are excusable, and others are not. Mistakes that people make because they don't know any better or due to ignorance are excusable. However, mistakes made not because of ignorance, but because of an unnatural or uncontrollable passion, are not excusable.

Since we have defined what it means to suffer and do injustice, we can now ask if Euripides' strange words hold any truth:

"I killed my mother, that's my story in short.
Were you both willing, or both unwilling?"

Is it really possible to be treated unjustly on purpose, or is suffering injustice always the opposite—something involuntary—just as doing injustice is voluntary? Is suffering injustice always involuntary, or can it be voluntary at times? The same question can be asked for being treated fairly: all fair actions are voluntary, so it seems reasonable that both being treated unfairly and being treated fairly could be either voluntary or involuntary. But it seems strange, even in the case of being treated fairly, that it could always be voluntary, since some people are treated fairly against their will.

Another question we might ask is whether everyone who suffers something unjust is being treated unjustly, or if it's like taking action. In both doing and receiving, it's possible to experience justice or injustice by accident. Doing something unjust isn't the same as acting unjustly, just as suffering something unjust isn't the same as being treated unjustly. The same is true for acting justly and being treated fairly. It's impossible to be treated unjustly if the other person isn't acting unjustly, or to be treated fairly if they aren't acting fairly.

Now, if acting unjustly means deliberately harming someone, and 'deliberately' means knowing the person you're acting on, the tool you're using, and how you're doing it, then someone who harms themselves because they lack self-control does it voluntarily. This means they can also be treated unjustly on purpose, which raises the question of whether someone can treat themselves unjustly. A person may harm themselves on purpose due to a lack of self-control while being harmed by someone else who also acts deliberately, so it's possible to be treated unjustly on purpose.

Or perhaps our definition is wrong. Should we add to 'harming another on purpose' the idea that it must also be 'against the will of the person being harmed'? In that case, a person may be harmed on purpose and suffer an unjust act on purpose, but no one is treated unjustly on purpose, because no one wants to be treated unjustly—not even the person who lacks self-control. They act against their own will since no one wants what they don't think is good, even though the person without self-control does things they believe they shouldn't.

Also, a person who gives away their possessions, like how Homer says Glaucus gave Diomede "armor of gold for bronze, worth a hundred oxen for nine," is not treated unjustly. Though giving is within his power, being treated unjustly isn't, because someone else must treat him unjustly. So, it's clear that being treated unjustly is not something done willingly.

Two questions still remain: whether it's the person who gives someone more than their share who acts unjustly, or the person who gets too much, and whether it's possible to treat yourself unjustly. These questions are connected. If the first case is true—that the one who distributes unfairly is unjust but not the person who receives too much—then if a person gives another more than they give themselves, knowing and choosing to do so, they treat themselves unjustly. This is what modest people seem to do, since the virtuous person tends to take less than their share. Or is this view too simple? Maybe they receive more of some other good, like honor or dignity. We can solve this by applying the same rule we use for unjust action: the person isn't treated unjustly if it's what they wanted, so they don't suffer injustice, though they may suffer harm.

It's clear that the one who distributes unfairly acts unjustly, but not always the person who gets too much. Injustice belongs to the person who deliberately acts unfairly, not the one who receives the unfair share. The responsibility lies with the person who makes the decision, and in this case, that's the distributor, not the recipient. Also, the word 'act' has different meanings: lifeless objects, a hand, or a servant carrying out an order can be said to 'kill,' but it's not really them acting unjustly, even though they carry out an unjust action.

If the distributor made their judgment in ignorance, they don't act unjustly according to the law, and their decision isn't legally unjust, though it may be unjust in another sense (since legal justice and natural justice are different). But if the distributor knowingly makes an unfair judgment, they are trying to get something extra, either gratitude or revenge. In this case, they get too much, just like if they had taken part of the spoils. It doesn't matter if what they get is different from what they distribute; for example, if they give out land but aim to receive money from it.

People think that it's easy to act unjustly, and so being just must be easy too. But it's not. It's easy to sleep with someone else's wife, hurt someone, or take a bribe. But doing these things as part of a bad character is neither easy nor within everyone's control. Similarly, people think it takes no great wisdom to know what's just and unjust, because understanding the laws isn't hard. But how actions should be done and goods divided fairly—that's harder to know than what's good for health. Even though knowing that honey, wine, or medicine can help is easy, knowing how, to whom, and when to use them requires the skill of a doctor.

For this reason, people think that being unjust can come as easily to a just person as it does to an unjust one. The just person would be even better at unjust actions because they know what to do. For example, they could sleep with someone or harm their neighbor, and the brave person could throw away their shield and run from danger. But to act cowardly or unjustly isn't just doing those things—it's doing them because of a bad character, just as being a doctor doesn't mean simply using or not using a knife, but knowing how to heal in the right way.

Just actions occur between people who share good things and can have too much or too little of them. Some beings, like the gods, can't have too much of them, and to others, like those who are beyond help, not even a little share is good—it harms them. But to others, these goods are helpful up to a certain point, so justice is a human concept.

Next, we'll talk about fairness and what it means to be fair. Fairness and justice seem to be neither entirely the same nor completely different. We sometimes praise fairness and fair people, so we use the term to praise other virtues as well. But when we think about it, it seems strange that fairness could be different from justice yet still praiseworthy. If they are different, then either justice or fairness can't be good. If both are good, they must be the same.

These thoughts give rise to questions about fairness. All of them are somewhat correct and not in opposition. Fairness is better than one type of justice, but it's still a kind of justice. Fairness isn't different in kind, just better in a certain way. The same thing can be just and fair, and while both are good, fairness is better. The reason we face this problem is that fairness corrects legal justice. All laws are general, but sometimes it's impossible to make a general law fit every case. The law takes the most common case, knowing that it won't always be right. This isn't the fault of the law or the lawmaker—it's because of the nature of human affairs. So, when the law speaks in general terms, but a specific case doesn't fit, fairness comes in to correct the mistake. Fairness allows us to make the decision that the lawmaker would have made if they were present and knew the situation.

Fairness is better than this kind of justice, though not better than justice in an absolute sense. It corrects errors that arise from the general nature of the law. This is why not everything can be decided by law—sometimes we need to make exceptions. Laws are like the flexible lead rulers used to make molds, which bend to fit the stone rather than staying rigid. In the same way, judgments are made to fit the facts.

It's clear now what fairness is and that it's a kind of justice, but better in certain ways. It's also clear who the fair person is—the one who chooses and acts fairly, not insisting on their rights to an extreme but often taking less than their share even when the law is on their side. This quality is fairness, which is a kind of justice, not a separate virtue.

Whether a person can treat themselves unjustly is clear from what we've said. One type of just actions is those based on virtue that are required by law. For example, the law doesn't allow suicide, and what it doesn't allow, it forbids. A person who harms another on purpose breaks the law and acts unjustly, knowing both the person they harm and the tool they use. So, if someone stabs themselves in anger, it goes against the right way to live, and the law doesn't permit it. They act unjustly, but toward whom? Surely toward the state, not themselves. They suffer willingly, but no one is treated unjustly willingly. This is why the state punishes suicide—because it's considered unjust to the state.

Also, in the sense of acting unjustly where a person acts unjustly but isn't completely bad, it's not possible to treat oneself unjustly. This is different from the first sense. The unjust person in this case is bad in a particular way, like a coward, not bad in every way. Their unjust action doesn't show full wickedness. In this case, it would mean that the same thing could be both added to and taken from the same person at the same time, which is impossible—justice and injustice always involve more than one person.

Additionally, unjust actions are voluntary and chosen. But if a person harms themselves, they are both the one suffering and the one causing the suffering at the same time. So, it's impossible to treat yourself unjustly. Besides, no one commits injustice without specific actions, and no one can commit adultery with their own spouse or steal from their own house.

The question of whether a person can treat themselves unjustly is solved in the same way as the question of whether a person can be treated unjustly willingly.

It's clear that both suffering injustice and acting unjustly are bad. One means getting less than the fair amount, and the other means getting more, similar to how health is the goal in medicine. But acting unjustly is worse, because it involves vice and deserves blame. Vice is either complete and absolute or close to it, though not every voluntary unjust action shows full injustice as a character trait. Being treated unjustly doesn't involve vice in oneself. In itself, being treated unjustly is less bad, but it can sometimes lead to a worse outcome. Theory doesn't care about that—it calls pleurisy a worse illness than a small injury, though the injury could become worse if it leads to being captured or killed.

Metaphorically, there is a kind of justice between a person and themselves, though not in the strict sense. It's like the justice between a master and servant or husband and wife. These relationships show how the rational part of the soul relates to the irrational part. People believe that a person can be unjust to themselves because these parts of the soul can conflict. This leads people to think there is a kind of justice between the parts of a person, like between ruler and ruled.

This is our account of justice and the other moral virtues.

Book 6

Since we have previously said that one should choose what is in the middle, not the extreme of too much or too little, and that this middle point is decided by the correct rule, let's discuss what these correct rules are. In all the states of character we have mentioned, as well as in other areas, there is a goal the person with the right rule aims for, and they either increase or decrease their actions to hit that goal. There is a standard that defines these middle points, which we call the balance between too much and too little, and this standard follows the right rule. But even though this statement is true, it's not very clear. It's like when we say in other areas of knowledge that we should not do too much or too little, but act in a balanced way as the right rule dictates. If someone only knew that, they wouldn't be much wiser, just as we wouldn't know what kind of medicine to use if someone only told us, "use what the medical art prescribes, as practiced by those who know it." That's why, when it comes to the soul, it's necessary not only to make the true statement but also to understand what the right rule is and what standard sets it.

We divided the virtues of the soul into two kinds: those related to character and those related to intellect. Now that we've talked in detail about moral virtues, let's talk about the others, starting with some comments about the soul. We said before that the soul has two parts: one part follows rules or reason, and the other part is irrational. Let's now make another distinction within the part that follows reason. There are two parts here as well: one part thinks about things that don't change, and the other thinks about things that can change. Since the things they focus on are different, the parts of the soul that deal with them must also be different. The part that deals with what doesn't change can be called the scientific part, and the part that deals with what can change can be called the calculating part. This is because calculating and reasoning are the same thing, and we never calculate about things that don't change. So, the calculating part is a part of the soul that deals with rational principles.

Next, we need to understand what the best state of these two parts is, as that will be their virtue. The virtue of anything is related to its proper function. In the soul, three things control action and truth: sensation, reason, and desire.

Sensation doesn't start any actions. This is clear because animals can sense things but don't take actions the way humans do. In the same way that thinking can affirm or deny something, desire can lead to pursuit or avoidance. Since moral virtue is about choosing, and choice is thoughtful desire, both the reasoning must be correct and the desire must be right for the choice to be good. The desire should go after what the reasoning points to. This kind of thinking and truth is practical. For the thinking that is contemplative (not practical or productive), the good state is truth, and the bad state is falsehood. But in the part that is both practical and rational, the good state is when truth and right desire work together.

The source of action (not its goal) is choice, and choice comes from desire and reasoning toward a goal. This is why choice can't exist without reason and intellect or without a moral state. Good and bad actions need both intellect and character to happen. But intellect by itself doesn't cause anything to happen. Only the kind of intellect that has a goal and is practical leads to action. This kind of intellect even controls the intellect that produces things because anyone who makes something does it for a goal. The thing they make isn't the ultimate goal, but good action is. So, choice is either reason driven by desire or desire driven by reason, and this leads to action. This is why humans act. (It's important to note that nothing in the past can be chosen. No one chooses to have destroyed Troy, for example, because we don't deliberate about the past, only about the future, which can still change. As Agathon said:

"Even God cannot change what is done.")

The work of both intellectual parts is truth. Therefore, the best state for each part is the one that leads to truth, and that is their virtue.

Let's start from the beginning and talk about these states again. The ways the soul holds on to truth through affirmation or denial are five in number: art, scientific knowledge, practical wisdom, philosophical wisdom, and intuitive reason. We don't include judgment and opinion because they can be wrong.

Now, what exactly is scientific knowledge? If we are going to be precise and not just rely on similarities, we say that scientific knowledge is knowing something that cannot be otherwise. For things that could be different, we don't know whether they exist once they are out of our sight. Scientific knowledge deals with things that must be as they are, and therefore, it deals with things that are eternal. Things that are necessary are all eternal, and eternal things don't have a beginning or an end. Science is also thought to be teachable, and its object is something that can be learned. All teaching comes from what is already known, as we explain in Analytics. Teaching can happen either by induction or by syllogism. Induction starts from specifics and leads to a general understanding, and syllogism starts from general truths. The starting points of syllogisms are not proven by more syllogisms; they are learned through induction. So, scientific knowledge is a state where we can prove things, and it has the other characteristics that we explain in Analytics. Scientific knowledge occurs when a person believes something in the right way and knows the starting points of their argument. Otherwise, they only know things incidentally.

Let this be our explanation of scientific knowledge.

Both things that are made and things that are done are part of the variable. Making and acting are different. We can trust even the discussions outside of our own school on this. The capacity to act and the capacity to make are also different. Therefore, making isn't the same as acting, and acting isn't the same as making. Architecture, for example, is an art and is essentially the capacity to make something. Art is the ability to make, based on a correct understanding of how to do it. All art deals with creating something—figuring out how something can come into being that might or might not exist. The origin of this creation lies in the maker, not the thing being made. Art isn't about things that exist by necessity or nature, as those things originate from themselves. Since making and acting are different, art is about making, not acting.

In some way, both chance and art deal with the same objects. As Agathon said, "art loves chance, and chance loves art." Art, then, is the ability to make something by following correct reasoning, while lack of art is the opposite—it involves incorrect reasoning. Both art and chance deal with things that can vary.

Now let's talk about practical wisdom. We can understand what it is by considering who we think has it. A person with practical wisdom is able to think well about what is good and beneficial for themselves, not just in one specific area like health or strength, but in terms of living a good life overall. We also give credit to people who have practical wisdom in a specific area when they can figure out the best way to reach a good goal that is not the object of any art. So, in the general sense, a person who can deliberate well has practical wisdom. No one deliberates about things that don't change or about things they can't control. Since scientific knowledge involves proving things, and there's no proof of things that change (since they could be otherwise), practical wisdom can't be scientific knowledge or art. It's not science because the things we can do might be otherwise, and it's not art because making and acting are different. Practical wisdom must be the ability to act well concerning what is good or bad for humans. Making has an end beyond itself, but action is an end in itself. That's why we say people like Pericles had practical wisdom—because they could see what was good for themselves and for others in general. We consider those who are good at managing households or states to have this wisdom. (This is also why we call temperance "sophrosune," which means it preserves practical wisdom. It helps preserve the kind of judgment we've described. Not all judgments are ruined by pleasure and pain—only those about what should be done. The starting point for actions lies in the goal they aim for. But someone who is corrupted by pleasure or pain can no longer see why they should choose certain actions. Vice destroys the cause of action.)

So, practical wisdom is the ability to act well concerning human goods. While there is excellence in art, there is no such thing as excellence in practical wisdom. In art, a person who makes mistakes on purpose is better than one who makes mistakes by accident, but in practical wisdom, the opposite is true, just as it is with the virtues. Practical wisdom is a virtue, not an art. There are two parts of the soul that can reason, and practical wisdom is the virtue of the part that forms opinions. Opinion is about things that can change, and so is practical wisdom. But practical wisdom isn't just reasoning. This is shown by the fact that reasoning can be forgotten, but practical wisdom cannot be.

Scientific knowledge is about things that are universal and necessary, and it deals with what can be proven. All scientific knowledge comes from first principles, but the first principles themselves cannot be the objects of science, art, or practical wisdom. Scientific knowledge deals with things that can be demonstrated, and art and practical wisdom deal with things that can change. First principles also can't be the objects of philosophical wisdom because philosophers need to prove things about them. So, if the mental states that give us truth are scientific knowledge, practical wisdom, philosophical wisdom, and intuitive reason, and first principles aren't objects of the first three, then it must be intuitive reason that grasps them.

Wisdom has two meanings. In the arts, we call people wise when they are highly skilled, like Phidias in sculpture or Polyclitus in making statues. Here, wisdom simply means excellence in art. But we also think some people are wise in general, not just in one specific area. As Homer says in Margites:

"The gods made him neither a digger nor a ploughman,
Nor wise in anything else."

So, wisdom must be the highest form of knowledge. The wise person must know not only what follows from first principles but also the first principles themselves. Wisdom must be intuitive reason combined with scientific knowledge of the highest things, which is as complete as it can get.

We're talking about the highest things because it would be strange to think that politics or practical wisdom is the best kind of knowledge since humans aren't the best things in the universe. If what is healthy or good is different for humans and fish, but what is white or straight is always the same, we can say that what is wise is the same for all but practical wisdom differs. It applies to those things that are concerned with themselves. That's why we say that some animals have practical wisdom when they can take care of their own lives. It's also clear that philosophical wisdom and politics are not the same. If philosophical wisdom were about a person's own interests, there would be many different kinds of philosophical wisdom, just as there are many different kinds of medicine, one for each kind of being.

But if someone argues that humans are the best of animals, this doesn't change the point. There are other things that are much more divine than humans, such as the heavenly bodies. So, philosophical wisdom is scientific knowledge combined with intuitive reason about the highest things in nature. That's why we say that people like Anaxagoras and Thales had philosophical wisdom, even though they were often ignorant of what was good for themselves. They knew remarkable, admirable, difficult, and divine things, but they were useless because they didn't focus on human goods.

Practical wisdom, on the other hand, is concerned with human things and things that can be deliberated about. We say that practical wisdom involves deliberating well, but no one deliberates about things that can't change or that don't have an end goal. The person who is good at deliberating is the one who can aim at the best outcome for humans, based on reason, from the things that can be done. Practical wisdom isn't just about general truths; it must also deal with specific details. Practice deals with specific things. That's why someone with experience may be more practical than someone with theoretical knowledge. For example, a person may know that light foods are easy to digest, but if they don't know what kinds of food are light, they can't create a healthy diet. However, someone who knows that chicken is light food will be better at creating a healthy diet.

Practical wisdom is about action, so we should have both general and specific knowledge, or at least specific knowledge. But even within practical wisdom and philosophical wisdom, there are different kinds of control.

Political wisdom and practical wisdom are the same kind of state of mind, but their essence is different. The practical wisdom involved in managing a city includes legislative wisdom, which is concerned with creating laws, while the political wisdom that deals with specific actions is known simply as 'political wisdom.' This kind of wisdom deals with actions and decisions since laws are meant to guide individual actions. This is why people involved in this art are said to 'participate in politics,' just as manual workers are said to 'do things.'

Practical wisdom is mostly identified with the type that deals with a person's own life, and this is generally called 'practical wisdom.' Other types include household management, legislation, and politics. Politics can be divided into two parts: deliberative and judicial. Knowing what is good for oneself is one kind of knowledge, but it is very different from other types. The person who knows and focuses on their own interests is considered to have practical wisdom, while politicians are often seen as meddling in other people's affairs. This is reflected in the words of Euripides:

"How could I be wise, when I could have had
An equal share among the soldiers,
Instead of aiming too high and doing too much?"

People who think this way believe that one should look out for their own good, and they think this is the right thing to do. This belief is where the idea that such people have practical wisdom comes from. But maybe one's own good can't exist without household management or some form of government. Additionally, knowing how to manage your own affairs isn't easy and requires investigation.

What has been said is supported by the fact that while young people can become experts in geometry, mathematics, and other similar subjects, it's believed that a young person cannot have practical wisdom. The reason is that practical wisdom deals not only with general ideas but also with specific situations, which come from experience. A young person doesn't have experience because experience comes with time. We might also wonder why a boy can become a mathematician but not a philosopher or a physicist. It's because the things studied in mathematics exist in theory, while the first principles of philosophy and physics come from experience. Young people don't have firm beliefs about these first principles; they only know the words. But the nature of mathematical objects is clear to them.

Additionally, mistakes in deliberation can be about either general principles or specific details. For example, someone might not know that all water that weighs heavy is harmful, or they might not realize that this specific water weighs heavy.

It's clear that practical wisdom is not the same as scientific knowledge. Practical wisdom, as we've said, is about specific facts because the things to be done are specific in nature. It is different from intuitive reason. Intuitive reason deals with general starting points, which can't be explained, while practical wisdom focuses on specific facts. These facts aren't known through scientific knowledge but through perception—a perception similar to how we recognize that a certain shape is a triangle. In this way, there is a limit, just as there is with general rules. But this kind of perception is closer to practical wisdom, though it's different from the perception that involves the senses.

There's a difference between inquiry and deliberation. Deliberation is a specific kind of inquiry. We need to understand what excellence in deliberation is and whether it's a form of scientific knowledge, opinion, skill in guessing, or something else. It isn't scientific knowledge because people don't inquire about things they already know. But good deliberation involves inquiring and thinking carefully. It also isn't a skill in guessing because guessing doesn't involve reasoning and happens quickly, while people take time to deliberate. We say that people should act quickly once they've finished deliberating but should deliberate slowly. Quick thinking is different from excellence in deliberation because it's more like guessing. Excellence in deliberation also isn't the same as opinion. But since someone who deliberates badly makes mistakes, while someone who deliberates well does so correctly, excellence in deliberation must involve correctness. This correctness is different from knowledge or opinion. There's no such thing as correct knowledge (since knowledge doesn't include error), and correctness of opinion is the same as truth. At the same time, everything that is a matter of opinion is already decided. Excellence in deliberation involves reasoning. The only option left is that it's the correctness of thinking. Opinion is not the same as inquiry because it has already reached a conclusion, while someone who is deliberating is still searching and calculating.

Excellence in deliberation means being correct in deliberation. So, we need to first understand what deliberation is and what it deals with. Since there are different kinds of correctness, it's clear that excellence in deliberation is not just any kind of correctness. For example, a person without self-control or a bad person, if they are clever, may achieve their goal through deliberation. But they will have ended up with something harmful. To deliberate well is considered a good thing because it means being correct in achieving good ends. However, (1) it's possible to reach something good through incorrect reasoning, by using false premises. This means that even if someone achieves the right result, they didn't reach it in the right way, so this isn't excellence in deliberation. (2) It's also possible to achieve a result after long deliberation, while someone else might reach it more quickly. In the first case, we don't yet have excellence in deliberation, which is about being correct in terms of the goal, the method, and the timing. (3) Additionally, it's possible to deliberate well either in a general sense or about a specific goal. Excellence in deliberation in the general sense is when someone achieves a goal that is good in general, while excellence in deliberation in a specific sense is when someone succeeds in reaching a particular goal. (4) If it's true that people with practical wisdom are good at deliberating, then excellence in deliberation will be about correctly determining what leads to the goals that practical wisdom recognizes.

Understanding and goodness of understanding, which make people known as having good judgment, are not exactly the same as opinion or scientific knowledge. If they were, everyone would have good understanding. Nor are they part of specific sciences like medicine or geometry. Understanding isn't about things that are always true and unchangeable, nor is it about everything that comes into existence. It deals with things that can be questioned and deliberated about. So, it deals with the same objects as practical wisdom. But understanding and practical wisdom aren't the same. Practical wisdom leads to decisions, as its goal is to determine what should or shouldn't be done. Understanding, on the other hand, only makes judgments. Understanding and good understanding are the same thing. Having understanding isn't the same as having or gaining practical wisdom. Just as learning is called understanding when it's the use of knowledge, understanding is about using opinion to judge what others say about matters related to practical wisdom—and doing so correctly. The term 'understanding' has come from the ability to grasp scientific truth, and we often use it to describe that ability.

Judgment, which makes people known as having good judgment or as sympathetic judges, is the ability to correctly recognize what is fair. This is shown by the fact that we say the fair person is also a person of good judgment. Fairness is closely related to good judgment in certain matters, and judgment is about correctly recognizing what is fair. Correct judgment is the ability to recognize what is true.

All the states we've discussed seem to come together. When we talk about judgment, understanding, practical wisdom, and intuitive reason, we give credit to the same people for having these qualities. We say that they have reached an age of wisdom and possess practical wisdom and understanding. All these qualities deal with specifics, or what we might call ultimate things. Being a person of understanding and good judgment means being able to make decisions about the matters that practical wisdom deals with. What is fair is something that all good people recognize in their dealings with others. Everything we need to do in life involves specifics or ultimate things. People with practical wisdom must know specific details, and understanding and judgment are also about things that need to be done. These are ultimate things. Intuitive reason deals with ultimate things in both directions. It deals with both the first principles and the last conclusions. The intuitive reason that we use in demonstrations grasps the first, unchangeable principles, while the intuitive reason we use in practical matters grasps the final, changeable fact, or the minor premise. These variable facts are the starting points for reaching a goal, and we understand universals by looking at specifics. So, we must have a perception of these facts, and this perception is intuitive reason.

This is why these qualities are thought to be natural abilities. No one is considered a natural philosopher, but people are thought to have natural judgment, understanding, and intuitive reason. We believe these qualities come with age, and a person's natural development brings with it judgment and intuitive reason. This suggests that these qualities come from nature. Intuitive reason is both the starting point and the end. Demonstrations are based on intuitive reason and are about intuitive reason.

This is why we should listen to the sayings and opinions of experienced and older people, as well as people with practical wisdom. Their experience has given them insight, and they see things clearly.

We've now explained what practical and philosophical wisdom are and what they deal with. We've also said that each is a virtue of a different part of the soul.

We might wonder about the usefulness of these mental qualities. (1) Philosophical wisdom doesn't seem to deal with anything that makes a person happy, since it isn't concerned with things that come into being. Practical wisdom, on the other hand, does deal with things that make a person happy. But why do we need it? Practical wisdom deals with things that are just, noble, and good for humans. These are the things a good person does, but knowing about them doesn't make us better at doing them. Just as knowing what is healthy doesn't make us better at creating health (since health comes from the state of the body, not from the art of medicine), knowing what is just doesn't necessarily help us act justly. (2) If we say that a person should have practical wisdom to help them become good, practical wisdom is still useless for people who are already good. It's also useless for people who don't have virtue because it doesn't matter whether they have practical wisdom or follow the advice of someone who does. In the same way, we want to be healthy, but we don't need to learn the art of medicine to become healthy. (3) It also seems strange that practical wisdom, which is inferior to philosophical wisdom, would be in charge of it. This seems to be implied by the fact that the art that produces something also controls and commands it.

These are the questions we need to consider. So far, we've only mentioned the difficulties.

(1) First, we should say that these mental states are worth choosing for their own sake, even if they don't produce anything, because they are the virtues of the two parts of the soul.

(2) Secondly, these states do produce something, but not in the same way that the art of medicine produces health. Philosophical wisdom produces happiness, not by making something, but by existing and being used. Since it's part of virtue as a whole, possessing and using philosophical wisdom makes a person happy.

(3) Additionally, a person can only achieve their purpose through both practical wisdom and moral virtue. Virtue helps us aim at the right goals, and practical wisdom helps us find the right way to achieve them. (The fourth part of the soul—the part that deals with nutrition—doesn't have a virtue like this because it doesn't have control over what it does.)

(4) As for the idea that practical wisdom doesn't help us do what is noble and just, let's start by discussing something else. We've said that some people do just actions without being truly just. This includes people who follow the laws but do so unwillingly, out of ignorance, or for reasons other than the actions themselves. Even though they do the right things, they don't do them because they are good. To be truly good, a person must be in the right state when they act—they must choose to do good and do it for its own sake. Virtue helps us make the right choices, but knowing what to do to carry out those choices belongs to another ability.

We need to pay attention to this and explain it more clearly. There is an ability called cleverness, which helps people achieve the goals they aim for. When the goal is good, cleverness is praiseworthy, but when the goal is bad, cleverness is just smartness. This is why we call people with practical wisdom clever or smart. Practical wisdom isn't the same as cleverness, but it can't exist without it. This insight into practical matters doesn't develop without the help of virtue. This is because the reasoning behind actions starts with an understanding of what is good, but only good people can fully understand this.

Wickedness leads us astray and makes us misunderstand the starting points for action.

It's clear that it's impossible to have practical wisdom without being good.

We must now consider virtue again. Virtue is related to cleverness in the same way that practical wisdom is related to cleverness. They aren't the same, but they are similar. Natural virtue is like cleverness, while virtue in the full sense is like practical wisdom. People believe that certain character traits are natural. From the moment we are born, we might naturally be just, self-controlled, or brave, or have other moral qualities. But we still look for something else—something better. Both children and animals have these natural traits, but without reason, these traits can be harmful. It's like a strong body that moves without sight—it can fall badly because it can't see. But once reason is added, everything changes. The person still has the same natural traits, but now they are true virtues in the full sense.

In the part of us that forms opinions, there are two kinds of qualities: cleverness and practical wisdom. Similarly, in the moral part of us, there are two types of virtues: natural virtue and true virtue, and true virtue involves practical wisdom. This is why some people say that all virtues are forms of practical wisdom. Socrates was partly right and partly wrong. He was wrong to think that all virtues were forms of practical wisdom, but he was right to say that virtues include practical wisdom. This is supported by the fact that when people define virtue, they say it's a state of character and then add that it follows the right rule. The right rule is the one that follows practical wisdom. So, people seem to sense that true virtue is the kind that follows practical wisdom.

But we need to go a little further. Virtue isn't just the state that follows the right rule—it's the state that involves the right rule. Practical wisdom is the right rule about these matters. Socrates thought that virtues were rules or principles because he believed they were all forms of knowledge. We, however, believe that virtues involve a rational principle.

It's clear from what has been said that it's not possible to truly be good without practical wisdom, and you can't have practical wisdom without moral virtue. This also disproves the argument that the virtues can exist separately from each other. Some might argue that a person is not naturally equipped for all virtues, so they might have one virtue but not yet have developed another. This can happen with natural virtues, but not with the kind of virtues that make a person fully good. When a person has practical wisdom, they will have all the virtues. Even if practical wisdom didn't have any practical use, we would still need it because it is the virtue of this part of ourselves. It's also clear that we can't make the right choices without practical wisdom any more than we can without virtue. One helps us determine the right goal, and the other helps us do the things that lead to that goal.

However, practical wisdom isn't higher than philosophical wisdom, which is the higher part of us. It's like how medicine isn't above health—it doesn't use health but helps bring it about. Practical wisdom gives instructions for the sake of philosophical wisdom, but it doesn't command it. Saying practical wisdom is higher than philosophical wisdom would be like saying that politics rules the gods just because it gives orders about the state's affairs.

Book 7

Let's start fresh and explain that there are three kinds of bad character traits to avoid: vice, lack of self-control, and being brutish. There are opposites to two of these traits. One is called virtue, and the other is self-control. As for being brutish, the opposite would be a kind of superhuman virtue, something heroic and almost divine. Homer shows this when Priam says about Hector that he was so good:

"For he didn't seem like the child of a mortal man but as if he was born from a god."

So, if people say that humans can become like gods by having an excess of virtue, then the state of being godlike must be the opposite of being brutish. This is because, just like a brute doesn't have vice or virtue, a god doesn't either. A god's state is higher than virtue, and a brute's state is different from vice.

Now, since it's rare to find a godlike person—using a term from the Spartans, who called someone 'godlike' when they admired them greatly—it's also rare to find a brutish person among humans. You mainly find them among barbarians, though some people develop brutish qualities because of disease or deformity. We also call people who are extremely wicked 'brutish.' We'll talk more about this type of character later. While we've already discussed vice, now we need to talk about lack of self-control and weakness (or softness), as well as self-control and endurance. We need to look at these as neither exactly the same as virtue or wickedness nor as a completely different category. As always, we should look at the facts and, after addressing the difficulties, try to prove that most of the common ideas about these traits are true—or at least the majority of them and the most trustworthy ones. If we can refute objections and leave the common beliefs untouched, we will have proven our case well enough.

Both self-control and endurance are seen as good and praiseworthy, while lack of self-control and softness are seen as bad and blameworthy. The same person can be considered either self-controlled and sticking to their decisions or lacking self-control and abandoning them. A person who lacks self-control knows what they're doing is wrong but gives in to passion, while a self-controlled person knows their desires are wrong but refuses to follow them because of their reasoning. Everyone calls a person with self-control and endurance 'temperate.' Some think that a person with self-control is always temperate, while others disagree. Some also use the terms 'self-indulgent' and 'lacking self-control' interchangeably, while others make a distinction between the two. Some say that a person with practical wisdom cannot lack self-control, while others claim that even some practically wise and clever people can lack self-control. People also say that someone can lack self-control not just with physical desires but also with anger, the desire for honor, and the desire for profit. These are the things people say.

Now we can ask how someone who makes the right judgment can still lack self-control. Some say it's impossible for someone to act this way when they have knowledge because, as Socrates thought, it would be strange if knowledge could be overpowered and controlled like a slave. Socrates completely disagreed with the idea of lack of self-control. He believed there was no such thing because he said that no one acts against what they believe is best—they only do wrong because of ignorance. But this view clearly goes against what we observe, so we must investigate what happens with such a person. If they act out of ignorance, how exactly are they ignorant? It's clear that the person who lacks self-control doesn't think, before they give in, that they should act this way. But some people agree with some of Socrates' points but not all of them. They accept that knowledge is stronger than anything else, but they don't think that someone acts against what they think is best. Instead, they say that the person who lacks self-control doesn't have knowledge when they're overpowered by their desires; they only have an opinion.

But if it's just an opinion and not true knowledge, if it's not a firm conviction but a weak one, like someone who hesitates, we can understand why they fail to stick to it against strong desires. However, we don't feel the same way about wickedness or other bad states. So, is it practical wisdom that's overpowered? That would be the strongest state of all, but that idea doesn't make sense. It would mean that the same person could be both practically wise and lack self-control, but no one would say that a practically wise person would willingly do the worst things. Besides, we've already shown that a practically wise person is someone who acts (because they're concerned with real-world situations) and has all the other virtues.

Furthermore, if self-control means having strong, bad desires, then a temperate person can't be self-controlled, and a self-controlled person can't be temperate. This is because a temperate person wouldn't have bad or excessive desires, but a self-controlled person must have them. If the desires are good, then the state of resisting them would be bad, so not all forms of self-control would be good. If the desires are weak and not bad, there's nothing impressive about resisting them, and if they're weak and bad, there's still nothing great about resisting them.

Additionally, if self-control means sticking to every opinion, then it would be a bad thing, especially if it means sticking to false opinions. And if lack of self-control means abandoning every opinion, then there could be a good form of lack of self-control, like in Sophocles' play "Philoctetes," where Neoptolemus is praised for not sticking to the plan Odysseus convinced him to follow because he was upset about telling a lie.

Moreover, there's a problem with certain clever arguments. These arguments are designed to create paradoxes in an opponent's viewpoint to make the person who proves the paradox seem clever. But these arguments can confuse us. For example, one argument might suggest that foolishness combined with lack of self-control could be a kind of virtue. The reasoning is that a person who lacks self-control acts against what they believe is right, but they wrongly believe that something good is bad and that they shouldn't do it. So, as a result, they end up doing the good thing and avoiding the bad one.

Further, a person who chooses to pursue what is pleasant through careful thought might seem better than someone who does it out of lack of self-control. The first person is easier to correct because they might be persuaded to change their mind. But with a person who lacks self-control, we might say, "When water chokes you, what do you wash it down with?" If they had been persuaded that what they were doing was right, they would have stopped when they were persuaded to change their mind. But now, they act even though they've been persuaded to do something different.

Finally, if lack of self-control and self-control apply to everything, then who exactly is lacking self-control in the general sense? No one seems to lack control in every way, yet we still call some people lacking self-control without qualification. These are the kinds of difficulties we face. Some of these points must be disproven, while others should be accepted, as solving these difficulties is the key to finding the truth.

We should first ask if people who lack self-control act knowingly or not, and in what way they act knowingly. Then, we should ask what kinds of things the self-controlled and the uncontrollable person are concerned with—whether they deal with all pleasures and pains or just certain ones. We should also ask if self-control and endurance are the same thing or different, and we should approach the other relevant questions similarly. Our starting point is whether a person is self-controlled or lacking self-control because of the specific things they desire or because of their attitude toward them, or perhaps because of both. The next question is whether lack of self-control and self-control apply to every type of thing or just some. A person who lacks self-control in the general sense doesn't apply this to every object. They are mostly concerned with the same things as a self-indulgent person, but they differ in how they approach them. One person is led by their choices, thinking they should always pursue immediate pleasure, while the other person doesn't think so but still pursues it.

As for the idea that it's opinion and not knowledge that people act against when they lack self-control, that doesn't make a difference. Some people have firm opinions and don't hesitate but feel as if they know for sure. If the idea is that people with opinion are more likely to act against their judgment because their convictions are weaker, we can respond that there's not much difference between knowledge and opinion in this respect. Some people are just as convinced of their opinions as others are of their knowledge. This is shown by the views of Heraclitus. But since we use the word 'know' in two ways—for a person who has knowledge but isn't using it and for a person who is using it—it makes a difference whether someone has knowledge but isn't exercising it or is exercising it when they act wrongly. The latter case seems strange, but not the former.

Also, since there are two kinds of premises, a person can have both premises but still act against their knowledge, provided they are only using the universal premise and not the particular one. This is because particular actions are what must be done. There are also two types of universal terms: one applies to the person acting, and the other applies to the object. For example, "dry food is good for everyone" and "I am a person," or "this food is dry." But whether the person knows "this food is such and such," the person who lacks self-control either doesn't have that knowledge or isn't using it. So there's a big difference between these types of knowledge, and knowing in one way but acting incontinently wouldn't seem strange, while knowing in the other way would be extraordinary.

There's also a way that people can have knowledge without using it, which is like when someone is asleep, mad, or drunk. This is similar to the state of people under the influence of their desires. It's obvious that anger, sexual desire, and other such passions can change our bodily condition and can even make some people act mad. So, we can say that people who lack self-control are like people who are asleep, mad, or drunk. The fact that they use language based on knowledge doesn't prove anything. Even people under these passions can recite scientific proofs or poetry by Empedocles. Those who have just started learning something can repeat the words but don't yet fully understand it. They haven't made the knowledge part of themselves, and that takes time. So we should think that when people in a state of lack of self-control use language, it's no different from an actor reciting lines on a stage.

We can also think about the cause by considering human nature. One opinion is universal, and the other is about particular facts. When both opinions are combined, the soul must accept the conclusion. In cases of practical decisions, the person must immediately act. For example, if "everything sweet should be tasted" and "this is sweet," the person who can act and isn't prevented must immediately act. When the universal opinion is present and tells the person not to taste, but the opinion that "everything sweet is pleasant" and "this is sweet" is active, and when appetite is also present, one opinion tells the person to avoid the sweet thing, but appetite leads them toward it. This is why a person acts against self-control, not because of a contrary opinion but because of appetite. This also explains why animals don't lack self-control—they don't have universal judgments but only imagination and memory of particular things.

The explanation for how ignorance is removed and the person who lacks self-control regains knowledge is the same as for someone who is drunk or asleep. This is something for natural scientists to explain. Since the last premise is about a particular object and it leads to action, the person in a state of passion either doesn't have this knowledge or has it in the sense that knowing doesn't mean fully understanding, like a drunken person reciting the lines of a poem. And because this final term is not universal and isn't an object of scientific knowledge like the universal term, it seems that Socrates was right in saying that true incontinence doesn't arise in the presence of proper knowledge. The problem lies in perceptual knowledge, not in true knowledge.

This is enough to answer the question of how people can act with or without knowledge and how it's possible to act incontinently even when they have knowledge.

We should now discuss whether some people are generally lacking in self-control or whether all of them are lacking in a particular sense, and if so, what kinds of things they are concerned with. It's clear that both people with self-control and people who lack it, as well as people with endurance and those who are soft, are concerned with pleasures and pains.

Some pleasures come from things that are necessary, while others are desirable for their own sake but can be excessive. The bodily pleasures are necessary, such as those related to food and sexual desire. These are the same physical pleasures we mentioned earlier when talking about temperance and self-indulgence. The other pleasures aren't necessary but are still desirable, like victory, honor, wealth, and other good and enjoyable things. So, people who go to excess with these latter pleasures, going against what they know is right, aren't called lacking self-control without qualification. Instead, we say they lack self-control "with respect to money, gain, honor, or anger," because they are different from those who lack self-control in general, and we call them this way because of their resemblance to those who do.

For example, Anthropos (Man) won a contest at the Olympic Games. While the general definition of 'man' didn't differ much from his specific case, it was still different. We can see this because incontinence in general or in relation to physical pleasure is blamed as both a fault and a vice, but no one blames the people who lack control in other respects like that.

As for those who lack self-control with respect to bodily pleasures, which are the same pleasures that temperance and self-indulgence are concerned with, the person who pursues too much pleasure and avoids pain—whether it's hunger, thirst, heat, cold, or other physical sensations—against their better judgment and without choice is called lacking self-control, not with a specific qualification like "with respect to anger," but simply lacking self-control. This is confirmed by the fact that we call people 'soft' with regard to these pleasures, but not with regard to any of the others. That's why we group together the person lacking self-control with the self-indulgent person, and the self-controlled person with the temperate one, but we don't do this with other types of people. This is because they are all concerned with the same pleasures and pains, though they don't respond to them in the same way. Some people make deliberate choices, while others don't.

This is why we should call someone self-indulgent if they seek too much pleasure without having much appetite, or avoid moderate pain, rather than someone who does this because of strong desires. What would the first person do if they also had strong desires and suffered greatly from missing the "necessary" things?

Now, some desires and pleasures are connected to things that are generally good and noble. Some pleasant things are naturally worth choosing, while others are the opposite, and some fall in between, like wealth, profit, victory, and honor. People aren't blamed for being drawn to these things, for desiring or loving them, but for wanting them in the wrong way—that is, for going to excess. This is why people who go against what's right and either are controlled by or pursue one of the naturally noble and good things, like honor or love for children and parents, aren't considered bad. These things are good, and people who focus on them are praised. But there can still be excess, like in the case of Niobe who fought against the gods, or someone as devoted to their father as Satyrus, nicknamed "the filial," who was considered silly for it. So, there's no wickedness connected to these things because they are naturally worth choosing for their own sake. But still, excess is harmful and should be avoided. Similarly, there's no incontinence with these things, because incontinence is not just something to avoid, it's also something blameworthy. But because the feeling is similar, people use the term "incontinence" and add what it refers to, just like we call someone a bad doctor or actor without saying they're completely bad. In the same way, we don't call it incontinence without a qualifier, because these conditions aren't entirely bad, but only like badness. So, it's clear that true incontinence and continence are connected with the same things as temperance and self-indulgence. We use the word incontinence with anger because of the similarity, and this is why we say "incontinent in respect of anger," just like we say "incontinent in respect of honor or gain."

Some things are naturally pleasant. Of these, some are pleasant without exception, while others are pleasant only to specific types of people or animals. There are other things that aren't naturally pleasant, but (1) some become pleasant because of damage to the body, (2) some because of habits, and (3) some because of bad natures. Given this, we can find similar traits in these types of people, like we do in the first type. These are the brutish traits, like in the case of the woman who, they say, rips open pregnant women and eats the babies, or the things that savage tribes near the Black Sea are said to enjoy—like raw meat or human flesh, or even lending their children to each other to eat. Or there's the story of Phalaris.

These traits are brutish, but others come from disease or sometimes madness, like the man who sacrificed and ate his mother, or the slave who ate the liver of his companion. Other cases are bad habits, like pulling out one's hair, biting nails, or even eating coal or dirt, and also pederasty. These can be caused by nature in some people, and in others, they develop as bad habits from childhood.

People whose nature causes them to act this way aren't considered incontinent, just like we don't call women incontinent because they take the passive role in sex. Nor do we call those who act this way because of bad habits incontinent. These habits go beyond vice, just like brutishness does. A man with these habits doesn't experience normal continence or incontinence, but something that's only similar. A man with this problem in regard to anger is called incontinent in anger, but not simply incontinent. All extreme states—whether of foolishness, cowardice, self-indulgence, or bad temper—are either brutish or caused by disease. A man who's naturally afraid of everything, even the squeak of a mouse, is brutish in his cowardice, while a man who feared a weasel did so because of illness. In the case of foolish people, those who are naturally thoughtless and live by their senses are brutish, like some remote barbarian tribes, while others are foolish because of disease (like epilepsy) or madness. Some of these traits only show up sometimes, and people aren't always controlled by them. For example, Phalaris might have resisted the urge to eat a child or avoided unnatural sexual urges. But it's also possible for people to be controlled by these feelings, not just to have them. Just like human wickedness is called wickedness, but not simply wickedness—it's called brutish or diseased. In the same way, some types of incontinence are brutish or diseased, but only the type connected to human self-indulgence is simply incontinence.

It's clear, then, that incontinence and continence are connected to the same things as self-indulgence and temperance. Incontinence related to other things is a different type of incontinence, called incontinence only by metaphor and not in the true sense. Also, incontinence related to anger is less shameful than incontinence related to desires, as we'll now explain. Anger seems to listen to reason in some way, but it mishears it, like hasty servants who run off before they've heard everything, and then mess up the instructions, or like dogs that bark just because they hear a knock, without checking to see if it's a friend. Anger, because it's hot and quick, hears but doesn't really understand an order, and it rushes to take revenge. Reason or imagination tells us that we've been insulted, and anger, reasoning that such things should be resisted, boils up immediately. On the other hand, desire jumps to enjoy something when reason or perception only says that it's pleasant. So, anger follows reason in a way, but desire doesn't. That's why incontinence connected to desires is more shameful, because someone who's incontinent in anger is in some way defeated by reason, while someone controlled by desire is defeated by appetite and not by reason.

Also, we forgive people more easily for following natural desires, because we forgive them more easily for following common desires that everyone has, as long as they aren't excessive. Anger and bad temper are more natural than desires for excessive, unnecessary things. For example, there's the man who defended hitting his father by saying, "Yes, but he hit his father, and he hit his," (pointing to his child) "this boy will hit me when he's grown up; it's a family tradition." Or the man who, when being dragged along by his son, asked him to stop at the doorway, because he himself had only dragged his father that far.

Also, those who plot against others are more blameworthy. An angry person doesn't usually plot, and neither does anger itself—it's open. But the nature of desire is like what the poets say about Aphrodite, the "cunning daughter of Cyprus," or Homer's description of her "embroidered girdle":

"And in it is the whisper of seduction,
which steals the wits of the wisest,
however sensible they are."

If this type of incontinence is worse than the type related to anger, then it's both incontinence in the strict sense and, in a way, vice.

Also, no one commits an act of violence because of anger without feeling pain, but everyone who acts violently because of anger feels pain, while someone who acts violently for pleasure does it with enjoyment. If acts done out of anger are the most justifiable, then incontinence driven by desire is worse because there's no justice in violent acts driven by desire.

It's clear, then, that incontinence connected to desire is more shameful than incontinence connected to anger, and continence and incontinence are tied to bodily desires and pleasures. But we need to understand the differences among these pleasures. As we said earlier, some are human and natural in both kind and amount, while others are brutish or result from illness and disease. Temperance and self-indulgence are only concerned with the first type of pleasure. That's why we don't call animals temperate or self-indulgent, except metaphorically, and only if one species of animal is more wanton, destructive, or greedy than another. Animals can't choose or plan; they're simply deviations from the norm, like how madmen deviate from normal humans. Brute behavior is less evil than vice, even though it's scarier, because there's no better part to corrupt in animals as there is in humans. Comparing a lifeless object to a living one in terms of badness is like comparing injustice itself to an unjust person. Both are bad, but a bad person will do far more evil than a brute.

When it comes to pleasures, pains, desires, and dislikes that arise from touch and taste, which temperance and self-indulgence are mostly concerned with, people can either be defeated by even the easiest of these, or they can resist the hardest ones. When it comes to pleasures, incontinence and continence are the relevant traits, while when it comes to pain, softness and endurance are the terms. Most people fall somewhere in the middle, though they often lean toward the worse traits.

Since some pleasures are necessary while others aren't, and since the necessary ones are only necessary to a point, but excesses of them aren't, the person who seeks out too many pleasures or pursues necessary things to an extreme, and does this by choice, for their own sake and not for some other result, is self-indulgent. This person is unlikely to regret their actions and is therefore incurable, because someone who can't regret their actions can't be fixed. The person who doesn't pursue them enough is the opposite of self-indulgent. The person who is in the middle is temperate. Similarly, there's a person who avoids physical pain, not because they're overwhelmed by it, but because they choose to. (Some people are drawn to certain acts because of the pleasure involved, others because they want to avoid the pain that comes from the desire for pleasure, so these types of people are different.) Now, we'd think worse of someone with no desire, or weak desires, if they did something disgraceful than we would if someone did it under the influence of strong desire. We'd also think worse of someone who hit someone else, not in anger, than if they did it out of anger. For what would they have done if they had been strongly affected? This is why the self-indulgent person is worse than the incontinent one. Of these states, softness is a kind of weakness, and self-indulgence is the opposite. The incontinent person is opposed by the continent one, while the soft person is opposed by the person of endurance. Endurance means resisting, while continence means conquering, and resisting and conquering are different, just like not being defeated is different from winning. This is why continence is better than endurance. A person who fails to resist things most people can handle is soft and effeminate. Effeminacy is also a type of softness. This kind of person drags their cloak to avoid the pain of lifting it, and pretends to be sick without thinking they're miserable, though the person they're imitating really is miserable.

The same goes for continence and incontinence. If someone is defeated by violent and overwhelming pleasures or pains, it's not surprising. We're even willing to forgive them if they tried to resist, like Theodectes' Philoctetes when bitten by a snake, or Carcinus' Cercyon in the Alope, or like people who try not to laugh but burst out in laughter anyway, like what happened to Xenophantus. But it's surprising when someone is defeated by, and can't resist, pleasures or pains that most people can handle, when it's not due to heredity or illness, like the softness that runs in the Scythian kings, or the softness that's more common in women than in men.

The person who loves amusement is thought to be self-indulgent, but is really soft. Amusement is a form of rest, since it's a break from work, and the person who loves amusement is one of those who go to excess with it.

There are two types of incontinence: impulsiveness and weakness. Some people, after deciding what's right, fail to stick to their decision because of their emotions. Others, because they don't deliberate at all, are led by their emotions. Some people, like those who first tickle others but don't get tickled themselves, if they've already seen what's coming and have stirred up their rational mind, aren't defeated by their emotions, whether the emotion is pleasant or painful. It's quick and excitable people who suffer the most from impulsive incontinence. Quick people, because they're so fast, and excitable people, because their passions are so strong, don't wait for reasoning to catch up, because they tend to follow their imagination.

The self-indulgent person, as we've said, is unlikely to regret their actions, because they stick to their choices. But the incontinent person is more likely to regret. This is why, contrary to how we initially framed the issue, the self-indulgent person is incurable, while the incontinent person can be cured. Wickedness is like a disease, like dropsy or tuberculosis, while incontinence is like epilepsy. Wickedness is a lasting problem, while incontinence comes and goes. In general, incontinence and vice are different in nature. Vice doesn't realize its own nature, but incontinence does. Of incontinent people, those who temporarily lose control are better than those who have reason but fail to follow it. The latter are defeated by weaker emotions and don't act without thinking first, unlike the former. The incontinent person is like someone who gets drunk easily and quickly on a small amount of wine, less than what most people would need.

It's clear, then, that incontinence isn't the same as vice (though in some cases it might be). Incontinence goes against choice, while vice aligns with choice. However, both lead to similar actions. As Demodocus said of the Milesians, "The Milesians aren't without sense, but they do senseless things." Similarly, incontinent people aren't criminals, but they do criminal acts.

Since the incontinent person tends to pursue excessive bodily pleasures against their better judgment, while the self-indulgent person pursues them because that's just who they are, it's easier to persuade the incontinent person to change, while it's harder to change the self-indulgent person. Virtue and vice either preserve or destroy the first principle, and in actions, the final cause is the first principle, just like in math the hypotheses are the first principles. In neither case does reasoning teach the first principles. Here, it's virtue, either natural or developed by habit, that teaches the right opinion about the first principle. A temperate person is like this. The opposite is the self-indulgent person.

But there's a person who is driven by passion and acts against the right rule. Their passion controls them so they don't follow the right rule, but it doesn't control them to the point where they believe they should pursue such pleasures without limit. This is the incontinent person, who is better than the self-indulgent person and not entirely bad, because the best part of them, the first principle, is still intact. Opposite to them is the person who sticks to their beliefs and isn't swayed by passion. From these points, it's clear that the latter state is good, and the former is bad.

Is someone continent if they stick to any rule or choice, or if they stick to the right rule? Is someone incontinent if they abandon any rule or choice, or if they abandon the right rule and the correct choice? We raised this question earlier. Or is it true that people only incidentally stick to any rule or choice, but in reality, they stick to the true rule and right choice, and abandon what is wrong? If someone chooses this for the sake of that, they're really choosing the latter, but only incidentally the former. When we speak without any qualification, we mean what is true in itself. Therefore, in a sense, the continent person sticks to any opinion, and the incontinent person abandons any opinion, but without qualification, the continent person sticks to the true opinion.

Some people are very stubborn and stick to their own opinions. We call these people "strong-headed." These people are hard to convince at first, and even after that, they don't easily change their minds. They are similar to people who have self-control, just like a person who wastes money is somewhat like a generous person, and a reckless person is a little like someone who is brave. But there are many differences between them. The strong-headed person doesn't give in to their feelings or desires, while someone with self-control might be convinced sometimes. The strong-headed person refuses to listen to reason. They still have desires, and many of them are led by their pleasures. These stubborn people are usually opinionated, ignorant, or rude, and their opinions are influenced by feelings of happiness or sadness. They feel proud if they don't change their minds, like they've won something, but they feel disappointed when their decisions are rejected, much like how sometimes a law can lose its power. In this way, they are more like people who can't control themselves than those who can.

However, some people don't stick to their decisions, not because they lack self-control, but for other reasons, like Neoptolemus in Sophocles' play Philoctetes. He changed his mind not because of shameful pleasure, but because of a good reason—he thought telling the truth was the right thing to do, even though Odysseus had convinced him to lie. So, not everyone who changes for pleasure is self-indulgent or bad; only those who do it for shameful reasons are.

There are also people who enjoy physical things less than they should and don't follow the proper path. A person who is somewhere between this kind of person and one who lacks self-control is a person with self-control. The person without self-control breaks the rules because they enjoy physical things too much, while the other breaks the rules by not enjoying them enough. The person with self-control, however, follows the rules and doesn't let either extreme affect them. Since self-control is good, both of these opposite states must be bad, as they usually seem to be. But because the other extreme is less common, we often think that self-control is only the opposite of self-indulgence, just as temperance is the opposite of self-indulgence.

Since many words are used similarly, we also use the word "self-control" to describe both a person with self-control and a temperate person. Both of these types of people don't do anything against the rules because of physical pleasures. The person with self-control still has bad desires but doesn't act on them, while the temperate person doesn't feel any pleasure that goes against the rules. The self-indulgent person and the person without self-control are similar, too. Both pursue physical pleasures, but the self-indulgent person believes they should, while the person without self-control does not.

A person cannot be wise and lack self-control at the same time. A person who has wisdom is also good in terms of character. A wise person not only knows what is right but can also act on it, while the person without self-control cannot. However, it's possible for a clever person to lack self-control. This is why some people mistakenly believe a clever person is wise, even if they lack self-control.

Cleverness and wisdom are similar in how they think, but they are different in their purpose. The person without self-control is not like someone who fully understands the truth but more like someone who is asleep or drunk. They act willingly in some way, knowing what they are doing and why, but they are not evil because their purpose is still good. In this way, they are only halfway to being bad. They are not criminals because they don't act out of malice. Of the two types of people without self-control, one type can't stick to their decisions after thinking things through, and the other doesn't think things through at all. So, a person without self-control is like a city that has good laws but doesn't follow them, like in Anaxandrides' joke, "The city made a law but doesn't care about laws." The wicked person is like a city that follows its laws, but those laws are bad.

Self-control and the lack of it deal with extremes compared to what is normal for most people. The person with self-control sticks to their decisions more than most people, and the person without self-control sticks to them less than most people can.

Among the types of people without self-control, those who act quickly are easier to fix than those who think things through but fail to follow their own decisions. People who lack self-control because of habit are easier to change than those who are naturally this way because it's easier to change a habit than to change one's nature. Even though habits are hard to break because they become like nature, as the poet Evenus says:

"I say that habit is just long practice, my friend, And it becomes people's nature in the end."

We have now explained what self-control, lack of self-control, endurance, and softness are, and how these states are connected to one another.

The study of pleasure and pain belongs to the political philosopher because it helps us understand what is good and bad in the purest sense. It's important to examine these things because we said that virtue and vice are tied to pleasures and pains. Most people also say that happiness includes pleasure, which is why we call happy people "blessed," using a word that suggests enjoyment.

Some people think that no pleasure is a good thing in itself, while others think that some pleasures are good, but most are bad. A third view is that even if all pleasures are good, the best thing in the world is not pleasure. The arguments for these views include: (1) Every pleasure is a process toward a natural state, and no process is the same as its result, like how building a house is not the same as the house itself. (2) A temperate person avoids pleasure. (3) A wise person seeks freedom from pain, not pleasure. (4) Pleasures get in the way of thinking, especially intense pleasures like sexual pleasure. (5) There is no art of pleasure, and all good things come from some kind of art. (6) Both children and animals seek pleasure.

The arguments for the idea that not all pleasures are good include: (1) Some pleasures are shameful, and (2) Some pleasures are harmful to health. Finally, the argument that the best thing isn't pleasure is based on the idea that pleasure is a process, not an end result.

These are the main points of these arguments. But these reasons don't necessarily prove that pleasure isn't a good thing, or even the best thing. First, good things can be good in different ways—some are simply good, while others are good for certain people. In the same way, natural states and the actions that come from them can be divided this way, too. Some things that seem bad might only be bad for some people or for a short time, but not bad in general. Others only seem like pleasures, but they actually involve pain and are just healing processes, like what happens to sick people.

Also, there are two types of good things: activities and states of being. The processes that restore us to our natural state are only pleasant by accident. The pleasure comes from the part of our nature that isn't damaged. Some pleasures, like those from contemplation, don't involve pain or desire at all. This shows that the other pleasures are only accidental because people don't enjoy the same things when they are healthy as when they are recovering. When they're recovering, they enjoy even things that are sharp or bitter, which aren't naturally pleasant.

It's also wrong to say that pleasure is always a process. Pleasures are more like activities that come from a natural state. Some people confuse pleasure with process because they think activities are processes, but they are not.

The argument that some pleasures are bad because they can harm your health is like saying that health is bad because some healthy things are bad for making money. Both are bad in certain ways, but not bad overall. Even thinking can sometimes harm your health.

Pleasures that come from the activity of practical wisdom don't get in the way, but foreign pleasures do. For example, the pleasures of learning and thinking help us do those activities better.

The fact that there is no art of pleasure is because there is no art for any other activity either—just for the ability to do them. But people think that the arts of cooking and perfume-making are arts of pleasure.

The arguments that temperate people avoid pleasure and that wise people seek a painless life, and that animals and children seek pleasure, are all answered in the same way. We've already pointed out in what way pleasures are good or not. Both animals and children seek the wrong kind of pleasures, the ones that involve desire and pain—bodily pleasures. Wise people seek calmness and freedom from these desires. That's why temperate people avoid bodily pleasures, though they still have pleasures of their own.

It's also widely agreed that pain is bad and something we should avoid. Some pain is bad without question, and other kinds of pain are bad because they get in the way of our lives. The opposite of something bad is good, so pleasure must also be good. Speusippus' argument that pleasure is opposed to both pain and good things, like how more is opposed to less and equal, doesn't work because he wouldn't say that pleasure is a kind of evil.

Even if some pleasures are bad, that doesn't mean the highest good can't be a pleasure. Just like how the highest good can be a kind of knowledge, even though some kinds of knowledge are bad. If happiness is the unimpeded activity of our natural state, and activities are pleasant, then the highest good might well be a pleasure. This is why all people think the happy life is also a pleasant one. No activity is perfect when it is blocked, and happiness is the most perfect state. That's why the happy person needs physical and external goods, not because happiness depends on them, but to avoid being hindered. People who say a person being tortured on the rack can still be happy because they are good are mistaken.

We need external things to be happy, which is why some people think good fortune is the same as happiness. But it isn't. Even good fortune, when it goes too far, can get in the way, and then it's no longer good fortune. Happiness has a limit when it comes to external things.

Finally, the fact that all animals and people pursue pleasure suggests that pleasure is somehow the highest good. Even though not everyone seeks the same pleasures, and not all pleasures are good, everyone still seeks pleasure because it is part of our nature. Bodily pleasures are common and shared by all, which is why people think they are the only pleasures.

It's also clear that if pleasure is not good, the happy person wouldn't need it. But if pleasure isn't a good, then pain can't be bad either, and the good person's life wouldn't be any more pleasant than anyone else's life. If their activities aren't more pleasant, why would they avoid pain?

Regarding bodily pleasures, some people think noble pleasures should be chosen but not bodily ones, like those the self-indulgent person pursues. But why, then, are the opposite of these pains considered bad? Necessary pleasures are good, even if not as good as noble ones, because their opposite, pain, is bad.

We also need to explain why bodily pleasures seem more desirable than they really are. First, it's because they relieve pain. People experience so much pain that they seek extreme bodily pleasure to get rid of it. Relief from pain makes these pleasures seem better than they are. Also, some pleasures come from a bad nature or bad habits, like those of animals or bad people. Others are meant to cure a problem, but being healthy is better than getting healthy. These pleasures only seem good because they are part of a healing process.

Second, some people pursue intense pleasures because they can't enjoy anything else. They create artificial desires, like thirst, just to satisfy them. When these desires aren't harmful, it's okay, but when they are harmful, it's bad. These people can't enjoy the more subtle pleasures because their nature is restless. Young people and those with a lot of energy are always in need of release. Their bodies are always uncomfortable because of their unique makeup, and they are driven by strong desires. This is why they seek intense pleasures and become self-indulgent. But pleasures that don't come with pain can't be excessive. These are the natural pleasures that are good on their own, not by accident.

When we talk about things that are pleasant by accident, we mean those that act as cures. We think these processes are pleasant because they help fix something that is wrong in our nature. Natural pleasures, on the other hand, are those that stimulate healthy parts of our nature.

There isn't one thing that is always pleasant because our nature isn't simple. We have another part to us since we are mortal creatures. So, if one part of us is doing something, it can feel unnatural to the other part of our nature. When both parts are balanced, what we do doesn't feel either painful or pleasant. If our nature were simple, the same action would always be the most enjoyable. This is why God experiences a single and simple pleasure all the time. There's not only an activity of movement but also an activity of stillness, and pleasure is found more in rest than in movement. But, as the poet says, "change in all things is sweet," and this is because of some kind of flaw. Just like how a flawed person is always changing, a nature that constantly needs change is flawed because it's not simple or good.

We've now talked about continence and incontinence, and about pleasure and pain—what each of these is and how some of them are good and others are bad. What's left is to discuss friendship.

Book 8

After everything we've discussed, it makes sense to now talk about friendship, because it is either a virtue or involves virtue, and it is essential for living well. No one would want to live without friends, even if they had all other good things in life. Even rich people and those with power are thought to need friends the most. What good is success without people to help and share it with, especially with friends, who deserve it the most? How can success be maintained without friends to protect it? The more success someone has, the more they are at risk of losing it. In times of poverty and misfortune, people feel that friends are their only source of comfort. Friendship helps young people avoid mistakes, and it supports older people by taking care of their needs and helping with the things they can't do because of weakness. Friendship also inspires people in their prime to do great things—"two people working together." With friends, people are better at both thinking and acting. Parents naturally feel friendship for their children, and children for their parents. This is true not just for humans but also for birds and most animals. People of the same race also feel friendship for each other, especially among humans, which is why we praise those who love humanity. We even notice this when we travel and see how every person seems to be connected to others. Friendship also seems to be what holds communities together, and lawmakers seem to value friendship even more than justice. Unity is something like friendship, and lawmakers strive for this, while removing division as their greatest enemy. When people are friends, they don't need justice, but when they are just, they still need friendship. The highest form of justice is thought to be something like friendship.

Friendship is not only necessary, but also noble. We praise those who love their friends, and it is considered a good thing to have many friends. We also believe that good people are the same people who make good friends.

There is much debate about friendship. Some say that friendship is based on similarity, and that similar people become friends. This is where sayings like "like attracts like" and "birds of a feather flock together" come from. Others, however, say, "two of a trade never agree." People have also asked deeper questions about this, like Euripides' saying that "dry land loves rain, and the sky filled with rain loves to fall to earth," or Heraclitus' idea that "what is opposite helps" and "the best harmony comes from different notes" and "all things are born from conflict." Empedocles, along with others, says the opposite: "like attracts like." These are physical questions that we can leave for now because they aren't part of this discussion. Let's focus on the human aspects, like whether friendship can form between any two people, or whether wicked people can be friends. Is there only one type of friendship, or are there different kinds? Those who believe there is only one kind of friendship say this because they think friendship can vary in degree. But even things that are different in kind can vary in degree. We've already discussed this point before.

The kinds of friendship may become clearer if we first understand what it is that people love. Not everything is loved—only what is lovable. The lovable is something that is good, pleasant, or useful. Something useful is what brings about some good or pleasure. So, the good and the useful are loved as ends. Do people love the good itself, or what is good for them? These things sometimes conflict. The same goes for what is pleasant. It's believed that each person loves what is good for themselves, and that what is good is lovable in general, but what is good for each person is lovable for them specifically. But each person doesn't love what is truly good for them, but what seems good to them. This difference doesn't matter much, though; we just have to say that "the lovable" is "what seems lovable."

There are three main reasons why people love something. We don't call the love of non-living things friendship, because it's not mutual love, and we don't wish good things for the non-living object itself. For example, it would be silly to say you wish wine well; if you wish anything for it, it's that it stays good so you can enjoy it. But for a friend, we should wish what is good for them for their sake. If someone wishes good for another person, but the feeling isn't returned, we call this goodwill, not friendship. Goodwill becomes friendship only when the feeling is returned and recognized. Many people feel goodwill toward those they've never met but believe to be good or useful. If this feeling is returned, they seem to have goodwill for each other, but we can't really call them friends if they don't know how the other person feels. To be friends, people must recognize that they both have goodwill and wish good for each other for one of the reasons mentioned.

These reasons are different from each other, and so are the types of love and friendship that come from them. There are three kinds of friendship, based on the three things that are lovable. For each of these, there is mutual and recognized love, and those who love each other wish each other well for the reason they love one another. People who love each other for their usefulness don't love each other for who they are, but for the good they get from each other. The same goes for those who love for pleasure—they don't love someone for their character but because they find them enjoyable. So, people who love for usefulness love for what is good for themselves, and those who love for pleasure love for what is pleasant to themselves. They don't love the person for who they are, but for how they are useful or enjoyable. These types of friendships are only based on circumstances. The loved person isn't loved for who they are, but for providing some good or pleasure. These friendships end easily if the person is no longer pleasant or useful.

What is useful doesn't last, and it always changes. When the reason for the friendship disappears, so does the friendship, because it only existed for a particular purpose. This kind of friendship is most common among older people, because at that age, people look for what is useful, not what is pleasant. Younger people, or those in their prime, seek friendships based on utility, too. These people don't spend much time together because they don't always enjoy each other's company. They only need each other when they are useful. They only find each other pleasant when they expect to get something good in the future. Friendships between host and guest also fall into this category.

Friendships between young people, on the other hand, seem to be based on pleasure. Young people live by their emotions and mostly chase what is pleasant to themselves at the moment. But as they grow older, their pleasures change. This is why young people become friends quickly and lose friendships just as fast. Their friendship changes with whatever they find enjoyable, and their pleasures change quickly. Young people also fall in love easily because most of their romantic friendships are based on emotions and the pursuit of pleasure. This is why they fall in love quickly and fall out of love just as fast, sometimes in a single day. But these people do want to spend their days and lives together, because this is how they fulfill the purpose of their friendship.

Perfect friendship is the friendship between good people who are alike in virtue. These friends wish well to each other because they are good, and they are good people themselves. People who wish well to their friends for their friends' sake are the truest friends. They do this because of who they are, not because of any outside factor. So, their friendship lasts as long as they are good—and goodness is something that lasts. These friends are good in general and good to each other, because good people are both good overall and useful to each other. They are also pleasant to each other because good people are pleasant in general and pleasant to each other. Each person finds their own activities and those of similar people enjoyable, and the actions of good people are either the same or similar. Such a friendship is permanent because it has all the qualities that friendship should have. All friendship is based on the desire for something good or pleasant— whether that good or pleasure is abstract or something the friend enjoys—and is based on a certain similarity. In the case of good people, all the qualities of friendship we've discussed belong to them because of who they are. For this kind of friendship, the other qualities are similar in both friends, and what is good without qualification is also pleasant without qualification. These are the most lovable qualities. Love and friendship, then, are found most often and in their best form between good people.

It is natural for such friendships to be rare because people like this are hard to find. Also, this kind of friendship takes time and familiarity to form. As the saying goes, people can't know each other until they've "eaten salt together." They can't become friends or be friends until each has been found lovable and trustworthy. Those who quickly show signs of friendship may want to be friends, but they aren't true friends until they both recognize the other as lovable and know this to be true. A desire for friendship can form quickly, but real friendship takes time.

This kind of friendship is perfect in both how long it lasts and in all other ways. In it, each friend gives and receives the same thing, or something similar to what they give. This is how things should be between friends. Friendships based on pleasure are similar to this kind of friendship, because good people also find each other pleasant. Friendships based on utility are also similar because good people are useful to each other, too. Friendships between lesser people tend to last longer when both friends get the same thing from each other, like pleasure, and also when they get this from the same source. This happens with witty people, for example, but not with lovers. Lovers do not enjoy the same things—the lover enjoys seeing their beloved, and the beloved enjoys receiving attention. When youth fades, the friendship often fades, too, because one no longer finds pleasure in seeing the other, and the other no longer receives attention. But many lovers stay together when they come to love each other's character through familiarity, especially if their characters are alike. Those who love each other for utility or pleasure are less likely to be true friends and less likely to stay friends for long. Those who are friends for utility part ways when they no longer benefit from each other, because they didn't love each other but loved the profit they gained.

When it comes to friendship for pleasure or utility, even bad people can be friends, or a good person can be friends with a bad person, or someone who is neither good nor bad can be friends with any kind of person. But when it comes to friendship for its own sake, only good people can truly be friends because bad people don't take pleasure in each other unless they get something from it.

Friendship between good people is the only type that cannot be harmed by slander. It's hard to believe bad things about someone you've known and trusted for a long time. Among good people, you find trust, the belief that "he would never wrong me," and all the other qualities that make true friendship. But in the other kinds of friendship, these problems can easily arise. People use the word "friend" even when their relationship is based on utility, like how alliances between states are made for mutual advantage. Friendships based on pleasure are like the friendships between children. So, we should probably call these people friends, too, and say that there are different kinds of friendship. The highest and truest form is the friendship between good people, but the other types are friendships by analogy. They are friends because of something good and something like what we find in true friendship, since even pleasure is good to those who love pleasure. These two kinds of friendship (pleasure and utility) are rarely combined, and people don't usually become friends for both pleasure and utility at the same time. Things that are only related by chance don't often come together.

Friendship is divided into these kinds. Bad people can be friends for the sake of pleasure or utility because they are alike in that way, but good people are friends for each other's sake because of their goodness. These are true friends, while the others are friends only by coincidence and because they resemble true friends.

Just as with virtue, some people are called good because of their character, while others are called good because of their actions. The same is true for friendship. Those who live together enjoy each other's company and help each other, but those who are apart or asleep aren't performing the activities of friendship, though they are ready to do so. Distance doesn't destroy friendship, but it stops the activity of it. However, if the distance lasts too long, people can forget their friendship. This is why people say, "out of sight, out of mind." Older people and sour people don't seem to make friends easily because they aren't very pleasant, and no one can spend time with someone who is unpleasant. Nature avoids what is painful and seeks what is pleasant. People who like each other but don't spend time together seem to have goodwill for each other rather than real friendship. There's nothing more characteristic of friends than living together. Even people who need something from others want their company, and those who are perfectly happy still want to spend their time with friends. Solitude is not good for these people. But people can't live together if they aren't pleasant and don't enjoy the same things, as friends who are companions do.

The truest friendship, as we've said many times, is the friendship of good people. What is good or pleasant without qualification is lovable and desirable, and for each person, what is good or pleasant to them is lovable. The good person is lovable and desirable to another good person for both reasons. It seems that love is a feeling, while friendship is more of a character trait. You can love non-living things, but friendship involves mutual choice, and choice comes from character. People wish good things for those they love, for their sake, not just because of a feeling but because of their character. When you love a friend, you love what is good for yourself, because a good person, in becoming a friend, also becomes a good thing for their friend. Each person loves what is good for themselves and returns this love equally with goodwill and pleasantness. Friendship is said to be based on equality, and this is most true in the friendship of good people.

Friendship doesn't easily form between sour or older people because they aren't as good-natured and don't enjoy company as much. These are considered the most important qualities for forming friendship. This is why younger people make friends more quickly than older people. It's because people don't become friends with those they don't find pleasant. The same goes for sour people—they don't make friends quickly. But these people may still have goodwill for each other because they wish each other well and help each other when needed. However, they aren't truly friends because they don't spend time together or enjoy each other's company. These two things are considered the most important parts of friendship.

You can't be a true friend to many people, just as you can't be in love with many people at once. Love is an intense feeling, and by nature, it can only be directed toward one person. It's also hard for many people to please the same person greatly, or to be considered good in the eyes of the same person. It also takes time to get to know someone and become familiar with them, and that's difficult to do with many people. However, when it comes to friendship based on utility or pleasure, it's possible to be friends with many people because many people can be useful or pleasant, and these kinds of relationships don't require as much time.

Of these two kinds of friendship, the one based on pleasure is more like true friendship, especially when both people get the same things from each other and enjoy each other's company, like in the friendships of young people. There is more generosity in these friendships. Friendships based on utility are more common among business-minded people. Those who are perfectly happy don't need friends for utility, but they do need friends for pleasure. They want to live with someone, and while they can endure what is painful for a short time, no one could put up with pain forever, not even if it came from something good. This is why they look for friends who are pleasant. Perhaps they should find friends who are both pleasant and good for them. That way, they will have all the qualities that friends should have.

People in positions of power tend to have friends who fall into two different groups: some are useful, and some are fun to be around. It's rare to find someone who is both useful and fun. They don't look for people whose fun side comes with virtue or whose usefulness is aimed at good things. Instead, they look for funny, witty people to entertain them, and other friends they choose are good at doing what they're told. These qualities rarely go together in one person.

We've already said that a good person is both fun and useful. However, a good person doesn't usually become friends with someone higher in status unless that person is also better in virtue. If they aren't, there's no equality in the friendship because one person isn't better in both ways. But finding someone who is better in both ways is not easy.

Still, the friendships we've talked about are about equality. Friends give and receive the same things from each other and want the same things for each other. Or, they might trade one thing for another, like fun for usefulness. However, we've already said that these types of friendships are less true and don't last as long.

People think these are friendships because they seem similar to friendships based on virtue. One involves fun, and the other involves usefulness. Both fun and usefulness are also part of virtuous friendships. However, these friendships don't last long and are not as strong against gossip and rumors as virtuous friendships are. So, they don't seem like true friendships because they are different from friendships based on virtue in many ways.

There's another type of friendship that involves inequality, like the friendship between a father and son, an older person and a younger person, or between a husband and wife. These friendships are also different from each other. The relationship between a parent and child isn't the same as the one between a ruler and a subject, and even a father's relationship with his son isn't the same as the son's relationship with his father. The same goes for husbands and wives. Each person has different roles and virtues, and they love each other for different reasons. This means the love and the friendship are different as well.

In these friendships, each person doesn't give or receive the same things from the other, and they shouldn't expect to. But when children give their parents what they owe them for bringing them into the world, and parents give their children what they need, these friendships will be lasting and excellent. In friendships where there is inequality, the love should also be unequal. The person who is better should be loved more than they love, and the more useful person should be loved more as well. When the love matches the merit of each person, a kind of equality is created, which is what we expect in friendship.

However, equality in friendship doesn't seem to work the same way as it does in justice. In justice, what's most important is proportional equality—each person gets what they deserve based on their merit. But in friendship, equal amounts of love and affection come first, and proportional merit comes second. This becomes clear when there's a big difference in virtue, wealth, or anything else between two people. They stop being friends because they no longer expect to be. This is especially clear with the gods, who are far greater than us in every way. It's also true for kings because people who are much lower in status don't expect to be friends with kings, just like ordinary people don't expect to be friends with the best or wisest people.

It's hard to say exactly how much difference two people can handle before they stop being friends. Friendship can still survive even if one person becomes a little different, but when one person becomes too different—like the difference between people and gods—friendship is no longer possible. This is why people wonder whether friends really want the greatest good for their friends, like becoming gods. If a friend becomes a god, they won't be friends anymore, and that wouldn't be a good thing for them. The answer is that a friend wants good things for their friend as long as they stay the same person they are now. So, they want the greatest good for their friend, but only as long as they stay human. But not every great thing; each person mostly wants the best things for themselves.

Most people seem to want to be loved more than they want to love. This is because of ambition, and it's why many people love flattery. The flatterer acts like a friend who is lower in status and pretends to love more than they are loved. Being loved is similar to being honored, which is something most people aim for. But people don't want honor for its own sake. Most people enjoy being honored by important people because they believe it will help them get what they want in the future. So, they like honor because it's a sign that good things will come. People who want honor from good people, or people who know them well, aim to confirm their own belief in their goodness. They enjoy honor because it makes them believe they are good based on what others think.

On the other hand, people enjoy being loved just for the sake of being loved. This makes it seem like being loved is better than being honored, and friendship seems to be desirable in itself. But it seems that loving is more important than being loved, as shown by how much mothers love their children. Some mothers give their children to others to raise, and as long as they know their children are okay, they love them even if they don't get love in return. They are happy just to see their children do well. Mothers still love their children even if the children don't know enough to return their love.

Since friendship depends more on loving, and people who love their friends are praised, it seems like loving is the main virtue of friendship. Only those who love in the right way can have lasting friendships, and only their friendships last over time.

This is also how unequal people can still be friends; their love can be made equal. Equality and similarity are what friendship is about, especially when it comes to people who are similar in virtue. Virtuous people are steady and loyal to each other. They don't ask for or offer bad favors, and they even stop each other from doing wrong. Good people try to keep themselves and their friends from doing anything bad.

Wicked people, however, are not steady. They don't even stay the same as themselves. They become friends for a short time because they enjoy each other's wickedness. Friendships based on usefulness or pleasure last longer because the friends continue to enjoy each other's company or benefit from each other. Friendships based on usefulness seem to happen most easily between opposites, like rich and poor, or ignorant and knowledgeable, because people want what they lack, and each gives something different in return. This can also be true in the case of lovers, where one is beautiful, and the other isn't.

Sometimes lovers seem ridiculous when they demand to be loved as much as they love, especially if they aren't equally lovable. Their demand might make sense if they were equally lovable, but if they aren't, it's silly. Still, opposites don't always seek each other out on purpose, but more by accident. What people really want is something in the middle, because that's what's best for them. For example, it's better for something dry not to become wet, but to reach a balanced, in-between state. The same goes for hot and cold and other opposites. We don't need to get too deep into this because it's not really the focus of our discussion.

Friendship and justice seem to focus on the same things and apply to the same people, as we said at the beginning. In every group, there seems to be some kind of justice and some kind of friendship. People call their fellow travelers and soldiers their friends, and the same goes for those they are connected to in other types of groups. The extent of their connection is the extent of their friendship, just as the extent of their connection determines how much justice exists between them. The saying "friends share everything" is true because friendship depends on sharing. Brothers and close friends share everything, but other friends share specific things—some more, some less. Friendships can be more or less true friendships, just like there are different levels of justice. The duties parents owe to their children aren't the same as those brothers owe each other, and the duties of close friends aren't the same as those of fellow citizens. The same is true for other kinds of friendship.

Because of this, there's also a difference in what it means to act unjustly toward each type of friend. It's worse to cheat a close friend than a fellow citizen, and worse not to help a brother than a stranger. It's also worse to hurt a father than anyone else. The demands of justice seem to grow stronger as the friendship becomes closer, which shows that friendship and justice apply to the same people and work in similar ways.

All kinds of groups are like smaller parts of a political community. People come together in groups for some specific advantage, to get something they need for their lives. This is also why political communities originally formed and why they still exist—people want what's best for the whole group. This is what lawmakers focus on when they create laws, and they call just what benefits everyone. Other groups aim for specific advantages, like sailors trying to make money on a voyage or soldiers trying to win a war. People in villages or religious groups act the same way. Some groups form for the sake of pleasure, like religious gatherings or social clubs. These groups exist for offering sacrifices and socializing.

But these groups are still part of the larger political community, which aims not just for short-term benefits but for what's good for life as a whole. They offer sacrifices, arrange gatherings, and assign honors to the gods, all while giving themselves some time to relax and enjoy life. These activities usually happen after the harvest when people have the most free time. So, all groups seem to be part of the larger political community, and the type of friendship depends on the type of group.

There are three main types of government, and each has a corrupted version of it. The good types are monarchy, aristocracy, and government based on property, which is often called "timocracy," although some people call it a "polity." Of these, monarchy is the best, and timocracy is the worst. The corrupted version of monarchy is tyranny. Both are types of one-man rule, but they are very different. A tyrant rules for his own benefit, while a king rules for the benefit of his people. A man is only a king if he doesn't need anything for himself and is better than his subjects in every way. A man like this doesn't have to worry about himself, so he focuses on what's good for his people. A king who doesn't act like this is just a king in name only.

Tyranny is the exact opposite of this. A tyrant only cares about himself. This is why tyranny is the worst form of government—it's the opposite of the best. Monarchy turns into tyranny when a bad king becomes a tyrant. Aristocracy turns into oligarchy when the rulers become corrupt. They divide the wealth of the city unfairly, keeping most of it for themselves and giving important jobs to the same small group of people. In this way, a few bad people end up in power instead of the best people. Timocracy turns into democracy because democracy is just timocracy taken a step further. Timocracy is government by the majority, and in democracy, everyone is considered equal if they meet the property requirement. Democracy is the least bad of the corrupted forms because it's only a small step away from timocracy.

These are the changes that governments are most likely to go through because they are the easiest and smallest transitions.

You can see examples of these types of governments even in households. The way a father deals with his children is like a monarchy because the father cares for them. This is why Homer calls Zeus "father." The ideal of monarchy is for it to be like a father's rule. However, in Persian families, the father's rule is more like a tyranny because they treat their sons like slaves. Tyranny is also like the way a master rules over his slaves because it's only for the master's benefit. This might seem like a proper form of government, but the Persian version is corrupt because different types of relationships should be governed in different ways.

The relationship between a man and his wife is like an aristocracy because the husband rules based on his worth. In matters where he should lead, he does, but in areas that suit his wife's abilities, he lets her handle them. If the husband tries to rule over everything, the relationship becomes more like an oligarchy because he's not ruling based on what's right. Sometimes, the wife rules because she's an heiress, and in that case, her rule is based on wealth and power rather than virtue, like in an oligarchy. The relationship between brothers is like timocracy because they are mostly equal, except for differences in age. If the age gap is too big, the friendship is no longer a brotherly one.

Democracy is seen in households where there's no clear leader, and everyone is treated equally. It's also found in households where the head of the family is weak, and everyone does as they please.

Each of these types of government involves friendship, just like they involve justice. The friendship between a king and his subjects depends on the king's ability to do good things for them. A good king takes care of his people like a shepherd cares for his sheep. This is why Homer called Agamemnon the "shepherd of the people." The friendship between a father and his children is even stronger because the father gives the greatest gifts: life, care, and upbringing.

Ancestors are respected for the same reasons. By nature, a father rules over his children, ancestors rule over their descendants, and a king rules over his people. These friendships are based on the superiority of one person over the other, which is why ancestors are honored. Justice in these relationships isn't the same for both sides. It's based on what each person deserves, just like the friendship is. The friendship between a man and his wife is like an aristocracy because the better person gets more of the good things, and each person gets what suits them. The same is true for justice in these relationships. The friendship between brothers is like the friendship between comrades because they are equal in age and similar in feelings and character. This is also similar to the friendship in timocratic governments, where the goal is for all citizens to be equal and fair. The leadership is shared equally, and the friendship fits this kind of equality.

In the corrupted forms of government, there is little friendship, just as there is little justice. The worst form of government, tyranny, has almost no friendship. Where there's nothing shared between the ruler and the ruled, there's no friendship because there's no justice. For example, there's no friendship between a craftsman and his tool, between the soul and the body, or between a master and a slave. The tool benefits its user, but there's no friendship or justice toward lifeless things. The same is true for horses or oxen, and even for slaves as slaves. There's nothing shared between a master and a slave. The slave is a living tool, and the tool is a lifeless slave. As a slave, a person can't be a friend, but as a human, they can be. There can be some justice between any two people who are part of a system of law or agreement, and so there can also be friendship between them as humans.

In tyrannies, there's almost no friendship or justice. But in democracies, there's more of both because the citizens are equal and have more in common.

Every type of friendship involves some kind of partnership, as we've said. But we can separate the friendships of family members and comrades from the rest. Friendships between fellow citizens, members of the same tribe, or people traveling together seem more like partnerships because they are based on agreements. We can also include the friendships between hosts and guests in this group. Family friendships seem to come in many forms, but they all depend on the parent-child relationship. Parents love their children because they are a part of themselves, and children love their parents because they come from them.

Parents know their children better than children know their parents, and the parent feels a stronger connection to the child than the child feels to the parent. The child comes from the parent, not the other way around. Also, parents start loving their children as soon as they are born, but children only start loving their parents later when they gain understanding. This explains why mothers love their children more than fathers do.

Parents love their children as they love themselves because children are like another version of them. Children love their parents because they were born from them, and brothers love each other because they share the same parents. This is why people talk about "the same blood" or "the same family." In a way, brothers are the same person in different bodies. Two things that help build friendship are being raised together and being close in age. "People of the same age stick together," and people who grow up together tend to be comrades. This is why the friendship between brothers is similar to that of comrades. Cousins and other relatives are connected because they come from brothers or the same ancestors. They are closer or more distant based on how close the original ancestor is to them.

The friendship between children and parents, and between humans and gods, is based on viewing them as something good and superior. Parents and gods give the greatest gifts—they are the reason for their existence, nourishment, and education from birth. This kind of friendship is more pleasant and useful than friendship with strangers because they live more closely together. The friendship between brothers is similar to that of comrades, especially when they are good people. In general, people who are alike become friends more easily because they share more with each other, and brothers naturally love each other from birth. Since they are born to the same parents, grow up together, and receive the same education, they tend to be more similar in character. The test of time strengthens and confirms their bond.

Friendship among other relatives is proportional to the closeness of the relationship. The friendship between a husband and wife seems to be natural because humans are naturally inclined to form couples, even more than to form cities. The household comes before the city, and reproduction is a common drive in both humans and animals. While animals unite only for reproduction, humans live together not just for this purpose but also for the various needs of life. From the start, their roles are divided, with men and women contributing different skills to the household. This cooperation makes their friendship both useful and pleasant. If the husband and wife are good people, their friendship can also be based on virtue, as each has their own virtues, and they take pleasure in them. Children seem to strengthen the bond between them, which is why childless couples tend to separate more easily. Children are a shared good, and what is shared tends to keep people together.

The way a husband and wife, or any friends, should treat each other is similar to how justice requires them to act. A person doesn't owe the same duties to a friend as they do to a stranger, a comrade, or a classmate.

There are three types of friendship, as we mentioned earlier: some friendships are between equals, while others are between those who are superior or inferior. Not only can equally good people become friends, but also a better person can be friends with someone worse off. In friendships based on pleasure or usefulness, the friends can be equal or unequal in the benefits they provide. When friends are equals, they should balance things equally in love and all other matters. When they are unequal, they should give and receive in proportion to their differences. Complaints and resentments arise mostly in friendships based on usefulness, which makes sense. Friends who care about virtue try to help each other, as this is a sign of both virtue and friendship. When people are competing to help each other, there are no complaints or quarrels. No one is upset with someone who loves them and treats them well. If a person is kind, they will repay kindness with kindness. A friend who excels at helping won't complain because they are achieving what they aim for, which is to do good. In friendships of pleasure, there aren't many complaints because both friends get what they want by enjoying each other's company. Even if one friend didn't bring enough pleasure, it would be silly to complain since they can simply stop spending time together.

Friendships of utility are full of complaints because each person uses the other for their own gain. They always want to get more than they give and feel like they are receiving less than they deserve. They often blame their partners for not meeting their expectations. Those who do favors for others can't always help as much as the other person wants.

It seems that, just as there are two kinds of justice—one unwritten and one legal—there are two kinds of friendship based on utility: moral and legal. Complaints arise when people don't end the friendship in the same way they started it. The legal kind is based on fixed terms. In purely business relationships, repayment happens immediately, while more generous relationships allow for delayed payment but still expect something in return. In these relationships, the debt is clear and not confusing, but the delay adds a friendly element. Some societies don't allow lawsuits over such agreements, believing that those who lend on credit should accept the risks. The moral kind of friendship isn't based on set terms. In this case, a person gives something to a friend without expecting immediate repayment, but they still expect to receive as much or more eventually. If they end up worse off after the friendship ends, they will complain. This happens because people often want to be noble but choose what benefits them. It's noble to help someone without expecting repayment, but receiving help is more beneficial. Therefore, if we can, we should repay what we received. We shouldn't force someone to be our friend against their will. We must acknowledge that we made a mistake by accepting a benefit from someone we shouldn't have and should settle the debt as if it were a business transaction.

There is some debate about whether we should measure a favor by how useful it was to the person who received it or by the kindness of the giver. The receivers often say they didn't get much because it was something small for the giver, or they could have gotten it from someone else, downplaying the favor. On the other hand, the givers say they gave the best they had and something that couldn't be easily obtained elsewhere, especially if it was given in a time of need. In friendships based on utility, it seems that the benefit to the receiver should be the measure. After all, the receiver asks for the favor, and the giver expects an equivalent return. The help given is equal to the advantage received, so the receiver should repay what they got or even more, as that would be nobler. In friendships based on virtue, complaints don't arise because the intention of the giver is the true measure. Intention is central to virtue and character.

Friendships between people of different status can also lead to disagreements because each expects to get more out of it. When this happens, the friendship falls apart. The superior friend thinks they should get more because they are better, while the more useful friend expects more because they believe a lesser person shouldn't receive the same benefits. They argue that, just like in business partnerships, those who invest more should receive more in return. But the friend in need argues the opposite, thinking that a good friend should help those in need. They ask, "What's the point of being friends with someone powerful or virtuous if it brings no benefits?"

Both sides seem justified in their expectations. Each should receive more from the friendship but in different ways. The superior friend should receive more honor, while the lesser friend should gain more material benefits. Honor is the reward for virtue and generosity, while material gain helps those in need.

This is also true in political arrangements. A person who doesn't contribute to the common good isn't honored. Public resources are given to those who benefit the public, and honor is one of these resources. It's impossible to receive both wealth and honor from the public at the same time because no one is willing to take the smaller share of everything. Therefore, the person who sacrifices wealth is given honor, while the person who wants to be paid receives wealth. This balance keeps the friendship intact, as we mentioned earlier. This is also how we should treat unequal friendships. The person who receives wealth or virtue should give honor in return, repaying what they can. Friendship asks a person to do what they are capable of, not necessarily what matches the merits of the situation. For example, no one can fully repay their debt to the gods or their parents. But a person who serves them to the best of their ability is considered good. This is why a person can't disown their father, although a father can disown his son. Since the son is always in debt, he should always try to repay it. However, just like creditors can forgive a debt, a father can forgive his son. At the same time, people think that a father wouldn't reject his son unless the son was extremely wicked. Besides the natural bond between father and son, it's human nature not to reject help from a child. But if the son is wicked, he will likely avoid helping his father or won't do so with much enthusiasm. Most people like to receive help but avoid giving it, seeing it as unprofitable. That covers these issues.

Book 9

In all friendships between people who are different, as we have said, it is balance that keeps things equal and preserves the friendship. For example, in political friendships, the shoemaker gets something back for his shoes that equals their value, and the weaver and all other workers do the same. Here, a common way to measure value is money, so everything is judged by this and compared to it. But in the friendship of lovers, sometimes the lover complains that their great love isn't returned (maybe because they aren't lovable), while the beloved might complain that the lover, who used to promise everything, now delivers nothing.

These problems happen when the lover loves the beloved for pleasure, while the beloved loves the lover for usefulness. They don't both have the qualities the other person expects. If these are the reasons for their friendship, it falls apart when they no longer get what they originally wanted. Each person didn't love the other for who they are but for certain qualities, and these qualities weren't lasting. That's why these friendships don't last. But the love between two good people, as we've said, lasts because it's based on their character.

Problems arise when what each person receives is different from what they wanted. It feels like you're getting nothing if you don't get what you were aiming for. There's a story of someone who promised rewards to a lyre-player, saying they would give more the better he played. But in the morning, when the player asked for his rewards, the person said they had given him pleasure for pleasure. Now, if both wanted the same thing, that would have been fine. But if one wanted enjoyment and the other wanted money, and only one person got what they wanted, then the friendship wasn't balanced. Each person focuses on what they want, and they give what they have in order to get that.

But who gets to decide the value of the service—the person making the sacrifice or the person who benefits from it? It seems like the second person leaves it up to the first. This is what Protagoras supposedly used to do; whenever he taught anything, he let the learner decide how much the teaching was worth and accepted whatever amount they set. But in situations like this, some people prefer the saying "let a man have his fixed reward." Those who get paid first and then don't do what they promised are naturally complained about, especially if their promises were exaggerated. This happens a lot with sophists because no one would pay for what they actually know. So, if these people don't do what they were paid to do, it's no surprise that others complain about them.

But where there is no official contract, people who give something up for the sake of someone else can't be complained about (as we said earlier). This is the nature of virtuous friendships. The return should be based on the intention behind the act because intention is what matters most in friendships and in virtue. This also applies to people who study philosophy together. The value of what they offer can't be measured in money, and no honor is enough to repay what they've done. Still, like with the gods or our parents, it may be enough to repay them by doing what we can.

If the gift wasn't like that but was given expecting something in return, then it's best to make sure the return is fair to both parties. If this can't be achieved, it seems fair and necessary that the person who got the service should set the value. If the person who gave the service gets back something equal to the benefit the other person received or what they would have paid for the pleasure, then they've gotten what's fair.

We see this happening with things that are sold. In some places, there are even laws that say no one can take legal action over voluntary agreements. This is because the law assumes that if you gave someone credit, you should settle with them based on the terms you originally agreed to. The law believes it's more fair for the person who received credit to set the terms than the one who gave it. Most people don't value things the same way when they have them as they did before they got them. They tend to think what they own is worth more than what others have. Still, the return is made based on what the receiver thinks it's worth. The receiver, though, should value the gift based on what they thought it was worth before they received it, not afterward.

There's another question: Should we always put our father first and obey him, or should we trust a doctor when we're sick? When choosing a general, should we pick someone with military skills? And, similarly, should we help a friend or a good person, or should we repay a benefactor or help a friend if we can't do both?

These kinds of questions are hard to answer clearly, aren't they? There are many variations depending on how important the help is and how noble it is. But it's clear that we shouldn't always put the same person first. Most of the time, we should repay benefits rather than do favors for friends, just like we should repay a loan before lending to someone else. But even this isn't always true. For example, if someone has been rescued from kidnappers, should they rescue the person who saved them, or should they save their father? It seems like they should save their father, even before saving themselves.

As we've said, the general rule is to repay what you owe, but if the gift is exceptionally noble or necessary, we should consider that first. Sometimes, it's not even fair to return an equal favor, like when one person does something good for someone they know is virtuous, but the other person repays someone they believe is bad. In such cases, it wouldn't be fair to repay the favor. Even if the person lent to you, expecting to be repaid, they might not expect the same if you believe they are bad. So, if the situation really is that way, the demand for repayment isn't fair. And if it only seems that way, people might still refuse to repay, thinking they aren't doing anything wrong.

As we've often said, discussions about emotions and actions can only be as precise as the topic allows.

It's clear that we shouldn't repay everyone in the same way, and we shouldn't always put our father first in everything, just like we don't sacrifice everything to Zeus. But we should give different things to our parents, brothers, friends, and benefactors. We should give each group what's appropriate and fitting. This seems to be what people actually do. They invite relatives to weddings because relatives are part of the family, and family events affect them. At funerals, relatives gather for the same reason. In matters of food, we should help our parents first because we owe our own nourishment to them. It's more honorable to provide for the people who gave us life, even before providing for ourselves. We should honor our parents like we honor the gods, but not with just any honor. We shouldn't give our parents the same honor we give a philosopher or a general. We should honor them as parents. We should also show respect to older people by standing when they enter and offering them seats. For friends and brothers, we should allow more freedom and sharing of everything. For other relatives, fellow citizens, and people from the same community, we should try to give each group what's appropriate, considering how close we are to them, their virtue, and their usefulness.

It's easier to compare people when they belong to the same group, but it's harder when they're from different groups. Still, we shouldn't avoid the task, but we should do our best to make a fair decision.

Another question is whether or not friendships should be ended when the other person changes. It seems natural to end a friendship based on usefulness or pleasure when the person no longer has those qualities. After all, we were only friends because of those qualities, and when they're gone, it's reasonable to stop loving them. But someone could complain if, while they loved us for our usefulness or pleasantness, we pretended to love them for their character. As we said earlier, most disagreements between friends come when they don't really understand the basis of their friendship. So, if someone believed they were being loved for their character when that wasn't the case, they should blame themselves. But if they were tricked by the other person pretending to love them for their character, then they have a right to complain. They could even argue that the deception was worse than counterfeiting money because the wrong was done to something more valuable.

If someone thought another person was good and that person turns out to be bad, should they still love them? It doesn't seem possible because not everything can be loved—only what is good. We can't and shouldn't love what is evil. It's not right to be a lover of bad things or to become like what's bad. We've said that people love what is similar to them. So, should we immediately end the friendship? Not always. This should only happen if the person's badness can't be fixed. If they can be reformed, it's better to help them improve their character or their situation. This is more in line with what friendship is about. But if someone breaks off a friendship with someone who can't be saved, they aren't doing anything wrong. After all, they didn't become friends with this bad person, and since their friend has changed and they can't help them, they give up on the friendship.

But what if one friend stays the same while the other gets better and becomes far more virtuous? Should the more virtuous person still treat the other as a friend? It seems they can't. When the gap between them becomes too large, it's obvious that the friendship can't continue. For example, in childhood friendships, if one friend remains childlike in their thinking while the other matures into an adult, how could they still be friends? They wouldn't enjoy or value the same things, and without that, they can't be friends because they can't share their lives together. We've already discussed these ideas.

Should the person who's changed treat their former friend as a complete stranger? Not exactly. They should still remember the old friendship, and just like we treat old friends better than strangers, we should also give some credit to people we used to be friends with, as long as the reason for ending the friendship wasn't too severe.

The way people treat their neighbors and the signs of friendship seem to come from how people relate to themselves. For example, we call someone a friend if they want and do what is good for their friend, or at least what seems good, for their friend's sake. Or we call someone a friend if they wish their friend to live and thrive, which is what mothers do for their children, and what friends do for each other even if they've fought. Others define a friend as someone who lives with you and has the same interests. Or they define a friend as someone who shares your joys and sorrows, which mothers do more than anyone. Friendship is defined by one or more of these traits.

Each of these traits applies to how a good person relates to themselves (and to everyone else in so far as they see themselves as good). Virtue and the good person, as we've said, seem to be the standard for everything. A good person's desires are consistent, and they want the same things with all their heart. So, they wish what's good for themselves and do what's good. It's part of being good to put good into action. They do this for their own sake because they do it for the part of them that thinks, which is considered to be the true self.

A good person wishes to live and be preserved, especially the part of them that thinks. Existence is good for a virtuous person, and everyone wishes good for themselves. No one would choose to possess everything if it meant becoming someone else. Even now, we believe God possesses the good. People only want good things if they can remain who they are while getting them. The part of us that thinks seems to be the real person, or at least more so than any other part.

A good person enjoys spending time with themselves. They find pleasure in remembering their past actions, and they have good hopes for the future, which makes them happy. Their mind is full of things to think about. They feel grief and joy with themselves more than anyone else because the same things are always painful or pleasant to them. Their feelings don't change from one moment to the next. It's like they never have anything to regret.

Since all these traits apply to how a good person relates to themselves, and they treat their friends the same way they treat themselves (because a friend is like another self), friendship is thought to be based on these traits. People who have these traits are friends.

Whether or not someone can be friends with themselves is a question we can put aside for now. But there does seem to be friendship within a person in so far as they are like two or more people. This can be seen from the traits of friendship we've mentioned and from the fact that the highest form of friendship is compared to a person's love for themselves.

Even though most people have these traits, even if they aren't great, should we say that when they are happy with themselves and think they are good, they share in these traits? Definitely, no one who is completely bad or irreligious has these traits or even seems to have them. These traits barely apply to less-than-great people either, because they are in conflict with themselves. They want one thing but logically know they should want something else. This happens to people who lack self-control; they choose things that feel good but are harmful instead of the things they know are better. Others, because they are afraid or lazy, avoid doing what they know is best for them. Those who have done many terrible things and are hated for their wickedness even avoid life and might hurt themselves. Wicked people often look for others to spend time with and avoid being alone with themselves. When they are by themselves, they remember all the awful things they've done and imagine doing more bad things, but when they're with others, they forget. Because they don't have anything lovable about them, they don't love themselves. This is also why they don't feel happy or sad with themselves. Their soul is split apart because of their wickedness. One part of them feels sad when they stop themselves from doing certain things, while the other part feels pleased. They feel pulled in different directions, almost like they are being torn apart. Even if a person can't feel happy and sad at the same time, they might soon feel sad because they were once happy, and they wish those things hadn't made them feel happy at all. Bad people are weighed down by regret.

Because of this, a bad person doesn't seem to even like themselves since there's nothing in them to love. If this is the height of misery, we should do everything we can to avoid wickedness and try to be good. Only then can someone be a friend to themselves or someone else.

Goodwill is a friendly feeling but is not the same as friendship. You can have goodwill toward someone you don't know and without them knowing it, but that's not true of friendship. This has been mentioned before. Goodwill isn't even the same as feeling friendly because it doesn't involve strong feelings or desire. Those feelings come with real friendship. Friendship means being close, but goodwill can happen suddenly, like when we feel it for competitors in a contest. We feel goodwill toward them and hope for the best for them, but we wouldn't necessarily do anything with them. As mentioned before, goodwill happens suddenly and is only a surface-level feeling of love.

So, goodwill seems to be the start of friendship, like how admiring someone's looks is the start of love. No one loves someone if they aren't first pleased by their appearance. But just liking someone's appearance doesn't mean you love them. Love only happens when you long for the person when they're not around and crave their presence. In the same way, people can't be friends unless they first feel goodwill for each other. But just because people feel goodwill doesn't mean they're friends. They only wish good things for each other, but they wouldn't go out of their way for each other or put in the effort. So you could say that goodwill is like friendship that hasn't been acted on yet. But when it grows stronger and leads to closeness, it can become friendship—not the kind based on usefulness or pleasure since goodwill doesn't start that way either. If someone has goodwill toward someone because they received help from them, that's just being fair. If someone wishes success for another person because they hope to get something from them in return, that's not really goodwill toward the other person but more like goodwill toward themselves. It's like how someone isn't truly a friend if they only care for someone because they can get something out of it. In general, goodwill comes from admiring something good in another person, like their beauty or bravery, as we pointed out earlier with competitors in contests.

Unanimity also seems to be a kind of friendly relationship. That's why it isn't just agreeing on the same opinion, because that could happen between people who don't even know each other. We don't say that people who agree about everything are unanimous, like people who agree on facts about the stars. Unanimity about things like that doesn't create a friendly bond. But we do say that a city is unified when everyone agrees on what's best for them and chooses to take the same actions together. Unanimity, then, is about actions, especially those that are important and where both or all parties can get what they want. For example, a city is unified when everyone agrees that government officials should be elected or that they should form an alliance with Sparta. Or, when they agree that Pittacus should be their ruler and he is willing to lead them. But when two people both want the same thing only for themselves, like the captains in the Phoenissae, they aren't unified; they are in conflict. Unanimity only happens when everyone agrees that the same person should have something. For example, both the common people and the upper class want the best people to lead. Only in this way can everyone get what they want. Unanimity, then, seems to be political friendship, and it is often said to be so. It deals with things that benefit everyone and that affect our lives.

True unanimity is only found among good people. They are unified with themselves and with others because they have one purpose. They want justice and what is beneficial, and these are the things they work toward together. But bad people can only be unified a little, just like they can't truly be friends. They try to take more than their fair share of benefits while avoiding their share of work and public service. Each person tries to get what they want for themselves and criticizes others for doing the same. They get in each other's way, and when people don't watch out for each other, things quickly fall apart. As a result, they end up in conflict, forcing others to do what's right while they refuse to do the same.

People often think that those who help others love the people they've helped more than the people who received the help love the person who helped them. This idea is often seen as strange. Most people think it's because the person who was helped feels like they owe something, while the person who helped is like a creditor. Just like in financial debts, the person who owes money wishes their creditor didn't exist, while the creditor wants the debtor to be safe so they can be repaid. So, people think that benefactors want those they've helped to be around so they can get gratitude, while the people who received help don't care much about returning the favor. Epicharmus might say that this way of thinking is negative, but it's natural for people to act this way. Most people are forgetful and would rather receive kindness than give it.

But the reason for this goes deeper. The comparison to financial debts doesn't even fit. Creditors don't necessarily feel friendship toward their debtors; they just want them to be safe so they can get their money back. But people who help others feel love and friendship toward the people they've helped, even if they never expect anything in return. This is similar to how a craftsman loves his work more than the work could ever love him if it came alive. Poets feel this way about their poems, loving them like their children. This is the same for benefactors. The people they help are like their creations, and that's why they love them more than the recipients of the help love them. The reason for this is that life itself is something everyone values and loves. We exist by living and doing things. When a person helps another, they are acting, and that action makes them feel alive. So, the person who helps loves the person they've helped because it is through their actions that they experience life.

At the same time, the benefactor sees something noble in their actions, so they feel pleasure in the person they helped. But the person who was helped doesn't necessarily see anything noble in the benefactor. At most, they see something useful, and that's less pleasant or lovable. What is pleasant is the act of doing something in the present, the hope of the future, and the memory of the past. But the most pleasant thing is the act itself, and that's also the most lovable. For the person who did the act, the memory of the good thing they did stays with them because what is noble lasts. But for the person who was helped, the benefit fades away. Memories of noble things bring joy, but memories of useful things are not as pleasant, though the opposite is true when we think about the future.

Also, loving is like doing something, while being loved is like being on the receiving end. Loving someone is more active, while being loved is more passive.

Everyone loves what they've worked hard for more than what they've gotten without effort. For example, people who earned their money love it more than those who inherited it. Being treated well doesn't require effort, but treating others well does. This is why mothers often love their children more than fathers do. They went through more pain to bring their children into the world, and they know for sure that the children are theirs. The same applies to benefactors.

There's also the question of whether people should love themselves the most or someone else. People criticize those who love themselves most, calling them selfish, and they use the term in a negative way. A bad person seems to do everything for themselves, and the worse they are, the more they do it. People criticize them for not acting on their own accord. But a good person acts for the sake of honor, and the better they are, the more they act for the sake of their friends, even sacrificing their own interests.

But this idea doesn't quite match the facts, which isn't surprising. People say that we should love our best friend the most. And our best friend is someone who wishes well for us for our own sake, even if no one else knows about it. These traits are found most of all in how a person relates to themselves. The other traits that define a friend are also true of how a person treats themselves. As we said, the way we treat ourselves is the model for how we treat our friends. The old sayings agree with this, like "a single soul," "what friends have is shared," "friendship is equality," and "charity begins at home." All these sayings apply most to how a person relates to themselves. We are our own best friend, so it makes sense to love ourselves the most. This makes it a reasonable question: which of the two views should we follow? Both seem reasonable.

We need to separate these arguments and figure out where and in what way each view is correct. If we understand how each group uses the term "self-love," the truth becomes clear. People use the term "self-love" as an insult when they talk about people who give themselves more wealth, honors, and physical pleasures than anyone else. These are the things most people want and compete for because they think they are the best things. So, people who are selfish in this way satisfy their desires and emotions, especially the irrational part of their soul. Most people act like this, which is why the term "self-love" has a negative meaning—it reflects this common but bad form of self-love. It's only fair, then, that people who are selfish in this way are criticized. It's clear that most people call someone selfish when they give themselves more of these things.

However, if someone was always concerned with acting justly, with self-control, or with other virtues, and always tried to do what is right, no one would call that person selfish or criticize them.

But that kind of person is actually more of a "self-lover" than the others because they are giving themselves the best and noblest things. They satisfy the most important part of themselves and always listen to it. Just like a city or any organized system is identified with its leading part, a person is most identified with their reasoning mind. So, the person who loves and follows this part of themselves is the true "self-lover." Besides, people are said to have self-control if their reason is in control because that part is considered to be the true self. The things we do based on rational thought are considered our most real and voluntary actions. It's clear that this is the true self, or at least more so than any other part. It's also clear that the good person loves this part of themselves the most. So, it follows that they are the truest "self-lover," but in a very different way from those who are criticized for being selfish. The difference is like the difference between living according to reason and living according to emotion, or between wanting what is noble and wanting what seems useful. People admire and praise those who focus on noble actions. If everyone aimed for what is noble and worked hard to do the best deeds, everything would be better for everyone. Each person would also get the greatest good for themselves, which is virtue, the highest good.

Therefore, a good person should love themselves because they will benefit from doing good deeds, and they will help others too. But a bad person shouldn't love themselves because they will harm themselves and those around them by following their bad desires. A bad person does things that go against what they should do, but a good person does what they ought to do. Reason always chooses what is best for itself, and a good person follows their reason. It's also true that a good person does many things for their friends and country, even giving up their life if necessary. They will give up wealth, honors, and other things people usually compete for in order to gain something greater—nobility. They prefer a short time of intense pleasure over a long period of mild enjoyment, a year of noble life over many years of dull living, and one great and noble action over many small ones. People who die for others achieve this kind of greatness. So, they are really choosing something wonderful for themselves.

They will also give up wealth if it means their friends will gain more because while their friend gains money, they achieve nobility. They are actually giving themselves the better good. The same goes for honor and power. They will give these things up for their friend because doing so is noble and praiseworthy. This is why they are rightly considered good because they always choose what is noble over everything else. Sometimes, they will even let their friend take action instead of them because it might be nobler to help their friend act than to act themselves. In all the ways people are praised for their actions, a good person takes the larger share of what is noble for themselves. In this way, as we said before, a person should love themselves, but not in the way most people do.

There is also a debate about whether a happy person needs friends. Some say that those who are perfectly happy and self-sufficient don't need friends because they already have everything good. If they are self-sufficient, they don't need anything else. A friend, who is like another self, provides something a person can't give themselves, which is why people say, "When fortune is kind, what need is there for friends?" But it seems strange to say that a happy person has everything good but not friends, who are considered the greatest of external goods. Also, if it's more characteristic of a friend to do good for someone else than to be helped themselves, and if doing good is the mark of a virtuous person, and it's nobler to help friends than strangers, then a good person needs people to help.

This is why people ask whether we need friends more in good times or bad. It's assumed that people need friends in bad times to help them, but those who are doing well also need friends to do good for. It would be strange to think of the happiest person as being all alone. No one would choose to have the whole world if it meant being alone. Humans are social beings who naturally live with others. Therefore, even a happy person needs to live with others because they have all the good things in life. It's clearly better to spend your time with friends and good people rather than with strangers or random people. So, the happy person needs friends.

What exactly is the first group saying, and in what way are they right? Do they mean that most people think of friends as useful? If so, then a truly happy person wouldn't need these kinds of friends because they already have everything they need. They also wouldn't need friends just for enjoyment, or they'd need them very little because their life is already pleasant without outside pleasures. And since they don't need these types of friends, people think they don't need friends at all.

But this isn't true. We said before that happiness is about activity, and activity happens over time, not all at once like owning something. If (1) happiness comes from living and being active, and a good person's actions are virtuous and naturally pleasant, as we mentioned earlier, and (2) doing something yourself makes it more enjoyable, and (3) we can observe other people's actions more easily than our own, and (4) the actions of virtuous friends are pleasant to good people— then, if this is all true, a truly happy person will need friends like these. Their goal is to think about worthy actions, especially their own, and a good friend's actions are both good and pleasant.

Moreover, people believe that a happy person should live a pleasant life. If they were alone, life would be difficult because it's not easy to stay active all the time by yourself. But with others, it's easier to stay active. With friends, their activity will be more constant, and it's naturally pleasant, as it should be for a truly happy person. A good person enjoys virtuous actions and is bothered by bad ones, much like a musician enjoys good music and dislikes bad music. Spending time with good people also helps train us in virtue, as Theognis said before.

If we think more deeply about it, it seems that a virtuous friend is naturally something a good person would want. That which is naturally good is good and pleasant for a virtuous person. Life for animals is defined by their ability to sense things, and for humans, it's defined by their ability to sense or think. Abilities are defined by the activities they lead to, and life is essentially about perceiving or thinking. Life itself is one of the things that are good and pleasant because it is definite, and definite things are naturally good. That which is naturally good is also good for a virtuous person. This is why life seems pleasant to everyone. But we shouldn't apply this to a wicked or painful life, since such a life is undefined, as are its qualities. The nature of pain will become clearer later. But if life is good and pleasant—and it seems to be, since everyone desires it, especially those who are good and truly happy—and if someone who sees knows they are seeing, and someone who hears knows they are hearing, and someone who walks knows they are walking, and this applies to all other activities too—if we know that we are being active, and if knowing we are active is also knowing we are alive (since being alive is defined as perceiving or thinking), and if knowing we are alive is itself pleasant (since life is naturally good, and it's pleasant to be aware of good things in ourselves), and if life is desirable, especially for good people because for them existence is good and pleasant (since they are happy to be aware of the good within them)—and if a good person feels about their friend the same way they feel about themselves (because their friend is like another self)—then, if all this is true, just as each person's own existence is desirable, so is the existence of their friend. A person's existence is desirable because they are aware of their own goodness, and this awareness is pleasant in itself. Therefore, a person needs to be aware of their friend's existence, which happens through living together and sharing thoughts and conversations. This is what "living together" means for humans, unlike animals who just share a space for feeding.

If being alive is naturally good and pleasant for a truly happy person, and their friend's life is much the same, then a friend is something they will desire. Since they desire this, they must have it, or they will be missing something important. Therefore, a truly happy person will need virtuous friends.

Should we then try to have as many friends as possible? Or, like with hosting guests, should we aim for something in between—not too many but not none at all? Should this apply to friendship as well?

When it comes to friendships based on usefulness, this idea makes sense. Doing favors for many people can be exhausting, and life isn't long enough to help everyone. So, having more friends than necessary is pointless and can get in the way of living a good life. We don't need too many of these friends. The same goes for friendships based on pleasure. Just a few are enough, like a little seasoning is enough in food.

But when it comes to good friends, should we have as many as possible, or is there a limit, like there is with the size of a city? You can't have a city with only ten people, but if there are 100,000, it's not really a city anymore. So, there's probably no single perfect number of friends, but there is a range. The largest number of friends we can have is probably the most we can live with, since living together is a key part of friendship. And it's clear that we can't live closely with too many people or divide ourselves among them. Also, these friends should all be friends with each other if they're going to spend time together. It's hard for this to happen with a large group. It's also difficult to share happiness and sadness deeply with many people because you might have to rejoice with one friend while mourning with another. So, it's best not to aim for as many friends as possible, but just enough to live well with. It's actually impossible to be a great friend to many people. This is why we can't truly love many people at once. Love is an intense form of friendship, and that can only be felt for one person. Great friendships, too, are only possible with a few people. We see this in real life—famous deep friendships are always between two people. Those who have many friends and are close with all of them are often thought to not really be close to anyone. These people are more like fellow citizens than true friends, and they may be seen as overly eager to please. In the case of fellow citizens, you can be friends with many without being seen as insincere, but you can't have deep, virtuous friendships with many people. We should be satisfied if we find even a few true friends.

Do we need friends more in good times or bad? We need them in both. In bad times, people need help, and in good times, they need people to share their lives with and to be generous toward. People want to do good for others. Friendship is more necessary in bad times because useful friends are needed, but it's more noble in good times because we seek good friends to help and share our lives with. The very presence of friends is comforting in both good and bad times because sorrow is lessened when friends share in it. Some might ask if they help carry the burden of our grief, or if their presence alone, and knowing they feel sad for us, makes our pain lighter. Whether it's this or something else that lightens grief doesn't matter. What we've said seems to be true.

Their presence seems to have a mix of effects. Simply seeing our friends is comforting, especially in tough times. They help us cope with grief, both by being there and by offering comforting words if they know us well. A friend knows what pleases and pains us, and seeing them upset by our problems can also be painful because no one wants to make their friends sad. That's why strong-willed people try not to burden their friends with their troubles. They avoid sharing grief because they don't want to cause their friends pain. They also don't like to grieve themselves, so they avoid having others mourn with them. On the other hand, people who are more sensitive enjoy sharing their sorrow with friends and see them as companions in their grief. But in all things, we should aim to imitate the better type of person.

In contrast, having friends around in good times makes life more enjoyable. It's pleasant to see friends happy for our success. This is why we should eagerly invite our friends to share in our good fortune. A generous spirit is a noble one. But we should hesitate to bring them into our bad times because we want to burden them as little as possible with our troubles. Hence the saying, "Enough with my misfortune." We should only ask for help when our friends can do something important for us with little effort.

On the other hand, it's right to go to a friend's aid without being asked and to do so quickly, especially when they're in need. This is a key part of friendship, and it's nobler to help without being asked. It's also more pleasant for both people. But when friends are doing well, we should join them in their activities, but we shouldn't be quick to take advantage of their kindness. It's not noble to be eager to receive help. Still, we should avoid seeming ungrateful or rude by turning down their kindness, as that can sometimes happen.

So, it seems that having friends around is desirable in all circumstances.

Doesn't it follow, then, that just like lovers want to see their beloved most of all, friends most desire to live together? Friendship is a partnership, and as a person feels about themselves, they feel about their friend. Just as we enjoy being aware of our own existence, we also enjoy being aware of our friend's existence. This happens when we live together, so it's natural that friends aim for this. Whatever life means to each person, whatever they value most, they want to share that with their friends. Some people drink together, others play games or sports, go hunting, or study philosophy. Each person spends time with their friends doing what they love most in life. This is how they experience living together. The friendship of bad people leads to bad things because they unite in harmful activities and become worse by being like each other. On the other hand, the friendship of good people is good because they improve each other through their companionship. They become better through their activities together and by influencing each other's virtues. That's why it's said that "noble deeds come from noble people." So much for friendship. Our next topic will be pleasure.

Book 10

Next, we should probably talk about pleasure. It seems to be deeply connected to human nature, which is why when we teach children, we guide them with pleasure and pain. It is also believed that knowing how to enjoy the right things and hate the wrong things is very important for developing good character. These feelings affect our whole lives and play a significant role in both virtue and happiness because people tend to choose what feels good and avoid what feels bad. For this reason, we shouldn't skip over discussing pleasure, especially since it's a topic of much debate. Some people say pleasure is the ultimate good, while others say it's entirely bad. Some believe this because they think it's true, while others say it's better to claim pleasure is bad, even if it's not, to help people avoid it. They think that since most people are naturally drawn to pleasure, they should push them in the opposite direction to reach a balanced middle ground. But this way of thinking isn't right.

Arguments about feelings and actions are less trustworthy than facts. When they go against what people actually experience, they are often dismissed, which hurts the truth. For example, if someone argues against pleasure but is then seen seeking it, people might assume that all pleasure is worth pursuing because they aren't good at making distinctions. So, truthful arguments are the most useful, not just for gaining knowledge, but for living well. Since truthful arguments match the facts, they are more believable and motivate people to live by them. That's enough on that topic; let's move on to reviewing the opinions people have had about pleasure.

Eudoxus believed pleasure was the ultimate good because he saw that both rational and irrational beings aim for it. In everything, what is most sought after is considered the best, and the fact that all living things seek pleasure suggests it is the greatest good for all. He argued that just as every being finds its own good, like how each species finds the right food, the good is what all living things aim for. His argument was taken seriously, not just because of what he said, but because of his reputation for self-control. People believed he wasn't just defending pleasure because he liked it, but because it really was the truth. He also believed that this was obvious when you consider the opposite of pleasure: pain. Since all living things avoid pain, its opposite, pleasure, must be something they choose. He also argued that the things we choose for their own sake are the most desirable, and pleasure fits this description because no one asks why they are pleased—they just are. Finally, he said that when pleasure is added to any good, such as a just or temperate action, it makes it even more desirable. This shows that pleasure is one of the goods and that it can increase the value of other good things.

This argument suggests that pleasure is a good but not necessarily the highest good, because every good thing is more desirable when paired with another good. This is how Plato argued that pleasure is not the highest good. He said that a life with both pleasure and wisdom is more desirable than one with only pleasure. If the combination of pleasure and wisdom is better than just pleasure, then pleasure can't be the highest good because the highest good wouldn't become better by adding something else. This idea shows that if any good thing becomes more desirable when combined with another good, then it's not the ultimate good. So, what exactly meets this standard and is something we can experience? That's what we're trying to figure out.

Some people argue that just because all living things aim for something doesn't mean it's good. But that idea seems wrong. We believe that what everyone seeks must be good, and anyone who challenges this belief probably doesn't have a better argument. If only unintelligent creatures sought after pleasure, maybe there would be something to this objection. But since intelligent beings also seek pleasure, this argument doesn't make sense. Even among lower animals, there seems to be a natural drive toward their own good.

The argument about pleasure's opposite also doesn't seem right. Some say that just because pain is bad doesn't mean pleasure is good because good and bad are opposites, and both are also opposed to neutral things. While this is true in some cases, it doesn't apply here. If both pleasure and pain were bad, we should avoid both. If they were both neutral, we shouldn't avoid or seek either one. But clearly, people avoid pain as something bad and seek pleasure as something good. This shows that they are opposed in nature, not both bad or both neutral.

They also argue that because pleasure isn't a quality, it can't be a good. But activities connected with virtue aren't qualities either, nor is happiness. Some say that the good is fixed and unchanging, while pleasure is changeable because it comes in different degrees. But if they're judging pleasure based on how it feels, then the same could be said about justice and other virtues. We often say people are more or less just or brave and that their actions can also be more or less virtuous. Just like people can act more or less justly, they can experience different degrees of pleasure. If they're judging based on the variety of pleasures, they aren't identifying the real cause, especially since some pleasures are pure and others are mixed. Just like health can come in degrees without being uncertain, why couldn't the same be true for pleasure? The same amount of health isn't always present, and its intensity can vary. The same could be true for pleasure.

They also say that the good is complete, while movement and change are incomplete. They try to show that pleasure is a type of movement or change. But this doesn't seem right either. Movements, like walking, are described as having speed or slowness, and if a movement doesn't have its own speed, it still has it in relation to something else. But pleasure doesn't work like that. While you can quickly become pleased or angry, you can't be pleased quickly in the same way you can walk or grow quickly. You can shift into a state of pleasure quickly, but you can't experience pleasure as a fast process. So, pleasure isn't a type of movement.

How can pleasure be something that comes into being? We don't think just anything can come from anything else. Something can only come from what it's made of, so if pain is the destruction of something, pleasure must be the creation of the same thing. They say that pain comes from lacking what's natural, and pleasure comes from being restored. But these are bodily experiences. If pleasure is the restoration of what's natural, then the body would be the one feeling pleasure. But that's not what people think. Therefore, restoration itself isn't pleasure, although being restored can cause pleasure, just like an operation can cause pain.

This idea seems to come from the pain and pleasure connected with hunger. When people are hungry, they feel pain, and when they eat, they feel pleasure from being filled. But this doesn't apply to all pleasures. Learning, and even some physical pleasures like smells, sounds, sights, memories, and hopes, don't come from a lack of something. So, what are these pleasures restoring?

To answer those who bring up shameful pleasures, we can say that these pleasures aren't truly pleasant. If things are pleasant to people with bad character, that doesn't mean they are pleasant for everyone else. Just like we don't trust the tastes of sick people when it comes to food, we shouldn't trust the judgments of people with poor character. Or we could say that while pleasure is desirable, not all sources of pleasure are. For example, wealth is desirable, but not if it comes from betrayal, and health is desirable, but not if it comes from eating anything and everything. It's also possible that pleasures differ in kind. The pleasure that comes from good things is different from the pleasure that comes from bad things. You can't experience the pleasure of a just person without being just, or the pleasure of a musician without being musical, and so on.

The fact that a true friend is different from a flatterer also shows that pleasure isn't the highest good or that pleasures differ in kind. A friend is thought to be with us for our good, while a flatterer is there for our pleasure. The friend is praised, and the flatterer is criticized because their intentions are different. No one would choose to have the mind of a child for their whole life, even if they could enjoy the things children enjoy. Nor would they want to gain pleasure from doing something disgraceful, even if they never had to feel pain afterward. There are many things we would pursue even if they brought no pleasure, like seeing, remembering, knowing, and having virtues. If pleasure does come with these things, that's fine, but we would still choose them even if they didn't bring pleasure. So, it seems clear that pleasure isn't the highest good, nor is all pleasure desirable. Some pleasures are good in themselves and differ from others in kind or in their sources.

What exactly pleasure is, or what kind of thing it is, will become clearer if we start again from the beginning. Seeing, for example, seems complete at any moment because it doesn't need anything else to finish it. Pleasure also seems to be like this. It's complete in itself, and you can't find a pleasure that needs to last longer to be complete. This is also why pleasure isn't a movement. All movements, like building, take time and are aimed at a goal. They are only complete when the goal is reached. During the process, each step is incomplete and different from the whole movement. For example, placing stones is different from shaping the columns, and both are different from finishing the temple. The temple is complete because it reaches its goal, but the parts are incomplete. Each part of the process is different, and the complete movement only happens when the entire project is finished. The same is true for walking and other types of movement. Moving from one place to another has many forms—walking, flying, jumping, and so on. Even within walking, there are differences depending on where you are going. But pleasure doesn't work this way. Pleasure is complete at every moment. So, clearly, pleasure is not a movement. It is whole and complete, unlike movement.

This shows that the thinkers who say pleasure is a movement or a process of becoming are wrong. These concepts only apply to things that are divisible and not complete. Seeing, a point, or a unit don't "come into being," and neither does pleasure, because it's already whole.

Since each sense is active in relation to its object, and a sense that's in good condition works perfectly when it encounters the best possible object, the best activity of any sense is when it's at its best and focused on the best object. This activity is the most complete and pleasant. While pleasure can come from any sense, as well as from thinking and contemplating, the most complete pleasure comes from the best-conditioned sense interacting with the best object. The pleasure completes the activity, not in the same way as the sense or object itself, but as something that adds to it, like the bloom of youth adds to a person's appearance. As long as the sense and the object are as they should be, pleasure will be part of the activity because the sense and the object naturally produce this result when they work together.

Why, then, can't anyone feel pleasure all the time? Is it because we get tired? That's likely, because no human can stay active all the time. Therefore, pleasure isn't continuous because it comes with activity. Some things delight us when they're new, but less so over time for the same reason. At first, our mind is highly engaged, but eventually, our activity slows down, and so does the pleasure.

One might think that everyone desires pleasure because they all seek life. Life is an activity, and each person is active in the things and with the abilities they love most. For example, the musician uses his hearing to listen to music, the student uses his mind to think about theories, and so on. Pleasure completes these activities and therefore completes life, which people desire. So, it makes sense that they also desire pleasure, since it completes life. But whether we choose life for the sake of pleasure or pleasure for the sake of life is a question we can set aside for now. It seems they are connected and can't be separated, because without activity, there's no pleasure, and every activity is completed by the pleasure that comes with it.

Because of this, pleasures seem to be different depending on the activity. For different things are completed by different things, as we see in nature and in man-made objects. For example, animals, trees, paintings, sculptures, houses, and tools are all completed by different processes. In the same way, activities are completed by different pleasures. The activities of thinking are different from those of the senses, and both are different from each other. So, the pleasures that complete these activities are also different.

This is clear because each pleasure is connected to the activity it completes. An activity is improved by its proper pleasure because when people enjoy an activity, they do it better. For example, those who enjoy geometry become better at it and understand its principles more easily. Similarly, people who enjoy music or building improve in those activities by finding pleasure in them. So, pleasure enhances activities, and what improves an activity is unique to it. But things that are different in kind have different pleasures.

This is even clearer when we see how activities are disrupted by pleasures from other sources. For example, people who love playing the flute can't focus on a conversation if they hear someone playing the flute because they enjoy flute-playing more than the conversation. So, the pleasure from flute-playing disrupts their ability to pay attention to the conversation. This happens in all cases where a person is doing two things at once; the more enjoyable activity takes over, and if it's much more enjoyable, it will cause them to stop the other activity. This is why when we enjoy something a lot, we don't do anything else, and when we don't enjoy something, we tend to do something else instead, like eating sweets during a boring play.

Since activities are made better by their proper pleasures and hindered by unrelated pleasures, it's clear that different kinds of pleasure are very distinct. Unrelated pleasures act similarly to pain because activities are harmed by their proper pains. For example, if someone finds writing or doing math unpleasant, they won't write or do math because the activity causes them pain. So, activities are affected in opposite ways by their own pleasures and pains. Unrelated pleasures can have the same effect as pain, but usually to a lesser degree.

Since activities differ in how good or bad they are—some are worth choosing, some are worth avoiding, and some are neutral—the same is true of pleasures. Each activity has its own proper pleasure. The pleasure that comes from a good activity is good, and the pleasure that comes from a bad activity is bad, just like desires for good things are praised, and desires for bad things are criticized. But the pleasures that come with activities are more closely tied to them than desires because desires are separate in time and nature, while pleasures are closely connected to the activities themselves. In fact, it can be hard to tell the difference between the activity and the pleasure, which leads some people to think they are the same thing. (Though it would be strange to think that pleasure is the same as thinking or perception, it can seem that way because they always happen together.) As activities differ, so do their corresponding pleasures. For example, sight is more refined than touch, and hearing and smell are superior to taste. The pleasures that come with these activities are also superior, and the pleasures of thinking are even greater. Within each category, some pleasures are also better than others.

Each type of animal seems to have its own specific pleasure, just as it has its own specific function. This corresponds to its unique activity. If we look at different species, this becomes clear. For example, horses, dogs, and humans enjoy different things. As Heraclitus said, "Donkeys would prefer trash to gold," because donkeys find food more enjoyable than gold. So, animals of different kinds experience different pleasures. It's reasonable to think that the pleasures of one species don't differ too much, but in humans, they vary quite a lot. The same things delight some people but cause pain to others, and what one person finds pleasant, another may find unpleasant. The same thing happens with food; what tastes sweet to a healthy person may not taste sweet to someone who is sick. The same is true for other experiences. But in all these cases, we trust what the good person finds pleasant. If this is correct—and it seems to be—then virtue and the good person are the standard by which we measure pleasure. The things that seem pleasant to a good person are truly pleasant. If someone enjoys things that a good person finds boring, it's no surprise, because people can be damaged and corrupted in many ways. In these cases, the things aren't truly pleasant but are only pleasant to those who are in this specific condition.

Clearly, shameful pleasures shouldn't be called true pleasures, except to those with a distorted sense of enjoyment. But of the pleasures that are considered good, what kind should be seen as the proper pleasure for humans? This can be understood by looking at the activities involved. Pleasures come from these activities. Whether a truly happy person has one or several activities, the pleasures that complete these activities will be considered the true pleasures for humans. The other pleasures will be secondary, just as the activities that bring them are secondary.

Now that we have discussed virtues, friendships, and the types of pleasures, we can outline the nature of happiness, which we say is the ultimate goal of human life. Our discussion will be shorter if we first summarize what we've already said. We've said that happiness is not a state of being because if it were, a person who slept through their life or someone who suffered terrible misfortunes could be considered happy. Since these implications are unacceptable, we must see happiness as an activity, as we've said before. If some activities are necessary and are chosen for the sake of something else, while others are desirable for their own sake, it's clear that happiness must be among those that are desirable for their own sake, not for the sake of something else. Happiness is self-sufficient and lacks nothing. The activities that are desirable for their own sake are those that don't aim for anything beyond the activity itself.

Virtuous actions are considered desirable for their own sake because doing good and noble deeds is valuable on its own. Fun activities are also thought to be like this because we don't choose them for the sake of something else. In fact, we might neglect our bodies and possessions for the sake of fun, which can actually harm us. But many people who are thought to be happy focus on these kinds of activities, which is why quick-witted entertainers are highly valued at the courts of tyrants. They make themselves enjoyable companions in the tyrants' favorite activities, which makes them desirable. But just because people in power enjoy these activities doesn't mean they represent true happiness. People in power don't prove anything about what true happiness is because virtue and wisdom, which lead to good activities, don't depend on having power. Just because these powerful people, who have never experienced pure and meaningful pleasure, choose physical pleasures doesn't mean those pleasures are more valuable. Even children think the things they value most are the best things. It's natural that just as different things seem valuable to children and adults, different things seem valuable to bad people and good people. As we've often said, the things that are valuable and pleasant are those that seem so to a good person. To each person, the activity that matches their character is most desirable, and for a good person, the activity that matches virtue is most desirable.

Therefore, happiness is not found in amusement. It would be strange if the goal of life were amusement and we went through all the struggles of life just to have fun. Almost everything we choose, we choose for the sake of something else—except happiness, which is the ultimate goal. Working hard just to have fun would seem childish. But having fun so that we can work hard, as Anacharsis said, seems right. Fun is a kind of relaxation, and we need relaxation because we can't work all the time. But relaxation isn't the goal of life; it's something we do so we can get back to activity.

A happy life is thought to be a life of virtue. A virtuous life requires effort and isn't focused on fun. Serious things are better than trivial, amusing things. The activity of the better part of ourselves—

or the better person—is the more serious activity. And the activity of what's better is automatically superior and more like happiness. Even a slave can enjoy physical pleasures just as much as the best person, but no one would say a slave shares in happiness unless they also think the slave shares in human life. Happiness isn't found in these kinds of activities but, as we've said before, in virtuous activities.

If happiness is activity according to virtue, it makes sense that it would come from the highest virtue, which is the best part of us. Whether this is reason or something else that is our natural guide and helps us think about noble and divine things, the activity that comes from this part of us will be perfect happiness. We've already said that this activity is contemplation.

This seems to fit with what we said before and with the truth. First, this activity is the best because reason is the best part of us, and the things reason thinks about are the best things to know. Second, it's the most continuous because we can think about the truth for longer periods than we can do anything else. Happiness is thought to include pleasure, and the activity of philosophical wisdom is considered the most pleasant of all virtuous activities. The pursuit of wisdom offers pleasures that are pure and lasting, and those who know the truth are expected to enjoy life more than those who are still searching for it. The self-sufficiency that we talk about must also belong most to the contemplative life. While a philosopher needs the necessities of life just like a just person or someone with any other virtue, once they have those things, the just person needs other people to act justly toward. The temperate person, the brave person, and everyone else needs other people to live out their virtues. But the philosopher, even when alone, can contemplate the truth, and the wiser they are, the better they can do this. They may do it better with companions, but they are the most self-sufficient. This activity is loved for its own sake because nothing comes from it except the act of contemplation itself. In contrast, practical actions give us something beyond the action itself. Happiness is thought to depend on leisure because we work so that we can have leisure, and we make war so that we can live in peace.

The practical virtues are shown in political and military actions, but these activities seem to be the opposite of leisure. Warlike actions are completely unleisurely because no one chooses to go to war for the sake of being at war. A person who starts fights just to fight would be considered murderous. Political actions are also unleisurely because they aim at something beyond themselves, like power, honor, or happiness for oneself and others.

So, even though political and military actions are considered noble and important, they are not leisurely and aim at something beyond themselves. But the activity of reason, which is contemplation, seems to be superior in value and doesn't aim for anything beyond itself. It also brings its own pleasure, which enhances the activity. The self-sufficiency, leisure, lack of exhaustion (as much as possible for a human), and all the other attributes of the truly happy person are connected to this activity. Therefore, this is the complete happiness of a person, if they are allowed to live a full life, because none of the qualities of happiness are incomplete.

However, such a life might seem too lofty for a human. A person doesn't live this way because they are human, but because there is something divine within them. The activity of this divine part is far greater than the activity of the other kind of virtue, just as this part of us is greater than our human nature. If reason is divine compared to a human being, then living according to reason is divine compared to living a human life. We shouldn't listen to those who say that since we are humans, we should focus only on human things, or that since we are mortal, we should think about mortal things. Instead, we should do our best to live according to the highest part of ourselves. Even if this part is small in size, it far surpasses everything else in power and worth. This part of ourselves seems to be our true self because it is the most authoritative and valuable part of us. It would be strange to choose to live according to something else instead of this.

What we said earlier applies here as well: what is natural to each thing is the best and most enjoyable for that thing. So, for humans, the life according to reason is the best and most pleasant, because reason is the most human part of us. Therefore, this life is also the happiest.

But in a secondary sense, a life lived according to the other kind of virtue is also happy. The activities that come from this virtue are suited to our human nature. Acts of justice, bravery, and other virtues are things we do in relation to each other. We fulfill our duties when it comes to contracts, services, and various actions, and we deal with emotions. All of these things seem to be distinctly human. Some of them seem to come from the body, and the virtues of character are closely tied to emotions. Practical wisdom is also connected to virtue of character, and virtue of character is linked to practical wisdom, since the principles of practical wisdom align with moral virtue, and moral virtue is guided by practical wisdom. Since moral virtues are connected to emotions, they belong to our human nature. Therefore, the life and happiness that come from these virtues are also human. The excellence of reason is something separate from this. We don't need to go into too much detail here because that would go beyond the scope of our discussion. However, it seems that this kind of life needs fewer external things than a life of moral virtue. Both need the basics, of course, but the work of a statesman is more concerned with the body and material things. For this reason, there is little difference between the two. But there is a big difference in what each life needs to carry out its activities. A generous person will need money to do generous things, and a just person will need money to repay others because intentions are hard to see, and even people who are unjust can pretend to act justly. A brave person will need power to carry out acts of bravery, and a temperate person will need the right circumstances to show their temperance. Otherwise, how can anyone recognize them?

People also debate whether virtue is more about intention or action, and virtue is assumed to involve both. It's clear that virtue is complete when both are present. But to carry out virtuous actions, many things are needed, and the greater and nobler the action, the more things are required. But someone who is focused on contemplating the truth doesn't need any of these things, at least not for the sake of their activity. In fact, these things can even be obstacles to contemplation. However, since they are human and live in society, they will choose to do virtuous acts, so they will need these aids to live a human life.

We can see that perfect happiness is a contemplative activity from this thought: we believe the gods are the most blessed and happy of all beings. But what kind of actions can we attribute to them? Do they perform acts of justice, like making contracts or returning deposits? Wouldn't it seem silly for gods to do such things? How about brave acts, where they face dangers because it's noble? Or generous acts? Who would they give to? It would be strange if gods had money or needed anything like that. What about self-control? Praising them for not having bad desires seems pointless. If we consider all kinds of human action, none of them seem to fit gods—they seem trivial and unworthy of divine beings. But everyone assumes gods are alive and active; we don't think they just sleep like the myth of Endymion. If we take away action and productivity from a living being, what is left except contemplation? So, the activity of God, which is superior in blessedness, must be contemplative. And of all human activities, the one most like this is contemplation, which makes it closest to true happiness.

We see this in the fact that other animals don't share in happiness because they are completely deprived of this kind of activity. The whole life of the gods is blessed, and humans can share in this blessedness when they engage in similar activity. But animals aren't happy because they can't contemplate. So, happiness extends as far as contemplation does, and those who contemplate more deeply are more truly happy—not as a side effect, but because contemplation itself is valuable. Therefore, happiness must be some form of contemplation.

However, being human means we also need external things for happiness. We aren't self-sufficient for contemplation—we need a healthy body, food, and other necessities. Still, we shouldn't think that a happy person needs a lot of material things. Just because we need some external goods doesn't mean we need an excess of them. We don't need to rule the earth and sea to do noble deeds. Even with modest means, people can live virtuously. This is clear enough because private individuals are seen to do virtuous acts as much as rulers—perhaps even more. So, having enough of the basics is sufficient for a happy life lived according to virtue. Solon may have been right when he described a happy person as having modest possessions but having performed noble acts and lived a temperate life. Anaxagoras also seemed to think the happy person didn't need wealth or power, saying that to most people, the happy person would seem strange because they judge happiness by external things. The opinions of wise people seem to support these ideas.

But even though such ideas are convincing, we must look at the facts of life because they are the final test. If what we've said matches the facts, we should accept it. If not, we should see it as just a theory. A person who uses reason and develops it is likely to be in the best state of mind and closest to the gods. If the gods care about human affairs, it makes sense that they would value what is best and closest to them—reason—and reward those who value and honor it most. Those who care for what the gods care about and act rightly and nobly will be most dear to the gods. It's clear that this best describes the philosopher, so the philosopher must be most dear to the gods. And because of this, the philosopher will also be the happiest.

If we've covered the topics of virtue, friendship, and pleasure well enough, are we done? Not quite. As the saying goes, when there are things to be done, the goal isn't just to recognize them but to do them. So, with virtue, it's not enough to know about it—we must try to have it and use it. We must find any way we can to become good. If arguments alone were enough to make people good, they would deserve great rewards, as Theognis said. Such rewards should be given, but in reality, while arguments can inspire and encourage young people with noble hearts, they can't make most people good. Most people don't naturally respond to shame but only to fear. They don't avoid bad actions because they are bad, but because they fear punishment. They live by their desires, chasing after their pleasures and avoiding pain, without understanding what is truly noble and pleasant because they've never experienced it. What argument could change such people? It's hard, if not impossible, to remove bad traits through argument alone, especially when those traits have become deeply rooted. We should be satisfied if, with all the available methods for developing virtue, we can get people to develop even a little bit of it.

Some think we are made good by nature, others by habit, and others by teaching. The role of nature is clearly beyond our control and comes from divine causes in the truly fortunate. Argument and teaching, on the other hand, don't work for everyone. A person's soul must already have been shaped by good habits to enjoy noble things and hate what is bad, like soil prepared to nourish seeds. Someone who follows their desires won't listen to arguments against their behavior, and even if they do, they won't understand them. How can we convince someone like that to change? Passion doesn't usually yield to reason but to force. So, people's character must already have a natural tendency toward virtue, where they love what is noble and hate what is base.

It's hard to train people in virtue from a young age if they aren't raised under good laws. Living a temperate and disciplined life isn't pleasant for most people, especially when they're young. That's why their upbringing and activities should be regulated by law. When something becomes a habit, it stops feeling painful. But it's not enough to raise children well—they must continue practicing good habits as adults. We'll need laws for this too, covering the whole of life, because most people obey necessity rather than reason, and punishments rather than what is noble.

This is why some believe that lawmakers should encourage people toward virtue by appealing to what is noble, assuming that those who are well-raised will respond to such influences. They think punishments and penalties should be used for those who disobey or have worse natures, while those who are incurably bad should be banished completely. Good people, who live with their minds focused on what is noble, will follow reason, while bad people, who seek pleasure, can be corrected by pain, like a beast of burden. This is why punishments should be opposite to the pleasures that bad people love.

If a person is to become good, they must be well trained and continue to practice good habits. They must spend their time on worthy activities and avoid doing bad things, either by choice or by necessity. This can only happen if people live according to reason and order, enforced by laws. The command of one person, even a parent, doesn't have the same power as the law, unless that person is a king or something similar. The law has force because it's based on reason and practical wisdom. While people often dislike those who oppose their desires, they don't find the law as burdensome when it directs them toward what is good.

In Sparta, the lawmaker seems to have focused on upbringing and activities, but in most states, these things are neglected, and people live as they please, like the Cyclops, making their own laws for their family. It's best when the state takes care of these matters publicly, but if the state neglects this, individuals should help their children and friends toward virtue. They should at least have the will to do this if not the power.

From what we've said, it seems a person can do this better if they become capable of making laws. Public life is governed by laws, and good governance requires good laws. It doesn't matter whether these laws are written or unwritten, or whether they guide individuals or groups—just as in music or athletics. In cities, laws and the character of the people hold power. In households, it's the father's guidance and habits that hold power, and these are even stronger because of the natural bond between parent and child. Children are naturally affectionate and obedient. Private education has an advantage over public education, just like private medical treatment. While rest and fasting are generally good for someone with a fever, they might not be good for a specific person. A boxing coach doesn't train all his students the same way. So, personal education can be more precise because it's tailored to the individual.

However, it's best if a doctor, coach, or teacher has general knowledge of what's good for everyone or people of a certain type. After all, sciences are concerned with what is universal. But an experienced, non-expert person can sometimes take good care of themselves because they've studied their own case carefully. Some people seem to be their own best doctors, even though they couldn't help anyone else. Still, if someone wants to master an art or science, they should study what is universal and understand it as well as possible. Sciences deal with general principles.

So, anyone who wants to make people better—whether a few or many—must learn how to make laws if we become good through laws. It's not just anyone who can guide people toward the right condition. If anyone can do it, it's the person with knowledge, just like in medicine or any other skill that requires care and wisdom.

We must now ask where or how someone can learn to make laws. Is it, like in other fields, from experts? It used to be considered part of being a statesman. Or is there a difference between statesmanship and other sciences and arts? In other fields, the same people who practice the art also teach it, like doctors or painters. But while sophists claim to teach politics, they don't actually practice it. Politicians seem to do their work through skill and experience, not theory. Politicians don't write or talk much about politics, even though it would be more valuable than writing speeches for courts or assemblies. They also don't train their own children or friends to become statesmen. If they could, it's reasonable to think they would have done so, because there's no greater skill they could have passed on to their cities or kept for themselves and their loved ones. Experience clearly plays a role. Otherwise, how could they have become politicians by practicing politics? So, those who want to understand the art of politics need both knowledge and experience.

But the sophists who claim to teach politics seem far from actually teaching it. They don't even know what kind of thing it is or what subjects it deals with. If they did, they wouldn't confuse it with rhetoric or think it's less important. They wouldn't believe that you can legislate well just by collecting laws that seem good. They think it's possible to choose the best laws as if doing so didn't require intelligence. But good judgment is the most important thing, as it is in music. People who are experienced in a field can judge whether something is well-made and understand how it was achieved and what works well together. But those without experience can only see whether a work is good or bad, like people judging a painting. Laws are like the 'works' of politics. How can someone learn to be a lawmaker from them or judge which laws are best? Even doctors aren't trained just by reading books. Some medical books include not only treatments but also how to treat specific types of people and their conditions. These books are helpful to experienced people but useless to beginners. So, while collections of laws and constitutions might be helpful to people who can study and judge them, those without experience won't be able to make good judgments unless they have some natural gift. Still, they might become more knowledgeable.

Our predecessors didn't fully study the subject of lawmaking, so we should take it up ourselves. We should study the constitution to complete our understanding of human nature. First, let's review what earlier thinkers said on the topic. Then, using the constitutions we've collected, we should study what helps or harms states and what influences preserve or destroy different types of constitutions. We should also consider why some states are well-governed while others are poorly run. Once we've studied these things, we'll be in a better position to understand which constitution is best, how it should be organized, and what laws and customs it should use to be at its best. Let's begin our discussion.

Rhetoric

Aristotle

Book 1

Rhetoric is the counterpart of Dialectic. Both of these arts deal with topics that are familiar to everyone and don't belong to any specific science. As a result, most people use both rhetoric and dialectic to some degree because, at some level, everyone tries to discuss and defend their ideas, as well as attack the ideas of others. Ordinary people do this either randomly or based on practice and habit. Since people succeed either by practice or naturally, it is clear that we can analyze why some succeed through training while others do so naturally. Everyone would agree that figuring this out is part of the skill involved.

The writers of current rhetoric treatises, however, have only dealt with a small part of this art. The true heart of rhetoric lies in the methods of persuasion, and everything else is just secondary. But these writers often neglect enthymemes (a core element of persuasion) and instead focus on unimportant details. Stirring emotions like pity, anger, or prejudice does not focus on the core facts but simply appeals to the personal feelings of the judge. In places where rules for trials are stricter—like in well-governed states—this kind of rhetoric would have no place. For instance, in the court of the Areopagus, they avoid such irrelevant talk. This is a wise legal practice. Just as you wouldn't bend a carpenter's ruler before using it, you shouldn't manipulate the judge's feelings to influence the case. A litigant should only focus on showing whether something is true or false and whether it happened or didn't. Questions about the importance or fairness of the case should be left to the judge, not to the disputants.

It's important for laws to be written in a way that clearly defines as many details as possible, leaving only a few matters to the discretion of judges. There are several reasons for this. First, it's easier to find a few people who are sensible and capable of making and applying laws than it is to find a large number of people who are just as wise. Second, laws are created after careful consideration, while court decisions are often made quickly, which makes it harder for judges to ensure justice and fairness. Most importantly, lawmakers make general, long-term decisions, while members of the assembly or juries are tasked with ruling on specific cases. These people can be swayed by personal feelings like friendship, hatred, or self-interest, which clouds their judgment. So, in general, we should limit the number of decisions left to judges. However, questions about whether something happened or will happen, or whether it is true or not, must be left to the judge, since these can't be predicted by lawmakers.

Given this, it's clear that those who write about things like how to construct an introduction or narration in a speech are focusing on unimportant matters as if they were essential to the art of rhetoric. What these writers care about is how to influence the judge's feelings, but they say little about the real methods of persuasion, particularly enthymemes.

This explains why, although the same principles apply to both political and legal speeches, most writers have focused on legal rhetoric. Political rhetoric deals with more important matters and is more suited to citizens, but it tends to involve fewer irrelevant tactics. In political speeches, the audience is more likely to focus on the facts, as they are making decisions that directly affect their own interests. In court, it's not enough to prove the facts—you must also win over the listener's favor. In courts, judges are making decisions about other people's affairs, so they may listen with bias and focus on their own satisfaction, allowing the speakers to influence them instead of focusing on the truth. This is why some places, as mentioned earlier, have strict rules that forbid irrelevant arguments in court, whereas in public assemblies, the audience is better equipped to protect themselves from such distractions.

It's clear, then, that the true focus of rhetorical study is the methods of persuasion. Persuasion is a form of demonstration, as we are most convinced when we believe something has been proven. The main tool of persuasion for a speaker is the enthymeme, which is a kind of syllogism. And the study of all syllogisms falls under the field of dialectic. So, the person who best understands how syllogisms work will also be best at understanding enthymemes, once they've learned the differences between the two. The same faculty understands both truth and what seems close to truth, and people generally have a natural instinct for recognizing truth. This is why someone who is good at guessing the truth is also likely good at guessing what seems probable.

We've now seen that most writers on rhetoric focus on non-essential topics and have explained why they lean more toward legal rhetoric.

Rhetoric is useful for several reasons. (1) Things that are true and just naturally tend to prevail over their opposites, so if a judge's decision isn't right, it's likely the fault of the speaker, who should be blamed. (2) Some audiences can't be convinced by even the most accurate knowledge, because convincing someone through facts requires teaching, and not everyone can be taught. In such cases, we need to use ideas that are familiar to everyone to persuade them, as mentioned in the Topics, which deals with how to address general audiences. (3) We should also be able to argue both sides of an issue, not because we should use this skill unethically, but so that we can better understand the truth and defend against unfair arguments. Only dialectic and rhetoric allow us to argue both sides of a case, though the truth is usually easier to defend. (4) It's strange to think it's acceptable for someone to be unable to defend themselves with words and reason, even though using speech is what makes us human. If someone argues that the ability to speak can be misused, they should remember that the same can be said about most good things, such as strength, health, wealth, or leadership. All of these can be used for great good or great harm.

It's clear, then, that rhetoric isn't limited to any specific subject but is as universal as dialectic. It's also clearly useful. And its purpose isn't just to persuade, but to discover the best way to persuade in any given situation. In this way, rhetoric is like other arts. For example, the purpose of medicine isn't always to make someone completely healthy, but to help them become as healthy as possible. In the same way, rhetoric seeks to come as close as possible to persuading the audience, given the circumstances. Just as dialectic can distinguish between real and fake syllogisms, rhetoric helps distinguish between real and fake persuasion. Whether someone uses rhetoric ethically or not depends on their moral intentions, not their skill in the art.

Let's now begin discussing the systematic principles of rhetoric, focusing on the right methods and techniques for achieving success. We need to take a fresh look and define exactly what rhetoric is.

Rhetoric can be defined as the ability to find the ways to persuade someone in any situation. This is not something any other art or science does. Each other art teaches or persuades people about its specific subject, like medicine about health, geometry about shapes, or arithmetic about numbers. But rhetoric is about finding ways to persuade on almost any topic, which is why we say it isn't focused on just one specific area.

Some methods of persuasion are a part of rhetoric, while others are not. The ones that aren't are things like witnesses, evidence from torture, or written contracts—things the speaker doesn't create but are already there. The ones that are a part of rhetoric are the methods the speaker creates by using the rules of rhetoric. The first kind of persuasion just needs to be used, while the second kind needs to be invented.

There are three types of persuasion that come from speaking. The first type depends on the speaker's character; the second depends on putting the audience in a certain mood; the third comes from the proof or argument given in the speech. Persuasion happens through the speaker's character when the speech is given in a way that makes the speaker seem trustworthy. We believe good people more easily than others, especially when the facts aren't completely certain, and people disagree. This kind of persuasion should come from what the speaker says, not from what people already think about the speaker's character before the speech starts. It's not true, as some writers say, that a speaker's good character doesn't help them persuade others. In fact, a speaker's character is one of the most powerful ways to persuade.

Second, persuasion happens when the speaker stirs the audience's emotions. Our opinions change when we are happy or friendly compared to when we are upset or angry. This is the focus of most modern writers on rhetoric, and we will talk more about emotions later. Third, persuasion happens through the speech itself when the speaker proves something is true or seems true by using arguments that fit the case.

So, there are three ways to persuade. To master them, a person must be able to: (1) reason logically, (2) understand human character and what makes someone good, and (3) understand emotions—what they are, what causes them, and how they are stirred. It seems that rhetoric is related to both dialectic and ethics. We can even call ethics a part of political science. This is why rhetoric is often seen as political science, and those who teach it are seen as political experts—sometimes because they lack real knowledge, sometimes because they want to show off, and sometimes for other reasons. In reality, rhetoric is a branch of dialectic and similar to it, as we said earlier. Neither rhetoric nor dialectic studies any one specific subject; they are both about creating arguments. This should be enough to explain their scope and how they are related.

When it comes to persuasion through proof, or what seems like proof, rhetoric is like dialectic. In dialectic, there is induction and syllogism, or apparent syllogism, and the same is true in rhetoric. In rhetoric, an example is like induction, and an enthymeme is like a syllogism. I call the enthymeme a rhetorical syllogism and the example a rhetorical induction. Anyone who persuades through proof uses either enthymemes or examples; there is no other way. And since anyone who proves something has to use either syllogisms or inductions, as we know from the Analytics, enthymemes are syllogisms, and examples are inductions. The difference between an example and an enthymeme is explained in the Topics, where induction and syllogism are discussed. When we base a proof on several similar cases, this is induction in dialectic and an example in rhetoric. When we show that because certain things are true, another separate thing must also be true, whether always or usually, this is called a syllogism in dialectic and an enthymeme in rhetoric.

Both styles of oratory have their advantages. In some types of speeches, examples are more important, while in others, enthymemes are more effective. Similarly, some speakers are better at using examples, while others are better at using enthymemes. Speeches that rely on examples can be persuasive, but speeches that rely on enthymemes usually get more applause. We will talk about where examples and enthymemes come from and how to use them properly later. Next, we need to define these processes more clearly.

A statement is persuasive and believable either because it is obvious on its own or because it seems to be proven by other statements that are obvious. In both cases, it persuades because someone is convinced by it. But none of the arts deals with individual cases. For example, medicine doesn't focus on how to cure Socrates or Callias, but on how to cure anyone with a certain type of illness. It focuses on the general class of patients. Individual cases are too different from each other for any art to fully explain them. In the same way, the theory of rhetoric doesn't focus on what seems likely to a specific person like Socrates or Hippias, but on what seems likely to people in general. This is also true of dialectic. Dialectic doesn't make arguments based on random ideas or the thoughts of crazy people; it uses ideas that are worth discussing. Rhetoric also deals with common subjects that are debated. Rhetoric focuses on topics we talk about when we don't have an exact science or system to guide us, and when we are speaking to people who can't easily follow long, complicated arguments. We discuss things that seem to offer us choices. No one wastes time discussing things that are or will always be the same, because we can't change them.

We can form syllogisms and conclusions from previous syllogisms or from premises that haven't been proven and aren't accepted by everyone. The first type of argument is hard to follow because of its length, especially for an audience of untrained thinkers. The second type won't convince people because it's based on ideas they don't already accept.

Enthymemes and examples deal with what usually happens. The example is an induction, and the enthymeme is a syllogism about things that are not certain but likely. Enthymemes use fewer steps than normal syllogisms because if one of the steps is something well known, there's no need to mention it. The listener can add it themselves. For example, to prove that Dorieus won a contest where the prize was a crown, you just need to say, "He won at the Olympic games," because everyone knows the prize for the Olympics is a crown, so you don't need to mention that.

There are not many necessary facts that can be used in rhetorical syllogisms. Most of the things we make decisions about are not certain but give us options. We deliberate about our actions, and our actions are rarely controlled by necessity. Also, conclusions about things that usually happen must come from premises that also deal with what usually happens, just like necessary conclusions come from necessary premises. We know this from the Analytics. So, the statements used in enthymemes are usually about what happens most of the time, though some may be necessary truths. The materials for enthymemes are probabilities and signs. Probabilities are things that usually happen, but only if they are part of something that could happen differently. A probability is like a general truth, while the thing it applies to is like a specific case. Signs are of two kinds: one is like a specific case leading to a general conclusion, and the other is like a general truth leading to a specific case. The infallible kind is a "complete proof," or tekmerion, while the fallible kind doesn't have a specific name. Infallible signs are those that can be used to form proper syllogisms, which is why they are called "complete proofs." When people think their argument can't be refuted, they call it a complete proof, meaning it has been demonstrated and finished.

The first kind of sign can be illustrated by saying, "The fact that Socrates was wise and just is a sign that all wise people are just." This is a sign, but even if the statement is true, the argument can still be refuted because it isn't a syllogism. The second kind of sign can be shown by saying, "The fact that he has a fever is a sign that he is sick," or, "The fact that she is producing milk is a sign that she recently had a child." These are examples of infallible signs that form complete proofs, because if the particular statement is true, it cannot be refuted. The other kind of sign, where the general truth leads to a specific case, would be something like, "The fact that he is breathing fast is a sign that he has a fever." This argument can be refuted, even if the fast breathing is true, because someone could breathe fast without having a fever.

So, we have now explained what a probability is, what a sign is, what a complete proof is, and how they differ. The Analytics explains why some arguments can be formed into syllogisms and others can't.

An example is one type of induction, and we have already explained how it is different from other kinds of arguments. An example compares two things that are alike. When two statements are about similar things, but one is more familiar, the more familiar one is called an example. For instance, we might argue that Dionysius, by asking for a bodyguard, is trying to become a dictator. We can support this by giving examples from the past: Peisistratus asked for a bodyguard in order to take power and did become a dictator, and so did Theagenes in Megara. These examples are used to show that Dionysius has the same goal because he is asking for the same thing. This is an example of the general principle that anyone who asks for a bodyguard is trying to become a dictator. We have now explained the sources of these types of persuasion, which are often seen as proofs.

There is an important difference between two types of enthymemes that almost everyone overlooks. This is the same difference we find between types of syllogisms in dialectic. One kind of enthymeme belongs to rhetoric, just as one kind of syllogism belongs to dialectic. The other kind actually belongs to other skills or areas of knowledge, whether we already use them or haven't learned them yet. When people miss this difference, they fail to notice that the more they focus on the details of their specific topic, the more they move away from pure rhetoric or dialectic. This will make more sense with further explanation.

The proper subjects of rhetorical and dialectical syllogisms are the things we say the general or universal arguments deal with. These are arguments that apply equally to questions about ethics, science, politics, and other topics that are unrelated to each other. For example, an argument about "more or less" can be used in a syllogism or enthymeme about ethics, science, or anything else. But there are also special types of arguments based on specific ideas that apply only to certain subjects. For example, some ideas about science cannot be used to create an enthymeme or syllogism about ethics, and vice versa. This rule applies across the board. The general arguments don't focus on one specific subject, so they don't help us understand any one topic better. On the other hand, when we choose ideas that fit a specific argument better, we might accidentally create a new science that is separate from rhetoric and dialectic. We may explain the right principles, but then we're no longer talking about rhetoric or dialectic. Instead, we've moved into the field of knowledge that those principles belong to. Most enthymemes are actually based on these specific arguments, while fewer are based on the general ones. So, just like in other areas, we need to distinguish between the specific and general arguments when dealing with enthymemes. By specific arguments, I mean those that are unique to each subject. By general ones, I mean those that apply to all subjects equally.

Now let's classify the different types of rhetoric. Once we have these categories, we can look at each one individually and figure out what elements they are made of and what ideas they must use.

Rhetoric is divided into three parts, based on the three types of audiences that listen to speeches. In a speech, there are three things to consider: the speaker, the topic, and the audience. The audience is the one that determines the goal of the speech. The audience may be a judge, deciding on things that happened in the past or will happen in the future, or they may just be observers. A person in an assembly decides about future events, a juror decides about things that happened in the past, while an observer only judges the skill of the speaker. From this, we can see that there are three types of rhetoric: (1) political, (2) legal, and (3) ceremonial or display speeches.

Political speeches encourage people to do or not do something. This is true for both private counselors and people who speak to public assemblies. Legal speeches either accuse or defend someone. These are the only two options in any legal case. Ceremonial or display speeches either praise or criticize someone. These three kinds of rhetoric are focused on different times. The political speaker is focused on the future. They give advice about things that will happen. A legal speaker is focused on the past. One person accuses, and the other defends, based on things that have already happened. The ceremonial speaker is mainly focused on the present because praise or criticism is usually about current events. But they also sometimes refer to the past or make predictions about the future.

Rhetoric has three goals, one for each type of speech. The political speaker wants to show that a proposed action is either helpful or harmful. If they argue for it, they say it will do good. If they argue against it, they say it will cause harm. Other points, like whether the action is fair or honorable, are only brought up if they support the main point. Legal speakers want to prove that an action was either just or unjust, and they treat all other points as secondary to this. Ceremonial speakers want to prove that someone is worthy of honor or the opposite, and they treat everything else as secondary to that goal.

We can tell that each type of rhetoric focuses on these specific goals because speakers often ignore everything else. For example, in court, someone might admit that they did harm but still argue they weren't acting unjustly. Otherwise, there wouldn't be a trial. Similarly, political speakers may avoid admitting that they're recommending something harmful. They don't always worry about whether it's fair for a city to conquer innocent neighbors. Ceremonial speakers often praise someone for doing something noble, even if it wasn't in their best interest. For example, Achilles is praised for defending his friend Patroclus, even though he knew it would lead to his own death. While dying may not have been the smart choice, it was the more honorable one.

From this, we can see that these three types of rhetoric are the most important topics for a speaker to understand. Rhetorical arguments use complete proofs, probabilities, and signs. Every kind of syllogism is made of these ideas, and an enthymeme is a special type of syllogism made from these parts.

Since only possible actions, not impossible ones, can have been done in the past or will be done in the future, it's important for political, legal, and ceremonial speakers to know how to argue about what is possible or impossible, what has or hasn't happened, and what will or won't happen. Also, people try to show that good or bad, honor or disgrace, justice or injustice can be large or small, either absolutely or relatively. So speakers must also be able to argue about the size or importance of these things. They must be able to say which is the greater good, which is the greater act of justice, and so on.

These are the main topics that speakers need to understand. Now we can look at each type of rhetoric: political, ceremonial, and legal.

First, let's look at the things that political speakers advise people about. Political speakers don't deal with every subject, but only with things that might or might not happen. There is no advice to give about things that must happen or can never happen. Also, not all uncertain things are worth discussing, since some good things happen naturally, and some happen by accident, and it's useless to give advice about those. We only give advice about things we can control, things that depend on our own actions. We think about these things until we figure out whether we can do them or not.

To make a detailed list of the usual topics of political speeches and to define them all clearly would take too long here. That belongs to another, more detailed art. Rhetoric has already been given a much wider range of subjects than it really needs. As we've said before, rhetoric is a mix of logic and the ethical side of politics. It's a little like dialectic and a little like sophistical reasoning. But the more we try to turn rhetoric or dialectic into sciences, the more we lose their true nature. They are practical skills, not sciences. If we try to make them something else, we stop dealing with words and arguments and start getting into the details of specific subjects. Still, we can mention some important points that are practical to know, even though they belong more to political science.

There are five main topics that all political speakers discuss: (1) ways and means, (2) war and peace, (3) national defense, (4) imports and exports, and (5) laws.

On the topic of Ways and Means, the speaker needs to know how much revenue the country has and where it comes from. This way, if any source of revenue is being ignored, it can be added, or if any is weak, it can be increased. The speaker should also know about the country's spending so that wasteful spending can be cut, or large expenses reduced. People become wealthier by both increasing income and cutting expenses. To give good advice on this, a speaker must also know about how other countries handle these things.

On the topic of Peace and War, the speaker needs to know the country's military strength, both what it has and what it could have, and the type of strength it is. The speaker also needs to know the country's history of wars and how they were fought. This knowledge is important for both the speaker's own country and neighboring ones, especially those that could be enemies. The speaker should know whether another country's military is similar or different from their own because this can affect their relative strength. They should also study the wars of other countries and how they ended because similar causes tend to lead to similar outcomes.

On the topic of National Defense, the speaker needs to understand the current defense system, including the strength of the forces and the locations of the fortifications. This requires knowledge of the country's geography. With this information, they can suggest increasing garrisons where they are too small, removing them where they aren't needed, and guarding key points with extra care.

On the topic of the Food Supply, the speaker needs to know how much money is needed to feed the country, what kinds of food are produced domestically, and what needs to be imported. They also need to know what products the country exports. This helps them make trade agreements and treaties with other nations. There are two types of countries to be careful with: those stronger than your own, and those that are important trading partners.

Finally, and most importantly, the speaker must understand laws. The well-being of a country depends on its laws. The speaker needs to know how many types of constitutions there are and what conditions help each one succeed or fail. I am talking about how constitutions can be destroyed either by not being fully developed or by going too far. For example, democracy can turn into oligarchy if it's not developed enough or if it goes too far. In the same way, a nose that's too flat or too curved eventually stops looking like a nose at all. It's important to study the history of your own country's laws to understand which type of government is best for it now. It's also helpful to know the laws of other nations to learn which type of government suits different types of people. From this, we can see that travel books can be helpful for making laws since they teach us about the customs of different countries. History books are also useful. But all of this belongs to political science, not rhetoric.

These are the most important types of information that political speakers need. Let's now look at the arguments they use to support or reject proposals on these and other topics.

We can say that every person, and people in general, aim for a specific goal that guides what they choose and what they avoid. This goal, in short, is happiness and everything that makes it up. So, let's try to figure out what happiness is and what parts make it up. All advice about what to do or not do is focused on happiness and the things that either help or harm it. Whatever brings or increases happiness, or even part of it, should be done. Whatever destroys or stops happiness, or causes its opposite, should not be done.

We can define happiness as success combined with virtue, or as living an independent life, or as safely enjoying as much pleasure as possible. It can also be described as having good health, wealth, and property, along with the ability to protect and use them. Almost everyone agrees that happiness is one or more of these things.

From this, we can say that the parts of happiness include: good family, many friends, good friends, wealth, good children, many children, a happy old age, and physical qualities like health, beauty, strength, height, and athletic ability. It also includes fame, honor, good luck, and virtue. A person who has these inner and outer goods can't help but be independent, because there's really nothing else left to want. (Inner goods are those of the mind and body. Outer goods are things like family, friends, money, and honor.) We also think that a person needs resources and luck to live a truly secure life. Now that we've looked at what happiness is in general, let's break down its parts.

Good family in a community or country means that its people have been there for generations, that their first leaders were great people, and that many others have been born into this group who are admired for their qualities.

For an individual, good family—whether from the father's or mother's side—means both parents are free citizens. It also means that, like with a community, the family's ancestors were known for things like virtue, wealth, or some other quality people value. It's important that many members of the family, both men and women, young and old, have been admired for these qualities.

When we talk about having good children or many children, it's pretty clear what that means. For a community, it means having many young people who are strong, tall, beautiful, and athletic. It also means having young people who show virtues like self-control and courage. For an individual, it means having many children with these same qualities. Both sons and daughters are included here. For daughters, the virtues are beauty, height, self-control, and hard work that isn't considered degrading. Both communities and individuals should make sure that both men and women have these qualities. When women in a community, like in Sparta, are not treated well, half of human life is negatively affected.

Wealth is made up of having plenty of money and land, owning many large and beautiful properties, and having a lot of useful and fine tools, animals, and slaves. These possessions should be secure, respectable, and helpful. Useful property is what brings in income, while respectable property is what brings enjoyment. By "useful," I mean things that give us financial gain. By "enjoyable," I mean things we don't get much from other than pleasure. Property is secure if we can use it freely, and it's ours if we have the power to keep it or give it away, including selling it. Wealth is really about using things rather than just owning them. It's the activity of using property that truly makes someone wealthy.

Fame is being respected by everyone or having a quality that is admired by most people, or by the good and wise.

Honor is when someone is recognized for doing good. It's mainly given to those who have already done good but can also be given to someone who can do good in the future. Doing good involves helping others either by preserving life, providing resources, or giving access to things that are hard to get. Many people gain honor for things that might seem small, but the time and place often make them more important. Honor can come in many forms: sacrifices, recognition in writing, special privileges, land grants, front-row seats at public events, state-funded funerals, statues, and public support. Among foreigners, honor might be shown by bowing, giving someone priority, or giving gifts that are seen as symbols of respect. Gifts can be more than just property—they're also symbols of honor. This explains why people who love honor and people who love wealth both like receiving gifts. Gifts bring both groups what they want: property for the wealthy and honor for the respected.

Physical excellence is having good health, which means being free from illness and able to use your body without restrictions. Some people, like the historical figure Herodicus, are "healthy" but can't do anything because they must avoid most activities. That's not really something to admire. Beauty depends on age. In a young person, beauty is having a body that's fit for running and physical challenges, and being pleasant to look at. That's why well-rounded athletes are considered the most beautiful—they are naturally suited for both strength and speed. For someone in their prime, beauty is being fit for war and looking strong yet pleasant. For an older person, beauty is being strong enough for basic tasks and avoiding the deformities that often come with age and bother others.

Strength is the ability to move someone else when you want to, either by pulling, pushing, lifting, pinning, or holding them down. To be strong, you must be able to do these things in at least some ways, if not all. Physical size is about being taller, thicker, and wider than the average person, but not so much that it slows you down. Athletic excellence is made up of size, strength, and speed. Speed depends on strength. A fast runner is someone who can move their legs quickly and powerfully. A good wrestler is someone who can hold their opponent down. A strong boxer is someone who can hit hard and knock their opponent back. A great athlete can do all of these things.

Happiness in old age means aging slowly and without pain. A person is not happy if they age quickly or if they age slowly but with pain. Happiness in old age depends on good physical health and luck. If a person isn't healthy or strong, they will suffer. And even if they are strong, they can't live a long, painless life without luck. Some people live long lives without being physically strong, but that's a different issue and not something we need to focus on here.

The meaning of "having many friends" and "having good friends" is easy to understand. We define a friend as someone who always tries to do what they think is good for you. A person who has many people willing to do this has many friends. If these friends are good people, then they have good friends.

Good luck means getting or having all, or most, or the most important things that come from luck. Some things that seem to come from luck may actually be due to skill, but many things are beyond our control and happen by chance. For example, health can sometimes be controlled through effort, but beauty and height are natural. People envy things that come from good luck. Luck also explains things that happen unexpectedly, like if all your siblings are unattractive, but you are handsome, or if you find a treasure no one else noticed, or if a weapon hits the person next to you but misses you. Or if you skip going to a place where you usually go, and the others go there for the first time and get hurt. All of these are examples of good luck.

As for virtue, it's closely connected to praise, so we'll wait to define it when we talk about that topic.

It's now clear what we should aim for in supporting a proposal and what to avoid when arguing against it. The goals of political or deliberative speakers are based on what is useful. The purpose of deliberation is not to decide on the ultimate goals, but to figure out the best way to achieve them, meaning what is most useful. Since usefulness is a good thing, we need to understand what is generally considered "good" and "useful."

We can define something good as something that should be chosen for its own sake, or as something that we choose to achieve something else. It could also be what all living things seek, or what things with the ability to think or feel will seek once they gain that ability. Another definition could be what should be recommended to someone by reason or by their own personal judgment of what is good for them. Goodness could also be what brings something to a satisfying or self-sufficient state, or simply self-sufficiency itself. Something can also be called good if it creates, maintains, or leads to these characteristics while stopping or getting rid of their opposites. One thing can lead to another in two ways: either at the same time, or afterward. For example, learning leads to knowledge over time, while health leads to life at the same time. Things can produce other things in three ways: first, by directly causing them, like how being healthy produces health; second, by helping produce them, like how food produces health; and third, by usually leading to them, like how exercise generally helps maintain health.

Given all this, it's clear that getting good things and removing bad things are both good. Getting rid of bad things frees us from them right away, while getting good things gives us their benefits over time. It's also good to trade a smaller good for a greater one, or to reduce a greater evil in exchange for a lesser one. Virtue must also be good because it puts us in a good condition and leads to good actions. Virtues should be named and explained elsewhere. Pleasure is also good, since all animals aim for it. This means that things that are pleasant or beautiful are good too, because pleasant things bring pleasure, and beautiful things are either pleasant or desirable for their own sake.

Here is a more detailed list of things that are good. Happiness is one, because it is desirable for itself, is self-sufficient, and is the reason we choose many other things. Justice, courage, self-control, greatness of spirit, and generosity are all good too, because they are virtues of the soul. Physical qualities like health, beauty, and strength are also good, since they lead to other good things. For example, health brings both pleasure and life, which is why people often see it as the greatest good, because pleasure and life are two of the things people value most. Wealth is good because it's useful and leads to many other good things. Friends and friendship are good because a friend is valuable on their own and also brings other benefits. Honor and reputation are good too because they are both pleasant and often lead to other good things. Also, having honor usually means you already possess the qualities that bring it. The ability to speak and act is good because these qualities can lead to good outcomes. Good memory, quick learning, intuition, and similar abilities are good because they help us achieve good things. The same is true for the sciences and arts. Life itself is also good because it's desirable, even if no other benefits come from it. Justice is good because it helps the whole community.

These are the things most people agree are good. For things that people disagree about, we can argue like this: if the opposite of something is bad, then that thing must be good. Something is also good if its opposite benefits our enemies. For example, if it helps our enemies for us to be cowards, then clearly courage is valuable to us. In general, the opposite of what our enemies want or celebrate must be good. This idea is shown in lines like:

"Surely Priam would rejoice."

This rule holds true most of the time, but not always. Sometimes what benefits us may also benefit our enemies. That's why it's said that "troubles bring people together," meaning that the same thing can harm both sides.

Also, something that's not excessive is good, while something that's too much is bad. Something is also considered good if we've spent a lot of time, effort, or money on it. The mere fact that we've invested in it makes it seem valuable, and things that are seen as an end goal after a long journey are considered good. This is reflected in lines like:

"And for Priam (and Troy-town's folk) should they leave behind them a boast," and

"Oh, it were shame to have tarried so long and return empty-handed as erst we came,"

as well as the proverb about "breaking the pitcher at the door."

Anything that many people strive for or compete over is also seen as good, because, as we said before, what many people want is considered valuable. If something is praised, it must be good, since people don't usually praise what isn't good. This also applies to things praised by our enemies or even people we don't like, because if even they think something is good, it seems like everyone must agree.

Another way to argue something is good is if a wise or virtuous person has approved of it. For example, Athena helped Odysseus, Theseus helped Helen, the goddesses favored Paris, and Homer praised Achilles. Generally, anything people choose to do willingly is seen as good. This includes the things already mentioned and anything that might hurt our enemies or help our friends. A thing is "possible" in two ways: either it can be done, or it can be done easily. Things that are easy to do are those that don't cause pain or can be done quickly. The "difficulty" of something depends on how painful or time-consuming it is.

Something is good if it's what people want. People want to avoid evil, or at least to have more good than evil in their lives. This happens when any punishment is either small or barely noticeable. Good things are also things that are unique to us, something no one else has, because this increases their value. Things that fit a person's background, abilities, or needs are also good, as are things they feel they should have but currently lack. Even if these things seem small, people still pursue them. Anything that is easy to achieve is good, especially if most people, people like us, or people we look up to have succeeded in getting it.

Good things are also those that make our friends happy or our enemies upset. Things chosen by people we admire are also good.

Things that we are naturally or experientially suited for are good because we think we'll succeed more easily in them. Things that no unworthy person can achieve are considered better because they bring more praise. Finally, something is good if it's something we really desire, because what we desire is seen as both pleasant and better.

People tend to go after things that fit their character. People who love winning pursue victory. People who love honor pursue honor. Those who love money go after wealth, and so on. These are the sources we should use when we argue about what is good and useful.

Since people often agree that two things are useful but don't agree on which one is more useful, the next step is to talk about relative goodness and usefulness.

When something is better than another thing, it can be seen as the other thing but with something extra. The thing that is not as good is included in what makes up the better thing. When we say something is "greater" or "more," we're comparing it to something that is "smaller" or "less." Words like "great" and "small," or "many" and "few," are used to compare something to the normal amount. "Great" means something that is more than normal, and "small" means something that is less than normal. The same goes for "many" and "few."

When we call something "good," we mean that it is desirable for its own sake, not because of something else. It's something that everything aims for, something that everything would choose if they had wisdom and understanding. It's also something that tends to create or maintain these good things or always comes with them. The reason why things are done is to achieve an end, and the end is the good that everything aims for. For each person, what is good is whatever fulfills these conditions for them. So, a larger number of good things is better than a smaller number if that smaller number is included in the larger. In this way, the larger group is better because it surpasses the smaller one.

Also, if the largest member of one group is better than the largest member of another, then that whole group is better than the other group. If one group is better than another, the best member of that group is also better than the best member of the other group. For example, if the tallest man is taller than the tallest woman, then men as a group are taller than women. Similarly, if men are generally taller than women, the tallest man will be taller than the tallest woman. The superiority of one group over another is based on the superiority of their best members.

Another way to compare is when one good thing always comes with another, but the second thing doesn't always come with the first. The first thing is greater because its use includes the second thing. There are three ways one thing can come with another: at the same time, afterward, or as a possibility. Life comes with health at the same time (but health doesn't always come with life). Learning comes with knowledge afterward. Cheating can come with sacrilege as a possibility because someone who commits sacrilege could always cheat.

When two things are better than a third thing, the one that is better by a larger amount is greater than the other. A thing that produces a greater good than another thing is itself a greater good. We've already discussed how producing a greater good implies being a greater good. Similarly, something that comes from a greater good is itself a greater good. For example, if what is healthy is more desirable than what is pleasurable, then health is a greater good than pleasure.

Also, something that is desirable on its own is a greater good than something that isn't desirable on its own. For example, bodily strength is a greater good than being healthy because we don't want health just for its own sake, but we do want strength for its own sake. This is how we define what is good.

If one of two things is an end and the other is not, the end is the greater good because it's chosen for itself and not for something else.

For example, exercise is done for physical well-being, not for the sake of exercise itself. Of two things, the one that needs less help from other things is the greater good because it is more self-sufficient. Needing less help means it either needs fewer things or easier things. So if one thing cannot exist without another, but the second thing can exist without the first, the second thing is better. The thing that doesn't need help is more self-sufficient and therefore a greater good.

Also, something that causes other things is a greater good than something that doesn't, for the same reason: without a cause, nothing can exist or come into existence. If two sets of consequences come from two different causes, the consequences of the more important cause are themselves more important. In the same way, the cause that leads to more important consequences is the greater cause.

We can show that one thing is more important than another from two opposite perspectives. Something can seem more important either because it is a cause or because it isn't. A cause might be more important because it starts something, but an end might be more important because it is the goal. For example, Leodamas, when accusing Callistratus, said that the person who planned the crime was more guilty than the one who did it because it wouldn't have happened without the plan. But when accusing Chabrias, he said that the doer was worse than the planner because nothing would have happened without someone to carry out the plan.

Rare things are considered better than plentiful things. For example, gold is better than iron even though iron is more useful because gold is harder to get, which makes it more valuable. However, you could also argue that plentiful things are better because they are more useful. What we use more often is better than what we use less often, which is why there's a saying: "The best thing is water."

In general, hard things are better than easy things because they are rarer. But on the other hand, easy things are better because they are more in line with what we want.

Something is a greater good if its opposite is a greater evil or if losing it affects us more. Positive good and bad are more important than just the absence of them because positive good and bad are the actual goals, while simply not having good or bad is not.

The more noble or lowly the function of something is, the more good or bad that thing is. Similarly, the better or worse a thing is, the better or worse its function will be. The nature of a cause matches the nature of its effect, and the nature of the effect matches the nature of its cause.

Things are greater goods if being better at them is more desirable or honorable. For example, sharp vision is more desirable than sharp smell because sight is generally more valuable than smell. In the same way, loving friends more is more honorable than loving money more, so normal love for friends is more honorable than normal love for money.

One thing is also more honorable or better than another if it is more honorable or better to want it. The importance of what we want is linked to the importance of the desire itself. For this reason, if one thing is more honorable or better than another, it is also more honorable or better to desire it.

If one science is more valuable than another, the activity it deals with is also more valuable. The more valuable the subject of the science, the more valuable the science itself becomes.

Lastly, something is better if all or most people agree it is or if experts say so. People of understanding or the majority of people usually get it right, or at least as far as they use their understanding to make their decision. This general rule applies to all judgments, whether about goodness, size, or any other quality. Something is what it is because knowledge and understanding declare it to be so.

A thing is better if it belongs to better people, either because they are better or because the thing is better itself. For example, courage is better than strength. A greater good is something that a better person would choose, like choosing to suffer wrong instead of doing wrong, because that's what a just person would do.

The more pleasant of two things is better because everything seeks pleasure. People desire pleasurable experiences for their own sake, and pleasure is one of the characteristics of "the good" and "the end." One pleasure is greater than another if it has less pain or lasts longer.

Something that is more noble is better than something less noble because the noble is either pleasant or desirable for its own sake. Greater goods are things people desire more eagerly for themselves or their friends. On the other hand, greater evils are things people least want to happen.

More lasting things are better than things that fade quickly, and more secure things are better than less secure things. Lasting things give us longer enjoyment, and secure things are more convenient because they are always available.

Also, related words follow the same rule: if one is better, the others are too. For example, if a "brave" action is more honorable than a "temperate" action, then "bravery" is more desirable than "temperance," and "being brave" is better than "being temperate."

Something that everyone chooses is better than something that not everyone chooses. What is desired by more people is better because, as we've said, what everyone desires is good.

Something is better if it is chosen by competitors, enemies, authorized judges, or their representatives. In the first two cases, the choice is almost universal. In the last two cases, it's the decision of experts.

Sometimes, what is shared by everyone is better because it's shameful not to have it. Other times, what is rare is better because it is harder to get.

Things that are more praiseworthy are nobler and better. The same goes for things that earn more honors, as honor measures value. Things that have more severe penalties for not having them are also better, as are things that are better than others known or believed to be good.

Things look better when divided into parts because they seem to be better than more things this way. That's why Homer described the horrors of war in detail, showing how cities are destroyed, men are killed, and children and women are taken as slaves.

This same effect can be created by piling up examples or making a climax, like the comedian Epicharmus used to do. The reason this works is partly because division makes something look superior, and partly because the original thing seems to be the cause of important results.

A thing is better if it's harder or rarer than others, and its superiority can depend on the season, age, place, time, or the abilities of the person. When someone does something beyond their natural ability, age, or what others like them can do, their action is more noble, good, or just.

That's why there's an old saying about an Olympic winner: "I once carried loads of fish from Argos to Tegea, with a wooden yoke on my shoulders."

Similarly, Iphicrates used to boast about how far he had risen from humble beginnings.

What is natural is better than what is learned because it's harder to come by. Homer reflects this when he writes, "I have learned from no one but myself."

The best part of a good thing is especially good. Pericles once said in a funeral speech that losing the country's young men in battle was like losing the spring from the year.

Things that are useful when needed are also better, like things that help in old age or sickness. Of two things, the one that leads more directly to the goal is better. What benefits both people in general and individuals is also better.

Something that can be achieved is better than something that can't because what can be achieved is good in that situation, while the other isn't.

Something that comes at the end of life is better because it's closer to the ultimate goal.

What aims for reality is better than what aims for appearance. If a person wouldn't choose something if no one knew about it, it's aiming for appearance, not reality. This would suggest that receiving benefits is more desirable than giving them, since people will still want to receive them even if no one knows about it. But people wouldn't necessarily choose to give benefits if no one knew about it.

What people want to be is better than what they want to seem, because wanting to be something means aiming for reality. This is why people say justice isn't as valuable—because it's more desirable to seem just than to actually be just. This isn't true for health.

Something is better if it's more useful for many purposes. That's why wealth and health are considered very valuable—they provide many benefits, like helping people live, live well, feel pleasure, and act nobly.

Something is better if it brings both pleasure and less pain, because it gives multiple benefits. That way, you get the good of feeling pleasure and the good of not feeling pain.

Of two good things, the better one is the one that, when added to a third thing, makes a better whole. Also, things we can be seen to have are better than those that are hidden because they seem more real. Wealth may be considered a greater good if people know you have it.

Things that are highly valued are better than things that are not. For example, a one-eyed man suffers more from being blinded than a man with two eyes suffers from losing some sight because the one-eyed man has lost what he valued most.

These are the reasons we must use when speaking for or against a proposal.

The most important and effective skill for persuading people and speaking well in public affairs is understanding the different forms of government and recognizing their customs, rules, and interests. This is because people are always persuaded by what benefits them, and their benefit is tied to keeping things the way they are. Additionally, the final authority to make decisions depends on who holds the most power, and this varies depending on the type of government. There are as many types of supreme authorities as there are types of governments. The main forms of government are four: democracy, oligarchy, aristocracy, and monarchy. So, the ultimate power to judge and make decisions will always lie with either part or all of one of these types of government.

In a democracy, the people choose who will run the state by drawing lots. In an oligarchy, only those with a certain amount of wealth can hold office, while in an aristocracy, it's those with a specific education. By education, I mean the kind of education that is established by law, because it's the people who follow the country's traditions and laws who hold office in an aristocracy. These people are considered "the best," and that's where this form of government gets its name (which means "the rule of the best"). Monarchy, as the name suggests, is a system where one person has power over everyone else. There are two types of monarchy: kingship, which has certain limits, and tyranny, which has no limits at all.

We also need to pay attention to the goals that each type of government aims for because people choose actions that help them achieve their goals. The goal of democracy is freedom. The goal of oligarchy is wealth. In aristocracy, the goal is to protect education and national traditions, while tyranny's goal is to protect the tyrant. So, we need to identify the specific customs, rules, and interests that help each government achieve its ideal, because people choose their methods based on their goals.

Persuasion through rhetoric doesn't only happen through logical arguments but also through moral character. A speaker is more convincing if people believe that he is good, has goodwill towards them, or both. In the same way, we need to understand the moral qualities of each form of government, because the specific values of each will give us the best way to persuade them. We can learn the qualities of governments in the same way we learn about individuals—by looking at the choices they make. These choices are based on the goals that drive them.

We have now talked about the goals we should aim for, whether in the short term or the long term, when promoting any proposal. We've also discussed the reasons we should use to support the usefulness of that proposal. Finally, we've briefly touched on how to learn about the moral values and institutions of the different types of government—but only as much as is necessary for now. A more detailed discussion of this topic can be found in Politics.

Book 2

We have now discussed the materials needed to support or oppose a political measure, to give praise or blame, and to make a case in court for either prosecution or defense. We have also looked at the common opinions that we can use to best build our arguments in order to persuade our audience. These opinions are the ones our enthymemes are based on and developed from in each of the three kinds of oratory, depending on the specific needs of each type.

But since rhetoric's purpose is to influence decisions—whether it's the audience deciding between political speakers or a legal decision being made—the speaker must not only make their argument logical and believable. The speaker must also make sure their own character seems trustworthy, and they must help the audience, who will be making the decision, feel the right way. This is especially true in political speeches, but also applies in legal cases. It's very helpful if the speaker's character seems trustworthy and if they seem to have the right attitude toward the audience. Similarly, the audience must be in the right frame of mind. A speaker's character is most important in political speaking, while the audience's mood is more important in legal cases. When people feel friendly and calm, they think one way. When they feel angry or hostile, they think differently, or at least with different intensity. For example, when they feel friendly towards the person being judged, they think the person has done little or no wrong. But when they feel hostile, they take the opposite view. Also, if they're excited about something and hope it will be good for them, they believe it's likely to happen and will be good for them. But if they're feeling indifferent or annoyed, they don't think so.

There are three things that make people trust the speaker's character—these are the qualities that make us believe someone even without proof: good sense, good moral character, and goodwill. False statements and bad advice usually come from one or more of these three failures. Someone might form a false opinion because they lack good sense. Or they might know the truth, but because of bad moral character, they don't say what they really believe. Finally, they may be sensible and good, but because they don't have goodwill towards their audience, they fail to recommend the best course of action. These are the only possible reasons for bad advice. Therefore, someone who is believed to have all three of these good qualities will inspire trust in their audience. The way to make yourself seem sensible and morally good is the same as the way you would show others to have these qualities. Goodwill and friendliness will be part of our discussion on emotions, which we will now move to.

Emotions are feelings that change how people make decisions and that are also connected with either pain or pleasure. These include feelings like anger, pity, fear, and their opposites. We need to explain each of these emotions in three ways. For example, take anger. First, we must figure out what state of mind makes people angry. Second, we need to know who they usually get angry with. Third, we need to understand what reasons make them angry at those people. It's not enough to know just one or two of these things. If we don't know all three, we won't be able to make anyone feel anger. This applies to all the emotions. So, just as we previously listed useful points for the speaker to use in their arguments, let's now move on to analyze this topic in the same way.

Anger can be defined as a feeling, mixed with pain, that drives someone to seek revenge for an insult or wrong done to them or their friends without reason. If this definition is correct, anger is always directed at a specific person, like Cleon, rather than at people in general. It happens because someone has done or intended to do something harmful to you or one of your friends. Anger is always followed by a certain pleasure—the pleasure of expecting revenge. Since no one aims at something they think they can't achieve, the angry person is aiming at something they believe they can get. The belief that they will succeed is pleasurable. That's why it's been said that anger is "sweeter than honey," and that it "spreads through people's hearts."

There's also pleasure in anger because people think about taking revenge, and the images that come to mind are enjoyable, just like images that come in dreams.

Now, to slight someone means to think that they, or something about them, is clearly not important. We believe that both good and bad things are important and that things that lead to these are important too. But things that don't seem to matter much, or that don't lead to anything important, are considered unimportant. There are three types of slighting: contempt, spite, and insolence.

1. Contempt: This is feeling like something is unimportant. You slight what you think doesn't matter.

2. Spite: This is when you stop someone else from getting what they want, not because you want it, but just to prevent them from getting it. This kind of slighting happens because you don't care about getting anything yourself. You don't think the person can hurt you—otherwise, you'd be afraid of them, not slighting them. And you don't think they can help you, or you'd want to be friends with them.

3. Insolence: This involves doing or saying things that cause someone else shame, not because you want anything to happen for yourself, but simply for the pleasure of it. (Getting back at someone isn't insolence—it's revenge.) The person enjoying the pleasure of insolence thinks they are much better than the other person, which is why young people and wealthy people often act insolently. They think they're better than others when they act this way. One type of insolence is taking away someone's honor. You certainly slight them this way, because no one honors things that don't matter, for good or bad. That's why Achilles says, in anger, "He has taken my prize and dishonored me," and "Like a stranger, honored by no one," meaning this is why he is angry.

A person expects to be respected by those who are beneath them in birth, talent, goodness, or any area where they feel superior. For example, a rich man expects respect from a poor man, a skilled speaker expects respect from someone who can't speak well, a ruler expects respect from those they rule, and someone who believes they should be ruling expects respect from the person they think they should rule. That's why it's said, "Great is the anger of kings, sons of Zeus," and "Their anger lasts long after," because their great anger comes from their great sense of superiority.

A person also expects respect from those who they believe owe them something, whether because they have treated them well, are treating them well, or plan to treat them well—either directly or through their friends or at their request.

From what has been said so far, we can now understand (1) the mindset people are in when they get angry, (2) the types of people they get angry with, and (3) the reasons why they get angry.

1. The mindset: Anger comes from feeling some kind of pain. A person in pain is always trying to achieve something. So, if someone stands in their way, whether by stopping them from drinking when they're thirsty or in some other way, it feels the same to them. Whether someone opposes them or simply doesn't help them, or

annoys them while they're in this state, they'll feel angry in all of these situations. That's why people who are suffering from sickness, poverty, love, thirst, or any other unsatisfied desire are more prone to anger. They are easily angered, especially by those who ignore their suffering. A sick person gets angry if their illness is ignored, a poor person gets angry if their poverty is ignored, a soldier at war gets angry if the war is ignored, and a lover gets angry if their love is ignored. Any other kind of slight can cause anger when a person is already suffering. Everyone has their own source of anger based on their current feelings. People are also more likely to get angry when they expected the opposite to happen. An unexpected bad event is especially painful, just as an unexpected good event is especially pleasant. So, we can see what times, seasons, and situations lead people to be easily angered, and the more someone is in these conditions, the more easily they are angered.

2. The people we get angry with: We get angry with people who laugh, mock, or make fun of us because this behavior is insolent. We also get angry with those who hurt us in ways that show insolence— when the harm is neither payback nor something that benefits the other person, it feels like pure insolence. We also get angry with people who speak badly of us or show disrespect for the things we care most about. For example, people who care about being known as philosophers get angry when their philosophy is disrespected. People who are proud of their looks get angry when their appearance is criticized, and so on in other cases. We get particularly angry if we suspect that we lack the very quality we're being criticized for or if we think others believe we lack it. If we're confident that we're good at the thing we're being mocked for, we can ignore the insult. We also tend to get angrier with friends than with strangers because we expect our friends to treat us well, not badly. We get angry with people who used to treat us with honor or respect but no longer do, because we believe they now think little of us. We also get angry with those who don't return our kindness or don't return it enough, and with those who challenge us when they are below us in some way. All these

people seem to be showing contempt for us—those who oppose us seem to think they're better than us, and those who don't return our kindness seem to think we were acting from a lower position.

We are especially angry when we are insulted by people we see as insignificant. Since the slight is felt to be unjust, and people who are beneath us have no right to slight us, we feel particularly angry.

We also get angry when friends don't speak well of us or treat us well, and even more when they do the opposite. We get angry when they don't notice our needs, like Plexippus in Antiphon's play, because this shows they're slighting us. We always notice the needs of people we care about.

We also get angry with people who seem happy about our problems or who stay cheerful when we're suffering, because this shows they either hate us or don't care about us.

We also get angry with those who don't care about the pain they cause us. This is why we get angry at people who bring bad news.

We also get angry with people who listen to negative stories about us or keep pointing out our weaknesses, because this seems like either they're slighting us or they hate us. People who love us share in our troubles, and it should bother anyone to constantly focus on their own weaknesses.

We also get angry with people who insult us in front of five specific groups: (1) our rivals, (2) those we admire, (3) those we want to admire us, (4) those we respect, and (5) those who respect us. If someone insults us in front of these people, we feel especially angry.

We also get angry with those who insult or neglect people we are bound to protect, like our parents, children, spouses, or subjects. We also get angry with people who don't return a favor because this kind of slight seems especially unjust.

We get angry with people who respond with jokes or sarcasm when we're speaking seriously because this shows disrespect.

We also get angry when we're treated worse than everyone else, which is another way people show disrespect by implying we don't deserve what others do. Forgetfulness also causes anger, such as when someone forgets our name, even though this seems like a small thing. Forgetting shows neglect, and neglect feels like disrespect.

Now that we've explained the people we get angry with, the mindset we're in when we feel anger, and the reasons behind our anger, it's clear that the speaker will need to talk in a way that puts the audience in a state of mind that makes them prone to anger. The speaker will also need to show the other side in a way that makes them seem like the kind of people who deserve the audience's anger.

Since calming down is the opposite of getting angry, and calmness is the opposite of anger, we need to understand what makes people feel calm, who they feel calm towards, and how they are calmed down. Calming down can be defined as settling down or quieting anger. We usually get angry with people who disrespect us, and since disrespect is done on purpose, it's clear that we feel calm towards those who don't act this way or who seem to do it accidentally. We also feel calm towards those who meant to do the opposite of what they actually did. We also feel calm towards those who treat themselves the way they treated us, because no one is believed to intentionally disrespect themselves. We feel calm towards those who admit their mistake and are sorry, because we take their regret as enough, and stop being angry. This is shown in how we punish servants: those who argue and deny their wrongdoing get punished more, but we stop being angry with those who admit they deserved their punishment. The reason for this is that it's shameless to deny something obvious, and when people act shamelessly, they disrespect and look down on us. In any case, we don't feel shame in front of people we totally look down on.

We also feel calm towards those who lower themselves in front of us and don't argue with us. We feel that this shows they admit they are beneath us, and people who are beneath us feel fear. No one can disrespect someone they are afraid of. The fact that our anger fades when people lower themselves in front of us can even be seen in dogs, which don't bite people when they sit down. We also feel calm towards people who are serious when we are serious, because then we feel like they are treating us seriously and not looking down on us. We also feel calm towards those who have done us more favors than we have done for them. We also feel calm towards those who pray to us and ask for mercy, because they lower themselves by doing so. We also feel calm towards people who don't insult, mock, or disrespect anyone, or at least not anyone worthy of respect or anyone like us.

In general, we can figure out what makes us calm by looking at the opposite of what makes us angry. We don't get angry with people we fear or respect, as long as we feel fear or respect. You can't fear someone and be angry with them at the same time. Also, we don't feel much anger towards people who did something because they were angry. We don't feel like they did it to look down on us because no one insults others when they are angry—insulting others is painless, while anger is painful. We also don't get angry with people who respect us.

As for the mindset that makes people calm, it is clearly the opposite of what makes people angry. People are calm when they are having fun, laughing, or enjoying a feast. They are calm when they feel successful, satisfied, or happy. Basically, they are calm when they feel no pain or when they're enjoying harmless pleasures or hopeful about something. Also, as time passes, anger fades because time ends anger. Taking revenge on one person also reduces even greater anger towards someone else. For example, when Philocrates was asked by someone why he wasn't defending himself when the public was angry with him, he answered, "It's not the right time yet." When they asked, "When is the right time?" he replied, "When I see someone else getting blamed." This was because people become calm once they've let out their anger on someone else. This also happened in the case of Ergophilus: although the people were angrier with him than with Callisthenes, they let him go free because they had sentenced Callisthenes to death the day before.

Also, people calm down when the person they are angry at has already been punished or if they have already suffered more than the punishment they would have been given in anger. This makes people feel like they've already gotten their revenge. People also calm down if they feel they were the ones in the wrong and deserved to suffer because people don't get angry at what is fair. Since anger means feeling like you've been treated unfairly, if you realize your suffering is justified, the anger goes away. This is why it's a good idea to punish people with words before giving a real punishment—if you do this, even slaves are less upset about the actual punishment.

We also calm down if we believe the person being punished won't realize that they are being punished because of how they treated us. Anger is personal, after all. This is clear from the definition of anger. This idea is also shown by the poet, who wrote: "Say that it was Odysseus, destroyer of cities." This means that Odysseus wouldn't have felt avenged unless the Cyclops knew both who had blinded him and why. Because of this, we don't get angry with people who can't be aware of our anger, and especially not with people who have died. Once someone is dead, we feel like the worst has already happened to them and that they can't feel pain or anything else, which is what we aim to make them feel when we're angry. This is why the poet wisely made Apollo say, to stop Achilles from being angry at the dead Hector, "For look, in his fury, he dishonors the lifeless body."

It is now clear that when you want to calm others, you must use these points in your arguments. You must help your audience feel calm, and show them that the people they are angry with are dangerous, deserving of respect, have helped them, acted unintentionally, or feel very sorry for what they did.

Now, let's look at friendship and enmity, and ask who we feel these emotions towards and why. We'll start by defining friendship. We can describe friendship as wishing good things for someone else, not because it benefits you, but because you want good things for them, and being willing to help make those things happen. A friend is someone who feels this way and causes you to feel the same way in return. When people feel this way toward each other, they think of themselves as friends.

With this understanding, it follows that a friend is someone who shares your happiness in good things and shares your pain in bad things, simply because they care about you. Their happiness and sadness reflect their good wishes for you, since we all feel happy when we get what we want and sad when we don't. So, friends are people who see the same things as good and bad, and who are friendly or unfriendly to the same people. This means they must share the same wishes, and by wanting for each other what they want for themselves, they show themselves to be true friends.

We feel friendly towards people who have treated us well or treated people we care about well—whether they helped us in a big way, willingly, or during a critical moment—as long as they did it for our sake. We also feel friendly towards people who we think want to treat us well. This includes the friends of our friends, and people who like or are liked by those we like. We also feel friendly towards people who are enemies of our enemies, and people who dislike those we dislike. These people seem to share our view of what is good, which makes us think they want good things for us, and this, as we've seen, is what friends do.

We feel friendly towards people who are willing to help us with our money or our personal safety. This is why we value generous, brave, and just people. We consider just people to be those who don't take advantage of others—these are people who earn their living, especially farmers and manual workers. We also like self-controlled people because they don't treat others unfairly, and for the same reason, we like those who mind their own business.

We also feel friendly towards people we want as friends, if it's clear they want to be our friends too. These are morally good people and those respected by everyone, by the best people, or by those we admire or who admire us.

We also feel friendly towards people who are fun to live with and spend time with, like those who are good-natured, who don't point out our mistakes too often, and who aren't argumentative or quarrelsome—people like this always want to fight, and we feel that those who want to fight us want the opposite of what we want. We like people who know how to joke and take a joke. Both sides enjoy the exchange when they can handle being teased and can tease back in a good-natured way.

We feel friendly towards people who praise the good qualities we have, especially if they praise qualities we're unsure of. We also feel friendly towards people who are clean in their appearance, their dress, and in how they live. We like people who don't remind us of things we've done wrong or of the help they've given us, because both actions feel like criticism. We like people who don't hold grudges or stay angry but are quick to make up because we assume they'll treat us like they treat everyone else.

We also feel friendly towards people who don't speak badly about others and who only notice the good qualities in us and others, as a good person would. We feel friendly towards people who don't try to oppose us when we are angry or serious, because opposing us would feel like they are trying to fight us.

We like people who admire us, believe in our goodness, or enjoy our company, especially if they admire us for the qualities we most want to be admired, respected, or liked for.

We feel friendly towards people who are like us in character or occupation, as long as they don't compete with us or earn their living in the same way we do. Otherwise, it's like the saying, "Potter against potter and builder against builder begrudge each other's success."

We also like people who want the same things we want, if it's possible for both of us to have those things. Otherwise, competition causes trouble here too.

We feel friendly towards people with whom we have a relationship where we respect their opinions but don't feel embarrassed around them when we do something that might not be seen as proper. We also feel friendly towards people in front of whom we would be ashamed to do something truly wrong.

We feel friendly towards our rivals and those who we want to envy us—though without any bad feelings. Either we like these people, or we want them to like us.

We feel friendly towards people we help to achieve something good for themselves, as long as helping them doesn't harm us. We also feel friendly towards those who treat us well even when we're not around, which is why everyone feels friendly towards those who stay loyal to their friends after they've died.

In general, we like people who are truly devoted to their friends and don't abandon them when times get tough. Of all good people, we feel friendliest towards those who show their goodness as friends.

We also like people who are honest with us, including those who admit their own weaknesses. As mentioned earlier, we aren't embarrassed to do something improper around our friends, and if we are embarrassed, it means we don't truly love them. So, if we aren't embarrassed, it seems that we do love them.

We also feel friendly towards people who don't make us feel scared or uncomfortable. No one can like someone they're afraid of.

Friendship has different forms—companionship, closeness, family relationships, and so on.

Things that create friendship are: doing kind things, doing them without being asked, and not bragging about them afterward. This shows that the kindness was done for our sake, not for some other reason.

Enmity and hatred can be understood by looking at the opposites of what creates friendship. Enmity can come from anger, spite, or slander. Anger comes from personal offenses, while enmity can happen without a personal offense. We might hate people simply because we think they have a bad character.

Anger is always directed at specific individuals, like Callias or Socrates, while hatred can be directed at whole groups: for example, we all hate thieves and informers. Anger can fade over time, but hatred doesn't. Anger aims to make someone feel pain, while hatred aims to harm them. Angry people want their victims to feel their anger, but haters don't care whether their victims feel anything at all. All painful things are felt, but the greatest evils—like injustice and foolishness—aren't always felt, since they don't cause physical pain.

Anger is always accompanied by pain, but hatred is not. An angry person feels pain, but a hater doesn't. Many things can make an angry person pity the one who offended them, but a hater never wants to feel pity for someone they hate. The angry person wants the offender to suffer for what they've done, while the hater wants them to cease to exist.

From all this, it's clear that we can prove whether people are friends or enemies. If they aren't, we can make them seem like they are. If they claim to be friends, we can disprove their claim. If there's a question of whether an action was motivated by anger or hatred, we can argue for whichever we choose.

Let's now talk about fear. The following will explain the things and people that make us feel afraid, and the situations in which we feel fear. Fear can be defined as a feeling of pain or disturbance caused by imagining something bad or harmful happening in the future. It's about harmful or painful things only, because there are some bad things, like wickedness or stupidity, that don't scare us. What I mean is things that cause serious pain or loss. And we only fear these things if they seem close, not far away. For example, we all know we're going to die, but we're not scared of it because death isn't near us yet. Based on this definition, fear is caused by whatever we think has the power to destroy or hurt us in a way that leads to great pain. This is why even the signs of such things scare us, making us feel like the bad thing is near. The idea of a bad thing coming close is what we call "danger."

Signs of danger include people who are angry at us and have the power to harm us. It's clear they want to do something to us, and they are ready to act. Also, when someone who has power is unjust, we fear them because unjust people want to do harm. Virtuous people who have been wronged and now have power are also scary because they want to retaliate. We also fear powerful people who are afraid because they're likely to strike first. Since most people are bad, greedy, and cowardly in danger, it's usually scary to be at someone else's mercy. So, if we've done something bad, we're scared those who know might betray or abandon us. People who can harm us are also scary if we're vulnerable. Usually, people harm others when they have the power to do so. We fear people we've wronged because they're looking for a chance to get back at us.

We also fear people who are feared by those stronger than us, because if they can hurt stronger people, they can definitely hurt us. The same goes for those who are already hurting weaker people. These people either are already strong or will be when they get stronger. Among those we've wronged or those who are our enemies, it's not the loud and emotional ones we should fear, but the quiet, sneaky, and dishonest ones. We never know when they'll strike, so we can't feel safe. All dangerous things are scarier if they don't give us a chance to fix our mistakes. And the worst things are the ones we can't stop or have little control over. In general, anything that causes us to feel pity when it happens to others will also cause us to feel fear when it threatens us.

These are the main things that cause fear. Now, let's look at the conditions in which we feel fear. If fear is connected to the belief that something bad will happen to us, then clearly, no one will feel afraid if they believe nothing bad can happen to them. We won't fear things we don't believe can happen to us, or people we think can't hurt us. And we won't fear things at times when we think we're safe from them. So, fear is felt by those who think something bad is likely to happen to them, at the hands of certain people, in a certain way, and at a certain time. People don't believe this when they're in the middle of great success and become arrogant, careless, or reckless—the kind of attitude that wealth, physical strength, lots of friends, and power can bring. Nor do they feel fear when they've already experienced every kind of horror and have become numb to what's coming, like people being beaten who are already close to death. If someone is going to feel the pain of uncertainty, they need to have some faint hope of escaping. This is because fear makes us think about what can be done, and no one does this when they feel completely hopeless. So, when an audience needs to be frightened, the speaker must make them feel they are truly in danger by pointing out that it has happened to others who were stronger than they are. The speaker should also show that it's happening now or has happened to people like them, at the hands of unexpected people, in unexpected ways, and at unexpected times.

Now that we understand the nature of fear, the things that cause it, and the different states of mind that lead to fear, we can also understand what confidence is. Confidence is the opposite of fear, and the things that cause confidence are the opposite of what causes fear. Confidence is the belief that what keeps us safe is near, and that what's harmful is either far away or absent. Confidence may come from the presence of things that make us feel safe or from the absence of things that scare us. We feel confident if we think we can do many or important things to fix or prevent trouble. We also feel confident if we haven't wronged others or been wronged by them, if we have no rivals or our rivals are weak, or if our strong rivals are our friends or have treated us well. We also feel confident if the people whose interests align with ours are more numerous or stronger than those against us.

We feel confident in ourselves if we believe we've succeeded many times and never faced defeat, or if we've often faced danger and come out safely. There are two main reasons people face danger calmly:

either they have no experience of it or they have ways to deal with it. For example, when people are in danger at sea, they feel confident either because they've never experienced a storm or because their experience has given them the skills to handle it. We also feel confident when nothing seems to scare people like us, people weaker than us, or people we believe we're stronger than. We believe this when we've defeated them or others as strong or stronger than they are.

We also feel confident if we think we have more and better resources than our rivals—things like wealth, physical strength, supporters, land, and weapons. We feel confident if we haven't wronged many people, or at least not the people we fear. And generally, we feel confident if we think our relationship with the gods is good, as shown by signs and oracles. Anger also makes us feel confident because it comes from the belief that we've been wronged, not that we are the ones doing wrong, and that divine powers support the wronged. We also feel confident when we start something new and believe we will not fail or that we will succeed completely.

Now, let's turn to shame and shamelessness. The following will explain the things that cause these feelings, the people in front of whom we feel them, and the situations in which they occur. Shame can be defined as a feeling of pain or disturbance about bad things, whether they're happening now, happened in the past, or are likely to happen in the future. These bad things seem like they will bring disgrace to us, while shamelessness is when we don't care about or look down on these same bad things. If this definition is true, it follows that we feel shame about things that we believe are disgraceful to ourselves or to those we care about.

These bad things are, first of all, caused by moral weakness. Examples are throwing away your shield or running away in battle because of cowardice. Also, refusing to return money or cheating others because of injustice. Engaging in sexual activities with forbidden people, at wrong times, or in wrong places shows a lack of self-control. Making money in petty or disgraceful ways, like taking advantage of the poor or the dead, also reflects greed and meanness. When it comes to money, we feel ashamed if we don't help others as much as we can, or if we take help from those worse off than ourselves. Similarly, borrowing when it looks like begging, or begging when it looks like asking for a favor to be returned, or asking for such a favor when it feels like begging—all of these actions show a lack of dignity. Praising someone just to get something out of them or being overly sympathetic to someone's sadness when you're with them also reveals a flatterer's mindset.

Refusing to endure hardships that are endured by people who are older, higher-ranking, or less capable than we are shows weakness. Accepting many favors from someone and then insulting them for giving those favors shows a low, ungrateful character. Talking too much about yourself, bragging loudly, or taking credit for others' achievements shows boastfulness. These, and similar actions, are disgraceful and show a lack of shame.

Another cause of shame is failing to have something honorable that everyone else, or nearly everyone like us, has. By "people like us," I mean people of the same race, country, age, family, or those on our level. Once we are on the same level as others, it's shameful to have less education or fewer advantages than they do. And it's even worse if it's our own fault. Whenever we are to blame for our past, present, or future situation, it's because of our own moral weakness. We also feel ashamed if we've had, or are about to have, something dishonorable done to us, like giving ourselves up to vile actions. Acts that involve giving in to others' desires are shameful, whether we do so willingly or unwillingly (being forced is an example of unwillingness), because surrendering without resistance shows weakness or cowardice.

These, and other similar things, cause us to feel shame. Since shame is a feeling connected to disgrace, and we want to avoid disgrace itself (not just its consequences), we care about the opinions of certain people. These are the people in front of whom we feel shame—the ones whose opinion matters to us. These people include those who admire us, those we admire, those whose admiration we seek, those with whom we compete, and those whose opinions we respect.

We admire people who have qualities we value, or those who can give us something we really want—just like a lover desires the approval of their beloved. We compete with those on our level. We respect the opinions of wise people, like our elders and those who are well-educated. We feel more shame if our actions are done publicly and everyone can see. This is why the saying goes, "Shame is in the eyes." For this reason, we feel the most shame in front of people who are always around us and notice what we do because they're always watching. We also feel ashamed in front of people who don't have the same faults as us, since it's clear their opinions are different from ours.

We feel ashamed in front of people who are harsh toward those they think are wrong. People usually don't mind their neighbors doing things they do themselves, but they get upset when their neighbors do things they don't do. We also feel ashamed in front of people who might tell others about what we've done. Not telling others is as good as not believing we've done something wrong. People are likely to spread news about us if we've wronged them because they're looking for ways to hurt us, or if they gossip about everyone, because those who attack innocent people will be even more eager to attack the guilty.

We also feel shame in front of people whose job is to criticize others, like satirists and comedy writers. These people are basically gossips and tale-bearers. We feel shame in front of people who don't yet know anything bad about us, because so far, they've admired us. That's why we feel embarrassed to refuse favors to those who ask us for something the first time—we haven't lost their good opinion yet. These people include those who want to become our friends for the first time because they've only seen our good side. They also include our old friends who don't know any bad things about us. We feel ashamed not only of shameful acts themselves but also of the evidence of those acts. For example, we're not just ashamed of engaging in sexual activities, but also of the signs of it. Similarly, we're ashamed not only of disgraceful actions but also of disgraceful talk.

We also feel shame not just in front of the people mentioned, but in front of those who might tell these people what we've done, like their servants or friends. And generally, we don't feel shame in front of people whose opinions we completely look down on as untrustworthy. No one feels ashamed in front of small children or animals. We don't feel ashamed of the same things in front of close friends as we do in front of strangers. In front of close friends, we feel ashamed of what we see as real faults, while in front of strangers, we feel ashamed of what are considered social faults.

The conditions that make us feel shame include having people in our lives who fit the description of those before whom we feel shame, as mentioned earlier. These people are those we admire, those who admire us, those whose admiration we seek, or those from whom we want something that we can't get if we lose their good opinion. These people might actually be watching us (like when Cydias told the Athenians to imagine that all the Greeks were watching how they voted), or they might be close enough to find out what we do. This is why we don't want to be seen by people who once wanted to be like us when we're in trouble—it reminds them of when they admired us.

We also feel ashamed when we're dishonoring actions or accomplishments that we or our ancestors are proud of. We feel shame before people for whose wrongdoings we would also feel shame, such as those we've mentioned before, those who take us as role models, those we've taught or advised, or others who are like us and with whom we compete. There are many things that shame in front of such people makes us do or avoid doing. And we feel even more shame when we'll be constantly seen by people who know about our disgrace. That's why, when the poet Antiphon was about to be beaten to death by Dionysius, and he saw the people who were about to die with him covering their faces, he asked them, "Why are you covering your faces? Is it because you're afraid these spectators will see you tomorrow?"

This is how shame works. To understand shamelessness, just think about the opposite of everything mentioned here.

Let's talk about Kindness now. Its definition will show us towards whom it is felt, why, and in what state of mind. Kindness is when someone helps a person in need, not to get anything in return, nor for their own benefit, but for the benefit of the person being helped.

Kindness is especially great when it's shown to someone who is in great need, or who needs something important and hard to get, or who needs it during an important and difficult crisis; or if the helper is the only one, the first, or the main person to give help. Natural desires make up such needs, especially strong desires accompanied by pain when they aren't fulfilled. These cravings include things like sexual desire and the urges that arise during injuries and dangers; because desire is active both in danger and in pain.

Therefore, those who stand by us in poverty or exile, even if they don't help us much, are truly kind to us because our need is great and urgent; like the man who gave the mat in the Lyceum. So, the help should ideally meet just this kind of need; and if not this kind, then some other kind that is as great or greater. Now we understand to whom, why, and under what conditions kindness is shown; and these facts must form the basis of our arguments.

We must show that the people helped are, or have been, in the kind of pain and need we've described, and that their helpers gave, or are giving, the kind of help described, in the kind of need described. We can also see how to remove the idea of kindness and make our opponents seem unkind: we might argue that they are being or have been helpful simply to promote their own interest—which, as we've stated, is not kindness; or that their action was accidental or forced upon them; or that they were not doing a favor but merely returning one, whether they know this or not—in either case, the action is just a repayment and is therefore not kindness even if the doer doesn't know the situation.

When considering this subject, we must look at all the categories: an act may be an act of kindness because (1) it is a specific thing, (2) it has a particular size or (3) quality, or (4) it's done at a particular time or (5) place. As evidence of the lack of kindness, we may point out that a smaller service had been refused to the person in need; or that the same service, or an equal or greater one, has been given to his enemies; these facts show that the service wasn't done for the sake of the person helped. Or we might point out that the thing desired was worthless and that the helper knew it: no one will admit they are in need of something worthless.

That's enough about Kindness and Unkindness. Now let's consider Pity, asking ourselves what things excite pity, for whom, and in what states of mind pity is felt. Pity can be defined as a feeling of pain caused by seeing some evil, destructive or painful, happen to someone who doesn't deserve it, and which we might expect could happen to us or a friend, and might happen soon.

To feel pity, we must be capable of thinking that some bad thing may happen to us or a friend of ours, and moreover, some such evil as we've defined or something similar. Therefore, pity is not felt by those completely ruined, who suppose that no further evil can befall them since the worst has already happened; nor by those who imagine themselves immensely fortunate—their feeling is rather arrogant pride, because when they think they possess all the good things in life, they believe that nothing bad can happen to them, which is one of the good things they think they have.

People who think bad things might happen to them include those who have already experienced it and have safely escaped from it; elderly people, due to their good sense and experience; weak people, especially those inclined to cowardice; and also educated people, since they can think ahead. Also, those who have parents living, or children, or wives; because these are close to us, and the evils mentioned above may easily befall them.

And those who are neither moved by courageous emotions like anger or confidence (these emotions ignore the future), nor by a disposition to arrogant insolence (arrogant people also ignore the possibility that something bad will happen to them), nor yet by great fear (panicked people do not feel pity because they are focused on themselves); only those who are between these extremes feel pity. To feel pity, we must also believe in the goodness of at least some people; if you think nobody is good, you will believe that everybody deserves bad fortune. In general, we feel pity whenever we are in the condition of remembering that similar misfortunes have happened to us or our loved ones, or expecting them to happen in the future.

That's enough about the mental conditions under which we feel pity. What we pity is clearly stated in the definition. All unpleasant and painful things excite pity if they tend to destroy or cause pain and ruin; and all such evils that are due to chance, if they are serious. The painful and destructive evils are: death in its various forms, bodily injuries and afflictions, old age, diseases, lack of food.

The evils due to chance are: being without friends, having few friends (it's a pitiful thing to be torn away from friends and companions), deformity, weakness, mutilation; evil coming from a source from which good ought to have come; and the frequent repetition of such misfortunes. Also, the coming of good when the worst has happened—for example, the arrival of the Great King's gifts for Diopeithes after his death. Also, when no good has come to a person at all, or when they can't enjoy it when it does come.

So, the reasons we feel pity are these or similar. The people we pity are those we know, as long as they aren't very closely related to us—in that case, we feel about them as if we were in danger ourselves. For this reason, they say Amasis did not weep at the sight of his son being led to death, but did weep when he saw his friend begging: the latter sight was pitiful, the former terrible, and the terrible is different from the pitiful; it tends to cast out pity and often helps to produce the opposite of pity.

Also, we feel pity when the danger is near ourselves. We also pity those who are like us in age, character, disposition, social standing, or birth; because in all these cases, it seems more likely that the same misfortune may befall us too. Here, we must remember the general principle that what we fear for ourselves excites our pity when it happens to others.

Furthermore, since it's when the sufferings of others are close to us that they excite our pity (we cannot remember what disasters happened a hundred centuries ago, nor look forward to what will happen a hundred centuries in the future, and therefore feel little pity, if any, for such things), it follows that those who enhance the effect of their words with suitable gestures, tones, dress, and dramatic action are especially successful in exciting pity: they put the disasters before our eyes and make them seem close to us, just happening or just past.

Anything that has just happened, or is going to happen soon, is particularly pitiful; so too are the signs and actions of sufferers—the garments and the like of those who have already suffered; the words and the like of those actually suffering—for instance, those who are on the point of death. Most pitiful of all is when, in such times of trial, the victims are persons of noble character: whenever they are so, our pity is especially excited, because their innocence, as well as seeing their misfortunes before our eyes, makes their misfortunes seem close to ourselves.

The feeling most directly opposed to pity is called Indignation. Feeling pain at someone's undeserved good fortune is, in one sense, opposite to feeling pain at someone's undeserved bad fortune, and comes from the same moral qualities. Both feelings are associated with good moral character; it is our duty both to feel sympathy and pity for undeserved distress, and to feel indignation at undeserved prosperity; because whatever is undeserved is unjust, and that's why we ascribe indignation even to the gods.

It might be thought that envy is similarly opposed to pity, on the ground that envy is closely akin to indignation, or even the same thing. But it's not the same. It's true that envy is also a disturbing pain caused by the prosperity of others. But it's excited not by the prosperity of the undeserving but by that of people who are like us or equal to us.

The two feelings have this in common: they are not due to something bad likely to happen to ourselves, but only to what is happening to our neighbor. The feeling ceases to be envy in one case and indignation in the other, and becomes fear if the pain and disturbance are due to the prospect of something bad for ourselves as a result of the other person's good fortune.

The feelings of pity and indignation will obviously be accompanied by the opposite feelings of satisfaction. If you are pained by the undeserved distress of others, you will be pleased, or at least not pained, by their deserved distress. Therefore, no good person can be upset by the punishment of parricides or murderers. These are things we are bound to rejoice at, as we must at the prosperity of the deserving; both these things are just, and both give pleasure to any honest person, since he cannot help expecting that what has happened to someone like him will happen to him too.

All these feelings are associated with the same type of moral character. And their opposites are associated with the opposite type; the person who is delighted by others' misfortunes is identical with the person who envies others' prosperity. Because anyone who is pained by the occurrence or existence of a given thing must be pleased by that thing's non-existence or destruction. We can now see that all these feelings tend to prevent pity (though they differ among themselves for the reasons given), so all are equally useful for countering an appeal to pity.

We will first consider Indignation—saving the other emotions for later—and ask with whom, on what grounds, and in what states of mind we may feel indignant. These questions are really answered by what we've already said. Indignation is the pain caused by seeing undeserved good fortune. So, it's clear to begin with that there are some forms of good whose sight cannot cause it.

For example, a person may be just or brave, or acquire moral goodness; but we will not be indignant with him for that reason, any more than we will pity him for the opposite reason. Indignation is aroused by the sight of wealth, power, and the like—by all those things, roughly speaking, which are deserved by good people and by those who possess the goods of nature—noble birth, beauty, and so on.

Also, what is long established seems similar to what exists by nature; therefore, we feel more indignation at those possessing a given good if they have only just gotten it and the prosperity it brings. The newly rich offend more than those whose wealth is long-standing and inherited. The same is true of those who have office or power, plenty of friends, a fine family, and so on.

We feel the same when these advantages of theirs secure them others. Because again, the newly rich give us more offense by obtaining office through their riches than do those whose wealth is long-standing; and so in all other cases. The reason is that what the latter have is felt to be really their own, but what the others have is not; what appears to have always been as it is, is regarded as real, and so the possessions of the newly rich do not seem to be really their own.

Also, not every person deserves any given kind of good; there is a certain appropriateness in such things. For instance, it's fitting for brave men, not just men, to have fine weapons, and for men of noble birth, not upstarts, to make distinguished marriages. Indignation may therefore be properly felt when anyone gets what is not appropriate for him, though he may be a good man.

It may also be felt when anyone sets himself up against his superior, especially against his superior in some particular respect—hence the lines:

"Only from battle he shrank with Aias, Telamon's son;

Zeus would have been angered with him, had he fought with someone stronger."

But also, even apart from that, when the inferior in any sense contends with his superior; a musician, for instance, with a just man, for justice is a finer thing than music.

Enough has been said to make clear the grounds on which, and the persons against whom, Indignation is felt—they are those mentioned and others like them. As for the people who feel it; we feel it if we ourselves deserve the greatest possible goods and moreover have them, because it is unjust that those who are not our equals should be considered to deserve as much as we have. Or, secondly, we feel it if we are really good and honest people; our judgment is then sound, and we loathe any kind of injustice.

Also, if we are ambitious and eager to achieve particular goals, especially if we are ambitious for what others are getting without deserving to get it. And, generally, if we think that we ourselves deserve something and that others do not, we are inclined to be indignant with those others concerning that thing. Therefore, servile, worthless, unambitious people are not inclined to Indignation, since there is nothing they can believe themselves to deserve.

From all this, it is clear what sort of people those are at whose misfortunes, distresses, or failures we ought to feel pleased, or at least not pained: by considering the facts described, we see at once what their opposites are. If, therefore, our speech puts the judges in such a frame of mind as that indicated and shows that those who claim pity on certain definite grounds do not deserve to receive pity but do deserve not to receive it, it will be impossible for the judges to feel pity.

Now, let's look at Envy: we can understand why we feel it, who we feel it towards, and what kind of state of mind we are in when we feel it. Envy is the pain we feel when we see someone else having good fortune, specifically the kinds of good things we've already talked about. We feel it towards people who are like us, not because we want what they have, but because they have it, and we don't. We feel envy when we consider someone our equal, and by "equal," I mean in terms of birth, relationships, age, personality, reputation, or wealth.

We also tend to feel envy if we fall just short of having everything we want. This is why people who are powerful and prosperous often feel envious—they think others are taking what should be theirs. We also feel it if we are especially known for something, especially if it's wisdom or good fortune. People who are ambitious tend to feel more envy than those who are not. The same goes for those who claim to be wise; they want to be seen as wise. In general, anyone who strives for a certain reputation tends to feel envy in that area. Small-minded people feel envy easily because everything seems big to them.

The types of good things that make people feel envious have already been mentioned. These include actions or possessions that bring respect, honor, and the desire for fame, and nearly all of them are things that can cause envy. This is especially true if we want the thing ourselves, believe we deserve it, or think that having it would make us a little better than others, while not having it would make us a little worse. It's also clear who we tend to envy—those who are close to us in time, place, age, or reputation.

This is why there is a saying: "Family members can be jealous of each other."

We also feel envy towards our competitors—people just like the ones we've been talking about. We don't compete with people who lived a hundred centuries ago, or those not yet born, or the dead, or people living far away. Nor do we compete with people we consider far below or far above us. Instead, we compete with those who want the same things we do—our rivals in sports or love, for example. So, it's these people we are most likely to envy.

Another saying goes: "Potter envies potter."

We also feel envy towards people whose success makes us feel like failures. These are people we see as our neighbors or equals because it feels like it's our own fault that we didn't get the good thing they have. This bothers us and makes us feel envy. We also envy people who have what we believe we should have, or who got something we used to have. This is why older people often envy the young, and people who spend a lot of money envy those who spend less but get the same thing.

People also feel envy when they don't have something, or haven't gotten it yet, and they see someone else getting it quickly. We can also understand what things and people bring joy to envious people, and in what states of mind they feel it. The states of mind that bring pain are the same ones that will bring joy when the opposite happens. So, if we ourselves are in an envious state of mind, and those who are asking for our pity or help are in the same position we have described, it's clear they won't get our pity.

Next, we'll look at Emulation, focusing on its causes, its objects, and the state of mind in which it occurs. Emulation is the pain we feel when we see someone like us enjoying good things that we also value and could have for ourselves, but don't yet. However, this feeling isn't caused by the fact that someone else has these good things, but because we don't have them. Therefore, emulation is a good feeling, felt by good people, while envy is a bad feeling, felt by bad people.

Emulation encourages us to work for the good things we want, while envy makes us try to take those things away from our neighbor. Emulation is more likely to be felt by people who think they deserve certain good things that they don't yet have. It's important to note that no one tries for things they believe are impossible to get. This feeling is common in young people and people with high ambitions. It is also felt by those who already possess good things that are fitting for people held in high regard—such as wealth, many friends, public office, and so on.

These people think that since they deserve to be honored, they should also get these goods. They are driven by emulation because they believe these things belong to people with good character. Also, we feel emulation when others believe we deserve something. We feel this way about anything for which our ancestors, relatives, close friends, race, or country are highly honored, seeing it as something we should have, too. Since all things that are greatly honored are objects of emulation, moral goodness in its various forms must be something people emulate, as well as any good thing that benefits others. People honor those who are morally good, as well as those who are helpful to them.

We also tend to emulate people who have wealth and beauty more than those who have health, because wealth and beauty can bring joy to others. It's easy to see who we tend to emulate. These are the people who have qualities like courage, wisdom, or public office. Generals, speakers, and others in high positions can do a lot of good for many people. We also emulate those we want to be like, those who have many friends, and those admired by others.

People of the opposite kind, however, are objects of contempt, since the feeling of contempt is the opposite of emulation. People who are able to emulate or be emulated by others tend to look down on those who have bad qualities that are the opposite of the good things we've mentioned. They despise them for this reason. We often despise people who are lucky when their luck seems undeserved because they don't have the qualities that should come with it.

This wraps up our discussion of the feelings that can be created or eliminated, and the ways these emotions influence persuasive arguments.

Let's now look at the different types of human character in relation to emotions and moral qualities, and how they match up with different ages and circumstances. When I say emotions, I mean things like anger, desire, and so on, which we've already talked about. When I say moral qualities, I mean virtues and vices, which we've also covered, as well as the things different types of people are likely to want or do. By "ages," I mean youth, middle age, and old age. By "circumstances," I mean birth, wealth, power, and their opposites—in other words, good and bad fortune.

Let's start with the character of young people. Young men are passionate and tend to give in to their desires without much thought. Of all their bodily desires, sexual desire has the most control over them, and they often lack self-control in this area. They are also changeable and inconsistent in what they want. Their desires are strong, but short-lived, like a sick person's sudden hunger or thirst. They are quick-tempered and often let their anger take over. This happens because they love honor and can't stand being disrespected. If they feel unfairly treated, they become indignant. While they love honor, they love winning even more. Youth is eager to prove itself and victory is one way of doing that.

They value both of these things more than money, because they haven't yet learned what it's like to live without it. This is why Pittacus once made a remark about Amphiaraus. Young men tend to see the good in things rather than the bad, because they haven't yet seen much wickedness. They trust others easily because they haven't been cheated very often. They are hopeful, their youthful energy making them optimistic like they've had too much wine, and they have had few disappointments so far.

Their lives are focused more on what's ahead of them than what's behind, as they have a long future and little past to remember. The further back they go, the less they have to recall, which is why they focus on what lies ahead. They are easily deceived because of their optimistic nature. Their tempers and hopeful outlook make them braver than older people. Anger reduces fear, and hope increases confidence. When people are angry, they don't feel afraid, and when they expect good things to happen, they feel sure of themselves.

They are shy, following the rules of society in which they were raised, and they haven't yet developed their own standards. They also have high ideals, as they haven't been humbled by life or learned about its limitations. Their hopeful outlook makes them believe they can achieve great things, which is another reason for their high ambitions. They would rather do what is noble than what is useful. They live more by their sense of right and wrong than by practical thinking, which is why they prefer noble actions over useful ones. They are more attached to their friends and companions than older people because they enjoy spending time with others and haven't yet come to value their friends for what they can offer.

They tend to go to extremes in everything they do. They don't follow Chilon's advice, overdoing everything—whether it's love, hate, or anything else. They think they know everything and are always completely sure of themselves, which is why they tend to go too far. If they wrong someone, it's usually because they mean to insult them, not because they want to cause actual harm.

Young people are also quick to feel pity because they assume everyone is as good as they are, or at least better than they actually are. They judge others by their own harmless nature and don't think anyone deserves to be treated badly. They enjoy having fun and are often witty, as wit is a form of well-bred mischief.

Now let's talk about older men, those who have passed their prime. Their character is mostly made up of traits that are the opposite of those of young men. They have lived a long time, been fooled many times, and made many mistakes. Life, for them, has been tough, so they are never sure of anything and do everything with caution. They 'think' instead of 'knowing,' and because they are hesitant, they often add 'maybe' or 'perhaps' to everything they say. They are cynical, always looking at the worst side of things.

Their experience has made them suspicious and distrustful, so they neither love deeply nor hate passionately. As Bias said, they love as if they will one day hate and hate as if they will one day love. They are small-minded because life has humbled them, and their desires are limited to just what they need to survive. They are not generous because they have learned how hard it is to get money and how easy it is to lose it.

Older people are more cowardly and constantly worry about danger. Unlike the hot-blooded nature of youth, their temperament is cold, making them more prone to fear. They love life even more as they get closer to death, because people tend to desire what they don't have. They are also more self-centered, which is another form of small-mindedness. They are driven more by practical considerations than by noble ones, as the practical is what benefits them personally, while the noble is good for everyone.

They aren't shy, but more shameless, because they care more about what's useful than about what people think of them. They have little confidence in the future, both because of their experience— since most things turn out worse than expected—and their cowardice. They live more in the past than in the future because they have little future left, and memory focuses on the past. This is why they tend to talk a lot, always discussing the past, as they enjoy remembering it.

Their anger is quick but weak. Their physical desires have either faded or become less intense, so they don't feel them much, and their actions are driven more by greed than by passion. This is why people often think older men are self-controlled, but the truth is their passions have weakened, and they are motivated by the love of money. Older men live by reasoning more than by moral feeling; reasoning focuses on practicality, while moral feeling focuses on goodness.

If they wrong someone, they intend to cause harm, not insult. Old men may still feel pity, but for different reasons than young men. Young men pity others out of kindness, while old men pity others because they see that anything bad that happens to someone else could happen to them too. This thought provokes pity. Older men are also more likely to complain and less likely to joke or laugh, as the love of laughter is the opposite of complaining.

These, then, are the traits of young men and older men. People always appreciate speeches that reflect their own character, and now we can see how to craft speeches that appeal to our audiences by reflecting both their character and ours.

Now, let's talk about Men in their Prime. It's clear that their character lies somewhere between that of the young and the old, without the extremes of either. They don't have the overconfidence of the young, which can lead to recklessness, nor do they have the fearfulness of the old. Instead, they show the right balance of confidence and caution. They don't trust everyone, but they don't distrust everyone either—they judge people fairly.

Their lives are guided by both noble and practical considerations, not just one or the other. They avoid being either stingy or wasteful, instead choosing what is appropriate for the situation. When it comes to anger and desire, they are both brave and self-controlled. The young are brave but lack self-control, while the old are cautious but often too fearful. To sum it up, the best qualities of youth and old age are combined in people who are in their prime, while the excesses or shortcomings of each are balanced by moderation and good judgment.

The body reaches its prime between the ages of thirty and thirty-five, while the mind matures around the age of forty-nine.

This concludes the discussion of the character types found in youth, old age, and middle age. Now, let's turn to the influence of Fortune on human character, starting with Good Birth. Being born into a respected family makes people more ambitious. Anyone who starts life with advantages tends to want to build on them, and good birth implies that their ancestors were important. People who are well-born often look down on others, even those who are just as good as their own ancestors. This is because we see far-off achievements as greater than those that are closer to us, and they are easier to boast about.

However, being well-born—meaning from a good family—must be distinguished from nobility, which refers to living up to the standards of one's family. Most well-born people lack this quality, and many of them turn out to be weak. Like crops from the earth, the quality of people varies from generation to generation. Sometimes, a good family line produces exceptional individuals for a while, but then it starts to decline. A family known for intelligence can give way to people with eccentric or even unstable characters, like the descendants of Alcibiades or the elder Dionysius. On the other hand, a family known for being steady can decline into dullness and laziness, like the descendants of Cimon, Pericles, and Socrates.

The character of people shaped by Wealth is easy for anyone to see. Wealthy people often become arrogant and rude. Their wealth affects how they think, making them feel as if they possess every good thing in the world. They begin to see wealth as the measure of everything else.

Book 3

When making a speech, you need to focus on three things: first, how to persuade the audience; second, the language or style to use; and third, how to arrange the different parts of the speech in the right order. We've already talked about the ways to persuade. We said there are three main ways to persuade:

1. by appealing to the emotions of the audience,
2. by making them trust the speaker's character, and
3. by proving that the speaker's statements are true.

We also discussed enthymemes and the sources of arguments for them, noting that there are both specific and general types of arguments for these.

Next, we'll look at style. It's not enough to know what you need to say; you also have to say it the right way. Good style helps make a speech more effective. The first thing we discussed was naturally how persuasion comes from the facts themselves. Now, the second thing is how to present those facts in a proper way through language. The third thing, which is also important, is the way the speech is delivered. Delivery plays a big part in how successful a speech is, but it's been neglected for a long time. Even in theater and epic storytelling, it took a while to become an art form. In the past, poets acted out their plays themselves. It's clear that delivering a speech is as important in oratory as it is in poetry. (In poetry, delivery has been studied by people like Glaucon of Teos.) Essentially, delivery is about controlling your voice to express different emotions—speaking loudly, softly, or somewhere in between; using a high, low, or medium pitch; and adjusting the rhythm to match the subject. A speaker needs to think about these three things: volume, pitch, and rhythm. Those who do this well often win prizes in dramatic competitions. In public life, actors are now more important than poets, due to flaws in our political systems.

No complete guide on the rules of delivery has been written yet. Even the study of language itself made little progress for a long time. Delivery is not considered a very high-class subject to study, and that's understandable. Still, because rhetoric is all about appearances, we must pay attention to delivery, even though it's not the most respected topic. This is because we can't succeed without it. Ideally, we shouldn't need to do more than avoid annoying our listeners, without trying to charm them too much. We should win our arguments based on facts alone, so nothing but the proof of those facts should matter. However, as I've already said, other factors do influence the result because of the flaws in our audience. The way we speak does have a small but real effect, no matter what we're talking about, because the way something is said affects how clear it is. But style doesn't matter as much as people think. Fancy language is just for show and meant to entertain the audience. Nobody uses flowery language when teaching math.

When the principles of delivery are fully developed, they'll have the same impact as performance does on stage. But so far, only a few people, like Thrasymachus in his "Appeals to Pity," have made small attempts to explain them. The ability to perform dramatically is a natural talent and is hard to teach in a systematic way. However, the principles of good diction can be taught, and that's why we have skilled speakers who win prizes for their ability, just like those who are good at delivering speeches. Written or literary speeches rely more on their style than on their ideas.

It was the poets who first started using elevated language because words represent things, and they could use the human voice to represent emotions, too. The voice is the best tool we have for that. This is how the arts of reciting and acting were developed, along with other arts. Poets seemed to become famous because of their fancy language, even when their ideas were simple, so orators began to imitate them. For example, Gorgias's prose had a poetic style. Even today, many uneducated people think that poetic language makes the best speeches. But that's not true—prose language should be different from poetry. This is proven by how things are today, as even the language of tragedy has changed. Just like iambic meter was adopted instead of tetrameter because it is the closest to natural speech, tragedy has dropped the flowery words used in the early dramas, which are still found in epic poems. So, it's silly to imitate a poetic style that even poets no longer use. It's now clear that we don't need to discuss the whole question of style in detail, just the part that concerns rhetoric. The poetic side of style was already covered in the work on the Art of Poetry.

So, let's start from the observations made there, including the definition of style. Good style should be clear, as we know from the fact that if a speech doesn't make its meaning clear, it fails to do what speech is supposed to do. Style should also be appropriate, avoiding both low and overly elevated language. Poetic language may avoid being low, but it's not suited for prose. Clarity is achieved by using common, everyday words for both nouns and verbs. To avoid sounding low and to add elegance, you can use the other kinds of words mentioned in the Art of Poetry. Using different kinds of words makes language sound more impressive. People don't feel the same about strangers as they do about their fellow citizens, and the same is true for language. So, it's a good idea to give everyday speech a slightly unfamiliar touch, as people like to be surprised by something different.

In poetry, this happens a lot, and it works well there because the subjects are often removed from ordinary life. In prose, this happens less often because the subjects are more down-to-earth. Even in poetry, fancy language isn't always right, like when it's used by a slave or a young person, or when the subject is something trivial. To be appropriate, the style sometimes needs to be toned down and sometimes raised.

It's clear now that a writer needs to hide their skill and make it seem like they're speaking naturally, not artificially. Naturalness is persuasive, while artificiality has the opposite effect. When people sense that you're being artificial, they think you're trying to trick them, like when you water down their wine. It's like the difference between the voice of Theodorus and other actors: his voice really sounds like the character he's playing, while theirs do not. We can hide our effort by using ordinary words, the kind people use every day. Euripides, a poet, was the first to show how this could be done in his plays.

Language is made up of nouns and verbs. The different kinds of nouns were discussed in the Art of Poetry. Unusual, compound, and made-up words should only be used sparingly and in certain cases, which we'll talk about later. The reason for this is that they go too far from what's appropriate. In prose, besides the regular words for things, metaphors are the only other useful tool. We know this because both regular words and metaphors are what everyone uses in conversation. We now understand that a good writer can create a style that is clear without being too fancy, which matches our idea of what good oratorical prose should be. Words with multiple meanings are mostly useful for sophists who want to mislead people. Poets benefit from synonyms—words that have the same general meaning, like 'advancing' and 'proceeding', both of which are common and mean the same thing.

The Art of Poetry, as we've said before, has definitions of these different types of words, a classification of metaphors, and explains that metaphors are important in both poetry and prose. However, prose writers should focus especially on metaphors because they have fewer resources than poets do. Metaphors give style clarity, charm, and distinction in a way nothing else can. But metaphors aren't something that one person can easily teach another. Like epithets, metaphors need to be appropriate, meaning they should fit the thing they describe. If not, their lack of fit will be obvious, and the mismatch will stand out. It's like picking the right clothes for an old man—he wouldn't look good in the bright red cloak that suits a young man.

If you want to compliment someone, use a metaphor that makes them sound better. If you want to insult them, use a metaphor that makes them seem worse. For example, since opposites are often in the same category, you could say that a person who begs is 'praying', and that a person who prays is 'begging', as both actions are forms of asking. Iphicrates called Callias a 'beggar priest' instead of a 'torch-bearer', and Callias replied that Iphicrates must be uninitiated, or else he would've called him a 'torch-bearer' instead of a 'beggar priest'. Both are religious titles, but one is honorable and the other is not. Similarly, someone once called actors 'followers of Dionysus', but the actors called themselves 'artists'. Both are metaphors, but one is meant as an insult and the other as a compliment. Pirates now call themselves 'suppliers'. In this way, we can describe a crime as a mistake or a mistake as a crime. You could say a thief 'took' something or that he 'plundered' his victim.

An example from Euripides' Telephus shows how a metaphor can be inappropriate: "King of the oar, on Mysia's coast he landed." Here, the word 'king' is too grand for the subject, making the metaphor stand out too much. A metaphor can also fail if the sounds of the words used in it are harsh or unpleasant. Dionysius the Brazen once called poetry 'Calliope's screech'. Poetry and screeching both involve sounds, but the metaphor is bad because screeching is harsh and unpleasant, unlike poetry.

When using metaphors for things that don't have a name, it's better to take them from similar things that are closely related, so the connection is clear as soon as the metaphor is spoken. For example, in the famous riddle, "I saw a man gluing bronze with fire to another man's body," the process described has no name. However, both this process and gluing are forms of attaching things, so it makes sense to call the use of a cupping-glass 'gluing'. Good riddles often provide good metaphors because a metaphor is like a riddle, and a good riddle usually has a good metaphor.

Additionally, the materials for metaphors should be beautiful. As Licymnius says, both the sound and the meaning of words can be beautiful—or ugly. There's also another consideration that disproves the false argument of the sophist Bryson, who said there is no such thing as offensive language because the meaning is the same no matter which words you use. This is not true. One word can describe something more accurately than another, bringing the idea to life more vividly. Different words can show the same thing in different ways, so one term can be more beautiful or uglier than another. Both words may express fairness or foulness, but not to the same degree.

Metaphors should be pleasing to the ear, to the mind, and to the senses. It's better to say 'rosy-fingered dawn' than 'red-fingered' or, even worse, 'crimson-fingered dawn'. The epithets we use can also have a good or bad connotation, like calling Orestes a 'mother-killer' or calling him 'his father's avenger'. Simonides once refused to write a poem for the winner of a mule race because he found it unpleasant to write about "half-donkeys." But after he was paid well, he wrote, "Hail to you, daughters of swift-footed steeds!" even though the mules were also daughters of donkeys. The same effect can be achieved with diminutives, which make bad things seem less bad and good things seem less good. For example, in Aristophanes' Babylonians, he makes fun by saying 'goldlet' instead of 'gold', 'cloaklet' instead of 'cloak', and 'plaguelet' instead of 'plague'. However, whether using epithets or diminutives, we must be careful and strike a balance.

Bad taste in language can show up in four ways:

1. The misuse of compound words. For example, Lycophron talks about the 'many-faced heaven' above the 'giant-headed earth' and the 'narrow-shore path.' Gorgias uses phrases like the 'poor-poet flatterer' and 'breaking promises while keeping others.' Alcidamas says things like 'the soul filling with rage, and the face turning flame-red,' and 'he thought their enthusiasm would lead to success,' or 'success was the result of his words.' He also says, 'the dark-colored floor of the sea.' All these compound words sound better suited for poetry. So, this is one way bad taste can appear.

2. Another way is using strange or unusual words. For instance, Lycophron speaks of 'the extraordinary Xerxes' and 'thieving Sciron,' while Alcidamas says 'a toy for poetry' and 'the foolishness of nature.' He also says, 'sharpened by the unbending spirit of his mind.'

3. A third form of bad taste is using too many long or unnecessary adjectives. A poet can describe 'white milk,' but in prose, this kind of description may feel out of place, or if used too often, it makes the writing sound like poetry. Of course, we need to use some adjectives because they make the writing stand out and give it a certain quality. But we should aim for a balance, or the result will be worse than not trying at all. Instead of improving the writing, it can make it worse. That's why Alcidamas's use of adjectives seems so overdone— he doesn't treat them like seasoning for a dish but like the dish itself. For example, he doesn't just say 'sweat' but 'the wet sweat.' Instead of saying 'to the Isthmian games,' he says 'to the world-gathering of the Isthmian games.' Instead of simply 'laws,' he says 'the laws that rule the states.' And instead of 'at a run,' he says, 'his heart urging him to run fast.' He also doesn't say 'a school of the Muses' but 'the natural school of the Muses that he inherited.' He uses phrases like 'frowning care of heart,' and instead of 'gaining popularity,' he says, 'gaining universal popularity.' This kind of overuse makes his language seem absurd and unclear. When the meaning is already obvious, using too many words just makes it harder to understand.

The usual time to use compound words is when there isn't a simple term for something, and a compound can be easily made, like the word 'pastime.' But if you do this too much, the writing stops sounding like prose. That's why compound words are more common for writers of dithyrambs (a type of ancient Greek hymn) who like loud, booming words. Strange words are for writers of epic poetry, which is grand and lofty, while metaphors are best suited for iambic verse, the meter often used today.

4. The fourth area where bad taste shows up is in the use of metaphors. Just like other things, metaphors can be misused. Some are ridiculous, and that's why comic poets and tragic poets both use them. Others are too grand and theatrical, and if they're too far-fetched, they can be confusing. For example, Gorgias speaks of 'events that are green and full of sap,' and says, 'you planted a bad deed, and a terrible harvest you reaped.' That sounds too much like poetry. Alcidamas once called philosophy 'a fortress threatening the power of law' and the Odyssey 'a beautiful mirror of human life.' He also spoke of 'not offering such a toy to poetry.' These expressions don't work for the reasons I've mentioned—they don't connect with the listener.

Another example is Gorgias's comment to a swallow that had dropped something on him as it flew by. He said, 'Shame on you, Philomela.' He was making a joke, addressing her as the girl she once was, not the bird she is now. It was a good jab because, as a bird, the act wasn't shameful, but as a girl, it would have been.

A simile is also a metaphor; the difference is small. When a poet says Achilles 'leapt on the enemy like a lion,' it's a simile. But if he says, 'the lion leapt on the enemy,' it's a metaphor—he's calling Achilles a lion because they're both brave. Similes can be useful in both prose and poetry, but not too often, since they're more like poetry. You should use similes the same way you use metaphors, as they are nearly the same thing except for this slight difference.

Here are some examples of similes. Androtion said that Idrieus was like a dog let off the leash, ready to attack and bite. Theodamas compared Archidamus to Euxenus, who couldn't do geometry. This simile shows that Euxenus is like an Archidamus who can't do math. In Plato's Republic, those who strip the dead are compared to dogs that bite the stones thrown at them but don't touch the person who threw them. There's also a simile comparing the Athenian people to a ship's captain who is strong but a little deaf. Another compares poets' verses to people who are fresh and youthful, but once the freshness fades, the beauty is gone—just like verses that lose their charm when broken into prose. Pericles compared the Samians to children who take their food but still cry. He compared the Boeotians to oak trees, saying they were destroying each other in civil wars, just as one oak tree causes another to fall. Demosthenes said the Athenian people were like seasick men on a ship. He also compared political speakers to nurses who swallow the food themselves but smear the children's lips with spit. Antisthenes compared the skinny Cephisodotus to frankincense, saying that his thinness was enjoyable, just like frankincense.

All these comparisons can be made as either similes or metaphors. A good metaphor will also work as a simile, and a simile can be turned into a metaphor by removing the explanation. But the proportional metaphor must always work both ways. For example, if a drinking bowl is called the shield of Dionysus, a shield can also be called the drinking bowl of Ares.

These are the elements that make up speech. The foundation of good style is correct language, which can be broken down into five main points.

1. First, the proper use of connecting words and arranging them in the right order. For example, the connective 'men' (as in ego men) requires the correlative de (as in o de). You must introduce the second word before the first is forgotten, and not let too many other words get in the way. Avoid inserting

too many connectives before finishing the thought. For example: "But as soon as he told me (because Cleon had come begging and pleading), he took them along and set out." If too many words get in the way before "set out," the meaning gets lost. So, one key to good style is the proper use of connecting words.

2. The second point is to use specific names for things instead of vague or general ones.

3. The third point is to avoid being unclear, unless you want to be vague on purpose, like those who have nothing to say but want to seem like they do. These people tend to use this style in poetry. Empedocles, for example, uses long-winded phrases to impress his audience, much like fortune-tellers who use unclear language to sound wise.

Fortune-tellers use general statements because they are less likely to be proven wrong. It's easier to guess 'even' or 'odd' in a guessing game than to guess the exact number. In the same way, fortune-tellers have a better chance of being right if they say something will happen, without specifying when it will happen. This kind of unclear language has the same effect and should be avoided unless you have a specific reason for using it. (4) The fourth rule is to follow Protagoras' classification of nouns as male, female, or inanimate and use them correctly. For example: "When she arrived, she spoke and then left." (5) The fifth rule is to express plurality, fewness, and unity correctly. For example: "When they arrived, they struck me."

In general, written work should be easy to read and therefore easy to deliver aloud. This isn't possible when there are too many connecting words or clauses, or when the punctuation is unclear, like in the writings of Heraclitus. His work is hard to punctuate because it's not always clear if a word belongs with what comes before or after it. For example, at the beginning of his treatise, he says, "Though this truth is always, men understand it not," and it's unclear whether "always" goes with the first part or the second part of the sentence.

Another thing that causes mistakes is when you attach a third idea to two ideas that don't fit with it. For example, "sound" and "color" don't both work with the same verbs: you can "perceive" both, but you can't "see" both. Finally, confusion happens if you try to give too much information without first making your main point clear. For example, saying, "I meant, after telling him this, that, and the other, to set out," is less clear than saying, "I meant to set out after telling him; then, this, that, and the other thing happened."

The following suggestions will help make your language more impressive:

1. Instead of simply naming something, describe it. For example, instead of saying 'circle,' say 'a shape where every point is the same distance from the center.' To be concise, do the opposite—use the name instead of a description. When mentioning something ugly or offensive, use the name if the description is ugly, and use a description if the name is ugly.
2. Use metaphors and epithets, but be careful not to make it sound too much like poetry.
3. Use the plural form instead of the singular, like in poetry, where you might see something like "the Achaean havens" even though only one harbor is meant, or "the many-leaved folds of my letter."
4. Don't group two words under one article—give each word its own, like 'that wife of ours.' But to be concise, you can combine them, like saying 'our wife.' Use plenty of connecting words, but if you want to be concise, leave them out while still keeping the connection, like saying 'having gone and spoken' versus 'having gone, I spoke.' (6) Another useful technique comes from Antimachus, who described something by talking about what it's not. For example, he described Teumessus by saying, "It is a small, wind-swept hill." You can apply this technique to good or bad qualities, depending on what you're talking about. Poets use this device to create phrases like 'stringless' or 'lyreless melody.' A good example is calling a

trumpet sound 'a lyreless melody.'

Your language will feel appropriate if it matches the emotion and character of the subject. 'Matching the subject' means you shouldn't speak casually about serious matters, or use solemn language for trivial things. You also shouldn't use fancy adjectives for simple nouns—otherwise, it will sound ridiculous, like in the works of Cleophon, who wrote absurd phrases like 'O queenly fig-tree.' To express emotion, you should use the language of anger when talking about injustice, the language of disgust or reluctance when talking about impiety or something foul, and the language of joy when telling a story of glory. Use the right tone for each situation.

This kind of language makes people believe your story. They think you're telling the truth because people usually behave the way you describe when facing similar situations. As a result, they believe what you're saying, whether it's true or not. An emotional speaker often makes the audience feel the same way, even if the argument itself isn't strong. That's why many speakers try to overwhelm their audience with just noise.

This way of presenting your story also reflects your character. Each type of person, and each kind of personality, will have its own way of expressing the truth. By 'type of person,' I mean differences like age—whether someone is a boy, a man, or an old man. I also mean differences in gender, like being a man or a woman, or nationality, like being Spartan or Thessalian. By 'personality,' I mean only those qualities that shape a person's character, as not every trait does this. If a speaker uses words that fit a certain personality, they will bring that character to life. For instance, a rustic person and an educated person won't say the same things or speak in the same way.

Another way to impress the audience is by using a common tactic of speechwriters—phrases like 'Who doesn't know this?' or 'Everyone knows.' The listener may feel embarrassed about not knowing, so they'll agree with the speaker to appear knowledgeable.

All the different styles of speech can be used either appropriately or inappropriately. One way to counteract exaggeration is to include a small criticism of yourself. People will think it's fine for you to speak this way because it seems like you know what you're doing. Also, it's better if not everything fits together too perfectly because then your audience won't see through your speech as easily. For example, if your words are harsh, don't also make your tone of voice and facial expressions harsh—otherwise, your speech will seem too rehearsed. But if you mix things up by using one technique and not the other, you'll still be using skill, but no one will notice it. (However, if you express mild feelings with a harsh tone or harsh feelings with a mild tone, you'll be less convincing.) Compound words, frequent adjectives, and unusual words fit best in emotional speeches. People tend to forgive an angry speaker who describes something as 'colossal' or 'sky-high.' We excuse this language when the speaker has already won over the audience and stirred their emotions, whether through praise, blame, anger, or affection, as Isocrates does at the end of his Panegyric with phrases like 'name and fame' and 'in that they brooked.' People do speak like this when they are deeply moved, so once the audience feels the same, they naturally approve of the speech. That's why this kind of language works in poetry, which is inspired. It should be used either when emotions are high or ironically, like Gorgias and some of the passages in Plato's Phaedrus.

The structure of prose should have rhythm, but not be metrical. If it sounds too much like poetry, the audience won't trust it because it will seem too artificial. It will also distract them, making them focus on the rhythm instead of the message, just like how children interrupt with answers to questions before the speaker finishes. But if your prose has no rhythm at all, it will feel too loose and unfocused. While we don't want the restrictions of meter, we do need some structure, or else the speech will feel vague and unsatisfying. Rhythm, which comes from numbers, provides that structure. Meters are just specific kinds of rhythm. So, prose should have rhythm, but not follow a specific meter, or it will become poetry instead of prose. The rhythm should not be too exact either, just enough to be noticeable.

Of the different types of rhythm, the heroic rhythm has dignity but lacks the natural flow of speech. The iambic rhythm is closest to everyday conversation, so it shows up more often in casual talk. However, in a speech, we need more dignity and the power to lift the listener beyond ordinary life. The trochaic rhythm feels too much like lively dancing, which you can see in tetrameter verse, one of the trochaic rhythms.

The paean is the best rhythm for prose. It was first used by speakers in the time of Thrasymachus, though they didn't have a name for it yet. The paean is a third type of rhythm, closely related to the others. It has a ratio of three to two, while the other rhythms have ratios of one to one, or two to one. The paean is a middle ground between these ratios.

The other two types of rhythm should be avoided in prose because they sound too much like meter. The paean should be used instead because it doesn't produce a clear meter, so it stands out less. Right now, the same type of paean is used at the beginning and end of sentences, but the end should be different from the beginning. There are two types of paean: one starts with a long syllable and ends with three short ones, as in

"Dalogenes | eite Luki | an,"

and

"Chruseokom | a Ekate | pai Dios."

The other type starts with three short syllables and ends with a long one, as in

"meta de lan | udata t ok | eanon e | oanise nux."

This kind of paean creates a true ending. A short syllable doesn't give a sense of completion, so the rhythm feels cut off. A sentence should end with a long syllable, signaling the end through rhythm, not just a period or punctuation.

We've now seen that prose should have rhythm but not follow strict meter, and which rhythms work best for this.

The style of prose can either be loose, with only connecting words linking the ideas, like the preludes in dithyrambs, or more structured and balanced, like the strophes of old poets. The loose style is the older one, like in the opening of Herodotus's work: "Here is the investigation of Herodotus the Thurian." Everyone used this style in the past, but few do so now. By 'loose style,' I mean writing that has no natural stopping points and only ends because there's nothing more to say. This kind of style is unsatisfying because it feels endless. People like to see a finish line in front of them. It's only when they reach the end that they relax. When people see the end of the course ahead of them, they keep going. This is how the loose style works. The more compact style, on the other hand, is written in periods.

A period is a section of speech with a clear beginning and end that's small enough to grasp all at once. This kind of language is satisfying and easy to follow. It's satisfying because it's definite. The listener feels like they've understood something and reached a conclusion, while endless speech leaves them feeling lost. It's easy to follow because it's easy to remember. Periodic language can be counted, and numbers are the easiest thing to remember. That's why verse, which has a clear structure, is easier to recall than prose.

A period should only be complete when the sense is complete— it shouldn't break off suddenly, like in these iambic lines from Sophocles:

"Calydon's soil is this; of Pelops' land

(The smiling plains face us across the strait.)"

By splitting the lines wrong, the meaning becomes unclear, and you might think Calydon is in the Peloponnesus.

A period can be either made up of several parts or be simple. A period with several parts is a section of speech

1. complete in itself,
2. divided into parts, and
3. able to be spoken in one breath.

Each part is called a member. A simple period only has one member. Both the members and the whole period should not be too short or too long. If a member is too short, it can trip up the listener, as they expect the rhythm to continue but are cut off. If it's too long, the listener feels left behind, like someone walking past the finish line without turning back for their friends. A period that's too long becomes a speech or a dithyrambic prelude. The result is much like the prelude that Democritus of Chios made fun of Melanippides for writing instead of antistrophic stanzas:

"He who sets traps for others' feet
Is likely to fall into them first;
And long-winded preludes do harm to us all,
But the preluder suffers the most."

This applies to speakers with long, drawn-out periods. Periods with too short members aren't really periods at all, and they make the audience feel jarred.

The periodic style with multiple members can be of two types. One type is simply divided, like in the sentence: "I have often wondered at the organizers of national gatherings and the founders of athletic contests." The other type is antithetical, where each part contains opposites or contrasts, like "They helped both groups—not only those who stayed behind but also those who went along with them. For the latter, they gained new land larger than what they had at home, and for the former, they left enough land at home." Here, the contrasts are 'staying behind' versus 'going along,' and 'enough' versus 'larger.' Another example: "It often happens that the wise fail, and the foolish succeed." Or: "They were awarded the prize of valor immediately and gained command of the sea shortly after." And:

"They sailed through the mainland and marched through the sea, by bridging the Hellespont and cutting through Athos." And: "Nature gave them their country, and law took it away again." And: "Some perished in misery, others were saved in disgrace." And: "Athenian citizens keep foreigners as servants in their homes, while the city of Athens allows its allies to live as slaves." And: "To possess in life or to leave behind at death."

Someone once said about Peitholaus and Lycophron in a court case: "These men used to sell you when they were at home, and now they have come here to buy you." All of these examples use the structure I just described. This kind of speech is satisfying because the listener can easily grasp the meaning of the contrasts, especially when they are placed side by side. It also gives the impression of logical reasoning, as placing two opposing ideas side by side helps prove one of them false.

This is how antithesis works. Parisosis is when the two parts of a period are equal in length. Paromoeosis is when the first or last words of each part are similar. At the beginning, the similarity is usually between whole words, while at the end, it's between the final syllables or forms of the same word. Here's an example at the beginning:

"agron gar elaben arlon par' autou"
and
"dorhetoi t epelonto pararretoi t epeessin"
And here's an example at the end:
"ouk wethesan auton paidion tetokenai,
all autou aitlon lelonenai"
and
"en pleiotals de opontisi kai en elachistais elpisin"
An example with the same word form:
"axios de staoenai chalkous ouk axios on chalkou."
An example of the same word repeated:
"su d' auton kai zonta eleges kakos kai nun grafeis kakos."
An example of one syllable:

"ti d' an epaoes deinon, ei andrh' eides arhgon?"

It's possible for a sentence to have all these features at once—antithesis, parisosis, and paromoeosis. (The ways to begin periods have been fully covered in the Theodectea.) There are also false antitheses, like the one from Epicharmus:

"There once I as their guest did stay,
And they were my hosts on another day."

Now that we've covered the points above, let's talk about how to come up with lively and interesting sayings. The ability to invent them comes from either natural talent or lots of practice, but this guide can show the general approach. We can do this by looking at the different types of sayings. First, we should note that we all enjoy getting new ideas easily. Words express ideas, so the best words are the ones that help us understand something new. Strange words confuse us, and ordinary words tell us what we already know. It's through metaphors that we can best grasp something fresh. When a poet calls 'old age a withered stalk,' he's giving us a new idea by connecting it to something we already understand, like how a plant blooms and then withers. The similes poets use do the same thing, and if they're good similes, they can be very striking. A simile is just a type of metaphor, but since it's longer, it's not as appealing. It doesn't say directly that 'this is that,' so the listener isn't as interested.

We can see that both speech and reasoning are more lively when they help us grasp a new idea quickly. This is why people don't respond well to obvious arguments (ones that are so clear they need no explanation) or to ones that confuse them. People prefer arguments that give them new information immediately, or that their minds can almost understand right away. These two types give us a sense of learning something new. But obvious and confusing arguments don't teach us anything at all. So, these are the things that make an argument interesting in terms of meaning. In terms of style, the antithesis (contrast) is appealing, like in the phrase, 'thinking that the peace for everyone else was a war against their own interests.' Here, there's a contrast between peace and war.

It's also good to use metaphors, but they shouldn't be too far-fetched, or they'll be hard to understand, nor too obvious, or they won't have any effect. The words should also paint a picture in the listener's mind—events should feel like they're happening right now, rather than being described as something in the future. So, we should aim for three things: Antithesis, Metaphor, and Making Things Feel Real.

Of the four types of metaphor, the most appealing is the proportional metaphor. For example, Pericles once said that the young men who had died in war had left the country 'as if the spring were taken out of the year.' Leptines, when talking about the Lacedaemonians, said that he didn't want the Athenians to let Greece 'lose one of her two eyes.' When Chares was being examined for his part in the Olynthiac war, Cephisodotus was upset and said that Chares wanted to be examined 'while he still had his fingers around the people's throat.' The same speaker once urged the Athenians to march to Euboea, 'with Miltiades' decree as their food rations.' Iphicrates, frustrated at the truce between the Athenians and Epidaurus, said that the Athenians had given up their travel money for the journey of war. Peitholaus called the state galley 'the people's big stick,' and he called Sestos 'the grain storage of the Peiraeus.' Pericles urged his fellow citizens to get rid of Aegina, calling it 'the eyesore of the Peiraeus.' Moerocles joked that he was no more of a crook than a certain respectable citizen, 'whose crookedness earned him over thirty percent profit every year, unlike my ten percent.'

There's also the iambic line of Anaxandrides about how his daughters delayed getting married: 'My daughters' wedding days are overdue.' Polyeuctus once said about a man named Speusippus, who was paralyzed, that he couldn't stay quiet 'even though fortune had locked him in the prison of illness.' Cephisodotus called warships 'painted millstones,' and Diogenes the Dog called taverns 'the dining halls of Attica.' Aesion said the Athenians had 'poured their town into Sicily,' which is a vivid metaphor. The phrase 'until all of Greece shouted out loud' is another vivid metaphor. Cephisodotus warned the Athenians not to hold too many 'parades,' and Isocrates used the same word when talking about those who 'parade around at national festivals.' Another example comes from the Funeral Speech: 'It's fitting that Greece should cut her hair in mourning beside the tombs of those who died at Salamis, because her freedom and their bravery are buried together.' Even if the speaker had only said that it was right to cry when bravery was being buried, it would have been a metaphor. But linking 'bravery' and 'freedom' also creates an antithesis.

Iphicrates once said, 'The path of my words goes straight through the middle of Chares' deeds.' This is a proportional metaphor, and the phrase 'straight through the middle' makes it vivid. The phrase 'calling in one danger to save us from another' is also a vivid metaphor. Lycoleon, while defending Chabrias, said, 'They didn't even respect the bronze statue of him standing over there, which pleads for him.' This was a metaphor for the moment, but it wouldn't always apply. It's still a vivid metaphor, though. Chabrias was in danger, and his statue seemed to plead for him, like a lifeless yet living thing that reminded people of his service to his country. The phrase 'practicing every form of pettiness' is metaphorical because practicing something means you're getting better at it. So is the phrase 'God lit our reason like a lamp inside our souls,' because both reason and light help us see things. The phrase 'we're not ending our wars, just postponing them' is also metaphorical, because both war and postponement deal with future actions. The saying 'This treaty is a nobler trophy than those we set up on battlefields' is another metaphor. It means that while trophies on the battlefield celebrate small victories, the treaty celebrates our success in the whole war. The saying 'A country pays a heavy price when it's condemned by the judgment of the world' is also metaphorical, because 'paying a price' refers to deserved damage.

We've already said that liveliness comes from using proportional metaphors and making people 'see things.' We still need to explain what we mean by 'seeing things' and how to make this happen. By 'making them see things,' I mean using words that show things in action. For example, saying a good man is 'four-square' is a metaphor because both a good man and a square are considered perfect. But the metaphor doesn't suggest any action. However, saying someone is 'in full bloom' does suggest action. The phrase 'you must wander like a free, sacred animal' also suggests action. The line 'Then the Greeks sprang to their feet' is another example—'sprang' shows both action and a metaphor, suggesting quick movement. Homer often uses this technique to bring life to lifeless things in his poetry. For example, 'The boulder bounced downward into the valley,' or 'The arrow flew,' or 'The spear struck the earth, still eager to feed on the flesh of the heroes.' All of these examples give action to things that aren't alive. Homer attaches these ideas to things using proportional metaphors, like comparing a shameless man to the boulder of Sisyphus. In his famous similes, he also makes non-living things seem alive, as in 'Curving and crested with white, wave after wave followed each other without stopping.' Everything here is described as moving and full of life.

Metaphors should be taken from things related to the original, but not in an obvious way—just like in philosophy, where a sharp mind can see similarities between very different things. For example, Archytas said that both an arbitrator and an altar serve the same purpose because injured people seek refuge in both. You could also say an anchor and an overhead hook are alike, because one holds things down from below, and the other holds them from above. Saying a state is 'leveled' is another metaphor, as it connects the idea of a flat surface with equal political power.

Liveliness is especially created by metaphor, and by surprising the listener. When the listener expects something different, they're more impressed when they hear the new idea. It's as if their mind says, 'Yes, of course, I hadn't thought of that.' Epigrams are lively because they don't mean exactly what the words suggest, like when Stesichorus said, 'The cicadas will chirp to themselves on the ground.' Well-written riddles are enjoyable for the same reason—they present a new idea and use metaphorical language. The surprising phrases of Theodorus work the same way. His thoughts are striking because they don't fit in with what you already know. This is also the effect of burlesque words in comic plays. Even jokes that change the letters of a word can create surprise. This happens in both poetry and prose. The word that comes next isn't what the listener expected, like in the line, 'Onward he came, his feet shod with—chilblains,' where the listener expected the word 'sandals.' But the joke should be clear as soon as the words are said. Jokes that change the letters of a word work by suggesting something different from the usual meaning. For example, Theodorus once said about Nicon, the harpist, 'Thratt' ei su' (which means 'you're a Thracian slave') instead of 'Thratteis su' (which means 'you're a harp player'), making a surprising joke. But this only works if you know that Nicon is from Thrace. Another example is the phrase 'Boulei auton persai.' In both cases, the joke has to fit the facts.

This is also true of sayings like, 'To the Athenians, their control of the sea wasn't the beginning of their troubles, since they gained from it,' or the opposite argument from Isocrates, that their empire was the beginning of their problems. In both cases, the speaker says something unexpected, and the listener recognizes it as true. There's nothing clever about saying, 'Empire is empire.' Isocrates means something more and gives new meaning to the word. The first example denies that 'beginning' in one sense means 'beginning' in another. In all these jokes, whether they use a word in two senses or as a metaphor, they're effective if they fit the facts. For example, if someone is named Anaschetos (which means 'unbearable'), and you say 'Anaschetos is unbearable,' the joke works if the person is really unpleasant. Another example is the saying, 'Don't be a stranger, stranger than you should be.' Here, you're using one word in two different senses. Another example is the famous line from Anaxandrides: 'Death is fitting before you do something that would make death fitting.' This is another way of saying, 'It's right to die before you do something that makes you deserve to die.' The point is that the shorter and more balanced these sayings are, the more effective they become. Antithesis makes the new idea stand out, and brevity makes it more impactful. They should always have some personal relevance or a clever expression if they're to be meaningful without being boring—two goals that aren't always met at the same time. For example, 'A person should die without doing wrong' is true, but not interesting. 'The right man should marry the right woman' is also true, but not engaging. To be effective, a saying needs both qualities, like 'It's right to die before you deserve to die.' The more a saying has these qualities, the more lively it feels. For example, if it uses metaphor in the right way, is antithetical, and balanced, it will give the sense of action.

Good similes are also metaphors, as they compare two things in the same way proportional metaphors do. For instance, we might say that a shield is 'the drinking bowl of Ares,' or that a bow is 'the stringless lyre.' This is a more complex way of using metaphor than just calling the bow a lyre or the shield a drinking bowl. There are also simpler similes, like saying a flute player is like a monkey, or comparing a near-sighted person's eyes to a flame flickering with water dropping on it. Similes work best when they're like converted metaphors. For instance, you could say that a shield is like the drinking bowl of Ares, or that a ruined building is like a house in tatters. Or you could say that Niceratus is like Philoctetes after being beaten by Pratys, which is a simile made by Thrasymachus after Niceratus lost to Pratys in a recitation contest and walked around unkempt and unwashed. Poets fail most when they don't capture the right resemblance, and succeed best when they do, as in the line 'His legs curled up like parsley leaves,' or 'Just like Philammon battling with his punch ball.' All of these are similes, and as we've said many times before, similes are metaphors.

Proverbs are also metaphors, as they compare one thing to another. For example, if a man starts a project hoping to profit, but ends up losing, someone might say, 'He's like the man from Carpathus and his hare.' This refers to both the man and the person in the proverb experiencing the same misfortune.

We've now explained how liveliness is created and why it works. Hyperboles, when successful, are also metaphors. For example, the saying about a man with a black eye, 'You'd have thought he was a basket of mulberries,' compares his black eye to a mulberry because of the color. The exaggeration lies in the amount of mulberries being suggested. The phrase 'just like so-and-so' can introduce a hyperbole in the form of a simile. For example, 'Just like Philammon battling with his punch ball' is the same as saying, 'You'd have thought he was Philammon battling with his punch ball,' and 'His legs curled up like parsley leaves' is like saying, 'His legs were so curly, you'd have thought they were parsley leaves.'

Hyperboles are best suited for young men to use because they show a lot of passion. This is why angry people tend to use them more than others. For example:

"Not though he gave me as much as the dust
Or the sands of the sea...
But her, the daughter of Atreus' son, I never will marry,
Not though she were fairer than golden Aphrodite,
And more skilled with her hands than Athene..."

The Attic orators often use this kind of speech. However, it doesn't suit an older speaker as well.

Each type of rhetoric has its own style. The style used for written works is not the same as the style for speaking, and political speeches differ from legal speeches. You need to know both styles. Knowing how to speak well helps you communicate clearly, while writing well allows you to share ideas with the public.

Written style is more polished, while spoken style allows for dramatic delivery, which can reflect character and emotion. This is why actors look for plays written with this in mind, and poets look for actors who can deliver those lines well. But poets who write for reading are different, like Chaeremon, who wrote in a polished, professional style. Professional writers' speeches may seem weak when performed, while the speeches of orators may sound impressive but look less professional when read. This happens because orators write speeches suited for live delivery, full of dramatic touches that lose their effect without the performance and can seem silly when written down. For example, strings of disconnected words or repeated phrases are fine in spoken speeches but would be criticized in written ones. Speakers often repeat phrases for dramatic effect, like "This is the man who deceived you, who cheated you, who meant to betray you." Actors like Philemon would use this technique in plays to great effect. But if it's not delivered with skill, it becomes awkward.

Another example is repeating unconnected statements like "I came to him; I met him; I begged him." These need to be acted out with variety in tone and pitch, or they sound flat. They make it seem like a lot has happened in a short time, as if several statements were made at once. It's similar to how conjunctions connect ideas in writing. Without conjunctions, a single statement can feel like many. For instance, "I came to him; I spoke to him; I pleaded with him," makes each part seem more important. Homer used this trick when he wrote:

"Nireus likewise from Syme (three well-fashioned ships did bring),

"Nireus, the son of Aglaia (and Charopus, bright-faced king),

"Nireus, the comeliest man (of all that to Ilium's strand)."

By repeating his name, it feels like Homer is saying a lot about Nireus, even though he only mentions him once and never talks about him again.

Public speeches are like painting a scene for a large audience. The larger the crowd, the less important fine details become. In legal speeches, though, more detail is needed, especially when speaking to a single judge who can pay closer attention to the arguments. In these cases, the speaker needs to be more careful with the facts, as the judge can judge more accurately without distraction. This is why speakers don't usually succeed in all areas of rhetoric at once. The less detailed speeches require a strong, clear voice, while ceremonial speeches need more literary quality, as they're meant to be read. Forensic speeches (legal ones) come next in terms of literary quality.

Going further, some may say that style should also be pleasant or grand, but that's not as necessary as being clear and appropriate. Style should balance ordinary and unusual words, include rhythm, and be persuasive by fitting the subject. If the speech is too long, it won't be clear, but if it's too short, it can feel incomplete. A middle path works best. The right balance of words, rhythm, and appropriateness will make the style pleasant.

This wraps up our discussion of style, both in general and in how it applies to different kinds of rhetoric. Now we'll move on to how to organize a speech.

A speech has two parts. You must present your case and then prove it. You can't present your case without proving it, and you can't prove something if you haven't stated what it is. The first part is called the Statement, and the second is the Argument, just like in reasoning we distinguish between a premise and proof. The common way of dividing speeches is not very useful. For example, "narration" is only a part of legal speeches, not political or display speeches. In political speeches, there's no need for "narration" or responding to an opponent, and an epilogue isn't always necessary either. In short speeches or those where the facts are easy to remember, an epilogue may not be needed at all. So, the only truly necessary parts of a speech are the Statement and the Argument.

Other parts, like refuting an opponent or comparing your case to theirs, are just part of the argument, because you're still proving something. The introduction doesn't do this, nor does the epilogue, which just summarizes what's been said. Dividing speeches into too many parts is pointless unless each part is truly distinct.

The introduction is the beginning of the speech, like the prologue in a play or the prelude in music. It sets the stage for what's to come.

Musical preludes are similar to introductions in speeches meant for display, where the speaker can begin with any impressive thought before leading into the main topic. For example, Isocrates' introduction to his Helen doesn't have much to do with Helen. It's acceptable to begin far from the main subject to avoid being monotonous.

Introductions to display speeches often involve praise or criticism. Gorgias, in his Olympic speech, praised the people of Greece for starting the festival gatherings. Isocrates, on the other hand, criticized them for honoring athletes but giving no prizes for intellectual achievement. Another way to begin is by offering advice, like saying, "We should honor good people, so I'm here to praise Aristeides," or "We should honor people who are not well-liked but are not bad, like Alexander, son of Priam." Sometimes, introductions may ask the audience to be patient if the topic is unusual or difficult, much like Choerilus did in his lines:

"But now when allotment of all has been made..."

Introductions to display speeches can include praise, advice, or requests for patience, and they can be either connected or disconnected from the main speech.

Introductions in legal speeches work like prologues in plays or epic poems, where the audience is given a preview of the main theme to avoid confusion. In epic poems, the introduction often tells what the story will be about, like:

"Sing, O goddess of song, of the Wrath..."

Or:

"Tell me, O Muse, of the hero..."

Tragic poets also give a hint of the story early on, as in Sophocles' play when he begins with "Polybus was my father..." The same happens in comedies. So, the main purpose of an introduction is to show what the speech is about. When the subject is short or simple, there's no need for a lengthy introduction.

Other types of introductions are used to address the speaker, the audience, or the subject. They can help to remove or build up prejudice. A defendant may start by clearing away any negative feelings the audience may have, while a prosecutor may wait until the end to stir up prejudice against the defendant.

Sometimes the introduction is used to gain the audience's attention, whether to make them take the subject seriously or, in some cases, to distract them. Speakers may also make the audience laugh to lighten the mood. You might use different strategies to make your listeners interested, like showing that you have a good character or that the topic is important or surprising. If you want to distract them, you could suggest that the subject isn't important or that it's unpleasant.

But none of this has to do with the speech itself. It's just about how easily the audience is swayed by things that aren't related to the topic. When the audience is focused, all you need is a summary of the subject at the start to help them follow along. In fact, it's better to call for attention later in the speech if necessary. It's silly to ask for attention at the beginning when the audience is already paying attention. Save these appeals for points where the audience might lose focus, saying something like, "Now I need you to pay attention to this point—it's just as important to you as it is to me," or "I'm going to tell you something more surprising than anything you've heard before."

These types of introductions are meant for real-life audiences, not ideal ones. They're often used to stir up emotions or remove doubts, like when a speaker says, "My lord, I will not say eagerly..." or "Why all this introduction?" Introductions are useful when the case seems weak. In these cases, it's better to focus on something other than the main facts.

To sum up, introductions help to get goodwill from the audience or to create certain emotions. In display speeches, it helps if the praise somehow includes the audience or their values, as Socrates said in his

Funeral Speech: "The challenge is not praising the Athenians in Athens, but in Sparta."

Introductions in political speeches are rare because the audience already knows the subject, but sometimes you need to address yourself or your opponents, or adjust the importance of the topic. Sometimes an introduction adds elegance to the speech, as in Gorgias' praise of Elis, where he begins without any preamble, saying, "Happy city of Elis!"

When dealing with prejudice, one way to defend yourself is to get rid of false assumptions that people may have about you. It doesn't matter if these assumptions have been spoken aloud or not; this difference doesn't change how you should handle them. Another approach is to confront the issue directly. You can deny the accusation, claim that you didn't cause harm, or argue that the harm wasn't as bad as claimed. You can say that you didn't act unfairly, or that if you did, it wasn't significant. These are the types of arguments you can use to respond. For example, Iphicrates, when replying to Nausicrates, admitted that he had caused harm but argued that he hadn't acted unjustly.

Another option is to admit that you did something wrong, but to balance it with other facts. You could say that even if what you did hurt the other person, it was still honorable, or that while it caused pain, it was for their benefit. Another approach is to say that the action was a mistake, or due to bad luck or necessity. For instance, Sophocles responded to someone accusing him of trembling to appear old by saying he was shaking because he couldn't help it—he didn't want to be eighty years old.

You could also explain that your intention was different from the actual result. For example, you might say, "I didn't mean to hurt him; I intended to do something else," or "The damage was an accident. I'd be terrible if I had planned this outcome." Another argument is that the person accusing you has faced similar suspicions or situations themselves. You could also point out that others who were suspected for the same reasons were later found innocent, like saying, "Am I a bad person just because I dress well? If that's true, then so-and-so must be too."

If others have been falsely accused by the same person or have faced suspicion like you, but were later proven innocent, you can use that to support your case. Another method is to accuse your accuser in return by saying, "It's outrageous to believe this person's claims when you can't even trust them."

You can also argue that the matter has already been settled. A good example is when Euripides responded to Hygiaenon, who accused him in court of encouraging perjury with a line in one of his plays that said:

"My tongue has sworn, but my heart has not."

Euripides replied by saying that his opponent was wrong to bring this issue to court when it should be decided in a theatrical contest. He said, "If I haven't already answered for my words there, I'm ready to defend myself if you take it to the proper place."

Thank You for Reading

Dear Reader,

We hope this timeless classic has sparked your imagination and enriched your literary journey. Now that you've turned the final page, we want to share a vision for the future of reading—one where every classic you've ever wanted to explore is at your fingertips, in a format that best suits your life.

We'd like to invite you to gain immediate, unlimited digital & audiobook access to hundreds of the most treasured literary classics ever written—along with the option to secure deluxe paperback, hardcover & box set editions at printing cost. Together, we can spark a new global literary renaissance alongside our small, independent publishing house called "The Library of Alexandria."

Thousands of years ago, the Library of Alexandria stood as a beacon of knowledge—until it was lost to history. We aim to reignite that spirit of preservation and discovery right now, in the modern age—only this time, it's accessible to all, in every language and every format.

Picture a world where every timeless classic, novel, poem, or philosophical treatise is not only available to read but also updated for today's readers—modernized, translated into any language or dialect, and ready to enjoy in any format you choose, whether that is in an eBook, audiobook, paperback, or deluxe hardcover & box set version a printing cost.

By joining our movement to rebuild the modern Library of Alexandria, you become part of an unprecedented mission to offer:

- **Unlimited Audiobook & eBook Access to the Greatest Classics of All Time**

  Instantly explore thousands of legendary works, from Plato and Shakespeare to Jane Austen and Leo Tolstoy. All are instantly ready to read or listen to, giving you a complete literary universe at your fingertips.

- **Paperback & Deluxe Editions at Printing Costs:**

  Purchase any title in a paperback, deluxe hardbound, or deluxe boxset edition at printing costs, shipped right to your doorstep. Curate your personal library of Alexandria with editions worthy of display—crafted to last, designed to captivate, and delivered straight to your door.

- **Modern translations for Contemporary Readers in all languages and dialects**

  Discover a vast selection of classics reimagined in clear, current language—no more struggling with outdated phrases or obscure references. Next to the original versions, we aim to offer translations in as many languages and dialects as possible.

  As we continue our translation efforts and add new languages, readers everywhere can connect with these works as if they were written today. By bridging linguistic divides, you're contributing to ensuring that these timeless stories become more meaningful, accessible, and inspiring for people across the globe.

- **Your Personal Library of Alexandria:**

  Over the months and years, you'll curate a unique physical archive of classics—each volume a testament to your taste, curiosity, and love of knowledge. It's not just about owning books—it's about curating a cultural legacy you'll cherish and pass down for generations to come.

- **Join a Global Literary Renaissance:**

  Your support fuels an ongoing mission: allowing us to reinvest in offering deluxe print editions (including special boxsets) at their true cost, broaden the range of available formats and translations, and extend the reach of these works to new audiences worldwide. By joining today, you're not just preserving a legacy of masterpieces; you set in motion a powerful wave of literary accessibility.

We are more than a publisher—we're a movement, and we can't do it alone. Your support lets us scale our mission, preserving and reimagining history's greatest works for tomorrow's readers.

Become a Torchbearer of knowledge.

Thank you for picking up this book and allowing us into your literary journey. As you turn the pages, know that you're part of something larger: a global effort to keep these stories alive, share their wisdom across borders and generations, and spark a true cultural revival for the modern era.

If this resonates with you—please consider taking the next step by visiting:

www.libraryofalexandria.com

With gratitude and a shared love of knowledge,

The Modern Library of Alexandria Team

Visit:

www.libraryofalexandria.com

Or scan the code below:

www.ingramcontent.com/pod-product-compliance
Lightning Source LLC
Chambersburg PA
CBHW011400010726
47495CB00009B/2717